Tolkien On Fairy-stories

Tolkien On Fairy-stories

Expanded Edition, with Commentary and Notes

J.R.R. TOLKIEN

Edited by
VERLYN FLIEGER
& DOUGLAS A. ANDERSON

HarperCollins*Publishers*

HarperCollins*Publishers*
1 London Bridge Street,
London SE1 9GF

HarperCollins*Publishers*
Macken House, 39/40 Mayor Street Upper
Dublin1, D01 C9W8, Ireland

www.tolkien.co.uk
www.tolkienestate.co.uk

Published by HarperCollins*Publishers* 2014

26

ISBN 978-0-00-758291-4

Set in Stempel Garamond

Printed and bound in the UK using 100% Renewable Electricity
by CPI Group (UK) Ltd

ACKNOWLEDGEMENTS

We are grateful for assistance from John Garth, Carl Hostetter, Colin Manlove, Vésteinn Ólason, and Ted Sherman. Thanks go to Marjorie Burns who directed us to Vésteinn Ólason for translation of a Norse ballad quote. Thanks also to Priscilla Tolkien for her memories of the extent of her father's research into Andrew Lang's "colour" Fairy Books. A special thanks goes to Rachel Hart, Muniments Archivist at the University of St. Andrews, for helping with many queries; and to the Lilly Library at Indiana University for supplying a copy of Andrew Lang's introduction to the rare large paper edition of *The Blue Fairy Book*. For permission to reprint newspaper accounts of the original 1939 lecture, we thank *The Scotsman*, and *The St. Andrews Citizen*. We are grateful to the Marion E. Wade Center at Wheaton College, Wheaton, Illinois, for permission to quote from the letter in their Archive from Margaret Douglas. And as always, we are grateful to the Bodleian Library, University of Oxford and to the Tolkien Estate for permission to use the manuscripts and for cooperation in making this edition possible.

CONTENTS

INTRODUCTION

J.R.R. Tolkien spent a large portion of his long and productive life writing on fairy-stories, from his 1910 poem, "Wood-sunshine" to his 1964–5 short story, *Smith of Wootton Major* and the more substantial works in between – the "Silmarillion", *The Hobbit*, and *The Lord of the Rings*. It was almost exactly in the middle of that span, in 1939, that he put the subject in capital letters. "On Fairy-stories" is Tolkien's defining study of and the centre-point in his thinking about the genre, as well as being the theoretical basis for his fiction. Thus it is both the essential and natural companion to his fiction.

Next after his essay on "*Beowulf*: The Monsters and the Critics", "On Fairy-stories" is his most reprinted critical work, and like the *Beowulf* essay it is a landmark in its field. Not only is it a definitive discussion of fairy-stories and their relationship to myth and fantasy, it is his most explicit analysis of his own art. It is in addition the hinge and pivot between his two most popular and influential books, *The Hobbit* and *The Lord of the Rings*. Not only in the context of his fiction, but in the larger context of his own and his century's fascination with myth and fantasy and their roles in the making of meaning, this is Tolkien's most important critical commentary. It is the template on which he shaped his idea of sub-creation, and the manifesto in which he declared his particular concept of what fantasy is and how it ought to work.

The judgment of Tolkien's biographer Humphrey Carpenter that "On Fairy-stories" makes "too many [points] for an entirely cogent argument" (Carpenter, 191) is somewhat off the mark, for Tolkien is not making a single argument, nor is he trying to prove a thesis. Rather, he is offering a wide-ranging overview, and while he does indeed make many points both major and minor along the way, they are all in the service of his larger declaration – that fairy-story is a legitimate literary genre, not confined to scholarly study but meant for readerly enjoyment by adults and children alike.

Nevertheless, the eminent Tolkien scholar Tom Shippey's considered opinion that the essay is lacking "a philological core, a kernel" (Shippey, 45), cannot altogether be dismissed, for it must be admitted that while "On Fairy-stories" is packed with information and erudition, it casts so wide a net as to appear at first glance lacking a core, philological or otherwise. There is philology, certainly, but not necessarily at the core, and what is there is chiefly in the service of a more wide-ranging vision. And though there is a traceable path through what seems at times an impenetrable thicket of names and theories, the first-time reader may need a hand-rail to hold on to. Fortunately, Tolkien has provided just such a hand-rail, one that if held to confidently will prove a reliable guide. The first page raises three questions: What are fairy-stories? What are their origins? What is the use of them? The essay unfolds Tolkien's answers to these questions, and if we remain faithful to his three-part guide, we will stay fairly close to the path.

THE ESSAY

The first sub-heading, "Fairy-story", addresses Tolkien's initial question – what are fairy-stories? After a brief look at the current usage of and assumptions about the word *fairy* (and what is wrong with both) he points out the obvious – that fairy-stories are not stories about fairies but stories about humans in Faërie, "the realm or state in which fairies have their being". He further defines the genre by citing types of stories that are not fairy-stories – travellers' tales, dream visions, beast-fables – and disqualifying them one by one.

The next section, "Origins", takes a historical look at where fairy-stories might have come from in the context of research into just that question by the joint disciplines of comparative philology and mythology. Having discovered the universality of folk and fairy tale motifs throughout the world's literature – that they shared the same few plots, character types and motifs – scholars of nineteenth-century comparative philology and mythology enquired into the mechanics of how this might have happened. Was it *independent invention* (an original story-teller), or *diffusion* (which Tolkien calls "borrowing in space") or *inheritance* (which he calls "borrowing in time")? Declaring that this can never be satisfactorily resolved, he concludes that it doesn't matter since it will all go back to an inventor somewhere in some time, and the important thing is the effect the stories have *now* on those who read them. Nevertheless, the fact that the original investigations were led by philologists engaged in the historical study of words leads Tolkien to a consideration of the power of language, and from there to the interlocking operations of human language, perception and imagination. Here, in the recombining of disparate words "new form is made". The ability of humankind to create an imagined world out of words is the theme that runs through the rest of the essay.

It is here that Tolkien jumps in at the deep end of the debate that raged among the founding fathers of the folklore movement in the nineteenth and early twentieth centuries. He does it by holding up to critical scrutiny both the "solar" theory proposed by Max Müller and the "anthropological" theory proposed by Müller's opponent, Andrew Lang. Finding neither theory adequate to account for the myths as they exist, Tolkien introduced his own term, *sub-creation*, to apply to the creative interaction of human imagination and human language that in his opinion gives rise to myth. Whatever may be or may have been their inspiration – celestial phenomena or totemism or history made into legend – myths take shape because human beings find words to describe and enshrine their experience. This leads Tolkien to two of his most vivid metaphors – the Cauldron of Story, in which the ingredients of history and legend endlessly simmer (over the fire of human imagination), and from which the Soup is served up as the tale told. Examples of ingredients range from the Norse god Thórr to the mother of Charlemagne, to King Arthur to Hrothgar of the *Beowulf* poem, as "new bits added to the stock" of the Soup.

Tolkien's way of addressing the next question – what is the use of them? – is more complex and difficult to disentangle. Unlike his procedure in the previous sections, he does not give here a (reasonably) simple answer under a simple heading, "Use", but subdivides "Use" into smaller but interrelated sections. These are (1) "Children": in which he critically considers a presumed audience; (2) "Fantasy": in which he discusses technique; and (3) three sub-divisions of the latter, "Recovery", "Escape", and "Consolation": in which he analyses the effect of fairy-stories on their readers.

Starting with "Children" Tolkien first acknowledges and then challenges the assumption that children are the natural and appropriate audience for fairy-stories, and that they were the original or even the ideal audience for such tales. The collections of fairy-stories, of which Andrew Lang's are pre-eminent, are in the main by-products of the scholarly study of comparative mythology, though they are made as and presented as books for children. This assumption, Tolkien maintains, is "an accident of domestic history". The tales have been relegated to the nursery like outworn but still serviceable furniture discarded by adults as old-fashioned. This does not mean that children are especially fond of the old tales, any more than they are especially fond of the old furniture. And like the outworn furniture banished to the nursery, the stories have been roughly treated, indeed, damaged by careless use.

Andrew Lang's assumption of the childish credulity that makes children (in Lang's opinion) the natural audience for fairy-stories leads Tolkien to consideration of that "willing suspension of disbelief" which Samuel Taylor Coleridge marked as the effect of fiction on the receiving mind, but which Tolkien characterizes rather as the involuntary suspension of disbelief. "What really happens", he says, "is that the story-maker proves a successful 'sub-creator'. He makes a Secondary World which your mind can enter." Belief in a Secondary World is not confined to or even typical of children *per se*, but is the hallmark of a certain kind of literary taste. Tolkien makes a plea that the fairy-stories not be assigned either to children or adults as a preferred reading audience, but that they be seen as worthy to be read by adults "as a natural branch of literature".

The next section, "Fantasy", contains some of Tolkien's most deeply considered thoughts on the particular appeal of fairy-stories and how that is achieved. His discussion here owes something to Coleridge's discussion of Imagination in his *Biographia Literaria*. Tolkien uses the word *fantasy*, with its derived meaning of "unreality" to encompass both the working of imagination and the result of that work, sub-creation, the making of a Secondary World. Focusing on narrative as the most effective literary vehicle for fantasy, he dismisses drama as already commanding secondary belief through the pretence that the actors are the characters they portray. To go a step further and accept that they are not just characters but fantastic ones – witches, talking animals, trees – is a step too far.

The section ends with Tolkien's defence of fantasy as a "natural human activity" illustrated by a quote from his poem "Mythopoeia", in which he reconfigures sub-creation as accomplished not with words but with light refracted through the human mind, light splintered "to many hues and endlessly combined in living shapes that move from mind to mind".

In "Recovery, Escape, Consolation", the essay moves to what Tolkien feels is the real "use" of fairy-stories, the important benefits to heart and soul they give their readers. "Recovery" is just that, the recovering or getting-back of something lost: in this case a fresh view of things too long taken for granted. He describes it as a cleaning of the windows, the wiping away of accumulated grime and triteness. The section on "Escape" is equally easy and straightforward, and the term means just what it says. Fairy-stories offer their readers escape from one world into another, a process which Tolkien defends as legitimate against the popular criticism of "escapist" as a term generally understood to mean light or inconsequential entertainment. Distinguishing the Escape of the Prisoner from the

Flight of the Deserter, Tolkien makes it clear that the former is not just understandable but commendable, while the latter is at the very least understandable in the face of the "Morlockian horror of factories". The final Escape satisfies the oldest and deepest desire of humankind, to Escape from Death, and in fairy-stories this Escape leads to the Consolation of the Happy Ending.

It was in this section particularly that Tolkien mounted his staunch defence of the Happy Ending, that element of fairy-stories popularly supposed to distinguish them from real life, but the sense of which, as he well knew, is necessary for the spiritual health and well-being of the human psyche. To accompany the Happy Ending he coined the word *eucatastrophe*, the "good catastrophe" to describe the sudden, miraculous "turn" from sorrow to joy that on the brink of tragedy rescues the story from disaster, which he called *dyscatastrophe*, and makes the Consolation of the Happy Ending possible.

By a kind of Faërian free association, Consolation leads Tolkien to Joy and Joy leads him to *evangelium* and the essay's "Epilogue", a vision of *eucatastrophe* that occurs not in the imaginary world but in the real one. In calling the Gospels of the New Testament, the story of Christ, the most successful fairy-story because it is the one that has been accepted as true Tolkien is not making light of the Gospels, but revealing the underlying gravity and essential truth of fairy-stories. The little *eucatastrophes* of fairy-tales, of "Snow White" and "Cinderella" wherein a dying heroine can be restored to life by a kiss, or of "The Black Bull of Norroway", when after the maiden's long sacrifice and suffering the knight wakens and turns to her, are foreshadowings of the Great Tale. "The presence of the greatest does not depress the small" said Tolkien. On the contrary, it hallows it.

It does not seem unreasonable to suppose that in attaching this "Epilogue" to what came before it, Tolkien was seeking to give "On Fairy-stories" its own "turn" and adding his own Consolation and Happy Ending to his essay.

THE IMMEDIATE CONTEXT

"On Fairy-stories" had its genesis in the Andrew Lang Lecture Tolkien gave at the University of St. Andrews on 8 March 1939. Asked to speak on some aspect of Lang's life and work, Tolkien chose fairy-stories, the subject for which Lang was and still is best known to the general public. We may speculate that when Tolkien picked the topic he might already have had fairy-stories on his mind, having just over a year before published his own extended fairy-story, *The Hobbit*, to critical and popular acclaim. While *The Hobbit* can be seen as prologue to the lecture, the lecture must be seen as both prologue and guide to that tale's sequel, *The Lord of the Rings*, on which Tolkien was just then beginning work. The lecture on fairy-stories came at a critical juncture in Tolkien's creative development. It marked the transition between his two best-known works, but it also functioned as the bridge connecting them, facilitating the perceptible improvement in tone and treatment from one to the other. *The Lord of the Rings* became the practical application and demonstration of the principles set forth at St. Andrews. Tolkien alluded to this in a letter to W.H. Auden *á propos The Lord of the Rings*:

I had been thinking about 'Fairy Stories' and their relation to children – some of the results I put into a lecture at St. Andrews and eventually enlarged and published in an Essay. (*Letters*, 216).

Not long after, he returned to the subject in a letter to his aunt, Jane Neave:

I am not interested in the 'child' as such . . . and have no intention of meeting him/her halfway, or a quarter of the way. . . . I have only once made the mistake of trying to do it, to my lasting regret, and (I am glad to say) with the disapproval of intelligent children: in the earlier part of

The Hobbit. But I had not then given any serious thought to the matter: I had not freed myself from the contemporary delusions about 'fairy-stories' and children. I had to think about it, however, before I gave an 'Andrew Lang' lecture at St. Andrews on Fairy-stories; and I must say I think the result was entirely beneficial to *The Lord of the Rings*, which was a practical demonstration of the views that I expressed. (*Letters* 309–310).

In respect of his own fiction, then, Tolkien's Andrew Lang lecture stands as a watershed in his development as a writer and marks an exponential improvement in Tolkien's own authorial development. It is a benchmark and a point from which, although this was ancillary to the defence of fairy-stories, he was able to look both backwards and forwards at the practice of his craft.

Reading it, we can find between the lines his recognition of the flaws in his own fairy-story, *The Hobbit*. Beyond that and far more important, we see him hammering out the principles for sub-creation and the inner consistency of reality in fantasy fiction by which he created *The Lord of the Rings*. What was effective and beguiling in *The Hobbit* – hobbit earthiness combined with fairy tale, the tentative beginnings of a Faërie Otherworld – has been retained and wrought to a high finish in *The Lord of the Rings*. What was problematic or ill-fitted – the heavy-handed jokes, the patchwork marvels, the inconsistent mixture of talking purses and third-act saviours – has been eliminated.

Simple comparison of the two books will show the advances in tone and technique from one to the other. Tolkien's criticism of Andrew Lang, that his fairy-stories too often display "an eye on the faces of other clever people over the heads of his child-audience", is equally applicable to *The Hobbit*, which casts a similar eye at "clever people". Gandalf's characterization of Bilbo as "fierce as a dragon in a pinch" is the narrator's cue to engage in a bit of word play on the word *pinch*: "If you have ever seen a dragon in a pinch, you will realize that this was only poetical exaggeration" (24). In itself, this might be funny, but the attempt at humour violates the integrity of the Secondary World that "On Fairy-stories" insists is necessary for Secondary Belief.

In contrast, when Frodo conquers his fear in the barrow, the narrator of *The Lord of the Rings* simply tells the reader that, "There is a seed of courage hidden (often deeply, it is true) in the heart of the fattest and most timid hobbit, waiting for some final and desperate danger to make it grow" (137). The speaker in the first sentence has somewhat the tone and stance of a stand-up comic getting a laugh at his character's expense, while the speaker in the second sentence conveys the assured confidence of a storyteller who likes his characters and respects his audience.

The Hobbit's jokey intrusive narrative voice has been abandoned without regret, together with the familiar relationship between authorial *I* and audience *you* – as in, "pretty fair nonsense I daresay you think it" after the relentlessly jolly elven song at Rivendell, or the editorial, "now you know enough to go on with" after the description of "what is a hobbit?". Instead, *The Lord of the Rings* presents a self-effacing third-person storyteller who begins by announcing simply and without comment that, "When Mr. Bilbo Baggins of Bag-end announced that he would shortly be celebrating his eleventy-first birthday with a party of special magnificence, there was much talk and excitement in Hobbiton". Now you do indeed "know enough to go on with", but neither that fact nor the narrator who communicates it without commentary has been plucked out of the world of the narrative. Nor have you as the reader.

Other changes show commensurate improvement. An exponential development in skill of introduction and integration into plot and theme distinguishes the shadowy Strider who becomes Aragorn from the "grim-voiced" man at Lake-town who turns into Bard the Bowman. The one, whose unannounced appearance in the Common Room of *The Prancing Pony* at Bree is not just integral to his character but is part of the plot, is credibly vouched for, first by Gandalf's letter and then by his own appearance and account of himself. The other, with no introduction and in less than a page of text is hastily given a history and genealogy that have all the appearance of an add-on. Whatever subsequent part he plays in the negotiations at the Lonely Mountain, Bard the Bowman is initially a plot device to relieve Bilbo of the un-hobbitlike deed of killing the dragon.[1] In contrast, the dual identity of Strider/Aragorn is part of the pre-history of *The Lord of the Rings*. That it did not start out as such is testament to Tolkien's increasing skill in re-weaving his material according to the principles developed in "On Fairy-stories".

It is in his practical approach to the writing of fantasy that Tolkien hits his critical stride. "Anyone", he says, "can say *the green sun*", but to make a Secondary World "inside which the green sun will be credible . . . will certainly demand . . . a special skill, a kind of elvish craft" ("On Fairy-stories", paragraphs 68–9, 140). The improvement in his own elvish craft from *The Hobbit* to *The Lord of the Rings* is the best example. In *The Lord of the Rings*, the realm of Faërie that is the home and source of other-world enchantment is more internally consistent and better integrated than it was in *The Hobbit*. The theatrical special effects of Mirkwood's disappearing elves, blinking lights, and talking spiders give way to the Old Forest's ominous silence and the hostility of its trees. In the yet more potent Faërie of Lórien, the elven magic which Sam Gamgee feels but cannot express does not reside in any particular special effects, but in the indescribable (though not imperceptible) atmosphere that suffuses that land.

The music-hall speech that marks *The Hobbit*'s comical trolls (and their talking purse) has been replaced by the authentic, coarsely realistic gutter-slang of the orcs. The trolls are caricatures; the orcs are drawn as if from life. All of these improvements can be subsumed under the heading of the most potent phrase in Tolkien's essay, "the inner consistency of reality". *The Lord of the Rings* has it; *The Hobbit* has it intermittently, but not consistently. What is more, *The Lord of the Rings* has it largely

---

[1] See John Rateliff's discussion of Bard in *Return to Bag End*, The History of *The Hobbit* Part Two, pp. 555–8.

because The Hobbit does not, and even more because the writing of "On Fairy-stories" allowed Tolkien to analyse and codify – and put into practice – the difference between them.[1]

Avoiding any reference to his own work, but pulling no punches in pointing out the flaws in that of other writers (such luminaries as Michael Drayton, William Shakespeare, Andrew Lang and Sir James M. Barrie), Tolkien established positive criteria by which fairy-stories – and by extension his own developing kind of fantasy literature – could be evaluated. He built up a working vocabulary for the craft of fantasy that could be used in its criticism, developing such terms as *sub-creation, Secondary World, Faërie, inner consistency of reality, Cauldron of Story, the Soup*. His fairy-story essay covers many more aspects of fairy tales than there is room or time to discuss here, but its chief concern is the essential nature of fairy-stories, their position in relationship to myth, the character of their intended audience, and their uses as a literary genre.

THE LARGER CONTEXT

Occupying a primary position in the context of Tolkien's own life and work, and of the genres of fairy-story and fantasy in general, the essay fits as well into a larger literary context. Ever since Aristotle set out to examine how tragedy affected an audience, writers and thinkers have explored the power of the word and its effect on the mind. Tolkien's essay is part of that tradition.

---

[1]   It must be acknowledged that although Tolkien profited from the mistakes he made in *The Hobbit* to develop the principles he laid out in "On Fairy-stories" and put into practice in *The Lord of the Rings*, the sum of his works surpasses his own critique of them. Tolkien could certainly have achieved *The Lord of the Rings* without delivering his lecture. In similar fashion, "On Fairy-stories" goes beyond its function as an instruction manual on the writing of fairy-stories, even novelistically extended ones. Tolkien's essay has now become a standard reference-work for fantasy criticism in general, a defence of the poet's art of making with words, and a capsule history of the study of folklore.

Exploring and commenting on the history, narrative strategies, contents and emotional effects of one of the oldest narrative forms, "On Fairy-stories" is part of a critical tradition on imaginative writing that reaches from Classical Greece to the late twentieth century. It belongs in the same line as Aristotle's *Poetics*, Sidney's *Defence of Poesey*, Wordsworth's Preface to the *Lyrical Ballads*, Coleridge on Imagination in *Biographia Literaria*, and T.S. Eliot's essay on "Tradition and the Individual Talent" in *The Sacred Wood*. Tolkien's analysis of the potency and potential of juxtaposed and recombined words to construct and/or deconstruct reality, and his psychological treatment of the interdependence of perception and reality, anticipate the modernist and post-modernist thinking of his own time and beyond.

"On Fairy-stories" is not just an exercise in literary or even theoretical analysis, however, any more than it is merely a personal statement of creative principles. It also engages with, and gives an abbreviated history of, one of the great intellectual explorations of the nineteenth and early twentieth centuries, comparative philology and its implications for the development of human perception. The discovery of the linguistic relationship between Sanskrit and Latin led to scholarly investigation into the origins of language and of myth, casting new light on history, culture, and national identity, and giving rise to the great folk and fairy tale collections that we now take for granted. Traditional though they might now seem, they had not always been there.

Europe's interest in the past had been awakened by the seventeenth and eighteenth-century antiquarians. These had focused largely on the physical monuments, the prehistoric standing stones and stone circles of Europe and the British Isles. This archaeological interest was re-fuelled by research into oral folktales. In Germany Jacob and Wilhelm Grimm were searching for the oldest remnants of the Germanic language in order to establish a German national identity (the best-known result being their huge collection of folk and fairy tales first published in 1812). Elias Lönnrot's 1835 *Kalevala*, expanded and republished in 1849, gave the Finns their mythic identity, and John Francis

Campbell's 1860 *Tales of the West Highlands* salvaged on the brink of disappearance the folktales and lore of Celtic Scotland. The Irish-American linguist and folklorist Jeremiah Curtin, who collected and studied the myths and folktales of Slavs and Native Americans, also published in 1890 *Myths and Folk-lore of Ireland* and in 1895 *Tales of the Fairies and of the Ghost World* collected from Munster. In 1901 John Rhys's two-volume *Celtic Folklore* did the same for Wales. Many more examples could be cited from the great nineteenth-century surge of interest in myth and nationalism. But by the time of Tolkien's essay, the great period of collection and interpretation was over, brought to an abrupt close by World War I and never afterward revived with the same force.

Nevertheless, the results of this research – the tales themselves – remained, and with them problems of interpretation. Examined closely, both myth and fairy tale revealed a preoccupation with uncomfortably raw material: murder, bestiality, rape, incest, child abuse, and cannibalism. So perturbing were these contents of humanity's ancestral attic that their discoverers were unable to take them at face value, and felt the necessity not just to explain them, but to explain them away. The messier aspects of myth and fairy tale could not really mean what they seemed to mean, so they were re-interpreted, first as metaphors for natural phenomena, then as carryovers without understanding of savage practices from the primitive "childhood" of humanity. Arguing against both schools of thought, Tolkien puts the major opponents in the mythology wars, Max Müller and Andrew Lang, in clear perspective.

Müller, a native German who spent his adult life in England, was the chief proponent of the theory of "solar mythology", though he soon acquired a cadre of followers. Relying on the findings of the new discipline of comparative philology interpreted by his own nineteenth-century rationalistic lights, Müller declared that the gods of ancient mythology were originally celestial phenomena such as dawn, sunset, lightning and thunder, whose names survived after their initial referents were forgotten. In a process Müller famously described as "a disease of language" the names were then applied to personifications such as Apollo and Zeus and Aurora, making them metaphors for the original phenomena and giving rise to stories about them. A hero slaying a dragon was the day overcoming the night; Cronus swallowing his children was the heavens devouring the clouds, and so on.

But the sprawling characters and plots of all the world's mythologies and folk tales cannot be crammed into a few nature metaphors, however pervasive and powerful they might seem; Tolkien stated that Müller's view of mythology as a disease of language could be "abandoned without regret". "Philology has been dethroned," he declared, "from the high place it once had in this court of inquiry". And Andrew Lang, as Tolkien well knew, was the man who pushed philology off its throne. Lang found and ruthlessly exposed the logical fallacies in using philological evidence to support the solar theory, turning for his own answers to another new discipline, anthropology. Lang and his supporters (like Müller he was not alone in the fight) proposed that rather than the degraded remnants of natural forces the problematic elements in the tales were the survivals of animal-worship and animistic magic. Lang's Darwinian assumption that fairy-stories were leftovers from the childhood of human development led to the corollary assumption that the tales were therefore leftover fare for human children, who would in the course of time, like the human race in general, mature into adulthood and put away childish things.[1]

Tolkien found fault with both schools of thought, criticizing them for their narrowness of vision and naiveté of approach, and proposed instead the simpler answer that fairy-stories, like myths, are the products of a potent sub-creative combination – human language and human imagination – responding to the surrounding world by recreating it in story. "To ask what is the origin of stories", he declared, "is to ask what is the origin of language and

---

[1] It seems never to occur to those who espouse this temporarily comforting analogy that if followed through consistent with its beginning, the logical next stage of such a progression is old age and senescence followed by death.

of the mind" ("On Fairy-stories", paragraph 22). Just as human beings are hard-wired for human language, so they are hard-wired to make stories out of that language, and to make a world out of those stories.

THE PUBLICATION HISTORY

Revised from the lecture over successive stages, the essay reached its first completed form in 1943, some four years after Tolkien first delivered his lecture. "On Fairy-stories" was first published four years after that by Oxford University Press in *Essays Presented to Charles Williams*, edited by C.S. Lewis. This volume had originally been intended as a festschrift for Williams, but on his untimely death in 1945 it was converted to a memorial volume. Subsequent to the publication of *The Lord of the Rings*, "On Fairy-stories" was issued together with Tolkien's short story "Leaf by Niggle" in 1964 in a slim volume titled *Tree and Leaf*.

The editors of the present volume would like to think that Tolkien would be pleased that this new edition will affirm the essay's importance, and will hopefully attract a new audience who may hitherto have been unaware of it. Above all, it will make plain the sound theoretical and conceptual structure that underlies and supports *The Lord of the Rings*. It is a structure that, as its author once declared of an older English poem in the same mode, the *Beowulf*, makes Tolkien's own masterpiece "strong to stand: tough builder's work of true stone".

VERLYN FLIEGER
DOUGLAS A. ANDERSON

PART ONE

THE ESSAY

ON FAIRY-STORIES

J.R.R. TOLKIEN

[Other than numbering the paragraphs for ease of reference with the Editors' Commentary, Tolkien's text is given here in its final form as edited by Christopher Tolkien and published in *The Monsters and the Critics and Other Essays*.]

1 I propose to speak about fairy-stories, though I am aware that this is a rash adventure. Faërie is a perilous land, and in it are pitfalls for the unwary and dungeons for the overbold. And overbold I may be accounted, for though I have been a lover of fairy-stories since I learned to read, and have at times thought about them, I have not studied them professionally. I have been hardly more than a wandering explorer (or trespasser) in the land, full of wonder but not of information.

2   The realm of fairy-story is wide and deep and high and filled with many things: all manner of beasts and birds are found there; shoreless seas and stars uncounted; beauty that is an enchantment, and an ever-present peril; both joy and sorrow as sharp as swords. In that realm a man may, perhaps, count himself fortunate to have wandered, but its very richness and strangeness tie the tongue of a traveller who would report them. And while he is there it is dangerous for him to ask too many questions, lest the gates should be shut and the keys be lost.

3   There are, however, some questions that one who is to speak about fairy-stories must expect to answer, or attempt to answer, whatever the folk of Faërie may think of his impertinence. For instance: What are fairy-stories? What is their origin? What is the use of them? I will try to give answers to these questions, or such hints of answers to them as I have gleaned – primarily from the stories themselves, the few of all their multitude that I know.

FAIRY-STORY

4   What is a fairy-story? In this case you will turn to the *Oxford English Dictionary* in vain. It contains no reference to the combination *fairy-story,* and is unhelpful on the subject of *fairies* generally. In the Supplement, *fairy-tale* is recorded since the year 1750, and its leading sense is said to be (*a*) a tale about fairies, or generally a fairy legend; with developed senses, (*b*) an unreal or incredible story, and (*c*) a falsehood.

5   The last two senses would obviously make my topic hopelessly vast. But the first sense is too narrow. Not too narrow for an essay; it is wide enough for many books, but too narrow to cover actual usage. Especially so, if we accept the lexicographer's definition of *fairies:* 'supernatural beings of diminutive size, in popular belief supposed to possess magical powers and to have great influence for good or evil over the affairs of man'.

6   *Supernatural* is a dangerous and difficult word in any of its senses, looser or stricter. But to fairies it can hardly be applied, unless *super* is taken merely as a superlative prefix. For it is man who is, in contrast to fairies, supernatural (and often of diminutive stature); whereas they are natural, far more natural than he. Such is their doom. The road to fairyland is not the road to Heaven; nor even to Hell, I believe, though some have held that it may lead thither indirectly by the Devil's tithe.

> O see ye not yon narrow road
> So thick beset wi' thorns and briers?
> That is the path of Righteousness,
> Though after it but few inquires.
>
> And see ye not yon braid, braid road
> That lies across the lily leven?
> That is the path of Wickedness,
> Though some call it the Road to Heaven.

> And see ye not yon bonny road
> That winds about yon fernie brae?
> That is the road to fair Elfland,
> Where thou and I this night maun gae.

7 As for *diminutive size:* I do not deny that the notion is a leading one in modern use. I have often thought that it would be interesting to try to find out how that has come to be so; but my knowledge is not sufficient for a certain answer. Of old there were indeed some inhabitants of Faërie that were small (though hardly diminutive), but smallness was not characteristic of that people as a whole. The diminutive being, elf or fairy, is (I guess) in England largely a sophisticated product of literary fancy.[1] It is perhaps not unnatural that in England, the land where the love of the delicate and fine has often reappeared in art, fancy should in this matter turn towards the dainty and diminutive, as in France it went to court and put on powder and diamonds. Yet I suspect that this flower-and-butterfly minuteness was also a product of 'rationalisation', which transformed the glamour of Elfland into mere finesse, and invisibility into a fragility that could hide in a cowslip or shrink behind a blade of grass. It seems to become fashionable soon after the great voyages had begun to make the world seem too narrow to hold both men and elves; when the magic land of Hy Breasail in the West had become the mere Brazils, the land of red-dye-wood.[2] In any case it was largely a literary business in which William Shakespeare and Michael Drayton played a part.[3] Drayton's *Nymphidia* is one ancestor of that long line of flower-fairies and

[1] I am speaking of developments before the growth of interest in the folk-lore of other countries. The English words, such as *elf,* have long been influenced by French (from which *fay* and *faërie, fairy* are derived); but in later times, through their use in translation, both *fairy* and *elf* have acquired much of the atmosphere of German, Scandinavian, and Celtic tales, and many characteristics of the *huldu-fólk*, the *daoine-sithe*, and the *tylwyth teg*.

[2] For the probability that the Irish *Hy Breasail* played a part in the naming of Brazil see Nansen, *In Northern Mists*, ii, 223–30.

[3] Their influence was not confined to England. German *Elf, Elfe* appears to be derived from *A Midsummer-night's Dream*, in Wieland's translation (1764).

fluttering sprites with antennae that I so disliked as a child, and which my children in their turn detested. Andrew Lang had similar feelings. In the preface to the *Lilac Fairy Book* he refers to the tales of tiresome contemporary authors: 'they always begin with a little boy or girl who goes out and meets the fairies of polyanthuses and gardenias and apple-blossom. . . . These fairies try to be funny and fail; or they try to preach and succeed.'

8   But the business began, as I have said, long before the nineteenth century, and long ago achieved tiresomeness, certainly the tiresomeness of trying to be funny and failing. Drayton's *Nymphidia* is, considered as a fairy-story (a story about fairies), one of the worst ever written. The palace of Oberon has walls of spider's legs,

> And windows of the eyes of cats,
> And for the roof, instead of slats,
> Is covered with the wings of bats.

The knight Pigwiggen rides on a frisky earwig, and sends his love, Queen Mab, a bracelet of emmets' eyes, making an assignation in a cowslip-flower. But the tale that is told amid all this prettiness is a dull story of intrigue and sly go-betweens; the gallant knight and angry husband fall into the mire, and their wrath is stilled by a draught of the waters of Lethe. It would have been better if Lethe had swallowed the whole affair. Oberon, Mab, and Pigwiggen may be diminutive elves or fairies, as Arthur, Guinevere, and Lancelot are not; but the good and evil story of Arthur's court is a 'fairy-story' rather than this tale of Oberon.

9   *Fairy,* as a noun more or less equivalent to *elf,* is a relatively modern word, hardly used until the Tudor period. The first quotation in the *Oxford Dictionary* (the only one before A.D. 1450) is significant. It is taken from the poet Gower: *as he were a faierie.* But this Gower did not say. He wrote *as he were of faierie,* 'as if he were come from Faërie'. Gower was describing a young gallant who seeks to bewitch the hearts of the maidens in church.

His croket kembd and thereon set
A Nouche with a chapelet,
Or elles one of grene leves
Which late com out of the greves,
Al for he sholde seme freissh;
And thus he loketh on the fleissh,
Riht as an hauk which hath a sihte
Upon the foul ther he schal lihte,
And as he were of faierie
He scheweth him tofore here yhe.[1]

This is a young man of mortal blood and bone; but he gives a much better picture of the inhabitants of Elfland than the definition of a 'fairy' under which he is, by a double error, placed. For the trouble with the real folk of Faërie is that they do not always look like what they are; and they put on the pride and beauty that we would fain wear ourselves. At least part of the magic that they wield for the good or evil of man is power to play on the desires of his body and his heart. The Queen of Elfland, who carried off Thomas the Rhymer upon her milk-white steed swifter than the wind, came riding by the Eildon Tree as a lady, if one of enchanting beauty. So that Spenser was in the true tradition when he called the knights of his Faërie by the name of Elfe. It belonged to such knights as Sir Guyon rather than to Pigwiggen armed with a hornet's sting.

10   Now, though I have only touched (wholly inadequately) on *elves* and *fairies,* I must turn back; for I have digressed from my proper theme: fairy-stories. I said the sense 'stories about fairies' was too narrow.[2] It is too narrow, even if we reject the diminutive

---

[1]   *Confessio Amantis,* v. 7065 ff.
[2]   Except in special cases such as collections of Welsh or Gaelic tales. In these the stories about the 'Fair Family' or the Shee-folk are sometimes distinguished as 'fairy-tales' from 'folk-tales' concerning other marvels. In this use 'fairytales' or 'fairy-lore' are usually short accounts of the appearances of 'fairies' or their intrusions upon the affairs of men. But this distinction is a product of translation.

size, for fairy-stories are not in normal English usage stories *about* fairies or elves, but stories about Fairy, that is *Faërie*, the realm or state in which fairies have their being. *Faërie* contains many things besides elves and fays, and besides dwarfs, witches, trolls, giants, or dragons: it holds the seas, the sun, the moon, the sky; and the earth, and all things that are in it: tree and bird, water and stone, wine and bread, and ourselves, mortal men, when we are enchanted.

11   Stories that are actually concerned primarily with 'fairies', that is with creatures that might also in modern English be called 'elves', are relatively rare, and as a rule not very interesting. Most good 'fairy-stories' are about the *aventures* of men in the Perilous Realm or upon its shadowy marches. Naturally so; for if elves are true, and really exist independently of our tales about them, then this also is certainly true: elves are not primarily concerned with us, nor we with them. Our fates are sundered, and our paths seldom meet. Even upon the borders of Faërie we encounter them only at some chance crossing of the ways.[1]

12   The definition of a fairy-story – what it is, or what it should be – does not, then, depend on any definition or historical account of elf or fairy, but upon the nature of *Faërie*: the Perilous Realm itself, and the air that blows in that country. I will not attempt to define that, nor to describe it directly. It cannot be done. Faërie cannot be caught in a net of words; for it is one of its qualities to be indescribable, though not imperceptible. It has many ingredients, but analysis will not necessarily discover the secret of the whole. Yet I hope that what I have later to say about the other questions will give some glimpses of my own imperfect vision of it. For the moment I will say only this: a 'fairy-story' is one which touches on or uses Faërie, whatever its own main purpose may be: satire, adventure, morality, fantasy. Faërie itself may perhaps most nearly be translated by Magic[2] – but it is magic of a peculiar mood and power, at the furthest pole from

---

[1]   This is true also, even if they are only creations of Man's mind, 'true' only as reflecting in a particular way one of Man's visions of Truth.

[2]   See further below, p. 63.

the vulgar devices of the laborious, scientific, magician. There is one proviso: if there is any satire present in the tale, one thing must not be made fun of, the magic itself. That must in that story be taken seriously, neither laughed at nor explained away. Of this seriousness the medieval *Sir Gawain and the Green Knight* is an admirable example.

13 But even if we apply only these vague and ill-defined limits, it becomes plain that many, even the learned in such matters, have used the term 'fairy-tale' very carelessly. A glance at those books of recent times that claim to be collections of 'fairy-stories' is enough to show that tales about fairies, about the fair family in any of its houses, or even about dwarfs and goblins, are only a small part of their content. That, as we have seen, was to be expected. But these books also contain many tales that do not use, do not even touch upon, Faërie at all; that have in fact no business to be included.

14 I will give one or two examples of the expurgations I would perform. This will assist the negative side of definition. It will also be found to lead on to the second question: what are the origins of fairy-stories?

15 The number of collections of fairy-stories is now very great. In English none probably rival either the popularity, or the inclusiveness, or the general merits of the twelve books of twelve colours which we owe to Andrew Lang and to his wife. The first of these appeared more than fifty years ago (1889), and is still in print. Most of its contents pass the test, more or less clearly. I will not analyse them, though an analysis might be interesting, but I note in passing that of the stories in this *Blue Fairy Book* none are primarily about 'fairies', few refer to them. Most of the tales are taken from French sources: a just choice in some ways at that time, as perhaps it would be still (though not to my taste, now or in childhood). At any rate, so powerful has been the influence of Charles Perrault, since his *Contes de ma Mère l'Oye* were first Englished in the eighteenth century, and of such other excerpts from the vast storehouse of the *Cabinet des Fées* as have become well known, that still, I suppose, if you asked a man to name at random a typical 'fairy-story', he would be most likely

to name one of these French things: such as *Puss-in-Boots,
Cinderella,* or *Little Red Riding Hood.* With some people
Grimm's Fairy Tales might come first to mind.

16   But what is to be said of the appearance in the *Blue Fairy
Book* of *A Voyage to Lilliput?* I will say this: it is *not* a fairy-
story, neither as its author made it, nor as it here appears 'condensed' by Miss May Kendall. It has no business in this place. I
fear that it was included merely because Lilliputians are small,
even diminutive – the only way in which they are at all remarkable. But smallness is in Faërie, as in our world, only an accident. Pygmies are no nearer to fairies than are Patagonians. I do
not rule this story out because of its satirical intent: there is
satire, sustained or intermittent, in undoubted fairy-stories, and
satire may often have been intended in traditional tales where
we do not now perceive it. I rule it out, because the vehicle of
the satire, brilliant invention though it may be, belongs to the
class of travellers' tales. Such tales report many marvels, but
they are marvels to be seen in this mortal world in some region
of our own time and space; distance alone conceals them. The
tales of Gulliver have no more right of entry than the yarns of
Baron Munchausen; or than, say, *The First Men in the Moon* or
The Time-Machine. Indeed, for the Eloi and the Morlocks there
would be a better claim than for the Lilliputians. Lilliputians are
merely men peered down at, sardonically, from just above the
house-tops. Eloi and Morlocks live far away in an abyss of time
so deep as to work an enchantment upon them; and if they are
descended from ourselves, it may be remembered that an
ancient English thinker once derived the *ylfe,* the very elves,
through Cain from Adam.[1] This enchantment of distance, especially of distant time, is weakened only by the preposterous and
incredible Time Machine itself. But we see in this example one
of the main reasons why the borders of fairy-story are
inevitably dubious. The magic of Faërie is not an end in itself,
its virtue is in its operations: among these are the satisfaction of
certain primordial human desires. One of these desires is to

[1] *Beowulf,* 111–12.

survey the depths of space and time. Another is (as will be seen) to hold communion with other living things. A story may thus deal with the satisfaction of these desires, with or without the operation of either machine or magic, and in proportion as it succeeds it will approach the quality and have the flavour of fairy-story.

17   Next, after travellers' tales, I would also exclude, or rule out of order, any story that uses the machinery of Dream, the dreaming of actual human sleep, to explain the apparent occurrence of its marvels. At the least, even if the reported dream was in other respects in itself a fairy-story, I would condemn the whole as gravely defective: like a good picture in a disfiguring frame. It is true that Dream is not unconnected with Faërie. In dreams strange powers of the mind may be unlocked. In some of them a man may for a space wield the power of Faërie, that power which, even as it conceives the story, causes it to take living form and colour before the eyes. A real dream may indeed sometimes be a fairy-story of almost elvish ease and skill – while it is being dreamed. But if a waking writer tells you that his tale is only a thing imagined in his sleep, he cheats deliberately the primal desire at the heart of Faërie: the realization, independent of the conceiving mind, of imagined wonder. It is often reported of fairies (truly or lyingly, I do not know) that they are workers of illusion, that they are cheaters of men by 'fantasy'; but that is quite another matter. That is their affair. Such trickeries happen, at any rate, inside tales in which the fairies are not themselves illusions; behind the fantasy real wills and powers exist, independent of the minds and purposes of men.

18   It is at any rate essential to a genuine fairy-story, as distinct from the employment of this form for lesser or debased purposes, that it should be presented as 'true'. The meaning of 'true' in this connection I will consider in a moment. But since the fairy-story deals with 'marvels', it cannot tolerate any frame or machinery suggesting that the whole story in which they occur is a figment or illusion. The tale itself may, of course, be so good that one can ignore the frame. Or it may be successful and

amusing as a dream-story. So are Lewis Carroll's *Alice* stories, with their dream-frame and dream-transitions. For this (and other reasons) they are not fairy-stories.[1]

19   There is another type of marvellous tale that I would exclude from the title 'fairy-story', again certainly not because I do not like it: namely pure 'Beast-fable'. I will choose an example from Lang's Fairy Books: *The Monkey's Heart,* a Swahili tale which is given in the *Lilac Fairy Book.* In this story a wicked shark tricked a monkey into riding on his back, and carried him half-way to his own land, before he revealed the fact that the sultan of that country was sick and needed a monkey's heart to cure his disease. But the monkey outwitted the shark, and induced him to return by convincing him that the heart had been left behind at home, hanging in a bag on a tree.

20   The beast-fable has, of course, a connection with fairy-stories. Beasts and birds and other creatures often talk like men in real fairy-stories. In some part (often small) this marvel derives from one of the primal 'desires' that lie near the heart of Faërie: the desire of men to hold communion with other living things. But the speech of beasts in the beast-fable, as developed into a separate branch, has little reference to that desire, and often wholly forgets it. The magical understanding by men of the proper languages of birds and beasts and trees, that is much nearer to the true purposes of Faërie. But in stories in which no human being is concerned; or in which the animals are the heroes and heroines, and men and women, if they appear, are mere adjuncts; and above all those in which the animal form is only a mask upon a human face, a device of the satirist or the preacher, in these we have beast-fable and not fairy-story: whether it be *Reynard the Fox,* or *The Nun's Priest's Tale,* or *Brer Rabbit,* or merely *The Three Little Pigs.* The stories of Beatrix Potter lie near the borders of Faërie, but outside it, I think, for the most part.[2] Their nearness is due largely to their strong moral element: by

---

[1] See Note A at the end (p. 79).

[2] *The Tailor of Gloucester* perhaps comes nearest. *Mrs. Tiggywinkle* would be as near, but for the hinted dream-explanation. I would also include *The Wind in the Willows* in Beast-fable.

which I mean their inherent morality, not any allegorical *significatio*. But *Peter Rabbit*, though it contains a prohibition, and though there are prohibitions in fairyland (as, probably, there are throughout the universe on every plane and in every dimension), remains a beast-fable.

21   Now *The Monkey's Heart* is also plainly only a beast-fable. I suspect that its inclusion in a 'Fairy Book' is due not primarily to its entertaining quality, but precisely to the monkey's heart supposed to have been left behind in a bag. That was significant to Lang, the student of folk-lore, even though this curious idea is here used only as a joke; for, in this tale, the monkey's heart was in fact quite normal and in his breast. None the less this detail is plainly only a secondary use of an ancient and very widespread folk-lore notion, which does occur in fairy-stories;[1] the notion that the life or strength of a man or creature may reside in some other place or thing; or in some part of the body (especially the heart) that can be detached and hidden in a bag, or under a stone, or in an egg. At one end of recorded folk-lore history this idea was used by George MacDonald in his fairy-story *The Giant's Heart*, which derives this central motive (as well as many other details) from well-known traditional tales. At the other end, indeed in what is probably one of the oldest stories in writing, it occurs in *The Tale of the Two Brothers* on the Egyptian D'Orsigny papyrus. There the younger brother says to the elder:

'I shall enchant my heart, and I shall place it upon the top of the flower of the cedar. Now the cedar will be cut down and my heart will fall to the ground, and thou shalt come to seek for it, even though thou pass seven years in seeking it; but when thou has found it, put it into a vase of cold water, and in very truth I shall live.'[2]

---

[1]   Such as, for instance: *The Giant that had no Heart* in Dasent's *Popular Tales from the Norse;* or *The Sea-Maiden* in Campbell's *Popular Tales of the West Highlands* (no. iv, cf. also no. i); or more remotely *Die Kristallkugel* in Grimm.

[2]   Budge, *Egyptian Reading Book*, p. xxi

22 But that point of interest and such comparisons as these bring us to the brink of the second question: What are the origins of 'fairy-stories'? That must, of course, mean: the origin or origins of the fairy elements. To ask what is the origin of stories (however qualified) is to ask what is the origin of language and of the mind.

ORIGINS

23 Actually the question: What is the origin of the fairy element? lands us ultimately in the same fundamental inquiry; but there are many elements in fairy-stories (such as this detachable heart, or swan-robes, magic rings, arbitrary prohibitions, wicked stepmothers, and even fairies themselves) that such can be studied without tackling this main question. Such studies are, however, scientific (at least in intent); they are the pursuit of folklorists or anthropologists: that is of people using the stories not as they were meant to be used, but as a quarry from which to dig evidence, or information, about matters in which they are interested. A perfectly legitimate procedure in itself – but ignorance or forgetfulness of the nature of a story (as a thing told in its entirety) has often led such inquirers into strange judgments. To investigators of this sort recurring similarities (such as this matter of the heart) seem specially important. So much so that students of folk-lore are apt to get off their own proper track, or to express themselves in a misleading 'shorthand': misleading in particular, if it gets out of their monographs into books about literature. They are inclined to say that any two stories that are built round the same folk-lore motive, or are made up of a generally similar combination of such motives, are 'the same stories'. We read that *Beowulf* 'is only a version of *Dat Erdmänneken*'; that '*The Black Bull of Norroway* is *Beauty and the Beast*', or 'is the same story as *Eros and Psyche*'; that the Norse *Mastermaid* (or the Gaelic *Battle of the Birds*[1] and its

[1] See Campbell, op. cit., vol. i

many congeners and variants) is 'the same story as the Greek tale of Jason and Medea'.

24   Statements of that kind may express (in undue abbreviation) some element of truth; but they are not true in a fairy-story sense, they are not true in art or literature. It is precisely the colouring, the atmosphere, the unclassifiable individual details of a story, and above all the general purport that informs with life the undissected bones of the plot, that really count. Shakespeare's *King Lear* is not the same as Layamon's story in his *Brut.* Or to take the extreme case of *Red Riding Hood:* it is of merely secondary interest that the re-told versions of this story, in which the little girl is saved by wood-cutters, is directly derived from Perrault's story in which she was eaten by the wolf. The really important thing is that the later version has a happy ending (more or less, and if we do not mourn the grandmother overmuch), and that Perrault's version had not. And that is a very profound difference, to which I shall return.

25   Of course, I do not deny, for I feel strongly, the fascination of the desire to unravel the intricately knotted and ramified history of the branches on the Tree of Tales. It is closely connected with the philologists' study of the tangled skein of Language, of which I know some small pieces. But even with regard to language it seems to me that the essential quality and aptitudes of a given language in a living moment is both more important to seize and far more difficult to make explicit than its linear history. So with regard to fairy-stories, I feel that it is more interesting, and also in its way more difficult, to consider what they are, what they have become for us, and what values the long alchemic processes of time have produced in them. In Dasent's words I would say: 'We must be satisfied with the soup that is set before us, and not desire to see the bones of the ox out of which it has been boiled.'[1] Though, oddly enough, Dasent by 'the soup' meant a mishmash of bogus pre-history founded on the early surmises of Comparative Philology; and by 'desire to see the bones' he meant a demand to see the workings and the

[1]   *Popular Tales from the Norse*, p. xviii

proofs that led to these theories. By 'the soup' I mean the story as it is served up by its author or teller, and by 'the bones' its sources or material – even when (by rare luck) those can be with certainty discovered. But I do not, of course, forbid criticism of the soup as soup.

26   I shall therefore pass lightly over the question of origins. I am too unlearned to deal with it in any other way; but it is the least important of the three questions for my purpose, and a few remarks will suffice. It is plain enough that fairy-stories (in wider or in narrower sense) are very ancient indeed. Related things appear in very early records; and they are found universally, wherever there is language. We are therefore obviously confronted with a variant of the problem that the archaeologist encounters, or the comparative philologist: with the debate between *independent evolution* (or rather *invention*) of the similar; *inheritance* from a common ancestry; and *diffusion* at various times from one or more centres. Most debates depend on an attempt (by one or both sides) at over-simplification; and I do not suppose that this debate is an exception. The history of fairy-stories is probably more complex than the physical history of the human race, and as complex as the history of human language. All three things: independent invention, inheritance, and diffusion, have evidently played their part in producing the intricate web of Story. It is now beyond all skill but that of the elves to unravel it.[1] Of these three *invention* is the most important and fundamental, and so (not surprisingly) also the most mysterious. To an inventor, that is to a storymaker, the other two must in the end lead back. *Diffusion* (borrowing in space) whether of an artefact or a story, only refers the problem of origin elsewhere.

[1]   Except in particularly fortunate cases; or in a few occasional details. It is indeed easier to unravel a single *thread* – an incident, a name, a motive – than to trace the history of any *picture* defined by many threads. For with the picture in the tapestry a new element has come in: the picture is greater than, and not explained by, the sum of the component threads. Therein lies the inherent weakness of the analytic (or 'scientific') method: it finds out much about things that occur in stories, but little or nothing about their effect in any given story

At the centre of the supposed diffusion there is a place where once an inventor lived. Similarly with *inheritance* (borrowing in time): in this way we arrive at last only at an ancestral inventor. While if we believe that sometimes there occurred the independent striking out of similar ideas and themes or devices, we simply multiply the ancestral inventor but do not in that way the more clearly understand his gift.

27   Philology has been dethroned from the high place it once had in this court of inquiry. Max Müller's view of mythology as a 'disease of language' can be abandoned without regret. Mythology is not a disease at all, though it may like all human things become diseased. You might as well say that thinking is a disease of the mind. It would be more near the truth to say that languages, especially modern European languages, are a disease of mythology. But Language cannot, all the same, be dismissed. The incarnate mind, the tongue, and the tale are in our world coeval. The human mind, endowed with the powers of generalisation and abstraction, sees not only *green-grass,* discriminating it from other things (and finding it fair to look upon), but sees that it is *green* as well as being *grass.* But how powerful, how stimulating to the very faculty that produced it, was the invention of the adjective: no spell or incantation in Faërie is more potent. And that is not surprising: such incantations might indeed be said to be only another view of adjectives, a part of speech in a mythical grammar. The mind that thought of *light, heavy, grey, yellow, still, swift,* also conceived of magic that would make heavy things light and able to fly, turn grey lead into yellow gold, and the still rock into a swift water. If it could do the one, it could do the other; it inevitably did both. When we can take green from grass, blue from heaven, and red from blood, we have already an enchanter's power – upon one plane; and the desire to wield that power in the world external to our minds awakes. It does not follow that we shall use that power well upon any plane. We may put a deadly green upon a man's face and produce a horror; we may make the rare and terrible blue moon to shine; or we may cause woods to spring with silver leaves and rams to wear fleeces of gold, and put hot fire into the

belly of the cold worm. But in such 'fantasy', as it is called, new form is made; Faërie begins; Man becomes a sub-creator.

28   An essential power of Faërie is thus the power of making immediately effective by the will the visions of 'fantasy'. Not all are beautiful or even wholesome, not at any rate the fantasies of fallen Man. And he has stained the elves who have this power (in verity or fable) with his own stain. This aspect of 'mythology' – sub-creation, rather than either representation or symbolic interpretation of the beauties and terrors of the world – is, I think, too little considered. Is that because it is seen rather in Faërie than upon Olympus? Because it is thought to belong to the 'lower mythology' rather than to the 'higher'? There has been much debate concerning the relations of these things, of *folk-tale* and *myth;* but, even if there had been no debate, the question would require some notice in any consideration of origins, however brief.

29   At one time it was a dominant view that all such matter was derived from 'nature-myths'. The Olympians were *personifications* of the sun, of dawn, of night, and so on, and all the stories told about them were originally *myths (allegories* would have been a better word) of the greater elemental changes and processes of nature. Epic, heroic legend, saga, then localised these stories in real places and humanised them by attributing them to ancestral heroes, mightier than men and yet already men. And finally these legends, dwindling down, became folk-tales, *Märchen,* fairy-stories – nursery-tales.

30   That would seem to be the truth almost upside down. The nearer the so-called 'nature myth', or allegory of the large processes of nature, is to its supposed archetype, the less inter-esting it is, and indeed the less is it of a myth capable of throw-ing any illumination whatever on the world. Let us assume for the moment, as this theory assumes, that nothing actually exists corresponding to the 'gods' of mythology: no personalities, only astronomical or meteorological objects. Then these natural objects can only be arrayed with a personal significance and glory by a gift, the gift of a person, of a man. Personality can only be derived from a person. The gods may derive their colour

and beauty from the high splendours of nature, but it was Man who obtained these for them, abstracted them from sun and moon and cloud; their personality they get direct from him; the shadow or flicker of divinity that is upon them they receive through him from the invisible world, the Supernatural. There is no fundamental distinction between the higher and lower mythologies. Their peoples live, if they live at all, by the same life, just as in the mortal world do kings and peasants.

31   Let us take what looks like a clear case of Olympian nature-myth: the Norse god Thórr. His name is Thunder, of which Thórr is the Norse form; and it is not difficult to interpret his hammer, Miöllnir, as lightning. Yet Thórr has (as far as our late records go) a very marked character, or personality, which cannot be found in thunder or in lightning, even though some details can, as it were, be related to these natural phenomena: for instance, his red beard, his loud voice and violent temper, his blundering and smashing strength. None the less it is asking a question without much meaning, if we inquire: Which came first, nature-allegories about personalized thunder in the mountains, splitting rocks and trees; or stories about an irascible, not very clever, red-beard farmer, of a strength beyond common measure, a person (in all but mere stature) very like the Northern farmers, the *bœndr* by whom Thórr was chiefly beloved? To a picture of such a man Thórr may be held to have 'dwindled', or from it the god may be held to have been enlarged. But I doubt whether either view is right – not by itself, not if you insist that one of these things must precede the other. It is more reasonable to suppose that the farmer popped up in the very moment when Thunder got a voice and face; that there was a distant growl of thunder in the hills every time a story-teller heard a farmer in a rage.

32   Thórr must, of course, be reckoned a member of the higher aristocracy of mythology: one of the rulers of the world. Yet the tale that is told of him in *Thrymskvitha* (in the Elder Edda) is certainly just a fairy-story. It is old, as far as Norse poems go, but that is not far back (say A.D. 900 or a little earlier, in this case). But there is no real reason for supposing that this tale is 'unprimitive', at any rate in quality: that is, because it is of folk-tale kind

and not very dignified. If we could go backwards in time, the fairy-story might be found to change in details, or to give way to other tales. But there would always be a 'fairy-tale' as long as there was any Thórr. When the fairy-tale ceased, there would be just thunder, which no human ear had yet heard.

33   Something really 'higher' is occasionally glimpsed in mythology: Divinity, the right to power (as distinct from its possession), the due worship; in fact 'religion'. Andrew Lang said, and is by some still commended for saying,[1] that mythology and religion (in the strict sense of that word) are two distinct things that have become inextricably entangled, though mythology is in itself almost devoid of religious significance.[2]

34   Yet these things have in fact become entangled – or maybe they were sundered long ago and have since groped slowly, through a labyrinth of error, through confusion, back towards re-fusion. Even fairy-stories as a whole have three faces: the Mystical towards the Supernatural; the Magical towards Nature; and the Mirror of scorn and pity towards Man. The essential face of Faërie is the middle one, the Magical. But the degree in which the others appear (if at all) is variable, and may be decided by the individual story-teller. The Magical, the fairy-story, may be used as a *Mirour de l'Omme;* and it may (but not so easily) be made a vehicle of Mystery. This at least is what George MacDonald attempted, achieving stories of power and beauty when he succeeded, as in *The Golden Key* (which he called a fairy-tale); and even when he partly failed, as in *Lilith* (which he called a romance).

35   For a moment let us return to the 'Soup' that I mentioned above. Speaking of the history of stories and especially of fairy-stories we may say that the Pot of Soup, the Cauldron of Story,

[1] For example, by Christopher Dawson in *Progress and Religion.*
[2] This is borne out by the more careful and sympathetic study of 'primitive' peoples: that is, peoples still living in an inherited paganism, who are not, as we say, civilised. The hasty survey finds only their wilder tales; a closer examination finds their cosmological myths; only patience and inner knowledge discovers their philosophy and religion: the truly worshipful, of which the 'gods' are not necessarily an embodiment at all, or only in a variable measure (often decided by the individual).

has always been boiling, and to it have continually been added new bits, dainty and undainty. For this reason, to take a casual example, the fact that a story resembling the one known as *The Goosegirl* (*Die Gänsemagd* in Grimm) is told in the thirteenth century of Bertha Broadfoot, mother of Charlemagne, really proves nothing either way: neither that the story was (in the thirteenth century) descending from Olympus or Asgard by way of an already legendary king of old, on its way to become a *Hausmärchen;* nor that it was on its way up. The story is found to be widespread, unattached to the mother of Charlemagne or to any historical character. From this fact by itself we certainly cannot deduce that it is not true of Charlemagne's mother, though that is the kind of deduction that is most frequently made from that kind of evidence. The opinion that the story is not true of Bertha Broadfoot must be founded on something else: on features in the story which the critic's philosophy does not allow to be possible in 'real life', so that he would actually disbelieve the tale, even if it were found nowhere else; or on the existence of good historical evidence that Bertha's actual life was quite different, so that he would disbelieve the tale, even if his philosophy allowed that it was perfectly possible in 'real life'. No one, I fancy, would discredit a story that the Archbishop of Canterbury slipped on a banana skin merely because he found that a similar comic mishap had been reported of many people, and especially of elderly gentlemen of dignity. He might disbelieve the story, if he discovered that in it an angel (or even a fairy) had warned the Archbishop that he would slip if he wore gaiters on a Friday. He might also disbelieve the story, if it was stated to have occurred in the period between, say, 1940 and 1945. So much for that. It is an obvious point, and it has been made before; but I venture to make it again (although it is a little beside my present purpose), for it is constantly neglected by those who concern themselves with the origins of tales.

36   But what of the banana skin? Our business with it really only begins when it has been rejected by historians. It is more useful when it has been thrown away. The historian would be likely to say that the banana-skin story 'became attached to the

Archbishop', as he does say on fair evidence that 'the Goosegirl *Märchen* became attached to Bertha'. That way of putting it is harmless enough, in what is commonly known as 'history'. But is it really a good description of what is going on and has gone on in the history of story-making? I do not think so. I think it would be nearer the truth to say that the Archbishop became attached to the banana skin, or that Bertha was turned into the Goosegirl. Better still: I would say that Charlemagne's mother and the Archbishop were put into the Pot, in fact got into the Soup. They were just new bits added to the stock. A considerable honour, for in that soup were many things older, more potent, more beautiful, comic, or terrible than they were in themselves (considered simply as figures of history).

37   It seems fairly plain that Arthur, once historical (but perhaps as such not of great importance), was also put into the Pot. There he was boiled for a long time, together with many other older figures and devices, of mythology and Faërie, and even some other stray bones of history (such as Alfred's defence against the Danes), until he emerged as a King of Faërie. The situation is similar in the great Northern 'Arthurian' court of the Shield-Kings of Denmark, the *Scyldingas* of ancient English tradition. King Hrothgar and his family have many manifest marks of true history, far more than Arthur; yet even in the older (English) accounts of them they are associated with many figures and events of fairy-story: they have been in the Pot. But I refer now to the remnants of the oldest recorded English tales of Faërie (or its borders), in spite of the fact that they are little known in England, not to discuss the turning of the bear-boy into the knight Beowulf, or to explain the intrusion of the ogre Grendel into the royal hall of Hrothgar. I wish to point to something else that these traditions contain: a singularly suggestive example of the relation of the 'fairy-tale element' to gods and kings and nameless men, illustrating (I believe) the view that this element does not rise or fall, but is there, in the Cauldron of Story, waiting for the great figures of Myth and History, and for the yet nameless He or She, waiting for the moment when they are cast into the simmering stew, one by one or all together, without consideration of rank or precedence.

38   The great enemy of King Hrothgar was Froda, King of the Heathobards. Yet of Hrothgar's daughter Freawaru we hear echoes of a strange tale – not a usual one in Northern heroic legend: the son of the enemy of her house, Ingeld son of Froda, fell in love with her and wedded her, disastrously. But that is extremely interesting and significant. In the background of the ancient feud looms the figure of that god whom the Norsemen called Frey (the Lord) or Yngvi-frey, and the Angles called Ing: a god of the ancient Northern mythology (and religion) of Fertility and Corn. The enmity of the royal houses was connected with the sacred site of a cult of that religion. Ingeld and his father bear names belonging to it. Freawaru herself is named 'Protection of the Lord (of Frey)'. Yet one of the chief things told later (in Old Icelandic) about Frey is the story in which he falls in love from afar with the daughter of the enemies of the gods, Gerdr, daughter of the giant Gymir, and weds her. Does this prove that Ingeld and Freawaru, or their love, are 'merely mythical'? I think not. History often resembles 'Myth', because they are both ultimately of the same stuff. If indeed Ingeld and Freawaru never lived, or at least never loved, then it is ultimately from nameless man and woman that they get their tale, or rather into whose tale they have entered. They have been put into the Cauldron, where so many potent things lie simmering agelong on the fire, among them Love-at-first-sight. So too of the god. If no young man had ever fallen in love by chance meeting with a maiden, and found old enmities to stand between him and his love, then the god Frey would never have seen Gerdr the giant's daughter from the high-seat of Odin. But if we speak of a Cauldron, we must not wholly forget the Cooks. There are many things in the Cauldron, but the Cooks do not dip in the ladle quite blindly. Their selection is important. The gods are after all gods, and it is a matter of some moment what stories are told of them. So we must freely admit that a tale of love is more likely to be told of a prince in history, indeed is more likely actually to happen in an historical family whose traditions are those of golden Frey and the Vanir, rather than those of Odin the Goth, the Necromancer, glutter of the crows, Lord of the Slain.

Small wonder that *spell* means both a story told, and a formula of power over living men.

39   But when we have done all that research – collection and com-parison of the tales of many lands – can do; when we have explained many of the elements commonly found embedded in fairy-stories (such as stepmothers, enchanted bears and bulls, cannibal witches, taboos on names, and the like) as relics of ancient customs once practised in daily life, or of beliefs once held as beliefs and not as 'fancies' – there remains still a point too often forgotten: that is the effect produced *now* by these old things in the stories as they are.

40   For one thing they are now *old,* and antiquity has an appeal in itself. The beauty and horror of *The Juniper Tree* (*Von dem Machandelboom*), with its exquisite and tragic beginning, the abominable cannibal stew, the gruesome bones, the gay and vengeful bird-spirit coming out of a mist that rose from the tree, has remained with me since childhood; and yet always the chief flavour of that tale lingering in the memory was not beauty or horror, but distance and a great abyss of time, not measurable even by *twe tusend Johr.* Without the stew and the bones – which chil-dren are now too often spared in mollified versions of Grimm[1] – that vision would largely have been lost. I do not think I was harmed by the horror *in the fairytale setting,* out of whatever dark beliefs and practices of the past it may have come. Such stories have now a mythical or total (unanalysable) effect, an effect quite independent of the findings of Comparative Folk-lore, and one which it cannot spoil or explain; they open a door on Other Time, and if we pass through, though only for a moment, we stand outside our own time, outside Time itself, maybe.

41   If we pause, not merely to note that such old elements have been preserved, but to think *how* they have been preserved, we must conclude, I think, that it has happened, often if not always, precisely because of this literary effect. It cannot have been we, or even the brothers Grimm, that first felt it. Fairy-stories are by

[1]   They should not be spared it – unless they are spared the whole story until their digestions are stronger.

no means rocky matrices out of which the fossils cannot be prised except by an expert geologist. The ancient elements can be knocked out, or forgotten and dropped out, or replaced by other ingredients with the greatest ease: as any comparison of a story with closely related variants will show. The things that are there must often have been retained (or inserted) because the oral narrators, instinctively or consciously, felt their literary 'significance'[1] Even where a prohibition in a fairy-story is guessed to be derived from some taboo once practised long ago, it has probably been preserved in the later stages of the tale's history because of the great mythical significance of prohibition. A sense of that significance may indeed have lain behind some of the taboos themselves. Thou shalt not – or else thou shall depart beggared into endless regret. The gentlest 'nursery-tales' know it. Even Peter Rabbit was forbidden a garden, lost his blue coat, and took sick. The Locked Door stands as an eternal Temptation.

CHILDREN

42 I will now turn to children, and so come to the last and most important of the three questions: what, if any, are the values and functions of fairy-stories *now?* It is usually assumed that children are the natural or the specially appropriate audience for fairy-stories. In describing a fairy-story which they think adults might possibly read for their own entertainment, reviewers frequently indulge in such waggeries as: 'this book is for children from the ages of six to sixty'. But I have never yet seen the puff of a new motor-model that began thus: 'this toy will amuse infants from seventeen to seventy'; though that to my mind would be much more appropriate. Is there any *essential* connection between children and fairy-stories? Is there any call for comment, if an adult reads them for himself? *Reads* them as tales, that is, not *studies* them as curios. Adults are allowed to collect and study anything, even old theatre programmes or paper bags.

[1] See Note B at end (p. 79).

43   Among those who still have enough wisdom not to think fairy-stories pernicious, the common opinion seems to be that there is a natural connection between the minds of children and fairy-stories, of the same order as the connection between children's bodies and milk. I think this is an error; at best an error of false sentiment, and one that is therefore most often made by those who, for whatever private reason (such as childlessness), tend to think of children as a special kind of creature, almost a different race, rather than as normal, if immature, members of a particular family, and of the human family at large.

44   Actually, the association of children and fairy-stories is an accident of our domestic history. Fairy-stories have in the modern lettered world been relegated to the 'nursery', as shabby or old-fashioned furniture is relegated to the play-room, primarily because the adults do not want it, and do not mind if it is misused.[1] It is not the choice of the children which decides this. Children as a class – except in a common lack of experience they are not one – neither like fairy-stories more, nor understand them better than adults do; and no more than they like many other things. They are young and growing, and normally have keen appetites, so the fairy-stories as a rule go down well enough. But in fact only some children, and some adults, have any special taste for them; and when they have it, it is not exclusive, nor even necessarily dominant.[2] It is a taste, too, that would not appear, I think, very early in childhood without artificial stimulus; it is certainly one that does not decrease but increases with age, if it is innate.

[1]   In the case of stories and other nursery lore, there is also another factor. Wealthier families employed women to look after their children, and the stories were provided by these nurses, who were sometimes in touch with rustic and traditional lore forgotten by their 'betters'. It is long since this source dried up, at any rate in England; but it once had some importance. But again there is no proof of the special fitness of children as the recipients of this vanishing 'folk-lore'. The nurses might just as well (or better) have been left to choose the pictures and furniture.

[2]   See Note C at end (p. 80).

45   It is true that in recent times fairy-stories have usually been written or 'adapted' for children. But so may music be, or verse, or novels, or history, or scientific manuals. It is a dangerous process, even when it is necessary. It is indeed only saved from disaster by the fact that the arts and sciences are not as a whole relegated to the nursery; the nursery and schoolroom are merely given such tastes and glimpses of the adult thing as seem fit for them in adult opinion (often much mistaken). Any one of these things would, if left altogether in the nursery, become gravely impaired. So would a beautiful table, a good picture, or a useful machine (such as a microscope), be defaced or broken, if it were left long unregarded in a schoolroom. Fairy-stories banished in this way, cut off from a full adult art, would in the end be ruined; indeed in so far as they have been so banished, they have been ruined.

46   The value of fairy-stories is thus not, in my opinion, to be found by considering children in particular. Collections of fairy-stories are, in fact, by nature attics and lumber-rooms, only by temporary and local custom play-rooms. Their contents are disordered, and often battered, a jumble of different dates, purposes, and tastes; but among them may occasionally be found a thing of permanent virtue: an old work of art, not too much damaged, that only stupidity would ever have stuffed away.

47   Andrew Lang's *Fairy Books* are not, perhaps, lumber-rooms. They are more like stalls in a rummage-sale. Someone with a duster and a fair eye for things that retain some value has been round the attics and box-rooms. His collections are largely a by-product of his adult study of mythology and folk-lore; but they were made into and presented as books for children.[1] Some of the reasons that Lang gave are worth considering.

48   The introduction to the first of the series speaks of 'children to whom and for whom they are told'. 'They represent', he says, 'the young age of man true to his early loves, and have his unblunted edge of belief, a fresh appetite for marvels'. '"Is it true?"' he says, 'is the great question children ask.'

---

[1]   By Lang and his helpers. It is not true of the majority of the contents in their original (or oldest surviving) forms.

49   I suspect that *belief* and *appetite for marvels* are here regarded as identical or as closely related. They are radically different, though the appetite for marvels is not at once or at first differentiated by a growing human mind from its general appetite. It seems fairly clear that Lang was using *belief* in its ordinary sense: belief that a thing exists or can happen in the real (primary) world. If so, then I fear that Lang's words, stripped of sentiment, can only imply that the teller of marvellous tales to children must, or may, or at any rate does trade on their *credulity*, on the lack of experience which makes it less easy for children to distinguish fact from fiction in particular cases, though the distinction in itself is fundamental to the sane human mind, and to fairy-stories.

50   Children are capable, of course, of *literary belief*, when the story-maker's art is good enough to produce it. That state of mind has been called 'willing suspension of disbelief'. But this does not seem to me a good description of what happens. What really happens is that the story-maker proves a successful 'sub-creator'. He makes a Secondary World which your mind can enter. Inside it, what he relates is 'true': it accords with the laws of that world. You therefore believe it, while you are, as it were, inside. The moment disbelief arises, the spell is broken; the magic, or rather art, has failed. You are then out in the Primary World again, looking at the little abortive Secondary World from outside. If you are obliged, by kindliness or circumstance, to stay, then disbelief must be suspended (or stifled), otherwise listening and looking would become intolerable. But this suspension of disbelief is a substitute for the genuine thing, a subterfuge we use when condescending to games or make-believe, or when trying (more or less willingly) to find what virtue we can in the work of an art that has for us failed.

51   A real enthusiast for cricket is in the enchanted state: Secondary Belief. I, when I watch a match, am on the lower level. I can achieve (more or less) willing suspension of disbelief, when I am held there and supported by some other motive that will keep away boredom: for instance, a wild, heraldic, preference for dark blue rather than light. This suspension of disbelief may thus

be a somewhat tired, shabby, or sentimental state of mind, and so lean to the 'adult'. I fancy it is often the state of adults in the presence of a fairy-story. They are held there and supported by sentiment (memories of childhood, or notions of what childhood ought to be like); they think they ought to like the tale. But if they really liked it, for itself, they would not have to suspend disbelief: they would believe – in this sense.

52   Now if Lang had meant anything like this there might have been some truth in his words. It may be argued that it is easier to work the spell with children. Perhaps it is, though I am not sure of this. The appearance that it is so is often, I think, an adult illusion produced by children's humility, their lack of critical experience and vocabulary, and their voracity (proper to their rapid growth). They like or try to like what is given to them: if they do not like it, they cannot well express their dislike or give reasons for it (and so may conceal it); and they like a great mass of different things indiscriminately, without troubling to analyse the planes of their belief. In any case I doubt if this potion – the enchantment of the effective fairy-story – is really one of the kind that becomes 'blunted' by use, less potent after repeated draughts.

53   '"Is it true?" is the great question children ask', Lang said. They do ask that question, I know; and it is not one to be rashly or idly answered.[1] But that question is hardly evidence of 'unblunted belief', or even of the desire for it. Most often it proceeds from the child's desire to know which kind of literature he is faced with. Children's knowledge of the world is often so small that they cannot judge, off-hand and without help, between the fantastic, the strange (that is rare or remote facts), the nonsensical, and the merely 'grown-up' (that is ordinary things of their parents' world, much of which still remains unexplored). But they recognise the different classes, and may like all

[1] Far more often they have asked me: 'Was he good? Was he wicked?' That is, they were more concerned to get the Right side and the Wrong side clear. For that is a question equally important in History and in Faërie.

of them at times. Of course the borders between them are often fluctuating or confused; but that is not only true for children. We all know the differences in kind, but we are not always sure how to place anything that we hear. A child may well believe a report that there are ogres in the next county; many grown-up persons find it easy to believe of another country; and as for another planet, very few adults seem able to imagine it as peopled, if at all, by anything but monsters of iniquity.

54   Now I was one of the children whom Andrew Lang was addressing – I was born at about the same time as the *Green Fairy Book* – the children for whom he seemed to think that fairy-stories were the equivalent of the adult novel, and of whom he said: 'Their taste remains like the taste of their naked ancestors thousands of years ago; and they seem to like fairy-tales better than history, poetry, geography, or arithmetic.'[1] But do we really know much about these 'naked ancestors', except that they were certainly not naked? Our fairy-stories, however old certain elements in them may be, are certainly not the same as theirs. Yet if it is assumed that we have fairy-stories because they did, then probably we have history, geography, poetry, and arithmetic because they liked these things too, as far as they could get them, and in so far as they had yet separated the many branches of their general interest in everything.

55   And as for children of the present day, Lang's description does not fit my own memories, or my experience of children. Lang may have been mistaken about the children he knew, but if he was not, then at any rate children differ considerably, even within the narrow borders of Britain, and such generalizations which treat them as a class (disregarding their individual talents, and the influences of the countryside they live in, and their upbringing) are delusory. I had no special 'wish to believe'. I wanted to know. Belief depended on the way in which stories were presented to me, by older people, or by the authors, or on the inherent tone and quality of the tale. But at no time can I remember that the enjoyment of a story was dependent on belief

---

[1]   Preface to the *Violet Fairy Book*.

that such things could happen, or had happened, in 'real life'. Fairy-stories were plainly not primarily concerned with possibility, but with desirability. If they awakened *desire*, satisfying it while often whetting it unbearably, they succeeded. It is not necessary to be more explicit here, for I hope to say something later about this desire, a complex of many ingredients, some universal, some particular to modern men (including modern children), or even to certain kinds of men. I had no desire to have either dreams or adventures like *Alice*, and the account of them merely amused me. I had very little desire to look for buried treasure or fight pirates, and *Treasure Island* left me cool. Red Indians were better: there were bows and arrows (I had and have a wholly unsatisfied desire to shoot well with a bow), and strange languages, and glimpses of an archaic mode of life, and, above all, forests in such stories. But the land of Merlin and Arthur was better than these, and best of all the nameless North of Sigurd of the Völsungs, and the prince of all dragons. Such lands were pre-eminently desirable. I never imagined that the dragon was of the same order as the horse. And that was not solely because I saw horses daily, but never even the footprint of a worm.[1] The dragon had the trade-mark *Of Faërie* written plain upon him. In whatever world he had his being it was an Other-world. Fantasy, the making or glimpsing of Other-worlds, was the heart of the desire of Faërie. I desired dragons with a profound desire. Of course, I in my timid body did not wish to have them in the neighbourhood, intruding into my relatively safe world, in which it was, for instance, possible to read stories in peace of mind, free from fear.[2] But the world that contained even the imagination of Fáfnir was richer and more beautiful, at whatever cost of peril. The dweller in the quiet and fertile plains may hear of the tormented hills and the unharvested sea and long for them in his heart. For the heart is hard though the body be soft.

[1] See Note D at end (p. 81).
[2] This is, naturally, often enough what children mean when they ask: 'Is it true?' They mean: 'I like this, but is it contemporary? Am I safe in my bed?' The answer: 'There is certainly no dragon in England today', is all that they want to hear.

56   All the same, important as I now perceive the fairy-story
element in early reading to have been, speaking for myself as a
child, I can only say that a liking for fairy-stories was not a dominant characteristic of early taste. A real taste for them awoke
after 'nursery' days, and after the years, few but long-seeming,
between learning to read and going to school. In that (I nearly
wrote 'happy' or 'golden', it was really a sad and troublous) time
I liked many other things as well, or better: such as history,
astronomy, botany, grammar, and etymology. I agreed with
Lang's generalised 'children' not at all in principle, and only in
some points by accident: I was, for instance, insensitive to
poetry, and skipped it if it came in tales. Poetry I discovered
much later in Latin and Greek, and especially through being
made to try and translate English verse into classical verse. A real
taste for fairy-stories was wakened by philology on the threshold of manhood, and quickened to full life by war.

57   I have said, perhaps, more than enough on this point. At
least it will be plain that in my opinion fairy-stories should not
be *specially* associated with children. They are associated with
them: naturally, because children are human and fairy-stories
are a natural human taste (though not necessarily a universal
one); accidentally, because fairy-stories are a large part of the
literary lumber that in latter-day Europe has been stuffed away
in attics; unnaturally, because of erroneous sentiment about
children, a sentiment that seems to increase with the decline in
children.

58   It is true that the age of childhood-sentiment has produced
some delightful books (especially charming, however, to adults)
of the fairy kind or near to it; but it has also produced a dreadful undergrowth of stories written or adapted to what was or is
conceived to be the measure of children's minds and needs. The
old stories are mollified or bowdlerised, instead of being
reserved; the imitations are often merely silly, Pigwiggenry
without even the intrigue; or patronizing; or (deadliest of all)
covertly sniggering, with an eye on the other grown-ups present.
I will not accuse Andrew Lang of sniggering, but certainly he
smiled to himself, and certainly too often he had an eye on the

faces of other clever people over the heads of his child-audience – to the very grave detriment of the *Chronicles of Pantouflia.*

59   Dasent replied with vigour and justice to the prudish critics of his translations from Norse popular tales. Yet he committed the astonishing folly of particularly *forbidding* children to read the last two in his collection. That a man could study fairy-stories and not learn better than that seems almost incredible. But neither criticism, rejoinder, nor prohibition would have been necessary if children had not unnecessarily been regarded as the inevitable readers of the book.

60   I do not deny that there is a truth in Andrew Lang's words (sentimental though they may sound): 'He who would enter into the Kingdom of Faërie should have the heart of a little child.' For that possession is necessary to all high adventure, into kingdoms both less and far greater than Faërie. But humility and innocence – these things 'the heart of a child' must mean in such a context – do not necessarily imply an uncritical wonder, nor indeed an uncritical tenderness. Chesterton once remarked that the children in whose company he saw Maeterlinck's *Blue Bird* were dissatisfied 'because it did not end with a Day of Judgement, and it was not revealed to the hero and the heroine that the Dog had been faithful and the Cat faithless'. 'For children', he says, 'are innocent and love justice; while most of us are wicked and naturally prefer mercy.'

61   Andrew Lang was confused on this point. He was at pains to defend the slaying of the Yellow Dwarf by Prince Ricardo in one of his own fairy-stories. 'I hate cruelty', he said, '. . . but that was in fair fight, sword in hand, and the dwarf, peace to his ashes! died in harness.' Yet it is not clear that 'fair fight' is less cruel than 'fair judgement'; or that piercing a dwarf with a sword is more just than the execution of wicked kings and evil stepmothers – which Lang abjures: he sends the criminals (as he boasts) to retirement on ample pensions. That is mercy untempered by justice. It is true that this plea was not addressed to children but to parents and guardians, to whom Lang was recommending his own *Prince Prigio* and *Prince Ricardo* as suitable for their charges.[1] It is

[1]   Preface to the *Lilac Fairy Book.*

parents and guardians who have classified fairy-stories as *Juvenilia.* And this is a small sample of the falsification of values that results.

62   If we use *child* in a good sense (it has also legitimately a bad one) we must not allow that to push us into the sentimentality of only using *adult* or *grown-up* in a bad sense (it has also legitimately a good one). The process of growing older is not necessarily allied to growing wickeder, though the two do often happen together. Children are meant to grow up, and not to become Peter Pans. Not to lose innocence and wonder, but to proceed on the appointed journey: that journey upon which it is certainly not better to travel hopefully than to arrive, though we must travel hopefully if we are to arrive. But it is one of the lessons of fairy-stories (if we can speak of the lessons of things that do not lecture) that on callow, lumpish, and selfish youth peril, sorrow, and the shadow of death can bestow dignity, and even sometimes wisdom.

63   Let us not divide the human race into Eloi and Morlocks: pretty children – 'elves' as the eighteenth century often idiotically called them – with their fairytales (carefully pruned), and dark Morlocks tending their machines. If fairy-story as a kind is worth reading at all it is worthy to be written for and read by adults. They will, of course, put more in and get more out than children can. Then, as a branch of a genuine art, children may hope to get fairy-stories fit for them to read and yet within their measure; as they may hope to get suitable introductions to poetry, history, and the sciences. Though it may be better for them to read some things, especially fairy-stories, that are beyond their measure rather than short of it. Their books like their clothes should allow for growth, and their books at any rate should encourage it.

64   Very well, then. If adults are to read fairy-stories as a natural branch of literature – neither playing at being children, nor pretending to be choosing for children, nor being boys who would not grow up – what are the values and functions of this kind? That is, I think, the last and most important question. I have already hinted at some of my answers. First of all: if

written with art, the prime value of fairy-stories will simply be that value which, as literature, they share with other literary forms. But fairy-stories offer also, in a peculiar degree or mode, these things: Fantasy, Recovery, Escape, Consolation, all things of which children have, as a rule, less need than older people. Most of them are nowadays very commonly considered to be bad for anybody. I will consider them briefly, and will begin with *Fantasy*.

FANTASY

65 The human mind is capable of forming mental images of things not actually present. The faculty of conceiving the images is (or was) naturally called Imagination. But in recent times, in technical not normal language, Imagination has often been held to be something higher than the mere image-making, ascribed to the operations of Fancy (a reduced and depreciatory form of the older word Fantasy); an attempt is thus made to restrict, I should say misapply, Imagination to 'the power of giving to ideal creations the inner consistency of reality'.

66 Ridiculous though it may be for one so ill-instructed to have an opinion on this critical matter, I venture to think the verbal distinction philologically inappropriate, and the analysis inaccurate. The mental power of image-making is one thing, or aspect; and it should appropriately be called Imagination. The perception of the image, the grasp of its implications, and the control, which are necessary to a successful expression, may vary in vividness and strength: but this is a difference of degree in Imagination, not a difference in kind. The achievement of the expression, which gives (or seems to give) 'the inner consistency of reality',[1] is indeed another thing, or aspect, needing another name: Art, the operative link between Imagination and the final result, Sub-creation. For my present purpose I require a word which shall embrace both the Sub-creative Art in itself and a

---

[1] That is: which commands or induces Secondary Belief.

quality of strangeness and wonder in the Expression, derived from the Image: a quality essential to fairy-story. I propose, therefore, to arrogate to myself the powers of Humpty-Dumpty, and to use Fantasy for this purpose: in a sense, that is, which combines with its older and higher use as an equivalent of Imagination the derived notions of 'unreality' (that is, of unlikeness to the Primary World), of freedom from the domination of observed 'fact', in short of the fantastic. I am thus not only aware but glad of the etymological and semantic connections of *fantasy* with *fantastic:* with images of things that are not only 'not actually present', but which are indeed not to be found in our primary world at all, or are generally believed not to be found there. But while admitting that, I do not assent to the depreciative tone. That the images are of things not in the primary world (if that indeed is possible) is a virtue not a vice. Fantasy (in this sense) is, I think, not a lower but a higher form of Art, indeed the most nearly pure form, and so (when achieved) the most potent.

67 Fantasy, of course, starts out with an advantage: arresting strangeness. But that advantage has been turned against it, and has contributed to its disrepute. Many people dislike being 'arrested'. They dislike any meddling with the Primary World, or such small glimpses of it as are familiar to them. They, therefore, stupidly and even maliciously confound Fantasy with Dreaming, in which there is no Art;[1] and with mental disorders, in which there is not even control: with delusion and hallucination.

68 But the error or malice, engendered by disquiet and consequent dislike, is not the only cause of this confusion. Fantasy has also an essential drawback: it is difficult to achieve. Fantasy may be, as I think, not less but more sub-creative; but at any rate it is found in practice that 'the inner consistency of reality' is more difficult to produce, the more unlike are the images and the rearrangements of primary material to the actual arrangements of the Primary World. It is easier to produce this kind of 'reality'

[1] This is not true of all dreams. In some Fantasy seems to take a part. But this is exceptional. Fantasy is a rational, not an irrational, activity.

with more 'sober' material. Fantasy thus, too often, remains undeveloped; it is and has been used frivolously, or only half-seriously, or merely for decoration: it remains merely 'fanciful'. Anyone inheriting the fantastic device of human language can say *the green sun.* Many can then imagine or picture it. But that is not enough – though it may already be a more potent thing than many a 'thumbnail sketch' or 'transcript of life' that receives literary praise.

69   To make a Secondary World inside which the green sun will be credible, commanding Secondary Belief, will probably require labour and thought, and will certainly demand a special skill, a kind of elvish craft. Few attempt such difficult tasks. But when they are attempted and in any degree accomplished then we have a rare achievement of Art: indeed narrative art, story-making in its primary and most potent mode.

70   In human art Fantasy is a thing best left to words, to true literature. In painting, for instance, the visible presentation of the fantastic image is technically too easy; the hand tends to outrun the mind, even to overthrow it.[1] Silliness or morbidity are frequent results. It is a misfortune that Drama, an art fundamentally distinct from Literature, should so commonly be considered together with it, or as a branch of it. Among these misfortunes we may reckon the depreciation of Fantasy. For in part at least this depreciation is due to the natural desire of critics to cry up the forms of literature or 'imagination' that they themselves, innately or by training, prefer. And criticism in a country that has produced so great a Drama, and possesses the works of William Shakespeare, tends to be far too dramatic. But Drama is naturally hostile to Fantasy. Fantasy, even of the simplest kind, hardly ever succeeds in Drama, when that is presented as it should be, visibly and audibly acted. Fantastic forms are not to be counterfeited. Men dressed up as talking animals may achieve buffoonery or mimicry, but they do not achieve Fantasy. This is, I think, well illustrated by the failure of the bastard form, pantomime. The nearer it is to 'dramatised fairy-story' the worse it

[1]   See Note E at end (p. 81).

is. It is only tolerable when the plot and its fantasy are reduced to a mere vestigiary framework for farce, and no 'belief' of any kind in any part of the performance is required or expected of anybody. This is, of course, partly due to the fact that the producers of drama have to, or try to, work with mechanism to represent either Fantasy or Magic. I once saw a so-called 'children's pantomime', the straight story of *Puss-in-Boots*, with even the metamorphosis of the ogre into a mouse. Had this been mechanically successful it would either have terrified the spectators or else have been just a turn of high-class conjuring. As it was, though done with some ingenuity of lighting, disbelief had not so much to be suspended as hung, drawn, and quartered.

71   In *Macbeth*, when it is read, I find the witches tolerable: they have a narrative function and some hint of dark significance; though they are vulgarised, poor things of their kind. They are almost intolerable in the play. They would be quite intolerable, if I were not fortified by some memory of them as they are in the story as read. I am told that I should feel differently if I had the mind of the period, with its witch-hunts and witch-trials. But that is to say: if I regarded the witches as possible, indeed likely, in the Primary World; in other words, if they ceased to be 'Fantasy'. That argument concedes the point. To be dissolved, or to be degraded, is the likely fate of Fantasy when a dramatist tries to use it, even such a dramatist as Shakespeare. *Macbeth* is indeed a work by a playwright who ought, at least on this occasion, to have written a story, if he had the skill or patience for that art.

72   A reason, more important, I think, than the inadequacy of stage-effects, is this: Drama has, of its very nature, already attempted a kind of bogus, or shall I say at least substitute, magic: *the visible and audible presentation of imaginary men in a story.* That is in itself an attempt to counterfeit the magician's wand. To introduce, even with mechanical success, into this quasi-magical secondary world a further fantasy or magic is to demand, as it were, an inner or tertiary world. It is a world too much. To make such a thing may not be impossible. I have never seen it done with success. But at least it cannot be claimed as the proper mode

of Drama, in which walking and talking people have been found to be the natural instruments of Art and illusion.[1]

73   For this precise reason – that the characters, and even the scenes, are in Drama not imagined but actually beheld – Drama is, even though it uses a similar material (words, verse, plot), an art fundamentally different from narrative art. Thus, if you prefer Drama to Literature (as many literary critics plainly do), or form your critical theories primarily from dramatic critics, or even from Drama, you are apt to misunderstand pure story-making, and to constrain it to the limitations of stage-plays. You are, for instance, likely to prefer characters, even the basest and dullest, to things. Very little about trees as trees can be got into a play.

74   Now 'Faërian Drama' – those plays which according to abundant records the elves have often presented to men – can produce Fantasy with a realism and immediacy beyond the compass of any human mechanism. As a result their usual effect (upon a man) is to go beyond Secondary Belief. If you are present at a Faërian drama you yourself are, or think that you are, bodily inside its Secondary World. The experience may be very similar to Dreaming and has (it would seem) sometimes (by men) been confounded with it. But in Faërian drama you are in a dream that some other mind is weaving, and the knowledge of that alarming fact may slip from your grasp. To experience *directly* a Secondary World: the potion is too strong, and you give to it Primary Belief, however marvellous the events. You are deluded – whether that is the intention of the elves (always or at any time) is another question. They at any rate are not themselves deluded. This is for them a form of Art, and distinct from Wizardry or Magic, properly so called. They do not live in it, though they can, perhaps, afford to spend more time at it than human artists can. The Primary World, Reality, of elves and men is the same, if differently valued and perceived.

75   We need a word for this elvish craft, but all the words that have been applied to it have been blurred and confused with other things. Magic is ready to hand, and I have used it above (p. 32),

---

[1]   See Note F at end (p. 82).

but I should not have done so: Magic should be reserved for the operations of the Magician. Art is the human process that produces by the way (it is not its only or ultimate object) Secondary Belief. Art of the same sort, if more skilled and effortless, the elves can also use, or so the reports seem to show; but the more potent and specially elvish craft I will, for lack of a less debatable word, call Enchantment. Enchantment produces a Secondary World into which both designer and spectator can enter, to the satisfaction of their senses while they are inside; but in its purity it is artistic in desire and purpose. Magic produces, or pretends to produce, an alteration in the Primary World. It does not matter by whom it is said to be practised, fay or mortal, it remains distinct from the other two; it is not an art but a technique; its desire is *power* in this world, domination of things and wills.

76   To the elvish craft, Enchantment, Fantasy aspires, and when it is successful of all forms of human art most nearly approaches. At the heart of many man-made stories of the elves lies, open or concealed, pure or alloyed, the desire for a living, realised sub-creative art, which (however much it may outwardly resemble it) is inwardly wholly different from the greed for self-centred power which is the mark of the mere Magician. Of this desire the elves, in their better (but still perilous) part, are largely made; and it is from them that we may learn what is the central desire and aspiration of human Fantasy – even if the elves are, all the more in so far as they are, only a product of Fantasy itself. That creative desire is only cheated by counterfeits, whether the innocent but clumsy devices of the human dramatist, or the malevolent frauds of the magicians. In this world it is for men unsatisfiable, and so imperishable. Uncorrupted, it does not seek delusion, nor bewitchment and domination; it seeks shared enrichment, partners in making and delight, not slaves.

77   To many, Fantasy, this sub-creative art which plays strange tricks with the world and all that is in it, combining nouns and redistributing adjectives, has seemed suspect, if not illegitimate. To some it has seemed at least a childish folly, a thing only for peoples or for persons in their youth. As for its legitimacy I will say no more than to quote a brief passage from a letter I once

wrote to a man who described myth and fairy-story as 'lies';
though to do him justice he was kind enough and confused
enough to call fairy-story making 'Breathing a lie through Silver'.

> 'Dear Sir,' I said – 'Although now long estranged,
> Man is not wholly lost nor wholly changed.
> Dis-graced he may be, yet is not de-throned,
> and keeps the rags of lordship once he owned:
> Man, Sub-creator, the refracted Light
> through whom is splintered from a single White
> to many hues, and endlessly combined
> in living shapes that move from mind to mind.
> Though all the crannies of the world we filled
> with Elves and Goblins, though we dared to build
> Gods and their houses out of dark and light,
> and sowed the seed of dragons – 'twas our right
> (used or misused). That right has not decayed:
> we make still by the law in which we're made.'

78 Fantasy is a natural human activity. It certainly does not destroy
or even insult Reason; and it does not either blunt the appetite
for, nor obscure the perception of, scientific verity. On the contrary. The keener and the clearer is the reason, the better fantasy
will it make. If men were ever in a state in which they did not
want to know or could not perceive truth (facts or evidence),
then Fantasy would languish until they were cured. If they ever
get into that state (it would not seem at all impossible), Fantasy
will perish, and become Morbid Delusion.

79   For creative Fantasy is founded upon the hard recognition that
things are so in the world as it appears under the sun; on a recognition of fact, but not a slavery to it. So upon logic was founded the
nonsense that displays itself in the tales and rhymes of Lewis
Carroll. If men really could not distinguish between frogs and
men, fairy-stories about frog-kings would not have arisen.

80   Fantasy can, of course, be carried to excess. It can be ill done.
It can be put to evil uses. It may even delude the minds out of
which it came. But of what human thing in this fallen world is

that not true? Men have conceived not only of elves, but they have imagined gods, and worshipped them, even worshipped those most deformed by their authors' own evil. But they have made false gods out of other materials: their notions, their banners, their monies; even their sciences and their social and economic theories have demanded human sacrifice. *Abusus non tollit usum.* Fantasy remains a human right: we make in our measure and in our derivative mode, because we are made: and not only made, but made in the image and likeness of a Maker.

RECOVERY, ESCAPE, CONSOLATION

81 As for old age, whether personal or belonging to the times in which we live, it may be true, as is often supposed, that this imposes disabilities (cf. p. 51). But it is in the main an idea produced by the mere *study* of fairy-stories. The analytic study of fairy-stories is as bad a preparation for the enjoying or the writing of them as would be the historical study of the drama of all lands and times for the enjoyment or writing of stage-plays. The study may indeed become depressing. It is easy for the student to feel that with all his labour he is collecting only a few leaves, many of them now torn or decayed, from the countless foliage of the Tree of Tales, with which the Forest of Days is carpeted. It seems vain to add to the litter. Who can design a new leaf? The patterns from bud to unfolding, and the colours from spring to autumn were all discovered by men long ago. But that is not true. The seed of the tree can be replanted in almost any soil, even in one so smoke-ridden (as Lang said) as that of England. Spring is, of course, not really less beautiful because we have seen or heard of other like events: like events, never from world's beginning to world's end the same event. Each leaf, of oak and ash and thorn, is a unique embodiment of the pattern, and for some this very year may be *the* embodiment, the first ever seen and recognised, though oaks have put forth leaves for countless generations of men.

82 We do not, or need not, despair of drawing because all lines must be either curved or straight, nor of painting because there

are only three 'primary' colours. We may indeed be older now, in so far as we are heirs in enjoyment or in practice of many generations of ancestors in the arts. In this inheritance of wealth there may be a danger of boredom or of anxiety to be original, and that may lead to a distaste for fine drawing, delicate pattern, and 'pretty' colours, or else to mere manipulation and over-elaboration of old material, clever and heartless. But the true road of escape from such weariness is not to be found in the wilfully awkward, clumsy, or misshapen, not in making all things dark or unremittingly violent; nor in the mixing of colours on through subtlety to drabness, and the fantastical complication of shapes to the point of silliness and on towards delirium. Before we reach such states we need recovery. We should look at green again, and be startled anew (but not blinded) by blue and yellow and red. We should meet the centaur and the dragon, and then perhaps suddenly behold, like the ancient shepherds, sheep, and dogs, and horses – and wolves. This recovery fairy-stories help us to make. In that sense only a taste for them may make us, or keep us, childish.

83   Recovery (which includes return and renewal of health) is a re-gaining – regaining of a clear view. I do not say 'seeing things as they are' and involve myself with the philosophers, though I might venture to say 'seeing things as we are (or were) meant to see them' – as things apart from ourselves. We need, in any case, to clean our windows; so that the things seen clearly may be freed from the drab blur of triteness or familiarity – from possessiveness. Of all faces those of our *familiares* are the ones both most difficult to play fantastic tricks with, and most difficult really to see with fresh attention, perceiving their likeness and unlikeness: that they are faces, and yet unique faces. This triteness is really the penalty of 'appropriation': the things that are trite, or (in a bad sense) familiar, are the things that we have appropriated, legally or mentally. We say we know them. They have become like the things which once attracted us by their glitter, or their colour, or their shape, and we laid hands on them, and then locked them in our hoard, acquired them, and acquiring ceased to look at them.

84   Of course, fairy-stories are not the only means of recovery, or prophylactic against loss. Humility is enough. And there is (especially for the humble) *Mooreeffoc,* or Chestertonian Fantasy. *Mooreeffoc* is a fantastic word, but it could be seen written up in every town in this land. It is Coffee-room, viewed from the inside through a glass door, as it was seen by Dickens on a dark London day; and it was used by Chesterton to denote the queerness of things that have become trite, when they are seen suddenly from a new angle. That kind of 'fantasy' most people would allow to be wholesome enough; and it can never lack for material. But it has, I think, only a limited power; for the reason that recovery of freshness of vision is its only virtue. The word *Mooreeffoc* may cause you suddenly to realise that England is an utterly alien land, lost either in some remote past age glimpsed by history, or in some strange dim future to be reached only by a time-machine; to see the amazing oddity and interest of its inhabitants and their customs and feeding-habits; but it cannot do more than that: act as a time-telescope focused on one spot. Creative fantasy, because it is mainly trying to do something else (make something new), may open your hoard and let all the locked things fly away like cage-birds. The gems all turn into flowers or flames, and you will be warned that all you had (or knew) was dangerous and potent, not really effec-tively chained, free and wild; no more yours than they were you.

85   The 'fantastic' elements in verse and prose of other kinds, even when only decorative or occasional, help in this release. But not so thoroughly as a fairy-story, a thing built on or about Fantasy, of which Fantasy is the core. Fantasy is made out of the Primary World, but a good craftsman loves his material, and has a knowledge and feeling for clay, stone and wood which only the art of making can give. By the forging of Gram cold iron was revealed; by the making of Pegasus horses were ennobled; in the Trees of the Sun and Moon root and stock, flower and fruit are manifested in glory.

86   And actually fairy-stories deal largely, or (the better ones) mainly, with simple or fundamental things, untouched by Fantasy, but these simplicities are made all the more luminous by

their setting. For the story-maker who allows himself to be 'free with' Nature can be her lover not her slave. It was in fairy-stories that I first divined the potency of the words, and the wonder of the things, such as stone, and wood, and iron; tree and grass; house and fire; bread and wine.

87   I will now conclude by considering Escape and Consolation, which are naturally closely connected. Though fairy-stories are of course by no means the only medium of Escape, they are today one of the most obvious and (to some) outrageous forms of 'escapist' literature; and it is thus reasonable to attach to a consideration of them some considerations of this term 'escape' in criticism generally.

88   I have claimed that Escape is one of the main functions of fairy-stories, and since I do not disapprove of them, it is plain that I do not accept the tone of scorn or pity with which 'Escape' is now so often used: a tone for which the uses of the word outside literary criticism give no warrant at all. In what the mis-users are fond of calling Real Life, Escape is evidently as a rule very practical, and may even be heroic. In real life it is difficult to blame it, unless it fails; in criticism it would seem to be the worse the better it succeeds. Evidently we are faced by a misuse of words, and also by a confusion of thought. Why should a man be scorned if, finding himself in prison, he tries to get out and go home? Or if, when he cannot do so, he thinks and talks about other topics than jailers and prison-walls? The world outside has not become less real because the prisoner cannot see it. In using escape in this way the critics have chosen the wrong word, and, what is more, they are confusing, not always by sincere error, the Escape of the Prisoner with the Flight of the Deserter. Just so a Party-spokesman might have labelled departure from the misery of the Führer's or any other Reich and even criticism of it as treachery. In the same way these critics, to make confusion worse, and so to bring into contempt their opponents, stick their label of scorn not only on to Desertion, but on to real Escape, and what are often its companions, Disgust, Anger, Condemnation, and Revolt. Not only do they confound the escape of the prisoner with the flight of the deserter; but they

would seem to prefer the acquiescence of the 'quisling' to the resistance of the patriot. To such thinking you have only to say 'the land you loved is doomed' to excuse any treachery, indeed to glorify it.

89   For a trifling instance: not to mention (indeed not to parade) electric street-lamps of mass-produced pattern in your tale is Escape (in that sense). But it may, almost certainly does, proceed from a considered disgust for so typical a product of the Robot Age, that combines elaboration and ingenuity of means with ugliness, and (often) with inferiority of result. These lamps may be excluded from the tale simply because they are bad lamps; and it is possible that one of the lessons to be learnt from the story is the realization of this fact. But out comes the big stick: 'Electric lamps have come to stay', they say. Long ago Chesterton truly remarked that, as soon as he heard that anything 'had come to stay', he knew that it would be very soon replaced – indeed regarded as pitiably obsolete and shabby. 'The march of Science, its tempo quickened by the needs of war, goes inexorably on . . . making some things obsolete, and foreshadowing new developments in the utilization of electricity': an advertisement. This says the same thing only more menacingly. The electric street-lamp may indeed be ignored, simply because it is so insignificant and transient. Fairy-stories, at any rate, have many more permanent and fundamental things to talk about. Lightning, for example. The escapist is not so subservient to the whims of evanescent fashion as these opponents. He does not make things (which it may be quite rational to regard as bad) his masters or his gods by worshipping them as inevitable, even 'inexorable'. And his opponents, so easily contemptuous, have no guarantee that he will stop there: he might rouse men to pull down the street-lamps. Escapism has another and even wickeder face: Reaction.

90   Not long ago – incredible though it may seem – I heard a clerk of Oxenford declare that he 'welcomed' the proximity of mass-production robot factories, and the roar of self-obstructive mechanical traffic, because it brought his university into 'contact with real life'. He may have meant that the way men were living

and working in the twentieth century was increasing in barbarity at an alarming rate, and that the loud demonstration of this in the streets of Oxford might serve as a warning that it is not possible to preserve for long an oasis of sanity in a desert of unreason by mere fences, without actual offensive action (practical and intellectual). I fear he did not. In any case the expression 'real life' in this context seems to fall short of academic standards. The notion that motor-cars are more 'alive' than, say, centaurs or dragons is curious; that they are more 'real' than, say, horses is pathetically absurd. How real, how startlingly alive is a factory chimney compared with an elm-tree: poor obsolete thing, insubstantial dream of an escapist!

91   For my part, I cannot convince myself that the roof of Bletchley station is more 'real' than the clouds. And as an artefact I find it less inspiring than the legendary dome of heaven. The bridge to platform 4 is to me less interesting than Bifröst guarded by Heimdall with the Gjallarhorn. From the wildness of my heart I cannot exclude the question whether railway-engineers, if they had been brought up on more fantasy, might not have done better with all their abundant means than they commonly do. Fairy-stories might be, I guess, better Masters of Arts than the academic person I have referred to.

92   Much that he (I must suppose) and others (certainly) would call 'serious' literature is no more than play under a glass roof by the side of a municipal swimming-bath. Fairy-stories may invent monsters that fly the air or dwell in the deep, but at least they do not try to escape from heaven or the sea.

93   And if we leave aside for a moment 'fantasy', I do not think that the reader or the maker of fairy-stories need even be ashamed of the 'escape' of archaism: of preferring not dragons but horses, castles, sailing-ships, bows and arrows; not only elves, but knights and kings and priests. For it is after all possible for a rational man, after reflection (quite unconnected with fairy-story or romance), to arrive at the condemnation, implicit at least in the mere silence of 'escapist' literature, of progressive things like factories, or the machine-guns and bombs that appear to be their most natural and inevitable, dare we say 'inexorable', products.

94 'The rawness and ugliness of modern European life' – that real
life whose contact we should welcome – 'is the sign of a biological inferiority, of an insufficient or false reaction to environment.'[1] The maddest castle that ever came out of a giant's bag in
a wild Gaelic story is not only much less ugly than a robot-
factory, it is also (to use a very modern phrase) 'in a very real
sense' a great deal more real. Why should we not escape from or
condemn the 'grim Assyrian' absurdity of top-hats, or the
Morlockian horror of factories? They are condemned even by
the writers of that most escapist form of all literature, stories of
Science fiction. These prophets often foretell (and many seem to
yearn for) a world like one big glass-roofed railway-station. But
from them it is as a rule very hard to gather what men in such a
world-town will *do*. They may abandon the 'full Victorian
panoply' for loose garments (with zip-fasteners), but will use
this freedom mainly, it would appear, in order to play with
mechanical toys in the soon-cloying game of moving at high
speed. To judge by some of these tales they will still be as lustful,
vengeful, and greedy as ever; and the ideals of their idealists
hardly reach farther than the splendid notion of building more
towns of the same sort on other planets. It is indeed an age of
'improved means to deteriorated ends'. It is part of the essential
malady of such days – producing the desire to escape, not indeed
from life, but from our present time and self-made misery – that
we are acutely conscious both of the ugliness of our works, and
of their evil. So that to us evil and ugliness seem indissolubly
allied. We find it difficult to conceive of evil and beauty together.

[1] Christopher Dawson, *Progress and Religion*, pp. 58, 59. Later he adds:
"The full Victorian panoply of top-hat and frock-coat undoubtedly
expressed something essential in the nineteenth-century culture, and
hence it has with that culture spread all over the world, as no fashion of
clothing has ever done before. It is possible that our descendants will
recognise in it a kind of grim Assyrian beauty, fit emblem of the ruthless
and great age that created it; but however that may be, it misses the
direct and inevitable beauty that all clothing should have, because like its
parent culture it was out of touch with the life of nature and of human
nature as well."

The fear of the beautiful fay that ran through the elder ages almost eludes our grasp. Even more alarming: goodness is itself bereft of its proper beauty. In Faërie one can indeed conceive of an ogre who possesses a castle hideous as a nightmare (for the evil of the ogre wills it so), but one cannot conceive of a house built with a good purpose – an inn, a hostel for travellers, the hall of a virtuous and noble king – that is yet sickeningly ugly. At the present day it would be rash to hope to see one that was not – unless it was built before our time.

95   This, however, is the modern and special (or accidental) 'escapist' aspect of fairy-stories, which they share with romances, and other stories out of or about the past. Many stories out of the past have only become 'escapist' in their appeal through surviving from a time when men were as a rule delighted with the work of their hands into our time when many men feel disgust with man-made things.

96   But there are also other and more profound 'escapisms' that have always appeared in fairy-tale and legend. There are other things more grim and terrible to fly from than the noise, stench, ruthlessness, and extravagance of the internal-combustion engine. There are hunger, thirst, poverty, pain, sorrow, injustice, death. And even when men are not facing hard things such as these, there are ancient limitations from which fairy-stories offer a sort of escape, and old ambitions and desires (touching the very roots of fantasy) to which they offer a kind of satisfaction and consolation. Some are pardonable weaknesses or curiosities: such as the desire to visit, free as a fish, the deep sea; or the longing for the noiseless, gracious, economical flight of a bird, that longing which the aeroplane cheats, except in rare moments, seen high and by wind and distance noiseless, turning in the sun: that is, precisely when imagined and not used. There are pro-founder wishes: such as the desire to converse with other living things. On this desire, as ancient as the Fall, is largely founded the talking of beasts and creatures in fairy-tales, and especially the magical understanding of their proper speech. This is the root, and not the 'confusion' attributed to the minds of men of the unrecorded past, an alleged 'absence of the sense of separation of

ourselves from beasts'[1] A vivid sense of that separation is very ancient; but also a sense that it was a severance: a strange fate and a guilt lies on us. Other creatures are like other realms with which Man has broken off relations, and sees now only from the outside at a distance, being at war with them, or on the terms of an uneasy armistice. There are a few men who are privileged to travel abroad a little; others must be content with travellers' tales. Even about frogs. In speaking of that rather odd but widespread fairy-story *The Frog-King* Max Müller asked in his prim way: 'How came such a story ever to be invented? Human beings were, we may hope, at all times sufficiently enlightened to know that a marriage between a frog and the daughter of a queen was absurd.' Indeed we may hope so! For if not, there would be no point in this story at all, depending as it does essentially on the sense of the absurdity. Folk-lore origins (or guesses about them) are here quite beside the point. It is of little avail to consider totemism. For certainly, whatever customs or beliefs about frogs and wells lie behind this story, the frog-shape was and is preserved in the fairy-story[2] precisely because it was so queer and the marriage absurd, indeed abominable. Though, of course, in the versions which concern us, Gaelic, German, English,[3] there is in fact no wedding between a princess and a frog: the frog was an enchanted prince. And the point of the story lies not in thinking frogs possible mates, but in the necessity of keeping promises (even those with intolerable consequences) that, together with observing prohibitions, runs through all Fairyland. This is one of the notes of the horns of Elfland, and not a dim note.

97   And lastly there is the oldest and deepest desire, the Great Escape: the Escape from Death. Fairy-stories provide many examples and modes of this – which might be called the genuine *escapist*, or (I would say) *fugitive* spirit. But so do other stories (notably those of scientific inspiration), and so do other studies.

[1] See Note G at end (p. 83).

[2] Or group of similar stories.

[3] The Queen who sought drink from a certain Well and the Lorgann (Campbell, xxiii); Der Froschkönig; The Maid and the Frog.

Fairy-stories are made by men not by fairies. The Human-stories of the elves are doubtless full of the Escape from Deathlessness. But our stories cannot be expected always to rise above our common level. They often do. Few lessons are taught more clearly in them than the burden of that kind of immortality, or rather endless serial living, to which the 'fugitive' would fly. For the fairy-story is specially apt to teach such things, of old and still today. Death is the theme that most inspired George MacDonald.

98   But the 'consolation' of fairy-tales has another aspect than the imaginative satisfaction of ancient desires. Far more important is the Consolation of the Happy Ending. Almost I would venture to assert that all complete fairy-stories must have it. At least I would say that Tragedy is the true form of Drama, its highest function; but the opposite is true of Fairy-story. Since we do not appear to possess a word that expresses this opposite – I will call it *Eucatastrophe*. The *eucatastrophic* tale is the true form of fairy-tale, and its highest function.

99   The consolation of fairy-stories, the joy of the happy ending: or more correctly of the good catastrophe, the sudden joyous 'turn' (for there is no true end to any fairy-tale):[1] this joy, which is one of the things which fairy-stories can produce supremely well, is not essentially 'escapist', nor 'fugitive'. In its fairy-tale – or otherworld – setting, it is a sudden and miraculous grace: never to be counted on to recur. It does not deny the existence of *dyscatastrophe,* of sorrow and failure: the possibility of these is necessary to the joy of deliverance; it denies (in the face of much evidence, if you will) universal final defeat and in so far is *evangelium,* giving a fleeting glimpse of Joy, Joy beyond the walls of the world, poignant as grief.

100   It is the mark of a good fairy-story, of the higher or more complete kind, that however wild its events, however fantastic or terrible the adventures, it can give to child or man that hears it, when the 'turn' comes, a catch of the breath, a beat and lifting of the heart, near to (or indeed accompanied by) tears, as

[1]   See Note H at end (p. 83).

keen as that given by any form of literary art, and having a peculiar quality.

101   Even modern fairy-stories can produce this effect sometimes. It is not an easy thing to do; it depends on the whole story which is the setting of the turn, and yet it reflects a glory backwards. A tale that in any measure succeeds in this point has not wholly failed, whatever flaws it may possess, and whatever mixture or confusion of purpose. It happens even in Andrew Lang's own fairy-story, *Prince Prigio,* unsatisfactory in many ways as that is. When 'each knight came alive and lifted his sword and shouted "long live Prince Prigio"', the joy has a little of that strange mythical fairy-story quality, greater than the event described. It would have none in Lang's tale, if the event described were not a piece of more serious fairy-story 'fantasy' than the main bulk of the story, which is in general more frivolous, having the half-mocking smile of the courtly, sophisticated *Conte.*[1] Far more powerful and poignant is the effect in a serious tale of Faërie.[2] In such stories when the sudden 'turn' comes we get a piercing glimpse of joy, and heart's desire, that for a moment passes outside the frame, rends indeed the very web of story, and lets a gleam come through.

> Seven long years I served for thee,
> The glassy hill I clamb for thee,
> The bluidy shirt I wrang for thee,
> And wilt thou not wauken and turn to me?

He heard and turned to her.[3]

---

[1]   This is characteristic of Lang's wavering balance. On the surface the story is a follower of the 'courtly' French *conte* with a satirical twist, and of Thackeray's *Rose and the Ring* in particular—a kind which being superficial, even frivolous, by nature, does not produce or aim at producing anything so profound; but underneath lies the deeper spirit of the romantic Lang.

[2]   Of the kind which Lang called 'traditional', and really preferred.

[3]   *The Black Bull of Norroway.*

EPILOGUE

102   This 'joy' which I have selected as the mark of the true fairy-story (or romance), or as the seal upon it, merits more consideration.

103   Probably every writer making a secondary world, a fantasy, every sub-creator, wishes in some measure to be a real maker, or hopes that he is drawing on reality: hopes that the peculiar quality of this secondary world (if not all the details)[1] are derived from Reality, or are flowing into it. If he indeed achieves a quality that can fairly be described by the dictionary definition: 'inner consistency of reality', it is difficult to conceive how this can be, if the work does not in some way partake of reality. The peculiar quality of the 'joy' in successful Fantasy can thus be explained as a sudden glimpse of the underlying reality or truth. It is not only a 'consolation' for the sorrow of this world, but a satisfaction, and an answer to that question, 'Is it true?' The answer to this question that I gave at first was (quite rightly): 'If you have built your little world well, yes: it is true in that world.' That is enough for the artist (or the artist part of the artist). But in the 'eucatastrophe' we see in a brief vision that the answer may be greater – it may be a far-off gleam or echo of *evangelium* in the real world. The use of this word gives a hint of my epilogue. It is a serious and dangerous matter. It is presumptuous of me to touch upon such a theme; but if by grace what I say has in any respect any validity, it is, of course, only one facet of a truth incalculably rich: finite only because the capacity of Man for whom this was done is finite.

104   I would venture to say that approaching the Christian Story from this direction, it has long been my feeling (a joyous feeling) that God redeemed the corrupt making-creatures, men, in a way fitting to this aspect, as to others, of their strange nature. The

---

[1]   For all the details may not be 'true': it is seldom that the 'inspiration' is so strong and lasting that it leavens all the lump, and does not leave much that is mere uninspired 'invention'.

Gospels contain a fairy-story, or a story of a larger kind which embraces all the essence of fairy-stories. They contain many marvels – peculiarly artistic,[1] beautiful, and moving: 'mythical' in their perfect, self-contained significance; and among the marvels is the greatest and most complete conceivable eucatastrophe. But this story has entered History and the primary world; the desire and aspiration of sub-creation has been raised to the fulfillment of Creation. The Birth of Christ is the eucatastrophe of Man's history. The Resurrection is the eucatastrophe of the story of the Incarnation. This story begins and ends in joy. It has pre-eminently the 'inner consistency of reality'. There is no tale ever told that men would rather find was true, and none which so many sceptical men have accepted as true on its own merits. For the Art of it has the supremely convincing tone of Primary Art, that is, of Creation. To reject it leads either to sadness or to wrath.

It is not difficult to imagine the peculiar excitement and joy that one would feel, if any specially beautiful fairy-story were found to be 'primarily' true, its narrative to be history, without thereby necessarily losing the mythical or allegorical significance that it had possessed. It is not difficult, for one is not called upon to try and conceive anything of a quality unknown. The joy would have exactly the same quality, if not the same degree, as the joy which the 'turn' in a fairy-story gives: such joy has the very taste of primary truth. (Otherwise its name would not be joy.) It looks forward (or backward: the direction in this regard is unimportant) to the Great Eucatastrophe. The Christian joy, the *Gloria*, is of the same kind; but it is pre-eminently (infinitely, if our capacity were not finite) high and joyous. But this story is supreme; and it is true. Art has been verified. God is the Lord, of angels, and of men – and of elves. Legend and History have met and fused.

But in God's kingdom the presence of the greatest does not depress the small. Redeemed Man is still man. Story, fantasy, still go on, and should go on. The Evangelium has not abrogated legends; it has hallowed them, especially the 'happy ending'. The

---

[1] The Art is here in the story itself rather than in the telling; for the Author of the story was not the evangelists.

Christian has still to work, with mind as well as body, to suffer, hope, and die; but he may now perceive that all his bents and faculties have a purpose, which can be redeemed. So great is the bounty with which he has been treated that he may now, perhaps, fairly dare to guess that in Fantasy he may actually assist in the effoliation and multiple enrichment of creation. All tales may come true; and yet, at the last, redeemed, they may be as like and as unlike the forms that we give them as Man, finally redeemed, will be like and unlike the fallen that we know.

NOTES

A

107   The very root (not only the use) of their 'marvels' is satiric, a mockery of unreason; and the 'dream' element is not a mere machinery of introduction and ending, but inherent in the action and transitions. These things children can perceive and appreciate, if left to themselves. But to many, as it was to me, *Alice* is presented as a fairy-story and while this misunderstanding lasts, the distaste for the dream-machinery is felt. There is no suggestion of dream in *The Wind in the Willows*. 'The Mole had been working very hard all the morning, spring-cleaning his little house.' So it begins, and that correct tone is maintained. It is all the more remarkable that A. A. Milne, so great an admirer of this excellent book, should have prefaced to his dramatised version a 'whimsical' opening in which a child is seen telephoning with a daffodil. Or perhaps it is not very remarkable, for a perceptive admirer (as distinct from a great admirer) of the book would never have attempted to dramatise it. Naturally only the simpler ingredients, the pantomime, and the satiric beast-fable elements, are capable of presentation in this form. The play is, on the lower level of drama, tolerably good fun, especially for those who have not read the book; but some children that I took to see *Toad of Toad Hall*, brought away as their chief memory nausea at the opening. For the rest they preferred their recollections of the book.

B

108   Of course, these details, as a rule, got into the tales, *even in the days when they were real practices,* because they had a story-making value. If I were to write a story in which it happened that a man was hanged, that *might* show in later ages, if the story survived – in itself a sign that the story possessed some permanent, and more than local or temporary, value – that it was

written at a period when men were really hanged, as a legal practice. *Might:* the inference would not, of course, in that future time be certain. For certainty on that point the future inquirer would have to know definitely when hanging was practised and when I lived. I could have borrowed the incident from other times and places, from other stories; I could simply have invented it. But even if this inference happened to be correct, the hanging-scene would only occur in the story, *(a)* because I was aware of the dramatic, tragic, or macabre force of this incident in my tale, and *(b)* because those who handed it down felt this force enough to make them keep the incident in. Distance of time, sheer antiquity and alienness, might later sharpen the edge of the tragedy or the horror; but the edge must be there even for the elvish hone of antiquity to whet it. The least useful question, therefore, for literary critics at any rate, to ask or to answer about Iphigeneia, daughter of Agamemnon, is: Does the legend of her sacrifice at Aulis come down from a time when human-sacrifice was commonly practised?

109   I say only 'as a rule', because it is conceivable that what is now regarded as a 'story' was once something different in intent: e.g. a record of fact or ritual. I mean 'record' strictly. A story invented to explain a ritual (a process that is sometimes supposed to have frequently occurred) remains primarily a story. It takes form as such, and will survive (long after the ritual evidently) only because of its story-values. In some cases details that now are notable merely because they are strange may have once been so everyday and unregarded that they were slipped in casually: like mentioning that a man 'raised his hat', or 'caught a train'. But such casual details will not long survive change in everyday habits. Not in a period of oral transmission. In a period of writing (and of rapid changes in habits) a story may remain unchanged long enough for even its casual details to acquire the value of quaintness or queerness. Much of Dickens now has this air. One can open today an edition of a novel of his that was bought and first read when things were so in everyday life as they are in the story, though these everyday details are now already as remote from our daily habits as the Elizabethan period. But that is a special modern situation. The anthropologists and folk-lorists do not imagine any conditions of that kind. But if they are dealing with unlettered oral transmission, then they should all the more reflect that in that case they are dealing with items whose primary object was story-building, and whose primary reason for survival was the same. The Frog-King (see p. 74) is not a *Credo,* nor a manual of totem-law: it is a queer tale with a plain moral.

C

110   As far as my knowledge goes, children who have an early bent for writing have no special inclination to attempt the writing of fairy-stories, unless that has been almost the sole form of literature presented to them; and they fail most markedly when they try. It is not an easy form. If children have any

special leaning it is to Beast-fable, which adults often confuse with Fairy-story. The best stories by children that I have seen have been either 'realistic' (in intent), or have had as their characters animals and birds, who were in the main the zoomorphic human beings usual in Beast-fable. I imagine that this form is so often adopted principally because it allows a large measure of realism: the representation of domestic events and talk that children really know. The form itself is, however, as a rule, suggested or imposed by adults. It has a curious preponderance in the literature, good and bad, that is nowadays commonly presented to young children: I suppose it is felt to go with 'Natural History', semi-scientific books about beasts and birds that are also considered to be proper pabulum for the young. And it is re-inforced by the bears and rabbits that seem in recent times almost to have ousted human dolls from the playrooms even of little girls. Children make up sagas, often long and elaborate, about their dolls. If these are shaped like bears, bears will be the characters of the sagas; but they will talk like people.

D

III I was introduced to zoology and palaeontology ('for children') quite as early as to Faërie. I saw pictures of living beasts and of true (so I was told) prehistoric animals. I liked the 'prehistoric' animals best: they had at least lived long ago, and hypothesis (based on somewhat slender evidence) cannot avoid a gleam of fantasy. But I did not like being told that these creatures were 'dragons'. I can still re-feel the irritation that I felt in childhood at assertions of instructive relatives (or their gift-books) such as these: 'snowflakes are fairy jewels', or 'are more beautiful than fairy jewels'; 'the marvels of the ocean depths are more wonderful than fairyland'. Children expect the differences they feel but cannot analyse to be explained by their elders, or at least recognised, not to be ignored or denied. I was keenly alive to the beauty of 'Real things', but it seemed to me quibbling to confuse this with the wonder of 'Other things'. I was eager to study Nature, actually more eager than I was to read most fairy-stories; but I did not want to be quibbled into Science and cheated out of Faërie by people who seemed to assume that by some kind of original sin I should prefer fairy-tales, but according to some kind of new religion I ought to be induced to like science. Nature is no doubt a life-study, or a study for eternity (for those so gifted); but there is a part of man which is not 'Nature', and which therefore is not obliged to study it, and is, in fact, wholly unsatisfied by it.

E

II2 There is, for example, in surrealism commonly present a morbidity or unease very rarely found in literary fantasy. The mind that produced the depicted images may often be suspected to have been in fact already morbid; yet this is not a necessary explanation in all cases. A curious disturbance of the mind is often set up by the very act of drawing things of this kind, a state similar in quality and consciousness of morbidity to the sensations in a high fever, when the mind develops a distressing fecundity and facility in figure-making, seeing forms sinister or grotesque in all visible objects about it.

113   I am speaking here, of course, of the primary expression of Fantasy in 'pictorial' arts, not of 'illustrations'; nor of the cinematograph. However good in themselves, illustrations do little good to fairy-stories. The radical distinction between all art (including drama) that offers a *visible* presentation and true literature is that it imposes one visible form. Literature works from mind to mind and is thus more progenitive. It is at once more universal and more poignantly particular. If it speaks of *bread* or *wine* or *stone* or *tree,* it appeals to the whole of these things, to their ideas; yet each hearer will give to them a peculiar personal embodiment in his imagination. Should the story say 'he ate bread', the dramatic producer or painter can only show 'a piece of bread' according to his taste or fancy, but the hearer of the story will think of bread in general and picture it in some form of his own. If a story says 'he climbed a hill and saw a river in the valley below', the illustrator may catch, or nearly catch, his own vision of such a scene; but every hearer of the words will have his own picture, and it will be made out of all the hills and rivers and dales he has ever seen, but especially out of The Hill, The River, The Valley which were for him the first embodiment of the word.

F

114   I am referring, of course, primarily to fantasy of forms and visible shapes. Drama can be made out of the impact upon human characters of some event of Fantasy, or Faërie, that requires no machinery, or that can be assumed or reported to have happened. But that is not fantasy in dramatic result; the human characters hold the stage and upon them attention is concentrated. Drama of this sort (exemplified by some of Barrie's plays) can be used frivolously, or it can be used for satire, or for conveying such 'messages' as the playwright may have in his mind – for men. Drama is anthropocentric. Fairy-story and Fantasy need not be. There are, for instance, many stories telling how men and women have disappeared and spent years among the fairies, without noticing the passage of time, or appearing to grow older. In *Mary Rose* Barrie wrote a play on this theme. No fairy is seen. The cruelly tormented human beings are there all the time. In spite of the sentimental star and the angelic voices at the end (in the printed version) it is a painful play, and can easily be made diabolic: by substituting (as I have seen it done) the elvish call for 'angel voices' at the end. The non-dramatic fairy-stories, in so far as they are concerned with the human victims, can also be pathetic or horrible. But they need not be. In most of them the fairies are

also there, on equal terms. In some stories they are the real interest. Many of the short folk-lore accounts of such incidents purport to be just pieces of 'evidence' about fairies, items in an agelong accumulation of 'lore' concerning them and the modes of their existence. The sufferings of human beings who come into contact with them (often enough, wilfully) are thus seen in quite a different perspective. A drama could be made about the sufferings of a victim of research in radiology, but hardly about radium itself. But it is possible to be primarily interested in radium (not radiologists) – or primarily interested in Faërie, not tortured mortals. One interest will produce a scientific book, the other a fairy-story. Drama cannot well cope with either.

G

115 The absence of this sense is a mere hypothesis concerning men of the lost past, whatever wild confusions men of today, degraded or deluded, may suffer. It is just as legitimate an hypothesis, and one more in agreement with what little is recorded concerning the thoughts of men of old on this subject, that this sense was once stronger. That fantasies which blended the human form with animal and vegetable forms, or gave human faculties to beasts, are ancient is, of course, no evidence for confusion at all. It is, if anything, evidence to the contrary. Fantasy does not blur the sharp outlines of the real world; for it depends on them. As far as our western, European, world is concerned, this 'sense of separation' has in fact been attacked and weakened in modern times not by fantasy but by scientific theory. Not by stories of centaurs or werewolves or enchanted bears, but by the hypotheses (or dogmatic guesses) of scientific writers who classed Man not only as 'an animal' – that correct classification is ancient – but as 'only an animal'. There has been a consequent distortion of sentiment. The natural love of men not wholly corrupt for beasts, and the human desire to 'get inside the skin' of living things, has run riot. We now get men who love animals more than men; who pity sheep so much that they curse shepherds as wolves; who weep over a slain war-horse and vilify dead soldiers. It is now, not in the days when fairy-stories were begotten, that we get 'an absence of the sense of separation'.

H

116 The verbal ending – usually held to be as typical of the end of fairy-stories as 'once upon a time' is of the beginning – 'and they lived happily ever after' is an artificial device. It does not deceive anybody. End-phrases of this kind are to be compared to the margins and frames of pictures, and are no more to be thought of as the real end of any particular fragment of the seamless Web of Story than the frame is of the visionary scene, or the casement of the Outer World. These phrases may be plain or elaborate, simple or

extravagant, as artificial and as necessary as frames plain, or carved, or gilded. 'And if they have not gone away they are there still.' 'My story is done – see there is a little mouse; anyone who catches it may make himself a fine fur cap of it.' 'And they lived happily ever after.' 'And when the wedding was over, they sent me home with little paper shoes on a causeway of pieces of glass.'

117   Endings of this sort suit fairy-stories, because such tales have a greater sense and grasp of the endlessness of the World of Story than most modern 'realistic' stories, already hemmed within the narrow confines of their own small time. A sharp cut in the endless tapestry is not unfittingly marked by a formula, even a grotesque or comic one. It was an irresistible development of modern illustration (so largely photographic) that borders should be abandoned and the 'picture' end only with the paper. This method may be suitable for photographs; but it is altogether inappropriate for the pictures that illustrate or are inspired by fairy-stories. An enchanted forest requires a margin, even an elaborate border. To print it conterminous with the page, like a 'shot' of the Rockies in *Picture Post*, as if it were indeed a 'snap' of fairyland or a 'sketch by our artist on the spot', is a folly and an abuse.

118   As for the beginnings of fairy-stories: one can scarcely improve on the formula *Once upon a time*. It has an immediate effect. This effect can be appreciated by reading, for instance, the fairy-story *The Terrible Head* in the *Blue Fairy Book*. It is Andrew Lang's own adaptation of the story of Perseus and the Gorgon. It begins 'once upon a time', and it does not name any year or land or person. Now this treatment does something which could be called 'turning mythology into fairy-story'. I should prefer to say that it turns high fairy-story (for such is the Greek tale) into a particular form that is at present familiar in our land: a nursery or 'old wives' form. Namelessness is not a virtue but an accident, and should not have been imitated; for vagueness in this regard is a debasement, a corruption due to forgetfulness and lack of skill. But not so, I think, the timelessness. That beginning is not poverty-stricken but significant. It produces at a stroke the sense of a great uncharted world of time.

EDITORS' COMMENTARY

1 – **Faërie**. Possibly the single most important term in Tolkien's critical lexicon, with a complex of referents. He used it to mean the Otherworld beyond the five senses – a parallel reality tangential in time and space to the ordinary world; he used it to mean the practice of enchantment or magic, especially through the use of words, for example spells or charms; and he used it to mean the altered mental or psychological state brought about by such practice. Tolkien deliberately employed the variant spelling in place of the more conventional "fairy", to distance himself and his reader from that spelling's connotations of daintiness and prettiness. Over the course of time, he experimented with various but always archaic spellings, including *Faery* and *Fayery*, but remained ever faithful to the same set of meanings.

His usage in the essay follows closely and further develops the definitions given in the OED, particularly senses 1: "The realm or world of the fays or fairies; fairyland, fairydom", and 4: "Of or belonging to 'faerie', resembling fairyland." Sense number one's connection with "fays" is etymological, for both derive from Middle English *faie*, "possessing magical powers", from Old French *fae* "fairy" from Latin *fātā* "the Fates", plural of *fātum*, Fate, the neuter past participle of fārī, "to speak", thus "spoken", demonstrating the power of the word. Clearly, then, *faërie* carries connotations older and considerably darker than its modern cousin.

The word was used in a number of medieval poems with which Tolkien was well-acquainted. Among these are *Sir Orfeo*, (c. 1350) and *Sir Gawain and the Green Knight* (c. 1400), both of which Tolkien edited and translated; Gower's *Confessio Amantis* (c. 1386–90) which he cites for its use of the word in the present essay, and Chaucer's "Wife of Bath's Prologue" (late fourteenth century). In these, the word is used to refer variously to fairies, fairyland, and magic or enchantment. Tolkien's translations took account of all different meanings, as the following examples show:

Sir Orfeo
    l. 193. *"with faierie was forth ynome"*
    Tolkien's translation: "by magic was she from them caught"
    l. 283. *"the king o Faierie with his route"*
    Tolkien's translation: "the king of Faërie with his rout"
    l. 404. *"and thider with fairie ycome"*
    Tolkien's translation: "and thither by fairy magic brought"
    l. 562. *"out of the londe of faiery"*
    Tolkien's translation: "out of the deeps of fairy land"

Sir Gawain and the Green Knight
    l. 240. *"for fantoum and fayry3 þe folk þere hit demed"*
    Tolkien's translation: "a phantom and fay-magic folk there thought it"

A note in Tolkien and Gordon's critical edition of *Sir Gawain and the Green Knight* calls the Green Chapel "nothing else than a fairy mound" (*Sir Gawain and the Green Knight* p. 86).

2 – filled with many things. In every draft up to and including the 1943 typescript, the phrase was "filled with many kings", not "many things'. Tolkien corrected it to "things" at the typesetting stage, probably in 1947.

   – lest the gates should be shut and the keys be lost. Cf. Tolkien's last short story published in 1967, *Smith of Wootton Major*, wherein the hero Smith has exactly this experience, being told by the King of Faery that he must relinquish the star that has allowed him access into that Otherworld. The key (in this case a "fay" star), although not lost, must pass to another owner, and it is clear both to Smith and to the reader, that the gate to Faery is definitely shut against his re-entry. Although *Smith of Wootton Major* goes far beyond the self-referential, and is perhaps Tolkien's most pure example of a fairy-story as described in the essay, some critics have seen in Tolkien's Smith a self-portrait, the depiction of an artist bidding farewell to the world of his creative imagination.

FAIRY STORY

6 – the Devil's tithe. The reference is plain, but its meaning in context less so. In Celtic folklore the Devil's tithe was an offering of food or drink to propitiate the Devil and avoid bad luck. On the Hebridean island of South Uist the Devil's tithe was a portion of dough from the *strùthan*, the St. Michael's Cake baked on Michaelmas, burnt and thrown over the left shoulder. Tolkien's use of the term may refer to the popular medieval notion that the road to fair Elfland, i.e. belief in fairies, was a pagan concept necessarily un-Christian and led to damnation.

An alternate, albeit related interpretation would associate the phrase with a line in the medieval ballad "Tam Lin", another tale of abduction to fairyland, this time of a woman, Fair Janet, rather than a man. Tam Lin tells Janet that "pleasant is the fairy land, / but, an eerie tale to tell, / Ay at the end of seven years/ we pay a tiend to hell". *Tiend* is an old Lowland term for *tithe*. It was the tribute paid by the fairies to the Devil every seven years.

– O see ye not yon narrow road. Verses from the Scottish ballad of "Thomas Rymer". Three versions are given in Francis Child's *English and Scottish Popular Ballads*. The version quoted here is closest to the C version of Child, but even closer to that printed as "Thomas the Rhymer" in *The Oxford Book of English Verse 1250–1900* (1900), edited by Arthur Quiller-Couch. Thomas Rymer or Rhymer, also called Thomas of Erceldoun or Ercildoune, was a poet and seer popularly supposed to have lived in Scotland sometime in the fourteenth century. His prophetic powers were the gift of the queen of Elfland, the speaker in the quatrains, who took Thomas with her to "fair Elfland" and kept him there for seven years (see Note on the Devil's tithe above).

In Tolkien's manuscript drafts, the second line of the third stanza reads "That winds about *the* fernie brae" (as it does in Quiller-Couch) – "*yon* fernie brae" in the final version is probably the result of a copying mistake.

7 – the Glamour of Elfland. Tolkien is using *glamour* in its archaic sense of magic or enchantment, a spell. A variant of *grammar* from Old French *gramaire*, *gramarye*, it is related to the ancient concept of letters as "spelling", therefore magic.

– the magic land of Hy Breasail. A mysterious island, an earthly paradise far to the west of Ireland. From Old Irish *Í* "island", *bres* "beauty, worth; great, mighty".

– footnote 1, the *huldu-fólk*, the *daoine-sithe*, and the *tylwyth teg*. These are all folk-euphemisms, epithets (such as the Greek "kindly ones" for the Furies) to be used for fear of offending the creatures thus referred to. As a courtesy to his hosts, Tolkien uses the Scottish term *daoine-sithe* rather than the more familiar Irish sound-alike, *daoine sidhe*, "the people of the mounds". The Icelandic *huldu-fólk* are the "hidden people"; the Scottish *daoine-sithe* are the "men of peace"; the Welsh *tylwyth teg* are the "fair family". All are specific terms for those supernaturals commonly called "elves".

– footnote 2, Nansen, *In Northern Mists*. Fridtjof Wedel-Jarlsberg Nansen (1861–1930) was a Norwegian explorer and the first to cross the Arctic ocean. He was also Rector of the University of St. Andrews from 1925 to 1928. *In Northern Mists: Arctic Exploration in Early Times* was published in 1911 in two volumes by Heinemann. Tolkien owned copies of this edition. The relevant part of the passage from Nansen (Nansen vol. ii pp. 228–230) is quoted as follows:

> In the ocean to the west of Ireland we find for the first time on this map [Angellino Dalorto/Dulcert p. 226] an island called "Insula de montonis suie de brazile." This island is met with again on later compass-charts under the name of "brazil" as late as the sixteenth and seventeenth centuries. It is evidently the Irish fortunate isle "Hy Breasail," afterward

called "O'Brazil" that has found its way on to this map, or probably on to the unknown older sources from which it is drawn. On this and the oldest of the later maps the island has a strikingly round form, often divided by a channel.

The Irish myth of Hy Breasail, or Bresail, the island out in the Atlantic [cf. vol. i. p. 357], is evidently very ancient; the island is one of the many happy lands like "Tír Tairngiri" [the promised land]. In the opinion of Moltke Moe and Alf Torp the name may come from the Irish "bress" [good fortune, prosperity], and would thus be absolutely the same as the Insulæ Fortunatæ. The Italians may easily have become acquainted with this myth through the Irish monasteries in North Italy, unless indeed they had it through their sailors, and in this way the island came upon the map. The form "brazil" may have arisen through the cartographer connecting the name with the valuable brazil-wood, used for dyeing. The channel dividing the island of Brazil on the maps may be the river which in the legend of Brandan ran through the island called "Terra Repromissionis," and which Brandan (in the Navigatio) was not able to cross. It is probably the river of death (Styx), and possibly the same that became the river at Hop in the Icelandic saga of Wineland (see vol. i p. 359). We this find here again a possible connection, and this strengthens the probability that Brazil was the Promised Land of the Irish, which on the other hand helped to form Wineland.

– **Michael Drayton** (1563–1631). An Elizabethan poet and playwright, contemporary of Shakespeare. His *Nymphidia* (also spelt *Nimphidia*) is a poem of just over seven hundred lines, first published in 1627. Influenced by Shakespeare's *A Midsummer Night's Dream* (printed in 1600, but written earlier), it tells of the intrigues at the Fairy Court, as revealed to the poet by Nymphidia, an attendant on Queen Mab.

– **footnote 3, in Wieland's translation.** Christoph Martin Wieland (1733-1813) translated twenty-two of Shakespeare's plays into German prose, save for *A Midsummer Night's Dream*, which he translated into verse.

– **Andrew Lang** (1844–1912). The Scotsman, in whose honour Tolkien's lecture was given, was in the nineteenth century one of Britain's foremost authorities on folklore and an early and energetic member of the British Folk-Lore Society. Lang was educated at St. Andrews University and at Balliol College, Oxford. He was first a Fellow and then an honorary Fellow of Merton College, Oxford, where Tolkien was also a Fellow. The author of *Custom and Myth* (1884), *Myth, Ritual and Religion* (1887) and *The Making of Religion* (1898) as well as numerous articles in nineteenth-century journals, Lang was a leading proponent of the anthropological theory of folklore, which sought to illuminate the messier aspects of myths and fairy tales by comparing them to the existing customs of "primitive". His contribution to the study of folklore was immense, but he is popularly remembered chiefly as the collector and editor of the twelve "colour" Fairy Books, the Blue, Red, Green, Yellow, Pink, Grey, Violet, Crimson, Brown, Orange, Olive and Lilac published from 1889 to 1910. Tolkien's mention of him is appropriate to the occasion of his lecture but even more, as the rest of the essay makes clear (notwithstanding Tolkien's disagreement with his theories), to his importance as a folklorist.

Tolkien's quote from the preface to *The Lilac Fairy Book* (1910) is imprecise in small details. Lang wrote: "the three hundred and sixty-five authors who try to write new fairy tales are very tiresome. They always begin with a little boy or girl who goes out and meets the fairies of polyanthuses and gardenias and apple blossoms: 'Flowers and fruits, and other winged things.' These fairies try to be funny, and fail; or they try to preach, and succeed. Real fairies never preach or talk slang. At the end, the little boy or girl wakes up and finds that he has been dreaming. Such are the new fairy stories. May we be preserved from all the sort of them!" (p. viii).

8 – And windows of the eyes of cats. The first word in Tolkien's quote is incorrect. The correct citation is:

> The windows of the eyes of cats,
> And for the roof, instead of slats,
> Is covered with the skins of bats, (lines 45–47)

– Oberon. King of the Fairies in Shakespeare's *A Midsummer Night's Dream.* The figure was derived from earlier tales in European romance and folktale where he is depicted as a dwarf or fairy.

– Pigwiggen. An Elizabethan term of contempt, possibly identified with "pigwidgeon", denoting an insignificant or simple person. Unlike Oberon and Mab, Pigwiggen is apparently a character of Drayton's own invention. His name tells you all you need to know about him.

– Mab. Mab or Medb was Queen of Connacht in the heroic Ulster cycle of Irish myth, which tradition assigns to the beginning of the Christian era. Over time her status dwindled from heroic myth to fairy tale, and her stature dwindled as well. She is mentioned in Shakespeare's *Romeo and Juliet* as Queen Mab, still royal but now "the fairies' midwife", and shrunk to a size "no bigger than an agate-stone perched on the forefinger of an alderman". This diminution clearly qualified her for inclusion in Drayton's *Nymphidia*, and illustrates the reductive treatment of fairies so disparaged by Tolkien in the previous paragraph.

– the waters of Lethe. Lethe was the river of forgetfulness in Greek mythology. When the spirits of the dead drank the waters of Lethe in Hades they lost all memory of their earthly lives.

– better if Lethe had swallowed the whole affair. An early draft (see MS. B p. 214) has "It would have been better if it had been beer at an inn."

– Arthur, Guinevere, and Lancelot. Principal figures in the story of the legendary King Arthur and participants in the best-known love triangle in English literature. Tolkien's point is that while Arthur and Guinevere may have been "real", for they had historical antecedents, their world still had more of Faërie, of true enchantment, than the diminutive, simpering cuteness of Drayton's poem.

9 – the poet Gower. John Gower, a Middle English poet (c. 1330–1408), contemporary and friend of Chaucer. His best-known work is the one cited here, the 33,000-line *Confessio Amantis* (The Lover's Confession), recounting, with moral commentary, the stories of famous lovers from antiquity and myth, set within a framework of the Seven Deadly Sins.

G.C. Macaulay's standard edition of *Confessio Amantis* was first published in two volumes as *The English Works of John Gower* in 1900 by the Early English Text Society. These were included as volumes two and three of Macaulay's four-volume set of *The Complete Works of John Gower* (1899–1902), which Tolkien owned. The passage quoted by Tolkien has slight differences in spelling and punctuation from Macaulay's text. Terence Tiller's modern English version, published in 1963, gives this passage as follows: "There he will let his body show, / Set on his well-combed crocquet-curl / A chaplet, or a brooch of pearl, / Or else a leafy coronal / New gathered from the grove – and all / To make himself look trim and fresh. / And then he gazes on their flesh / Like any falcon at the sight / Of prey on which to stoop and light; / As if he came from fairyland, / Thus will he pose before them . . ."

– His croket kembd. According to the OED, a *croket* is "a curl or roll of hair" and the word is also used for the decorative rolls on columns or finials. The sense then is that the "young gallant" has gone to excessive lengths to style his hair fashionably.

– Eildon Tree. Possibly a thorn tree, traditionally associated with magic. According to the British folklorist Katharine Briggs, the hawthorn tree was "primarily thought of as a tree sacred to or haunted by the fairies". In the poem it marks the intersection of the earthly and faery worlds, the place where the Queen of Elfland appeared to Thomas. Though it is no longer where it stood when she carried off Thomas the Rymer, a memorial stone marks the spot at the foot of the Eildon hills on the Scottish-English border overlooking Teviotdale.

– Spenser ... called the knights of his Faërie by the name of Elfe. Edmund Spenser (1552–1599). Elizabethan poet whose long allegorical poem in praise of Elizabeth I, *The Faerie Queene*, was based in part on Arthurian legend and mingled myth, history and Elizabethan politics in a poetic Otherworld. The first three books of *The Faerie Queene* were published in 1590, and the second three followed in 1596.

– Sir Guyon. Hero of Book II of *The Faerie Queen*, the personification of Temperance.

10 – **footnote 2, the Shee-folk.** The more traditional spelling is "Sidhe" but the pronunciation is the same. Although *sidhe* as a term has come to refer to the inhabitants of fairy mounds, the word properly refers to the mounds themselves. The Sidhe were the fairy folk of Ireland, the Tuatha Dé Danann who retreated into the mounds when the Sons of Mil conquered them in the last prehistoric invasion of Ireland.

11 – *aventures*. The unexpected absence of "d" in the spelling is worth noting (it was erroneously inserted in the version printed in the 1966 American compilation of some of Tolkien's shorter works *The Tolkien Reader*). Instead of the usual English word *adventures* Tolkien chooses the French *aventures*, which conveys, in addition to the usual meaning of "exciting experiences", the darker implications of hazard, uncertainty and outright danger that his following phrase "the Perilous Realm" underscores. The Old French spelling, found in medieval *lais* and romances, was *avanture*. Related to *avant* "forward", it carried as well as implications of risk or peril the notion of moving into unknown territory. In Chrétien de Troyes twelfth-century romance *Erec and Enide*, the final, Otherworld episode "The Joy of the Court" is called an *avanture*, one from which the hero, Erec, is warned that he will not return.

12 – *Sir Gawain and the Green Knight*. A medieval Arthurian romance/fairy tale in Middle English alliterative verse recounting Sir Gawain's perilous journey to the Green Chapel to have his head cut off by the Green Knight. With his colleague E.V. Gordon, Tolkien prepared in 1925 a scholarly critical edition of this text, which, although it has necessarily been updated, is still used in British universities. Tolkien's modern English translation of the poem, edited by his son Christopher, was published in 1975 together with translations of two other medieval poems, *Pearl* and *Sir Orfeo*.

15 – Charles Perrault (1628–1703). French writer best known for his literary versions of eight traditional oral folktales, including "Sleeping Beauty", "Cinderella", "Bluebeard", "Puss-in-Boots" and "Little Red Riding-hood", which he collected and published as *Histoires ou Contes du Temps passé, avec des Moralités* ("Stories of Past Times with Morals", 1697). Perrault recast the traditional stories to reflect the manners and lifestyles of the French upper classes of his time, and added moral tags. The first English translations of Perrault's tales were made by Robert Samber, published as *Histories or Tales of Past Times* (1729). Perrault's are the versions of the stories mentioned here with which most English-speaking readers are familiar.

 – *Contes de ma Mère l'Oye*. Later editions of Perrault's collections, some with added verse fairy tales, were renamed *Les Contes de ma Mère l'Oye* ("Stories of Mother Goose"), the subtitle to Perrault's *Histoires*. Mother Goose was a legendary female figure traditionally associated with folk and fairy tales. A popular folk-belief associates her with Bertha Broadfoot, "La Reine Pédauque". See paragraph 35.

 – *Cabinet des Fées*. A 40-volume collection of French fairy tales brought together in the years 1785–89 by Charles-Joseph Mayer (1751–1825).

 – *Grimm's Fairy Tales*. Jacob (1785–1863) and Wilhelm (1786–1859) Grimm are best-known for their collection of traditional German tales first published in two volumes in 1812 and 1815 as *Kinder- und Hausmärchen* ("Children's and Household

Tales"). Later editions were numerous, with varying contents – new tales, substitutions and rewritings. Wilhelm concentrated on the orally transmitted stories themselves. Jacob, though he contributed to the collection, was more interested in searching for linguistic evidence of ancient Germanic culture to support the burgeoning movement for German national unity. The first English translations appeared as *German Popular Stories* (two volumes, 1823 and 1826). Grimm's fairy tales (issued under many and various titles) are probably the most frequently published folk and fairy tales in the world.

16 – *A Voyage to Lilliput.* Part One of what is best known as *Gulliver's Travels* (originally published in 1726 as *Travels into Several Remote Nations of the World in Four Parts by Lemuel Gulliver*), a biting condemnation of human folly and petty pretension by the Irish satirist Jonathan Swift (1667–1745). The small size of the inhabitants of the kingdom of Lilliput compared to that of Gulliver allows him (and the reader) to see them as a mockery of human pretension and self-importance. However, this does not make Lilliputians fairies, nor Lilliput a fairyland.

    – Miss May Kendall. May Kendall (1861–1943), assisted Lang and his wife with retelling and adapting stories for the fairy tale collections. Her first book, the novel *That Very Mab* (1885), was written in collaboration with Lang. It tells of Mab, the queen of the fairies, and her visit to England, and serves as a thinly-veiled criticism of English society.

    – included merely because Lilliputians are small. At variance with this judgment is Tolkien's inclusion of lilliputians [*sic*] with hobbits and dwarves as "small people" in chapter one of the first edition of *The Hobbit*. The reference to Lilliputians was removed in the 1966 revision to the text.

    – Pygmies . . . Patagonians. The term Pygmy/Pygmies usually refers to various people of short stature (under five foot tall) in central Africa. It derives from Latin *Pygmaei* and Greek *Pygmaio*, the name used by Homer and Herodotus to refer to tribes of dwarfs that were reputed to inhabit Ethiopia and India.

Conversely, the native inhabitants of Patagonia in southern South America were, according to the exaggerations of seventeenth- and eighteenth-century travellers and romancers, said to be the tallest known people.

– **Baron Munchausen**. A fictional teller of tall tales. *Baron Münchausen's Narrative of his Marvellous Travels and Campaigns in Russia* (1785), variously retitled in later editions, was an eighteenth-century collection of tall stories by Rudolph Erich Raspe (1737–1794) based on the real-life German adventurer Karl Friederich von Münchausen (1720-1797), who was noted for his exaggerated accounts of his own experiences. In the nineteenth century Raspe's book was a popular classic.

– *First Men in the Moon, The Time Machine*. Two science fiction novels by H.G. Wells (1866–1946), one of the twentieth century's masters of the genre. *The Time Machine* was published in 1895, and *The First Men in the Moon* followed in 1901. Tolkien was particularly taken with *The Time Machine* (as a venture into time-travel; he calls the machine itself "preposterous and incredible"). In a letter to his son Christopher about early English history he remarked "I'd give a bit for a time-machine" (*Letters* 108).

– **Eloi and Morlocks**. The two major species of intelligent creatures of human descent encountered by Wells's Time-Traveller when he journeys into the future. The Eloi are small, delicate creatures living on the surface of the earth; the more ominous, fur-covered Morlocks live underground. The Morlocks are cannibals, and the Eloi are their food.

17 – In dreams strange powers of the mind may be unlocked. See Note to paragraph 74 on Faërian Drama.

18 – Lewis Carroll's *Alice* stories. Charles Lutwidge Dodgson (1832-1898), whose pen name was Lewis Carroll, wrote two fantasy classics, *Alice's Adventures in Wonderland*, published in 1865 and *Through the Looking Glass and What Alice found There*, published 1871 (though the imprint says 1872). Both books qualify as dream visions, since in each the child Alice wakes up at the end of her adventure. When both *The Hobbit* and *The Lord of the Rings* were first published they were (erroneously) compared with Carroll's two books, and superficial reviewers seized on the circumstance that both Tolkien and Carroll were Oxford scholars to promote the similarity.

20 – footnote 2, *The Tailor of Gloucester, Mrs. Tiggywinkle, The Wind in the Willows.* All three come close to having the quality of Faërie about them, for the animals in these books are not stand-ins for people, but enchanting (and enchanted) creatures with personalities of their own. As the text notes, the first two are stories by Beatrix Potter. The Tailor of Gloucester falls ill three days before Christmas, with the Mayor's coat and waistcoat cut out but not sewn. In a variation of the folktale of "The Shoemaker and the Elves" the mice (instead of elves) finish the sewing for him, and on Christmas Day, to the Tailor's astonishment, the Mayor's coat and waistcoat are ready for him. From that day he becomes rich, and the mice stitch all his buttonholes. Potter herself called it a fairy-tale, maintaining that she heard it in Gloucestershire, and that it was "true".

In *The Tale of Mrs. Tiggy-winkle*, when Lucie loses her pocket-hankies she finds them being washed and ironed by Mrs. Tiggy-winkle, the animals' laundry-woman (though she looks suspiciously like a hedgehog), who also washes Peter Rabbit's blue jacket. Lucie and Mrs. Tiggy-winkle deliver all the clean laundry to the appropriate recipient, but when Lucie turns to thank Tiggy-winkle, the tiny laundress is "running, running, running up the hill" and without her cap and shawl and petticoat. She is now an animal and no longer an aspect of Lucie's imagination.

Except for the character of Mr. Toad (a human-type of automobile-enthusiast blatantly satirised in true beast fable style), the animals in *The Wind in the Willows* live enchanting lives by the River-bank and have enchanting adventures. Some of the chapters come very close to prose poems, for example "Dulce Domum", where the Mole emotionally rediscovers his old home, "Wayfarers All" where the Rat longs to go adventuring, and "The Piper at the Gates of Dawn", where the god Pan watches over a baby otter lost from home. Tolkien's comments in early drafts suggest that he felt the "Pan" chapter was out of place and spoiled the "palette" of colours of the fields and woods and rivers of Oxfordshire.

21 – footnote 1, Campbell's *Popular Tales of the West Highlands.* This work originally appeared in four volumes in 1860-6. Tolkien owned another four-volume edition, published in 1890-93.

– *Die Kristallkugel* **in Grimm.** "The Crystal Ball", a story in which the enchanter's power is hidden in a crystal ball inside an egg inside a fiery bird inside a wild bull. The third brother can only retrieve the crystal ball and free the princess from the enchanter with the aid of his two shape-changed brothers, one an eagle and one a whale.

– **George MacDonald.** (1824–1905). Scottish preacher and writer of mystical fantasy best known for his children's books, *At the Back of the North Wind* (1871), *The Princess and the Goblin* (1872), and *The Princess and Curdie* (1883). He also wrote two adult fantasies, *Phantastes* (1858) and *Lilith* (1895), as well as a number of fairy tales, including "The Golden Key", "The Light Princess", "The Giant's Heart", and "The Day Boy and the Night Girl". His fairy tales were first collected in *Dealings with the Fairies* (1867), and reappeared in variously retitled collections. MacDonald's two important essays, forerunners of and influences on Tolkien's essay "On Fairy-stories", are "The Imagination: Its Functions and its Culture", collected with other essays in *Orts* (1882), and "The Fantastic Imagination", originally written for the American compilation *The Light Princess and Other Fairy Tales* (1893) but added to the expanded edition of MacDonald's essay collection, retitled *A Dish of Orts* (1893).

– **D'Orsigny papyrus.** Tolkien's citation is consistent throughout his drafts, but it is incorrect. The attribution should be to the D'Orbiney papyrus, so named because the British Museum had, in 1857, acquired the papyrus from Madame Elizabeth d'Orbiney, who had earlier purchased it in Italy. Tolkien's footnote cites "Budge, *Egyptian Reading Book* p. xxi".

But Budge correctly gives the source as "the D'Orbiney Papyrus, Brit. Mus. No. 10, 183". The papyrus is a 19th dynasty text dated to the reign of Seti I (c. 1306–1290 B.C.). Budge's book, whose full title is *An Egyptian Reading Book for Beginners*, describes itself as "a Series of Historical, Funereal, Moral, Religious and Mythological Texts printed in Hieroglyphic Characters together with a Transliteration and a Complete Vocabulary". It also reproduces hieroglyphic texts, with transliterations, and English translations, including "The Tale of the Two Brothers". This combination would have attracted Tolkien's notice as both a teller of tales and an inventor of alphabets, and Tolkien had a copy of the 1896 first edition in his personal library.

22 – origin of language and of the mind. This is Tolkien's compressed version of what has come to be called the Sapir-Whorf linguistic theory, also treated by his fellow-Inkling Owen Barfield in *Poetic Diction* (1928) and other works, that a symbiotic relationship exists between the word spoken and the speaker's perception, hence understanding, of the surrounding world. Language conditions its users, and both create the world they live in and describe. Anthropologist and linguist Edward Sapir (1884–1939) published *Language: An Introduction to the Study of Speech* (1921), a copy of which Tolkien had in his personal library. Benjamin Whorf (1897–1941) studied linguistics at Yale in the early 1930s under Sapir. A selection of Whorf's writings, *Language, Thought, and Reality*, appeared in 1956.

ORIGINS

23 – the pursuit of folklorists or anthropologists. Here begins Tolkien's discussion and capsule history of the discipline of folklore studies, which began with the Brothers Grimm and their search for German national identity in folk and fairy tales (see note to paragraph 15 above), and which ended (at least in its earliest, most energetic nationalistic phase) with World War I, which effectively cut off all inter-European study and exchange for four years. While Tolkien's low opinion of the folklorists' methods is clear, his description of their approach to stories is accurate.

– *Beowulf* '**is only a version of *Dat Erdmänneken***'. "Dat Erdmänneken" is a tale from Grimm, usually translated under the title "The Gnome". It does not appear in Lang's twelve collections, but is translated as "The Elves" in volume two of *Grimm's Household Tales* (1884), which Lang introduced. The tale bears virtually no resemblance to *Beowulf*. Twice in Tolkien's research notes for his Andrew Lang lecture Tolkien queried himself: once briefly, "Is Beowulf in any of A[ndrew] L[ang's] F[airy] B[oo]ks" (Bodleian Tolkien MS. 14, fol. 55 recto); and another time more extensively, "<u>Beowulf</u>. Is it in any of the A[ndrew] L[ang] Books. A Fairy Story. But when retold (seldom) it is not retold as such. For what the poet did to it was for his own purposes—rel[ated] to the substance but not the manner of the story. It should be retold as a fairy-story" (Bodleian Tolkien MS. 14, fol. 45 recto). The second note is on paper that seems to be associated with the revision made during the spring and summer of 1943, and may be the germ of Tolkien's story "Sellic Spell", a fairy-tale reworking into modern form of the folktale elements in *Beowulf*. "Sellic Spell" is known to have been in existence by June 1945. Tolkien's friend Gwyn Jones planned to publish it in *The Welsh Review*, but the magazine folded and Jones returned the story to Tolkien. It remains unpublished.

– '*The Black Bull of Norroway . . .* **Jason and Medea**'. These examples of how (in Tolkien's opinion) fairy-stories should *not* be read come from pp. xi–xii of Andrew Lang's Introduction to the large-paper edition of *The Blue Fairy Book*, of which only 113 copies were printed.

24 – **Layamon.** Layamon (more properly written Laȝamon, translated as Lawman) was a thirteenth-century English priest and historian (most early British history was written by clerics). His Middle English *Brut* (short for Brutus, descendent of Aeneas and popularly presumed to be the founder of Britain) was derived from an earlier *Brut* (a generic title for a history of Britain and its kings) written by the Channel Islander Wace, which in turn was derived from Geoffrey of Monmouth's twelfth-century *Historia Regum Britanniae*. Laȝamon's *Brut*, like the histories of his precursors, does indeed tell the story of King Leir and his daughters Gornoille, Regau, and Cordoille.

25 – Dasent. George Webbe Dasent (1817–1896) English scholar of Norse antiquities, translated Peter Christen Asbjørnsen and Jørgen Moe's *Norske Folkeeventyr* (1843–44; enlarged 1852) as *Popular Tales from the North* (1859; second edition, enlarged, 1859; third edition 1888). Dasent's "Introduction", often cut or omitted from later editions, appears in its fullest form (nearly one hundred and fifty pages) in the 1859 second edition, a copy of which Tolkien owned. It is divided into five sections, "Origin", "Diffusion", "Norse Mythology", "Norse Popular Tales", and "Conclusion". In the first two sections Dasent expounded the Indo-European, or as it was then called, the Indo-Aryan theory of the development of language. The quote that Tolkien cites come from page xviii of the first section of Dasent's "Introduction".

26 – *invention, inheritance, diffusion.* Tolkien's ensuing discussion gives a good, if brief, account of these competing theories as rationales for the worldwide prevalence and similarity of folktales, one of the early issues raised by the comparatists. It seems likely that Tolkien was here drawing directly on Andrew Lang, both Lang's Introduction to *The Blue Fairy Book*, p. xii (see paragraph 23 above), and his Introduction to *Grimm's Household Tales* include a critical examination of the theories of the solar mythologists Sir George Cox and Max Müller on Diffusion and Origin (*Grimm's* xix–xxiii).

27 – Philology has been dethroned. One of the principal dethroners was Andrew Lang. Tolkien noted Lang's part in this revolution in an early draft, but later excised it. Although the whole vast field of myth and folklore study had begun with comparative philology and the idea that cognate words in different languages might imply a related – possibly even an originally shared – linguistic and cultural background, other disciplines, such as anthropology, had challenged the primacy of language as the "key to all mythologies" (as George Eliot's Mr. Casaubon put it in *Middlemarch*).

– **Max Müller's view of mythology as a "disease of language".** Friedrich Max Müller (1823–1900), was born in Germany but lived his adult life in England, where he did the bulk of his work in the burgeoning field of comparative philology and mythology. Müller was a major proponent of "solar mythology", a theory, based largely on Sanskrit and Greek texts, proposing that the gods of mythology were originally celestial phenomena. Over time, so went the theory, the primary referents were forgotten although the names survived and developed through a "disease of language" (that is, a deviation from an original condition) into stories or myths. Thus, for example, the nightly descent of the sun below the horizon became the story of a hero's descent into the underworld.

The earliest appearance of Müller's famous phrase appears to be in the first of his *Lectures on the Science of Language* (1861), where he elaborated: "Mythology, which was the bane of the ancient world, is in truth a disease of language. A mythe [*sic*] means a word, but a word which, from being a name or an attribute, has been allowed to assume a more substantial existence. Most of the Greek, the Roman, the Indian, and other heathen gods are nothing but poetical names, which were gradually allowed to assume a divine personality never contemplated by their original inventors" (p. 11).

– **in our world coeval,** cf. paragraph 22.

– **another view of adjectives, a part of speech in a mythical grammar.** Tolkien's discussion here of the fluidity of words and their power to change meaning and alter reality anticipates by several decades the post-modern critical theories of interpretation and construction/deconstruction of the seventies and eighties of the twentieth century.

– **Man becomes a sub-creator.** The concept expressed here, and the phrase that describes it, are rivalled only by Faërie in their importance to Tolkien's theory of art. With its partner term *sub-creation*, *sub-creator* expresses Tolkien's profoundest views on the creative process, that the Prime Creator is God. His creation is the world of humankind who, following in God's creative footsteps, both make and are made in God's image, using – again, like God – the Word as the primary creative instrument. The character of Aulë in Tolkien's "Silmarillion" comes closest to expressing Tolkien's idea of sub-creation when Aulë explains to his own creator Ilúvatar his independent creation of the dwarves, saying that "the making of things is in my heart from my own making by thee" (*Silmarillion*, 43).

28 – to the 'lower mythology' rather than to the 'higher'? Essentially, oral tradition versus written text. In the terminology of the early folklorists the "lower" mythology was what Lang called "the lively oral tradition of Mährchen", of fairy tales and folklore, while the "higher" mythology was the written tradition exemplified by the Vedas of India, the myths of Greece and Rome, and the Icelandic Eddas. That both "higher" and "lower" contained the same motifs and patterns was explained by Max Müller as progressive degradation and diminution of the material over time. Thus, "the gods of ancient mythology were changed into the demigods and heroes of ancient epic poetry, and these demigods again became at a later age the principal characters in our nursery tales" (*Chips from a German Workshop*, ii, 243; quoted in *Peasant Customs and Savage Myths* vol. 1, 194).

29 – 'nature-myths'. Tolkien here gives cogent, if abbreviated presentation of Max Müller's theory of solar mythology and its extension by other folklorists such as George William Cox.

32 – *Thrymskvitha*. "The Lay of Thrym", a very funny poem detailing Thórr's efforts to retrieve his hammer from the giant Thrym in the underworld. Thrym will only give back the hammer in return for the fertility goddess Freya as his bride. Outraged at the idea, Freya refuses, so the gods gleefully dress the equally outraged Thórr in women's clothes and pass him off as Freya. When his hammer is laid in the "bride's" lap, Thórr grabs it and dispatches the giant with one blow.

– which no human ear had yet heard. See paragraph 22 above. A deliberately sweeping statement to emphasize the connection between the word and the phenomenon. The name creates the thing; without the name, we cannot identify the phenomenon, or our experience of it.

33 – footnote 1, Christopher Dawson in *Progress and Religion*. Dawson (1889–1970), an ecumenical Catholic thinker and historian, was an independent scholar who wrote on religion and culture. *Progress and Religion: An Historical Enquiry* was first published in London in 1929 by Sheed and Ward. Tolkien used the Unicorn Books paperback edition published in London in 1938, which has different pagination from the numerous Sheed and Ward hardcover printings. See commentary to paragraph 94 below.
– footnote 2, (often decided by the individual). Tolkien's comments show how far he is ahead of Lang, not to mention other anthropologists such as Lévi-Strauss, whose methods will not catch up with the opinions expressed here until the eighth decade of the twentieth century.

34 – *The Golden Key*. Written in 1867. MacDonald's mystical/allegorical short story about the progress through the life of two children, the boy Mossy and the girl Tangle. The golden key unlocks the door to the rainbow stair, up which they climb to an unspecified but fairly obvious higher plane of existence.
– *Lilith*. Written in 1895, MacDonald's novel-length allegorical dream vision about the progress of the individual towards salvation.

35 – Bertha Broadfoot, called "La Reine Pédauque" because of her large, gooselike flat foot, has been suggested as the origin of Mother Goose. The "casual example" Tolkien cites as a story told about her, "The Goosegirl", is a traditional tale of the servant girl who takes the place of the princess. Tolkien is following on Andrew Lang's discussion of the associations between Grimm's story and Bertha Broadfoot in his 1873 essay "Mythology and Fairy Tales".

– **between, say, 1940 and 1945.** The years spanning World War II. In wartime England, bananas, like all imported fruit, were severely rationed. Hence, the probability of a discarded banana peel being encountered on the street would have been unlikely. Useful as a dating device, this detail could not have been a part of the original 1939 lecture.

38 – Frey, Gerdr, Vanir. Figures in the Icelandic Prose and Poetic Eddas, the two chief medieval repositories of Scandinavian myth. In the Northern pantheon Frey was one of the Vanir, early Northern European fertility deities overrun by the later, warlike Æsir. Frey's love for the giant maiden Gerdr (whose name is related to "earth") has been seen as derived from a spring planting ritual, or conversely, from an autumn harvest rite. The love story, not its ritual or that ritual's implications, is what survives.

– **Odin, Necromancer, glutter of crows.** Chief of the gods in Norse mythology. Unlike Frey, Odin is one of the Æsir, the warlike skygods. Associated with magic, Odin is also a battle god and god of the slain, hence "glutter of crows", battlefield scavengers who feed off the bodies of dead warriors. Also unlike Frey, no love stories are told of Odin.

40 – *The Juniper Tree.* One of the Grimm's fairy tales. The story is both horrific and transcendent. A stepmother kills her stepson, butchers him and serves him to his unwitting father in "black-puddings". His tearful stepsister buries her brother's bones under the Juniper tree, and from them his spirit arises as a bird who first sings about his murder and then drops a millstone on the stepmother. This is just the kind of story of child abuse, cannibalism, and murder that so horrified nineteenth-century folklorists that they had to find a reason for its existence outside the story itself, either as a forgotten celestial phenomenon or as a primitive rite.

– *twe tusend Johr.* From the first sentence of the story as it appeared in Grimm's *Kinder- und Hausmärchen*. "*Dat is nu all lang heer, wol twe dusend Johr*", "It is now long ago, quite two thousand years". The dialect here is plattdeutsch, unlike the hochdeutsch or conventional German used for most of the tales. Thus *Johr* appears in place of the more familiar *Jahr*. Tolkien misspells the second word, which in the German edition is *dusend*, not *tusend*. See note 1, p. 137.

41 – Fairy-stories are by no means rocky matrices. The geologic comparison here is both timely and intentional: geology and mythology being coeval disciplines arising in roughly the same period and out of the same human impulse to dig into origins.

– derived from some taboo once practised long ago. A reference to the anthropological theory championed by Andrew Lang.

CHILDREN

42 – Children the natural or specially appropriate audience for fairy-stories. In 1955 Tolkien wrote to W.H. Auden à propos *The Lord of the Rings*, "I had been thinking about 'Fairy Stories' and their relation to children – some of the results I put into a lecture at St. Andrews and eventually enlarged and published in an Essay. . . . As I had [there] expressed the view that the connexion in the modern mind between children and 'fairy stories' is false and accidental and spoils the stories in themselves and for children, I wanted to try and write one that was not addressed to children at all (as such)" (*Letters*, 216).

48 – The introduction to the first of the series. Lang's twelve page "Introduction" was intended for adults, and it was published only in the large paper edition of *The Blue Fairy Book*, limited to 113 copies. Tolkien made notes from the copy in the Bodleian Library.

– 'They represent', he says 'the young ... appetite for marvels.' Quoted from the first paragraph of Lang's Introduction to the large paper edition of *The Blue Fairy Book* (p. xi).

– "'Is it true?'" he says, 'is the great question children ask'. We have been unable to find this quotation in the writings of Andrew Lang. In Tolkien's research notes, the phrase is in with his notes on Lang's "Introduction" to the large paper edition of *The Blue Fairy Book*. It occurs directly between the above quote from Lang's first paragraph and some of Tolkien's own observations (Bodleian Tolkien MS. 14, folio 40 recto), but the quote does not in fact appear in Lang's "Introduction". It seems likely that after some time had elapsed from making the notes, Tolkien mistakenly attributed to Lang a phrase he wrote in response to Lang.

50 – 'willing suspension of disbelief'. A phrase used by Samuel Taylor Coleridge in his *Biographia Literaria* (1817), chapter 14: "In this idea originated the plan of the 'Lyrical Ballads'; in which it was agreed, that my endeavours should be directed to persons and characters supernatural, or at least romantic; yet so as to transfer from our inward nature a human interest and a semblance of truth sufficient to procure for these shadows of imagination that willing suspension of disbelief for the moment, which constitutes poetic faith."

51 – a wild, heraldic, preference for dark blue rather than light. Dark and light blue are respectively the colours of Oxford and Cambridge universities. Tolkien, an Oxonian, would naturally prefer the dark blue.

54 – I was born about the same time as the *Green Fairy Book*. The *Green Fairy Book* was published in 1892, the year in which, on January 3, Tolkien was born in Bloemfontein, in the Orange Free State of Africa. There is no record of when he was introduced to the *Green Fairy Book*, but it is likely to have been after his return to England with his mother and younger brother in 1895. Worth noting is that one of the stories in *The Green Fairy Book*, "The Enchanted Ring", concerns a young man who is given a ring which will not only make him invisible, but will make him "the most powerful of men" provided he never makes "bad use of it". After many adventures, the young man, "fearing that if he kept the ring he might be tempted to use it", tries to give it back. The last sentences in the story need no comment: "Oh! How dangerous it is to have more power than the rest of the

world! Take back your ring, and as ill fortune seems to follow on all whom you bestow it, I will implore you, as a favour to myself, that you will never give it to anyone who is dear to me."

– **naked ancestors.** Another reference to Lang's anthropological theory of folklore, the analogy being between the ritual and practices of primitive societies, the "childhood" of human development, and the children presumed to be the audience for fairy stories.

55 – the prince of all dragons. Fafnir in the Eddas, one of a family of shape-changers. The story of "otter-payment" in Snorri Sturluson's Prose Edda tells how the god Loki killed an otter who turned out to be the son of a farmer, Hreidmar. To compensate Hreidmar for Otter's death, Loki commandeered a golden hoard from the dwarf Andvari. Otter's two brothers, Fafnir and Regin, killed their father for the gold, but Fafnir refused to share it with Regin. Taking the shape of a dragon he guarded the gold on Gnita Heath. Regin persuaded Sigurd to kill the dragon, but was killed in his turn by Sigurd, who then took the gold but fared little better, for the treasure embroiled him in a family feud that ended in his death.

– **worm.** An old word for dragon.

56 – a sad and troublous time. Tolkien describes this time rather vaguely as being "after the years between learning to read and going to school". The best likelihood would make it a reference to the years following his mother's death when he was twelve years old. He and his younger brother Hilary were left in the guardianship of Father Francis Morgan, a priest from the Birmingham Oratory who had been their mother's counsellor and friend. Father Francis arranged for them to stay with their aunt Beatrice Suffield, who had a room to let in her boarding house in Birmingham. This would have been a sad and troublous time indeed for a grief-stricken, orphaned boy, and it is no wonder that he turned to fairy tales. See Tolkien's discussion of Escape, Consolation and the Happy Ending in the section on "Fantasy".

58 – bowdlerized. Thomas Bowdler (1754–1825), produced expurgated, "family" editions of Shakespeare and Gibbon. Thus to bowdlerize is to remove from a text material considered objectionable, especially anything bawdy or obscene.

60 – 'He who would enter the Kingdom of Faërie . . . heart of a little child'. Lang actually wrote: "He who would enter into the Kingdom of Faery should have the heart of a little child, if he is to be happy and at home in that enchanted realm" (p. xiii of the "Introduction" to the large paper edition of *The Blue Fairy Book*).

– **Chesterton.** Gilbert Keith Chesterton (1874–1936). Catholic author, essayist, poet, social and literary critic, newspaper columnist and editor, defender of Christianity. Although he wrote one hundred books, his best-known is probably *The Man Who Was Thursday*, a mystery thriller with strong Christian overtones. His mystery series featuring the priest-detective Father Brown is still in print, has been a television series, and is available on DVD. Chesterton was a notable wit, and generated a vast number of quotable aphorisms, such as the one cited here. References to Chesterton appear more frequently in the early drafts (see notes to MS. A and MS. B).

– **Maeterlinck's *Blue Bird*.** A dramatic fantasy by the Belgian playwright Maurice Maeterlinck (1862–1949). Two children, a brother Tytyl and sister Mytyl, seek all over the world for the blue bird of happiness, only to find that it is in the home they left to go on their search. The play is highly symbolic, and the characters and situations allegorical.

Chesterton's anecdote on Maeterlinck comes from the opening paragraph of "On Household Gods and Goblins" in *The Coloured Lands*: "Sometime ago I went with some children to see Maeterlinck's fine and delicate fairy play about the Blue Bird that brought everybody happiness. For some reason or other it did not bring me happiness, and even the children were not quite happy. I will not go so far as to say that the Blue Bird was a Blue Devil, but it left us in something seriously like the blues. The children were partly dissatisfied with it because it did not end with a Day of Judgment; because it was never revealed to the hero and heroine that the dog had been faithful and the cat faithless. For children are innocent and love justice; while most of us are wicked and naturally prefer mercy" (p. 195).

63 – Eloi and Morlocks. See note to paragraph 16.

FANTASY

65 – Fancy ... the older word Fantasy. Tolkien's discussion here and in the succeeding paragraphs is essentially an expanded paraphrase of definition 4 under the entry for "Fancy" (a contraction of FANTASY as noun and adjective) in the first edition of *The Oxford English Dictionary*. Since he drew on it so heavily, the entire definition merits inclusion here: "In early use synonymous with IMAGINATION: the process and the faculty of forming mental representations of things not present to the senses; chiefly applied to the so-called creative or productive imagination, which frames images of objects, events, or conditions that have not occurred in actual experience. In later use the words *fantasy* and *imagination* (esp. as denoting attributes manifested in poetical or literary composition) are commonly distinguished: *fancy* being used to express aptitude for the invention of illustrative or decorative imagery, while *imagination* is the power of giving to ideal creations the inner consistency of realities."

– 'the power of giving to ideal creations the inner consistency of reality'. See the preceding entry. It is worthy of note that Tolkien changes the final word from *realities* to *reality*, thus shifting the reference from plural phenomena to a singular concept, an abstraction. The phrase "inner consistency" is used by Aristotle in his *Poetics*, but not in relation to "ideal creations".

– a cancelled early version of Tolkien's discussion from MS C reads: I propose to use Fantasy φαντασία a making visible to the mind) of the operation whereby mental images 'of things not actually present' are expressed, shown forth, created. The faculty of conceiving the images is properly called Imagination. But in recent times (in technical not normal language) Imagination has often been held to be something higher than Fantasy (or the reduced and depreciatory form Fancy); to be 'the power of giving to ideal creations the inner consistency of reality'. That distinction seems to me confused. The mental part of image-making is one thing, and should naturally be called Imagination. The grasp, and vivid perception of the image, a necessary preliminary to its successful expression, is a difference not of kind but of degree. The achievement of that expression which gives, or seems to give, 'the inner consistency of reality' – that is, commands Secondary Belief – is indeed another thing: the gift of Art, the link between Imagination and the final marvel of Subcreation: Fantasy, the showing forth, that power which the Elves have to the highest degree. (Bodleian MS.Tolkien 14, folio 160 verso)

66 – the powers of Humpty-Dumpty. In Lewis Carroll's *Alice Through the Looking-Glass*, Humpty-Dumpty declares that "When I use a word it means just what I choose it to mean – neither more nor less."

68–9 – *the green sun.* This image is striking not only because it invokes light as a determinative sub-creative force in a Secondary World, but also because it recalls the blue sun Allpain in David Lindsay's 1920 fantasy, *A Voyage to Arcturus*, a book well-known to Tolkien. In Lindsay's Secondary World of the planet Tormance, the extraordinary light of the blue sun created new colours, *jale* and *ulfire*. One of the jotted notes among Tolkien's early drafts for the lecture contains the isolated phrase "Blue Sun". However, in this instance it seems more likely that Tolkien is referring to "The Plattner Story" by H.G. Wells, first published in *New Review*, April 1896, and collected in *The Plattner Story and Others* (1897) and in *The Short Stories of H.G. Wells* (1927). In this story, a schoolteacher disappears from the everyday world and finds himself in a dark alternate landscape watching a green sun rise.

70 – children's pantomime. A particularly British theatrical tradition dating back to the eighteenth century, the pantomime, or "panto", is not actually mime in the sense of wordless physical action, but a story-spectacle, usually presented during the

Christmas season and featuring song, dance and slapstick comedy, often based on folk or fairy tale and aimed at a child audience.

74 – 'Faërian Drama.' While plainly intended to contrast Faërian drama with the kind of "human" drama discussed in the preceding paragraphs, no definition of what the faërian version consists of is given, except "those plays which according to abundant records the elves have often presented to men," a reference which does little to clarify the concept. No examples of such "plays" or "abundant records" are given. Moreover, Tolkien's description of a Faërian drama as "very similar to dreaming", albeit qualified as "a dream that some other mind is weaving", seems at variance with his exclusion earlier in the essay of the mechanism of dream as a vehicle for fairy-story. The paragraph's final sentence, if taken seriously and at face value, suggests that to Tolkien the difference between the Primary ("ordinary") world and the Otherworld of the elves is a matter of perception, not a clearly marked separation between reality and unreality.

See Tolkien's revisions to this passage in "The History of the Essay" pp. 138 ff. and MS. B Misc. pages [MS. 14, folio 36 verso:] "The real desire [in fairy-stories] is not to enter these lands as a natural denizen (as a knight, say, armed with a sword and courage adequate proper to this world) but to see them in action & being as we see our objective world – with the mind free from the limited body: a Faerian Drama (see p. 294).

75 – Enchantment. To *enchant* (the word is derived from Middle English *enchanten*, from Old French *enchanter*, from Latin *incantare*, "to chant magic words" – an incantation) is "to cast under a spell, to bewitch". Thus *enchantment* is the act of enchanting, as well as the state or condition of being enchanted, bewitched or en-spelled. It is important to note that this particular altered state is dependent on *words spoken or sung*.

77 – combining nouns and redistributing adjectives. These words make clear Tolkien's assumption that Fantasy and Enchantment are most effectively created by words, and that the chief instruments of sub-creation are the nouns and adjectives so combined and/or redistributed. Compare with the lines in the quoted poem about "refracted Light" splintered "to many hues" and "endlessly combined in living shapes that move from mind to mind".

– a letter I once wrote to a man. The man was C.S. Lewis, and the "letter" was in actuality a poem, "Mythopoeia" (Myth-making), subtitled "Philomythus to Misomythus" ("Myth-lover" to "Myth-hater"). "Mythopoeia" is Tolkien's reconfiguration into poetic imagery of the theories of Sapir-Whorf and Owen Barfield, which hold that it is through naming things – establishing them with words – that humankind comes to perceive and relate to its world. According to Christopher Tolkien, the occasion that led to the writing of "Mythopoeia" was the after-dinner stroll taken by Tolkien, Lewis and Hugo Dyson along Addison's Walk on the grounds of Magdalen College that is mentioned in Humphrey Carpenter's *J.R.R. Tolkien: A Biography*. Lewis wrote to his friend Arthur Greeves that on that occasion the three men talked about myth and metaphor. Lewis gave some credit to the talk for his subsequent embrace of Christianity.

– 'Dear Sir,' I said. According to Christopher Tolkien there is no evidence among the drafts of "Mythopoeia" that it was ever a verse epistle of the kind Tolkien describes. His conclusion is that the letter was a device by which to include part of the poem in the essay (*Tree and Leaf* 1989).

80 **– It can be put to evil uses.** A marginal emendation to the proof stage at the time of the essay's first publication in *Essays Presented to Charles Williams* adds the following sentence: "All things in this fallen world are subject to corruption, even the elves it seems, certainly human [seekers?]." Although the notation (in ink) is quite clear, and the place for insertion plainly marked, the sentence was not incorporated into the text as published.

– *Abusus non tollit usum.* "Abuse [misuse] does not preclude [i.e. is not argument against] use."

RECOVERY, ESCAPE, CONSOLATION

83 – regaining of a clear view. For comparison, see G.K. Chesterton's short story about a boy regaining his appreciation for the ordinary colours of the world around him, "The Coloured Lands" in the book of the same title. It was published in 1938, at about the time Tolkien was working on the lecture.

– locked them in our hoard. A recurring motif in Tolkien's work is that of treasure locked or hidden away. The most salient example is Feänor's locking of the Silmarils in an iron chamber in his fortress, but see also Tolkien's poem "The Hoard" in *The Adventures of Tom Bombadil*, and "Iúmonna Gold Galdre Bewunden", versions of which were published in the Leeds University literary magazine *Gryphon* in 1923, in the *Oxford Magazine* in 1937, and in *The Annotated Hobbit*, ed. Douglas A. Anderson, 1988, 2002.

84 – Mooreeffoc. Chesterton's anecdote comes from his book *Charles Dickens* (1906):

> "Herein is the whole secret of that eerie realism with which Dickens could always vitalize some dark or dull corner of London. There are details in the Dickens descriptions – a window, or a railing, or the keyhole of a door – which he endows with demoniac life. The things seem more actual than things really are. Indeed, that degree of realism does not exist in reality: it is the unbearable realism of a dream. And this kind of realism can only be gained by walking dreamily in a place; it cannot be gained by walking observantly. Dickens himself has given a perfect instance of how these nightmare minutiae grew upon him in his trance of abstraction. He mentions among the coffee-shops into which he crept in those wretched days one in St. Martin's Lane, "of which I only recollect that it stood near the church, and that in the door there was an oval glass plate with 'COFFEE ROOM' painted on it, addressed towards the street. If I ever find myself in a very different kind of coffee-

room now, but where there is such an inscription on glass, and read it backwards on the wrong side, MOOR EEFFOC (as I often used to do then in a dismal reverie), a shock goes through my blood." That wild word, "Moor Eeffoc," is the motto of all effective realism; it is the masterpiece of the good realistic principle – the principle that the most fantastic thing of all is often the precise fact. And that elvish kind of realism Dickens adopted everywhere. His world was alive with inanimate objects." (Quoted from *The Collected Works of G. K. Chesterton*, Volume XV, 1989, page 65.)

However, Tolkien seems to have responded not to this original source but to Maisie Ward's retelling in her "Introduction" to *The Coloured Lands*, where she reads more into Chesterton's words than is perhaps appropriate (note that in her usage, "Mooreeffoc" is, as in Tolkien's, one word, with only the initial letter capitalized):

"In Dickens, fantasy holds the next place to humour. But just as the humour is true human laughter, so the fantasy grows in that strange eerie twilight where trees and men have alien shapes that melt and merge back into realities. The things in Dickens that are most haunting are christened by Chesterton, 'Mooreeffocish' – and 'Mooreeffoc' is only 'coffee-room' read backwards as the child Dickens read it in the gloom and despondency of a foggy London night during his slavery at Murdstone and Grinby. Gloomy fantasy is truth read backwards. Cheerful fantasy is the creation of a new form wherein man, become creator, co-operates with God." (*The Coloured Lands*, pp. 14–15).

Ward's final sentence anticipates what Tolkien called sub-creation.

85 – the forging of Gram. (*Gram* translates as Old Norse "wrath") In the Icelandic Eddas Gram was the sword given by Odin to the Norse hero Sigmund. It was broken when Sigmund died in battle, but re-forged from its shattered pieces by the smith Regin for Sigmund's son Sigurd. With Gram, Sigurd killed the dragon Fáfnir (Regin's brother) and also Regin.

– Pegasus. Winged horse of Greek mythology, in some stories ridden by the hero Perseus, in others by Bellerophon.

88 – Führer. German "leader". Capitalized as the title assumed by Adolf Hitler, leader of the German Nazi party and head of the German state from 1934 until his death in 1945. Hitler was the prime instigator of World War II, and his image would have been as fresh in Tolkien's mind in 1939 as his memory was in 1947.

– Reich. German "realm". The territory of a German government. Hitler called his regime the Third Reich, the First Reich being the Holy Roman Empire, from the ninth century to 1806, and the Second Reich being the German Empire from 1871 to 1919 (the formal end of World War I).

– 'quisling'. A term used to describe traitors and collaborationists, after the Norwegian fascist politician Vidkun Quisling (1887–1945), who from 1942 until the end of World War II held the office of Minister President in occupied Norway, while the elected leadership was in exile. After the war Quisling was found guilty of high treason and executed.

89 – Chesterton truly remarked that . . . 'had come to stay'. In chapter one, "The Wheel of Fate", of part four, "Some Aspects of Machinery", in *The Outline of Sanity* (1926), G.K. Chesterton elaborated on the idea of something that has come to stay:

> "Suppose we ourselves had actually manufactured Uncle Humphrey; had put him together, piece by piece, like a mechanical doll. Suppose we had so ardently felt at the moment the need of an uncle in our home life that we had constructed him out of domestic materials . . . Under those conditions, it might be graceful enough to say, in the mere social sense and as a sort of polite fiction, 'Uncle Humphrey has come to stay.' But surely it would be very extraordinary if we afterwards found the dummy relative to be nothing but a nuisance, or that his materials were needed for other purposes – surely it would be very extraordinary if we were forbidden to take him to pieces again; if every effort in that direction

were met with the resolute answer, 'No, no; Uncle Humphrey has come to stay.' Surely we should be tempted to retort that Uncle Humphrey never came at all." (p. 144 in volume V, 1987, of *The Collected Works of G. K. Chesterton*).

– **The march of Science . . . : an advertisement.** Tolkien has quoted an advertisement, ironically headed "Foresight", for the House of Philips, a supplier of electricity. This advertisement is known to have appeared in *Punch* in 1943, as the House of Philips proudly celebrated its "fifty years of progress, . . . ever looking ahead to the needs of tomorrow."

90 – a clerk of Oxenford. In early drafts first described as "the head of an Oxford college", later as "an Oxford don".

91 – Bletchley station. At the time of Tolkien's lecture/essay a Victorian railway station built in 1846 of stone and iron. He apparently chose it as an example (good or bad) of Victorian utilitarian architecture. Bletchley was a major intercity station serving the Oxford to Cambridge line and is now a junction of the London to Glasgow line. "Bletchley station" was originally written "Paddington station", with "Paddington" crossed out and replaced with "Bletchley".

– **Bifröst.** In Norse mythology the rainbow bridge between Asgard, home of the gods, and Midgard (middle earth), home of humankind.

– **Heimdall.** Old Norse "world-brightener". Heimdall, the son of nine mothers, the watchman of the gods. At Ragnarök, the Doom of the Gods, Heimdall will blow the Gjallarhorn ("yelling horn") to summon the gods to the last battle.

94– footnote 1, Later he adds. The Dawson quote is given more fully in the note as it appears in *Essays Presented to Charles Williams*, where the first sentence is "Why is the stockbroker less beautiful than an Homeric warrior or an Egyptian priest? Because he is less incorporated with life: he is not inevitable but accidental. . . . The full Victorian panoply . . ." The sentence was first omitted in *Tree and Leaf*.

– 'improved means to deteriorated ends'. By its presentation this appears to be a quotation from Christopher Dawson's *Progress and Religion*. However, though the sentiment expressed is very much in line with Dawson's thesis, we do not find this phrasing in his book. Certainly it echoes a sentence in Aldous Huxley's *Ends and Means: An Inquiry into the Nature of Ideals and into the Methods Employed for Their Realization* (1937), chapter XIV: "We are living now, not in the delicious intoxication induced by the early successes of science, but in a rather grisly morning-after, when it has become apparent that what triumphant science has done hitherto is to improve the means for achieving unimproved or actually deteriorated ends."

– the fear of the beautiful fay. *Fay* from Old French *fae*, "fairy". See note to paragraph 1. In medieval poems and ballads the fay was almost invariably female, and was usually depicted as a fatal woman who lured mortal men to their doom. The queen of Elfland who abducted Thomas Rymer was one such figure, though she was kind enough to return Thomas to his own world after a stay of seven years in Elfland. In Tolkien's poem "Aotrou and Itroun" (Breton "Lord and Lady") the fay who appears to the Lord (first as a crone, then as a beautiful woman) is more malevolent. When the Lord refuses to wed her in return for the potion that has enabled his wife to bear children, she curses him to the death. Tolkien's poem has been compared to medieval models such as the Breton "Nann Hag ar Corrigan" (Lord Nann and the Corrigan) and the English ballad "Clerk Covill". In *The Lord of the Rings* Boromir expresses his suspicion of Galadriel as just such a figure, saying "I do not feel too sure of this Elvish lady and her purposes", calling Lórien a "perilous land" (p. 349), cf. Tolkien's description of Faërie in the opening paragraph of the essay. Éomer, too, associates the "Lady in the Golden Wood" with "net-weavers and sorcerers" (p. 422).

96 – 'absence of the sense of separation of ourselves from beasts'. This refers to a passage in Andrew Lang's essay, "Mythology and Fairy Tales", in the *Fortnightly Review*, May 1873: "to construct this myth [of swan-maidens], the notion of enchantment or magic, and the absence of our later sense of separation from the beasts, is required as necessary form, and these notions belong to the human mind before it reaches to the personification and worship of the higher and more abstract aspects of the world" (p. 627).

– 'How came such a story ever to be invented? . . . was absurd'. This quotation from Max Müller comes from page 250 of "Tales of the West Highlands" in volume two of the 1868 second edition of his *Chips from a German Workshop*, but it is more likely that Tolkien was here quoting from Andrew Lang's use of the exact same words in his Introduction to *Grimm's Household Tales*, p. xxxvii.

97 – the Escape from Deathlessness. A reference to what Tolkien described in a letter as the "real theme" of *The Lord of the Rings*: "The real theme for me is about something much more permanent and difficult [than power]: Death and Immortality: the mystery of the love of the world in the hearts of a race 'doomed' to leave and seemingly lose it; the anguish in the hearts of a race 'doomed' not to leave it until its whole evil-aroused story is complete" (*Letters*, 246).

98 – *Eucatastrophe*. Built on *catastrophe* (Greek *kata* "down" and *strephein* "to turn'). Though in a general sense *catastrophe* can mean any kind of cataclysmic disaster, in its narrower definition it marks the downturn of fortune in Greek tragedy that leads to the protagonist's fall. By adding Greek *eu* "good" as a prefix, Tolkien has reversed the meaning (and the direction) so that the "turn" leads upward to the happy ending.

99 – *evangelium*. Late Latin "good news". Tolkien is using the word literally but also with a consciousness of its Christian reference to the Gospels (Old English *godspel*, a direct translation of *evangelium*) of the New Testament.

101 – footnote 1, Thackeray's *Rose and the Ring*. Properly titled *The Rose and the Ring*, this was a kind of jeux d'esprit by William Makepeace Thackeray (1811–1863) whose masterpiece, *Vanity Fair*, a sharply satirical look at English high life in the

nineteenth century, was considered cynical and critical when the novel was published in 1848. Thackeray published his "fairy tale" spoof *The Rose and the Ring* in 1855. Much of its content and approach can be deduced from the names of its principal characters, King Valoroso of Paflagonia, the Fairy Blackstick, Prince Bulbo of Crim Tartary, the Countess Gruffanuff, the Chancellor Squaretoso and the Captain Kutasoff Hedzoff.

EPILOGUE

104 – footnote 1, The Art is here. Shortened from the note as it appeared in *Essays Presented to Charles Williams*, where it began; "The Gospels are not artistic in themselves." The change was first introduced in *Tree and Leaf*.

NOTES

107 – *The Wind in the Willows*. A children's classic by Kenneth Grahame, published in 1908, about the adventures of Rat and Mole and Badger and Mr. Toad along the riverbank.

– A.A. Milne. Author of the children's classics *Winnie-the-Pooh* and *The House at Pooh Corner* about the young boy Christopher Robin (modelled on Milne's own son), his stuffed bear Pooh and Pooh's friends Piglet, Rabbit, Eeyore the donkey, Kanga and Roo. Milne's *Toad of Toad Hall* (1929), a dramatic adaptation of *The Wind in the Willows*, focused on the "Toad" chapters of the book in which Rat and Mole and Badger play subsidiary roles.

108 – Iphigeneia, daughter of Agamemnon. In Euripides's Trojan War play *Iphigeneia at Aulis*, Agamemnon, leader of the Greek forces against the Trojans, sacrifices his daughter Iphegeneia when his ships are becalmed at Aulis, in order to gain a favourable wind so the Greek ships can sail for Troy.

114 – some of Barrie's plays. Sir James M. Barrie (1860–1937), Scottish journalist, novelist and playwright. Barrie wrote a memoir

Margaret Ogilvy, about his mother, as well as the novels *The Little Minister*, *Sentimental Tommy*, *and* its sequel *Tommy and Grizel*, and *The Little White Bird*, which introduced the character of Peter Pan (the relevant chapters from this book were later published separately as *Peter Pan in Kensington Gardens*). He wrote a series of successful plays produced in London's West End, including *Quality Street*, *The Twelve Pound Look*, *Dear Brutus*, *Mary Rose*, *The Admirable Crichton*, and his best-known work, *Peter Pan*.

– **In *Mary Rose* Barrie wrote a play on this theme.** See Manuscript B. pp. 272–4, MS. 6 folios 20–21 for Tolkien's longer and more detailed discussion of Barrie and *Mary Rose*.

116 – And if they have not gone away they are there still. We can find no exact use of this formulaic ending, but similar ones are found in three stories in *Popular Tales from the Norse*: "if they haven't left off their merry-making yet, why, they're still at it" in "Princess on the Glass Hill"; "and if the priest hasn't got out, why I daresay he's lying there still" in "Goosey Grizzel"; and "and if they're not dead, why, they're alive still" in "Doll i' the Grass".

– **My story is done – see there is a little mouse . . . a fine fur cap of it.** Slightly misquoted from the ending of "Hansel and Grettel" in *The Blue Fairy Book*, which reads: "My story is done. See! there runs a little mouse; anyone who catches it may make himself a large fur cap out of it" (p. 244).

– **And they lived happily ever after.** This archetypal fairy-tale ending occurs in three stories out of Lang's collections: "Prince Hyacinth and the Dear Little Princess" in *The Blue Fairy Book*; "Allerleirauh; or, the Many-furred Creature" in *The Green Fairy Book* ; and "The Frog" in *The Violet Fairy Book*. "The Twelve Brothers" in *The Red Fairy Book* ends "and they all lived happily ever afterwards".

– **And when the wedding was over . . . causeway of pieces of glass.** This is the ending of "The Knight of the Glens and Bens and Passes", the first story in *Folk Tales and Fairy Lore in Gaelic and English*, collected by James MacDougall.

THE HISTORY OF
"ON FAIRY-STORIES"

THE EVIDENCE

The material which constitutes "On Fairy-stories" exists in a multitude of rough workings: lists, notes, drafts in pencil, further drafts in ink (sometimes over pencil), cancelled and fair-copied manuscripts and a final typescript (with hand-written corrections) and carbon copy. The manuscript drafts are in varying states of readability, from a careful, sometimes calligraphic italic hand to a progressively less and less legible scribble that becomes at times indecipherable. Some pages (often the most illegible) show pencil underneath that is almost obliterated by pen, and all give evidence of extensive re-thinking as well as re-writing.

While the manuscripts are in a state of considerable disarray, it has been possible to distinguish three consecutive versions – one incomplete but initial draft which we have labeled MS. A, a much longer and heavily worked-over draft MS. B (both included in this edition as separate sections), and a final fair copy MS. C (which is essentially the form in which the essay was first published in 1947). MS. A was probably written between December 1938 and March 1939. The much longer and much amended MS. B is a very difficult text, a large proportion of which seems written for oral delivery but which also shows evidence of considerable revision undertaken probably in 1943. Developed from A, MS. B was the rough draft for MS. C which was in turn the copy-text for the typescript made in August of 1943. This was corrected and made ready for the printer by Tolkien in 1945 and published as "On Fairy-stories" in 1947.

THE BACKGROUND

On 25 November 1938, the University Court of St. Andrews, the oldest university in Scotland (founded between 1410 and 1413), announced the appointment of J.R.R. Tolkien, Rawlinson and Bosworth Professor of Anglo-Saxon at Pembroke College, Oxford, to deliver the Andrew Lang Lecture for 1938–39. Named for one of St. Andrews's most illustrious alumni, the Andrew Lang Lectureship was founded in 1926 and continues to this day.

On 29 June 1938 the St. Andrews Faculty of Arts had made recommendations to the Senatus Academius for the Andrew Lang lecturers for the coming three years; they were, in order, Gilbert Murray, Regius Professor of Greek at the University of Oxford; the Right Honourable Lord Hugh Macmillan, a Law Lord in the House of Lords; and Tolkien. Tolkien may well have been suggested as a candidate for the lectureship by Malcolm Knox (1900–88), then the professor of moral philosophy at St. Andrews. Knox had significant ties to Oxford, particularly with Pembroke College, where he had been an undergraduate and where Tolkien's professorial fellowship was based. Knox's former teacher and friend R.G. Collingwood was also a fellow at Pembroke. And before Knox moved to St. Andrews in 1936, he had been a lecturer and fellow in Oxford at Jesus College, and a lecturer at Queen's College. Knox and Tolkien would have known each other as members of the faculty at Oxford.

On 8 July 1938, the University Court announced that, on the recommendation of the Senatus Academius, it was agreed to invite Murray to deliver the Andrew Lang Lecture for 1938–9. Murray, however, was unable to undertake the lectureship due to the number of his engagements, and subsequently the University Court invited Lord Macmillan, who was also unable because of his commitments. On 7 October 1938 the Senatus agreed that Professor Tolkien be asked to undertake the lecture in the current session, and that Professor Murray be asked whether he could undertake it for 1939–40, and Lord Macmillan for 1940–1.

Accordingly, Tolkien was approached by the Secretary to the University, on 8 October 1938:

> Dear Sir,
> The Senatus Academicus of the University of St Andrews have agreed to invite you to deliver, during the current academic year, the Andrew Lang Lecture in the University, and they hope that it may be convenient for you, and that you would be willing to undertake this Lecture. The amount of the stipend is small, being only £30. The Lecturer is supposed to deliver at least one Lecture during his tenure of office, the subject to be "Andrew Lang and his Work" or one or other of the many subjects on which he wrote. There have already been ten lectures delivered under the foundation on Andrew Lang in relation to different aspects of his activities; but, as you will see, the subject of the lecture need not be concerned directly with Andrew Lang but may be upon any of the many subjects in which he was interested. The lecture is usually delivered soon after the opening of the session, say, in November or December; but a later date could be arranged, say, in January or February.
> Yours faithfully,
> Andrew Bennett, Secretary.[1]

Tolkien's reply does not survive, but Andrew Bennett's response does:

> 14 October 1938
> Dear Sir,
> I have to thank you for your letter of the 12th inst. in which you indicate your willingness to undertake the Lang Lecture this session. I should think there would be no difficulty in arranging a date about the end of January or beginning of

[1] St. Andrews Muniments, Copy out-letter books, UYUY7Sec/b/118/56. All quotations from the St. Andews records are used by the kind permission of the Keeper of Muniments of the University of St. Andrews.

February. When you are in a position to give a more definite date and state the subject you propose to lecture on, I shall be glad to hear from you again.
Yours faithfully,
Andrew Bennett, Secretary.[1]

Meanwhile, both Gilbert Murray and Lord Macmillan were contacted, and each had agreed to undertake the lectures for one of the subsequent years. On 25 November 1938 *The Scotsman* announced the appointments of Tolkien for 1938–9, Murray for 1939–40, and Macmillan for 1940–1[2]

Andrew Bennett wrote again to Tolkien on 18 January 1939, noting that he had not heard anything since his letter of 14 October, and that he hoped that Tolkien could now fix a date for the lecture[3]. According to a subsequent letter from Bennett to Tolkien of 3 February 1939, Tolkien finally replied on February 1, suggesting the 8th of March as the date for his lecture, and informing St. Andrews that the topic of his lecture would be "Fairy-stories"[4].

The minutes of the meeting of the Senatus Academius for 10 February 1939 record that: "A letter was read from Professor J.R.R. Tolkien intimating that he is prepared to deliver the Andrew Lang Lecture on the subject of "Fairy Stories" on Wednesday, 8th March. The Senatus approved the proposal and appointed Professor Rose to preside at the Lecture and to introduce Professor Tolkien."[5] On the following day, Andrew Bennett wrote to Tolkien that the date of March 8th was set for Tolkien's lecture.

[1] St. Andrews Muniments, Copy out-letter books, UYUY7Sec/b/118/42.
[2] World War II interrupted the series for six years. Murray finally gave his lecture on "Andrew Lang the Poet" on 7 May in 1947; Macmillan's lecture on "Law and Custom" was given the following year on 5 April 1948.
[3] St. Andrews Muniments, Copy out-letter books, UYUY7Sec/b/119/170.
[4] St. Andrews Muniments, Copy out-letter books, UYUY7Sec/b/119/421.
[5] St. Andrews Muniments, Senatus minutes UYUY452/41.

In accordance with the requirement that the lectures focus on some aspect of Lang's life and work, previous speakers had addressed such varied subjects as Lang's poetry, his place as a historian, his translations of Homer, his interest in the Scottish Borders, or in the House of Stuart. It would not be out of order to assume that in 1938 the idea of fairy-stories, lecture aside, was in the front of Tolkien's mind. Late in the previous year (September of 1937) he had published a children's book cum fairy-story, *The Hobbit*, to considerable success. Furthermore, he was currently embarked on the writing of its sequel, the extended fairy-story that was to become *The Lord of the Rings*. In addition (perhaps due to the success of *The Hobbit*), he had been scheduled in February of 1938 to address the Lovelace Society of Worcester College, Oxford, on the subject of fairy-stories in general. However, according to his biographer Humphrey Carpenter, when the time came, the talk on fairy-stories "had not been written" (Carpenter, 165), and instead Tolkien entertained his audience by reading another fairy-story of his own, this one the then-unpublished, "Farmer Giles of Ham". Whatever the preliminary circumstances in his own life, the title Tolkien chose for his lecture, "Fairy Stories" (not, as it later became, "On Fairy-stories"), named a topic for which both he and Andrew Lang were and are best known.

The lecture took place, as scheduled, on Wednesday evening, 8 March 1939. It was held in the United College Hall at St. Andrews, with the Professor of Greek, Herbert J. Rose, presiding. While visiting St. Andrews Tolkien enjoyed the hospitality of Malcolm Knox and his wife. Tolkien's lecture was reported in three Scottish newspapers, two weeklies of local origin, *The St. Andrews Citizen* and *The St. Andrews Times*, and the nationally-circulated daily *The Scotsman*. The first report to be published was in *The Scotsman*, but it is clearly based on the much longer local reportage that would appear a few days later in *The St. Andrews Citizen*. (The subsequent shorter report in *The St. Andrews Times* also derives directly from the one in the *Citizen*.) We reprint the reports from *The Scotsman* and *The St. Andrews Citizen* in Part Two of this volume.

The first ten Lang lectures were published as individual pamphlets by Oxford University Press, in all but one instance in either the year in which they were delivered, or the year after.[1] In 1949 all ten were collected as *Concerning Andrew Lang: being the Andrew Lang Lectures delivered before the University of St. Andrews*. No copy of Tolkien's lecture as delivered survives, but it is certainly the case that after its initial presentation at St. Andrews his text went through successive stages of re-writing for publication, and these drafts are available in the Bodleian Library. In the years 1943 to 1945–6 the lecture underwent its major revision from a talk designed for a listening audience to an essay directed toward a reading audience. It was published by Oxford University Press in December of 1947 in C.S. Lewis's collection, *Essays Presented to Charles Williams*.

On 7 December 1947 Tolkien sent a letter to Malcolm Knox, now Principal of St. Andrews, together with a copy of *Essays Presented to Charles Williams* just off the press. Referring to his 1939 lecture, Tolkien wrote, "In the end I took your advice and just published the 'lecture' in full (with all the little revisions and excisions) without reference to the University" (Hart, 5). Two things here are noteworthy: The first is the enclosure of the word *lecture* in quotation marks, suggesting that Tolkien had discussed the piece with Knox in the intervening years. The second is Tolkien's comment that it was published "without reference to the University" when in fact the essay opens by noting that it was "originally intended to be one of the Andrew Lang lectures at St. Andrews" (*EPCW*, 388).

Some years later, in 1963–4, the now-published essay was itself given further (albeit less extensive) revision for *Tree and Leaf*, its second appearance in print. After Tolkien's death in 1973, "On Fairy-stories" was re-published in Christopher

---

[1] The exception being Bernard Darwin's "Andrew Lang and the Literature of Sport", which was delivered in 1936 but not published until 1949.

Tolkien's 1983 edition of his father's essays. The status of "On Fairy-stories" among Tolkien's works at the present writing is that of a canonical piece, a standard text in the criticism of fantasy literature, and one necessary for a full understanding of Tolkien's own fiction. The progress of "On Fairy-stories" from lecture to published and twice re-published essay is an index of Tolkien's developing views and continuing engagement with the subject.

THE LECTURE

Starting presumably at the end of November 1938 (surely not before his appointment was officially announced), Tolkien had a scant three months in which to write his lecture. For a man of his painstaking, perfectionist work habits, this was not much time, for he had also to fulfill his University duties, which included preparing and delivering a course of lectures, and sitting on several committees. His work on the sequel to *The Hobbit* seems to have been temporarily put aside, since he wrote to Charles Furth at Allen & Unwin on 2 February 1939, "Since the beginning of December I have not been able to touch it" (*Letters*, 42).[1] As he began his preparations, two special aspects of his task were clearly in the forefront of his mind. One aspect was the importance of fairy-story, a branch of literature often dismissed as both childish and trivial, but relevant, indeed essential to modern life. The other aspect was his particular audience, which could be expected to be more than usually knowledgeable on the subject.

The most important was the topic, which, though he was both a reader and a writer in the genre, Tolkien readily acknowledged was far larger than could be covered in an evening's talk.

[1] See also his Introductory Note to *Tree and Leaf* (published in 1964). Here he wrote that the lecture was "written in the same period (1938–9) when *The Lord of the Rings* was beginning to unfold itself. . . . At about that time we had reached Bree" (p. 5).

Nevertheless, he did his best to cover the territory, researching the history of fairy-stories as a genre, re-familiarizing himself with the work of the Grimms, Perrault, and other collectors, even speculating about the folklore of folktales, as the Bertha Broadfoot example bears witness. While it is safe to assume that he was already familiar with much of this background through his studies in comparative philology, he nevertheless surveyed all twelve of Lang's *Fairy Books* for their content and approach to the subject (and predictably found them wanting), and made notes on individual tales to be used as illustration of his text. Not all of his painstaking research could be crammed into the final presentation, but the thoroughness of his preparation gave substance and authority to what he did include.

He began his preparations with an intensive program of exploration into the history, sociology, scholarly study and current status of folk and fairy tales. He drew up extensive lists of fairy tale collections to examine (all of the Lang "Colour" books), and jotted memos of particular items. For example, the back of a Pembroke College memo[1] scheduling "A Meeting of the Masters and Fellows" on Saturday, 25 February[2] contains the reminder, "<u>You must mention</u> Hans Andersen" (in the end he did not), as well as making some unexpected references, such as the single name "<u>Jung</u>", and again on the same page "Jung Psych of the unconscious". Not surprisingly, in view of the lecture's occasion, he concentrated chiefly on the voluminous publications of Andrew Lang. He made careful notes on all of Lang's *Fairy Books*.[3] He read and commented on Lang's more scholarly work on mythology and his seminal article on "Mythology and Fairy Tales" from *Fortnightly Review* (May 1873) as well as his lengthy and

---

[1] Reproduced on page 170.

[2] This must have been in 1939, less than a month before the lecture was delivered at St. Andrews, since according to a perpetual calendar the 25th did not fall on a Saturday in 1937–8, or 1940–6.

[3] Priscilla Tolkien remembers seeing the colour *Fairy Books* "all over the house" while her father was working on the lecture (personal communication).

erudite Introduction and Notes to the 1884 Margaret Hunt translation of *Grimm's Household Tales*.

Of less concern than the primary topic, but nevertheless a circumstance which Tolkien went out of his way to address, was the special nature of his audience. Not only could it be expected to be familiar with Lang and with fairy-stories, it was presumably and preponderantly Scottish. Tolkien was well aware that Scotland, an indigenously Celtic country, was not just a natural home of the folk and fairy lore traditionally associated with the Celts, but had been for many years a locus for research into the subject.

One book that figured largely as a springboard for Tolkien's thoughts was *The Coloured Lands,* a posthumously published collection of fairy-stories, satirical verse, pictures and commentary by G.K. Chesterton. It was published in late November 1938, so Tolkien's use of material from this book must post-date its appearance in print. Another important springboard was Christopher Dawson's *Progress and Religion: An Historical Enquiry*, originally published in 1929. Based on the page numbers referenced in Tolkien's manuscripts, we have determined that the edition Tolkien used (the only reset edition with page numbers that match Tolkien's usage) was the paperback published in the "Unicorn Books" imprint in the autumn of 1938. Thus two important resources that Tolkien used became available to him in late 1938.

In the days immediately following the lecture three newspaper reports were published, one in *The Scotsman*, a national daily newspaper, one in the weekly *St. Andrews Citizen*, and one in *The St. Andrews Times*. The newspaper reports give some indication of what the original audience heard, but equally worth attention is what was not reported – there is no mention of eucatastrophe or the parallel drawn in the published essay between fairy-stories and the Gospels of the New Testament. Judging from these reviews, the lecture given in 1939 was in the main a defence of fairy-stories as a legitimate literary genre, based on the very things for which fairy-stories were usually criticized – their "escapist function", their insistence on the Happy Ending, and their acceptance of the marvellous and the supernatural.

ESSAYS PRESENTED TO CHARLES WILLIAMS

It is difficult to determine with certainty either the exact time or the original reason for which Tolkien began his first major revision – whether for publication in the war-delayed Oxford University Press series of pamphlets of the Lang lectures, or for the much later volume of *Essays Presented to Charles Williams*. What is certain is that the latter marks the first appearance of Tolkien's lecture in print. During the London blitz early in World War II, Oxford University Press, and with it Charles Williams as one of its editors, were relocated for safety from London to Oxford. There Williams formed friendships with C.S. Lewis and Tolkien, and became a part of the informal literary group that called itself the Inklings and gathered weekly in Lewis's college rooms for drinks and conversation. As the war in Europe was winding down in early 1945 the press began preparations for its return to London. Williams's Oxford friends (chiefly C.S. Lewis) proposed putting together a volume of essays, a festschrift to honour him. Sadly, Williams did not live to see it published. Following an operation, he died suddenly and unexpectedly on 15 May 1945, and the festschrift, now changed to a memorial volume, was published to honour his memory. Its royalties became a posthumous gift to his widow.

The publication in 1947 of this revision made it the de facto basis for all future versions. Here, Tolkien was able to include more of the results of the vast research he had undertaken, much of which could not be crammed into an hour or so of lecture time. Indeed, a note jotted at this time raises the question of how much of Tolkien's lecture was actually delivered to the primary audience. Written on a 1943 calendar for the week of 16–22 August, during the time when Tolkien was engaged in developing the lecture into the essay, it reads,

This essay was originally written as the A[ndrew] L[ang] lecture in Univ[ersity] of St. A[ndrews], and some part of it

~~such as could be~~ was actually delivered there. Its present form is somewhat enlarged from the form it had had in that, and is of course much longer and I hope clearer than the lecture. But it was not materially altered, and A[ndrew] Lang

The note breaks off at this point, but the comment that "some part of it" was "actually delivered", plus the struck through phrase "such as could be" would indicate that Tolkien, keeping an eye on the time, may have edited for length as he went along. In any case, it is frequently difficult to distinguish between material originally drafted for the lecture and that written for its expansion or during its transformation into essay form, but the general progression can be determined. The opening pages of Manuscript B are transferred and overwritten in ink from Manuscript A's pencil, becoming the bridge between the first draft and an expansion to nearly twice the length of its precursor. Manuscript B, with all its cancelled pages and addenda, was the basis for Manuscript C, the final manuscript copy. This in turn was the basis for a typescript, itself emended in ink before being sent to the press for publication.

Tolkien made several starts (mostly discarded) on an elaborate opening analogy developing, as an Englishman in Scotland, his conflicting feelings of honour, unworthiness, and temerity.

I feel like a blundering mortal conjuror who finds himself, by some mistake, called on to speak of magic to the counsellors of an Elf king

. . . as if some mortal guest were politely asked for his views on magic by an Elflord

. . . a blundering mortal asked for his views on magic

. . . making an after-dinner speech on the subject of magic at the banquet of Elves

. . . give a display of magic to the court of an Elf king. After producing his rabbit, he may consider himself lucky if he is allowed to go home in his proper shape, or to go home at all. There are dungeons in Fairyland for the over-bold

These variations on the mock-humble stance of a stranger in fairyland, or even worse, an Englishman in Scotland, the natural home of fairy-stories, need not be taken at face value. They are similar to the opening of his 1955 O'Donnell Lecture[1] on "English and Welsh", where again he apologized as an Englishman for presuming to speak about things Celtic, even though the O'Donnell Lecture was delivered in Oxford to an audience largely English. Nevertheless, even with the sometimes minute changes from draft to draft, the mock-apologetic posture and the cluster of images he settled on – the Englishman in Scotland, the conjuror, the Elf-king or elflord, even the rabbit – were retained for publication, as was the following paragraph.

The land of Fairy Story is wide and deep and high, and is filled with many kings and all manner of men, and beasts, and birds; its seas are shoreless and its stars uncounted, its beauty an enchantment and its perils ever present; but its joy and sorrow are poignant as a sword. In that land a man may (perhaps) count himself fortunate to have wandered, but its very mystery and wealth make dumb the traveler who would report. And while he is there it is dangerous for him to ask too many questions, lest the gates shut and the keys be lost. The fairy gold (more or less) turns to withered leaves when it is brought away. All that I can ask is that you, knowing all these

[1] A series of annual lectures established in the will of Charles James O'Donnell (1850–1934) as a bequest to each of the Universities of Oxford, Wales, Edinburgh, National University of Ireland and Trinity College. The will stipulated that lectures were to be on the "British or Celtic element in the English Language and the dialects of English Counties and the special terms and words used in agriculture and handicrafts and the British or Celtic element in the existing population of England" (Prefatory Note, *Angles and Britons*). Tolkien was the first O'Donnell lecturer in Oxford, appointed in 1954 and speaking about "English and Welsh" on 21 October 1955 A selection of some of the lectures, those by Tolkien, T.H. Parry-Williams, Kenneth Jackson, B.G. Charles, N.K. Chadwick and William Rees, were published by University of Wales Press as *Angles and Britons* in 1963.

things, will receive my withered leaves, as a token at least that
my hand once held a little of the gold.

The only notable change in the published text is one of tense
from "I feel like a conjuror" to "I felt like a conjuror" made late
in the process as a correction to the typescript.

Internal evidence clearly places a major revision to 1943. One
page is written on the back of the cancelled draft of a syllabus
(for a war-time Naval Cadet's course) noting "The Course
begins on Th. 8 April and ends on Th. 6 Sept." Checked against
a perpetual calendar, these days and dates place the time of
writing as 1943, as does the wry allusion in the text to the
improbability of a story about an archbishop slipping on a
banana-skin being current in England between 1940 and 1943
(updated to 1945 in a correction made to the typescript).
Corroborative evidence comes in a letter written on 5 August
1943 by Williams' friend and occasional typist, Margaret
Douglas.

> I have at Charles's request undertaken to type a long essay by
> Professor Tolkien which is going to mean about fifty pages of
> typing, and not too easy a writing to read. I gather it was orig-
> inally a lecture which he gave some time or other in St.
> Andrews; it is all about fairy-stories, and rather fascinating.
> (manuscript letter to Raymond Hunt, Charles Williams
> Papers, The Marion E. Wade Center, Wheaton College,
> Wheaton, IL).

The "not too easy a writing to read" was that of MS. C, developed from MS. B as a copy-text in preparation for publication.

Like the manuscript copy, the typescript had no proper title,
but the heading "On Fairy-stories" was added in pen at centre
top in Tolkien's hand, and below it, also in pen, the name,
"J.R.R. Tolkien". An opening sentence, superscribed in pen like
the title, explains that the essay was "originally written intended
to be one of the Andrew Lang lectures at St. Andrews, and it
was, in abbreviated form, delivered there in 1940". Tolkien's

memory was off by a year, but the mistake was perpetuated in the published text, which reproduces the manuscript note verbatim. Pencilled instructions for typesetting (not in Tolkien's handwriting), such as "Bask 30 pt.", "caps." for the title, and "small caps" for the author's name, show that the typescript was being readied for the printer.

All indications are that the material on the Gospels as fairy-story was added at the time of the 1943 revision. No contemporary review of the lecture makes any reference to the Gospels, or to *eucatastrophe* and *evangelium*; simply concluding with the "escapist" function.

A year later Tolkien mentioned in a letter to his son Christopher dated 7–8 November 1944, "that fairy-story essay that I so much wish you had read that I think I shall send it to you. For it I coined the word 'eucatastrophe'" (*Letters*, 100). His use of the word "essay" points to a text prepared for publication, while the citation of *eucatastrophe* as coined for the essay would indicate that neither word nor concept were part of the original lecture. When plans for the Williams festschrift were altered by Williams's death, C.S. Lewis wrote on 17 May 1945 to Dorothy Sayers, inviting her to contribute to what was now a memorial volume. Lewis mentions that Tolkien, Barfield and Lewis himself "had in fact written our contributions" (Lewis *Letters*, Vol. II, 649). Barfield's essay, "Poetic Diction and Legal Fiction" had been delivered as a paper some ten years earlier (Barfield, "Introduction" to *The Rediscovery of Meaning and Other Essays*. 3), and Lewis's essay was originally read to an undergraduate literary Society at Merton College (Hooper, Introduction to C.S. Lewis's *Of Other Worlds*, viii).

And finally, on 26 May 1945, less than two weeks after Charles Williams's death, Margaret Douglas, who had produced the typed copy from Tolkien's "difficult to read" manuscript, wrote once more about the essay, this time to Tolkien himself.

Dear Professor Tolkien,
    I have been helping young Michael Williams to sort some of his father's papers, and we came across this which I recognized

as the lecture I typed for you at Charles's suggestion some time ago, so I thought you might perhaps like to have it returned to you.

I did so much work for Charles, and feel lost without it and without his friendship, which has meant so much to us all.

Of course do not trouble to acknowledge this.

       Yours sincerely,
          Margaret Douglas
          [Bodleian Tolkien MS. 14 fol. 121]

Douglas's brief note gives no indication of which copy it was that she and Michael Williams "came across" in the sorting of Williams's papers.

Tolkien made some further emendations to the proofs for the *Charles Williams* volume, which are stamped (presumably by the press) "Dec. 1946". A letter to Tolkien from the editor at the Oxford University Press dated 18 December asks him to return the marked proofs "passed for press" to C.S. Lewis at Magdalen College. With the exception of one major revision (about which more below) the preponderance of his corrections at this point are relatively minor changes to paragraphing or word-choice.[1]

These include the removal of a disparaging footnote reference to "the work of Disney", criticized for uniting "beautiful external detail with inner vulgarity", the systematic deletion of qualifiers such as "I feel" or "I guess", the excision of unnecessary sentences such as, "This is what I feel about it", as in the example cited above of the archbishop and the banana-skin. He removed from his illustrations of comparative folklore the example of Tertullian's *turris lamiae, pectin solis* as a precursor of "Rapunzel", replacing it with the example of *Beowulf* as a version of *Dat Erdmänneken*. He corrected the German title of "The Juniper Tree" from *Der Machandelboom* to *Von dem Machandelboom*, and emphasized the archaic flavour of that particular tale and its "distance and great abyss of time" by

[1]   And see note to paragraph 80 above.

adding the phrase "not measurable even by *twe tusend Johr*", which thereafter became part of the text.[1]

It should not be unexpected in a man who staunchly championed the power of narrative over other forms of art to create illusion and to cast a spell, that it was around his analysis of drama as a vehicle for fantasy that Tolkien made greater emendations and sought more precise refinements than to any other section of the essay. This is at best a debatable portion of his discussion, not only for his evaluation of drama as the vehicle for fantasy, but also for his criticism of "special effects" (though he did not use that term), in particular some of the fantastic effects written for the stage by England's greatest literary figure, William Shakespeare. Tolkien's observation that, "Very little about trees as trees can be got into a play" ("On Fairy-stories, paragraph 73) is a gloss on his later statement to W.H. Auden that the presence of the ents in *The Lord of the Rings* was due to his "bitter disappointment and disgust from schooldays with the shabby use made in Shakespeare of the coming of 'Great Birnam Wood to high Dunsinane Hill'" (*Letters* 212n). His elaborate strictures in the essay concerning the effect on stage of the witches in *Macbeth*, however, are worth closer examination, for what they reveal both about his ideas and about his concern for precision in diction.

Printed below are the four successive phases in the emendation at the proof stage of one brief passage on the witches. The left-hand column gives the passage as printed in the proofs. The two centre columns give Tolkien's two successive handwritten

---

[1] The italicized phrase, "*twe tusend Johr*", comes from the first sentence of the story as published in the 1812 German edition, where unlike some of the other tales, which appear in hochdeutsch, *The Juniper Tree* is presented in plattdeutsch, the Pomeranian dialect in which it was told to the Grimms. Thus the word for "year" is *Johr* instead of the more conventional *Jahr*. It is worthy of note that the 1812 text has *dusend* rather than *tusend*. However, it is impossible now to determine whether Tolkien's initial 't' was his own deliberate change to the text or was simply a spelling error made in a spur-of-the-moment marginal emendation and perpetuated thereafter by a succession of non-German copy-editors and typesetters.

emendations, one on the left and one on the right margin of the proofs. On the far right is the passage as published in *Essays Presented to Charles Williams*. That the four versions are not different from one another in meaning is obvious; all of them make essentially the same point.

Proof fol. 27	L. marg. emend	R. marg.emend	Published text
That argument gives the point to me, I think. And it also shows what degradation Fantasy must undergo, before it becomes fit even for the drama of Shakespeare.	Not degradation (as I think), near dissolution is a likely fate for Fantasy when Drama tries to use it.	An [argument] that concedes my point. To be dissolved, then, or to be degraded is the likely fate of Fantasy when Drama tries to use it.	That argument concedes the point. To be dissolved, or to be degraded, is the likely fate of Fantasy when a dramatist tries to use it, even such a dramatist as Shakespeare.

Tolkien did not stop there. The major revision mentioned above also entered in at this point in the essay's history, perhaps not surprising at so problematical a juncture as his discussion of fantasy and drama. As noted above (Note to paragraph 74) the passage in the published book beginning "Now Faërian Drama, those plays which according to abundant records the elves have often presented to men" contains some of Tolkien's most striking statements. Neither defining nor explaining what he means by Faërian Drama, he launches directly into a description of its effects on human beings. Here he talks about going beyond Secondary Belief, being bodily inside a Secondary World, experiencing it directly, about the power in such a too-strong potion to lead to Primary Belief in a Secondary World. So vivid and immediate is Tolkien's report on these extraordinary conditions that readers may find it hard to believe he was not speaking out of his own encounter with the phenomena he describes.

While the paragraph on Faërian Drama remains unchanged from typescript to galley proof to printed version, the paragraphs directly following it alter substantially, clear evidence that even at the proof stage Tolkien felt compelled to revise, enlarge and clarify. Rough and fragmentary manuscript workings precede three distinct revisions on three separate typewritten pages. These typewritten passages show Tolkien working his way through a thicket of related ideas, ever refining his terminology in his endeavour to map the boundary between illusion and experience that is the territory of the imagination and the very threshold of Faërie.

Read in consecutive order, the revisions speak for themselves. When compared with the passage they were intended to replace in the galleys, they show the direction of Tolkien's thought more clearly than could any second-hand digest or synopsis of their content. Given below is the original passage as it appeared in the galley proofs, followed by the draft revisions.

BODLEIAN LIBRARY TOLKIEN MS. 16 FOL. 28

PROOF p. 59

That is Art for them. They do not live in it, though they can, perhaps, afford to spend more time at it. The primary World, Reality, of elves and men is the same, if differently valued and perceived.

So we may observe the difference between Art, Enchantment, and Wizardry. Art is the human process that produces by the way (it is not its only or ultimate object) Secondary Belief; Enchantment is the elvish craft that produces a Secondary World into which artist and audience can actually enter, and which upon a man may work a delusory belief; Wizardry produces (or desires or pretends to produce) a real alteration in the Primary World. Wizardry is not an Art in the aesthetic sense, but allied to Science: Science as a technique, rather than an investigation of physical Truth. Fantasy is that form of human Art which when successful comes nearest to the elvish. To all these things, Enchantment and Magic are loosely applied. It is to the third only that Magic properly applies.

The Secondary Belief of human Art is not a delusion, though it may be or approach an illusion: willing submission to an illusion might be used of certain human attitudes to works of art (especially to Drama). A character in a fairy-story may be 'enchanted' in the elvish sense, or even spell-bound by a necromancer, but you, when according to the event Secondary Belief – and that is quite independent of your views of the possibility of elvish craft or wizards' spells in your Primary World – are not enchanted nor spell-bound. The words *enchantment* and *magic* can, in fact, be used of the effects of human Art, if at all, only by a metaphor, and a dangerous one.

The flurry of terms deployed here – *Art, Enchantment, Wizardry, Magic, Science, delusory belief, elvish craft, Fantasy* – is confusing and is itself confused. Tolkien was not satisfied with the distinctions among the words, and we may approve his attempts to clarify and differentiate among them. He cancelled the proof passage cited above, drawing a line round it in pen, slashing a diagonal line through it from corner to corner, and writing in the margin a notation for substitution. He then re-wrote the entire passage three times, struggling repeatedly to get his thoughts in order, to make this clearly important passage come out to his satisfaction. Printed below are his revision attempts labeled in order of composition Typescripts 'A', 'B', and 'C', with the final 'C' draft being the one he selected to replace the cancelled galley paragraphs in the final text. It is both obvious and worthy of note that the first draft is by far the longest as Tolkien searches for the best way to capture on paper some precise concepts and the minute distinctions among them. The second draft is the shortest; and the third is a compromise between the two both in length and conciseness. Editorial comments are enclosed in square brackets [ ].

BODLEIAN TOLKIEN MS. 6, FOL. 92

TYPESCRIPT 'A' DRAFT

This is for them a form of Art, and wholly distinct from Wizardry or Magic, properly so-called. They do not live in it, though they can, perhaps, afford to spend more time at it than human artists can. The primary World, Reality, of elves and men is the same, if differently valued and perceived.

We need a word for this elvish craft, but all the words that have been applied to it have been blurred and confused with other things. Magic is ready to hand, and I have ~~already~~ used it above, but I should not have done so: magic should be reserved for the operations of the Wizard or Magician. Art can be used by men, and also (according to report) by elves, and is the process that produces by the way (it is not its only or its ultimate object) Secondary Belief. The elvish craft, which for lack of a less ill-defined word I would call Enchantment, produces a Secondary World into which both designer and audience can enter, to the satisfaction of their senses, while they are inside; but in its purity it is artistic in desire and purpose. Magic produces, or pretends to produce, a real alteration in the Primary World. It does not matter by whom it is said to be practised, fay or mortal, it remains distinct from the other two; it is not an art but a technique; its desire is <u>power</u> in this world, domination (~~or delusion~~) of things and wills.

To the elvish craft, enchantment, Fantasy aspires, and when it is successful of all forms of human art most nearly approaches. At the heart of (man-made) stories of the elves lies, open or concealed, pure or alloyed, ~~this~~ a desire for a living, realized, sub-creative art, which is inwardly wholly different, however much it may outwardly resemble it, from the greed for self-centred power which marks the mere Magician. ~~It~~ and it is ~~thus~~ from the[m] ~~elves even if they are only the product (one of the highest) of human Fantasy~~ that we may learn what is the central aspiration and desire of human Fantasy – even if they elves are, all the more in so far as they are, only the product, one of the highest ~~products~~ , of that Fantasy itself.

But to the effects of human art neither the words <u>enchantment</u> nor <u>magic</u> should be applied, even by a metaphor: the metaphor is too dangerous. The Secondary Belief of human art is not a delusion, though it may be or approach an illusion: willing submission to an illusion might be used of certain human attitudes to works of Art, especially those of dramatic art. A character in a fairy-story may be 'enchanted' in the elvisg [*sic*] sense, or even spell-bound by a magician, but you, when according to the event Secondary Belief – and that is quite independent of your views of the possibility of elvish craft or wizards' spells in your Primary World, are not enchanted nor spell-bound.

This desire is one of the elements of which the elves, in their better ~~na~~ (but still perilous) part ~~of their nature, have been~~ are made; and it is from them that we may learn what is the central aspiration and desire of Fantasy – even if the elves are, all the more so in so far as they are, only the product, one of the highest, of that Fantasy itself. ~~But~~

and that desire ~~is not~~ does not seek delusion, nor bewitchment and domination; it seeks ~~partners in delight~~ shared enrichment, partners in making and delight not slaves. ~~Though~~ all things are subject to the peril of corruption, even the elves, not to mention human authors.

BODLEIAN TOLKIEN MS. 6, FOL. 93

THE TYPESCRIPT 'B' DRAFT

This is for them a form of Art, and wholly distinct from Wizardry (or Magic, properly so-called). They do not live in it, though they can, perhaps, afford to spend more time at it than human artists can. The primary World, Reality, of Elves and Men is the same, if differently valued and perceived.

The words applied to these things have been blurred and confused by vague and careless usage, and the things themselves are often mixed in the minds of men, and so in the tales men have told. Art can [illeg] used both by men and also by elves (as appears from stories); but for the peculiar elvish ~~craft~~ [form?] I would, for lack of a less ill-defined word reserve Enchantment; and ~~for~~ to the third thing, Magic. Art is the process that produces by the way (it is not its only or ultimate object)[,] Secondary Belief[.] Enchantment is the elvish craft that produces a Secondary World into which both artist and audience can enter, to the satisfaction of all their senses, while they are inside. But Magic produces (or desires or pretends to produce) a real alteration in the Primary World; it is not an art, but a technique. It does not matter by whom it is said to be wielded, fay or mortal, it remains distinct from the other two: its desire is power in this world, and its tendency (at least) inevitably evil. Fantasy is the form of human Art which when successful comes nearest to the elvish craft of ~~Enchantment: and at the heart of many man-made stories of the elves may be found the desire of a living realized sub-creative art, rather than the greed for self-centred power that marks the Magician~~
To the elvish craft of Enchantment

To this craft Fantasy aspires, and when it is successful of all forms of human art most nearly approaches. At the heart of many (man-made) stories of the elves lies, open or concealed, the desire of a realized sub-creative art, rather than greed for self-centred power that marks the mere Magician. Of this desire the elves, in their better ~~part~~ (though still perilous) part, are largely made – in so far as we in our tales have made them. But Magic, whether in Faerie or on Middle-earth, whether used by elf or any ~~other inhabitant of Faerie~~ other mind or will

This is not Magic, for its desire is different, though to it the word is usually applied

We need a word for this elvish craft [subsequent words in brackets too faint to read] but all the words that have been applied to these difficult and ill-explored regions [final words too faint to read]

BODLEIAN TOLKIEN MS. 6, FOL. 94

THE TYPESCRIPT 'C' DRAFT [MARKED AT BOTTOM IN SCRIPT "RIDER P. 59"]

This is for them a form of Art, and wholly distinct from Wizardry or Magic, properly so-called. They do not live in it, though they can, perhaps, afford to spend more time at it than human artists can. The primary World, Reality, of elves and men is the same, if differently valued and perceived.

We need a word for this elvish craft, but all the words that have been applied to it have been blurred and confused with other things. Magic is ready to hand, and I have used it above (p. 36[1]), but I should not have done so: Magic should be reserved for the operations of the Magician. Art is the human process that produces by the way (it is not its only or ultimate object) Secondary Belief. Art of the same sort, if more skilled and effortless, the elves can also use, or so the reports seem to show; but the more potent and especially elvish craft I will, for lack of a less debatable word, call Enchantment. Enchantment produces a Secondary World into which both designer and spectator can enter, to the satisfaction of their senses, while they are inside; but in its purity it is artistic in desire and purpose. Magic produces, or pretends to produce, a real alteration in the Primary World. It does not matter by whom it is said to be practiced, fay or mortal, it remains distinct from the other two; it is not an art but a technique; its desire is <u>power</u> in this world, domination of things and wills.

[1] This refers to the page proofs of *Essays Presented to Charles Williams*.

To the elvish craft, Enchantment, Fantasy aspires, and when it is successful, of all forms of human art most nearly approaches. At the heart of many man-made stories of the elves lies, open or concealed, pure or alloyed, the desire for a living, realized, sub-creative art, which (however much it may outwardly resemble it), is inwardly wholly different from the greed for self-centred power which is the mark of the mere Magician. Of this desire the elves, in their better (but still perilous) part, are largely made; and it is from them that we may learn what is the central desire and aspiration of human Fantasy – even if the elves are, all the more so in so far as they are, only ~~the~~ a product, ~~one of the highest,~~ of ~~the~~ Fantasy itself. That creative desire is only cheated by counterfeits, whether the innocent but clumsy devices of human dramatists, or the malevolent frauds of magicians. In this world it is for men unsatisfiable, and so imperishable. Uncorrupted, it does not seek delusion, nor bewitchment and domination; it seeks shared enrichment, partners in making and delight, not slaves.

To many, Fantasy, this . . . .

The 'C' draft represents the passage as it appeared in the published book in 1947 and as it has appeared in all subsequent publications. It seems clear that the terms Tolkien deployed here: *Art*, *Enchantment*, *Wizardry*, *Magic*, *Fantasy*, are not just the practical components of a critical vocabulary which he was in the process of developing, but are important in themselves as markers of discrete but often overlapping experiences, experiences which he goes to extraordinary lengths to distinguish and categorize.

With an Introduction by C.S. Lewis and contributions by Tolkien, Lewis, Owen Barfield, Dorothy Sayers, Warren Lewis, and Gervase Mathew, *Essays Presented to Charles Williams* was published on December 4, 1947, but was subsequently, as Tolkien wrote to W.H. Auden in 1955, "most scurvily allowed to go out of print" (*Letters, 216*).

TREE AND LEAF

The next opportunity for revision came nearly a decade and a half later with a new prospect for publication. In addition to his grumble to Auden in 1955 Tolkien had complained to his American publisher Houghton Mifflin that, "the O.U.P. [Oxford University Press] have infuriatingly let ["On Fairy-stories"] go out of print, though it is now in demand" (*Letters*, 220). The 1955 "demand" was a direct result of the publication in 1954–5 of *The Lord of the Rings*. Eager to follow up and capitalize on that book's unexpected success, Tolkien's British publishers George Allen & Unwin proposed bringing out "On Fairy-stories" as a stand-alone volume. Predictably, this led Tolkien to revise the essay further in preparation for re-publication. However, and although in his autobiography Rayner Unwin referred to this project as being "on the point of completion for so many years" (*George Allen and Unwin: A Remembrancer*, 105), it was not until 1959 that Tolkien actually signed a contract for a new publication.

Even with this hopeful development, however, no visible progress was made. Other projects intervened and the volume remained out of print for several years.[1] In 1963 Unwin revived the proposal, now suggesting that Allen & Unwin pair "On Fairy-stories" with Tolkien's short story "Leaf by Niggle", which could serve as a fictive illustration of the principles discussed in the essay[2], as well as helping to "bulk out" what would otherwise be a very slim stand-alone volume (Unwin, 117). In May 1964, the essay was published by Allen and Unwin together with "Leaf by Niggle" in a single volume titled *Tree and Leaf*, with an American edition brought out by Houghton Mifflin in March 1965.

---

[1] It was reissued in soft cover in 1966 by William B. Eerdmans publishers in Grand Rapids, Michigan, and reprinted several times, but at the present writing this edition, too, is out of print.

[2] Not, as it turns out, the best illustration, since "Leaf by Niggle" is more allegory than fairy-story. Tolkien's best short fairy-story, *Smith of Wootton Major*, would have served the essay better, indeed would have been ideal, but this story was not yet written.

Tolkien's Introductory Note to *Tree and Leaf* is worthy of attention for several reasons. First, because he here notes that both "On Fairy-stories" and "Leaf by Niggle" are, "no longer easy to obtain" (in fact, "Leaf by Niggle", published in *The Dublin Review* in January of 1945, had never been easy to obtain). He adds that essay and story "are related: by the symbols of Tree and Leaf, and by both touching in different ways on what is called in the essay 'sub-creation'" (*T&L*, vii). Second, because he dates the Andrew Lang Lecture as given in 1938, appending a footnote "Not 1940 as incorrectly stated in 1947" [i.e. in *Essays Presented to Charles Williams*] (*T&L*, [5]). In fact, he had both dates wrong, bracketing the correct year of 1939 by a year on either side. And third, because with equal inaccuracy, he stated that the essay was "reproduced with only a few minor alterations" (*T&L*, 6). There were, in fact substantial revisions to at least two passages, and a host of lesser revisions at the sentence level.

It would hardly be surprising if at this time Tolkien decided to make some alterations. Much had changed since the publication of *Essays Presented to Charles Williams*, not just his added years of experience as a writer but also his growing reputation as an author. By 1964, *The Lord of the Rings* had been in print for ten successful years and its popularity showed no signs of abating. Just as the publication many years before of *Farmer Giles of Ham* had capitalized on the success of *The Hobbit*, so the re-publication of "On Fairy-stories" in *Tree and Leaf* was intended to take advantage of the success of *The Lord of the Rings*. In the latter case, however, the time of publication had a more marked influence on the essay in question. Tolkien was in some significant respects a different man from the one who had written *The Hobbit* and given the lecture, different even from the writer of the essay as published in 1947.

He was now the author of one of the most popular pieces of fiction in the English-speaking world, a work published to enthusiastic critical acclaim and an equal measure of critical vilification. He would be speaking now to an audience many times larger than in 1939, or even in 1947, an audience moreover, that was already familiar with his work. He was confident not just of his opinions but of his art, sure of its quality, its value and its place in the tradition about which he was speaking. He took this fresh publication of "On Fairy-stories" as the opportunity for some re-thinking and re-writing, a reconsideration that had as much to do with the ongoing development of his vision as with the immediate occasion.

As had been the case with *Essays Presented to Charles Williams*, some substantial as well as some minor emendations were made at the proof stage. Most obvious is the addition at this time of the subheadings, "Fairy-story", "Origins", "Children", "Fantasy", and "Recovery, Escape, Consolation", as well as "Epilogue". These do much to make this densely packed essay easier to follow and to understand. Other emendations range from such fine-tuning as the changing or deletion of a word or phrase to the complete replacement – in two cases of a paragraph or more – of existing text with new material. These changes themselves make the trajectory of Tolkien's thinking clear. Minor copy-editing corrections for typographical style, spelling and punctuation – changes which do not affect meaning – have been omitted from the present discussion.

First and most arresting are the changes to the opening paragraphs. While some sentences are retained from one version to the other, there are sufficient differences between the two to merit reproducing both at length for comparison. For ease of reference, page numbers are cited from the British editions of both books.

EPCW, P. 38 PASTED OVER

This essay was originally intended to be one of the Andrew Lang lectures at St. Andrews, and it was, in abbreviated form, delivered there in 1940.[1] To be invited to lecture in St. Andrews is a high compliment to any man; to be allowed to speak about fairy-stories is (for an Englishman in Scotland) a

[1] See p. 126 above.

perilous honour. I felt like a conjuror who finds himself, by some mistake, called upon to give a display of magic before the court of an elf-king. After producing his rabbit, such a clumsy performer may consider himself lucky, if he is allowed to go home in his proper shape, or indeed to go home at all. There are dungeons in fairyland for the overbold.

And overbold I fear I may be accounted, because I am a reader and lover of fairy-stories, but not a student of them, as Andrew Lang was. I have not the learning, nor the still more necessary wisdom, which the subject demands. The land of fairy-story is wide and deep and high, and is filled with many things: all manner of beasts and birds are found there; shoreless seas and stars uncounted; beauty that is an enchantment, and an ever-present peril; both sorrow and joy as sharp as swords. In that land a man may (perhaps) count himself fortunate to have wandered but its very richness and strangeness make dumb the traveller who would report it. And while he is there it is dangerous for him to ask too many questions, lest the gates shut and the keys be lost. The fairy gold too often turns to withered leaves when it is brought away. All that I can ask is that you, knowing these things, will receive my withered leaves as a token that my hand at least once held a little of the gold.

CANCELLED P. 38

But there are some questions that one who is to speak about fairy-stories cannot help asking, whatever the folk of Faërie think of him or do to him. For instance: What are fairy-stories? What is their origin? What is the use of them? I will try to give answers to these questions, or rather the broken hints of answers to them that I have gleaned – primarily from the stories themselves: such few of their multitude as I know.

T&L PASTE-OVER P. 9

I propose to speak about fairy-stories, though I am aware that this is a rash adventure. Faërie is a perilous land, and in it are pitfalls for the unwary and dungeons for the overbold. And overbold I may be accounted, for though I have been a lover of fairy-stories since I learned to read, and have at times thought about them, I have not studied them professionally. I have been hardly more than a wandering explorer (or trespasser) in the land, full of wonder but not of information.

The realm of fairy-story is wide and deep and high and filled with many things: all manner of beasts and birds are found there; shoreless seas and stars uncounted; beauty that is an enchantment, and an ever-present peril; both joy and sorrow as sharp as swords. In that realm a man may, perhaps, count himself fortunate to have wandered, but its very richness and strangeness tie the tongue of a traveller who would report them. And while he is there it is dangerous for him to ask too many questions, lest the gates should be shut and the keys be lost.

There are, however, some questions that one who is to speak about fairy-stories must expect to answer, whatever the folk of Faërie may think of his impertinence. For instance: what are fairy-stories? What is their origin? What is the use of them? I will try to give answers to these questions, or such hints of answers as I have gleaned – primarily from the stories themselves, the few of all their multitude that I know.

The shifts in tone and approach are unmistakable. Gone is the quasi-apologetic explanation of the essay's origin as a lecture. Gone are the Englishman in Scotland, the diffident conjuror, the elf-king and the rabbit. Gone are the romantic withered leaves and the plea for their acceptance, together with the fairy gold of which they were the token (though the shut gates and lost keys were retained). Now, without preamble or apology, Tolkien begins authoritatively with a confident, straightforward announcement, "I propose to speak about fairy-stories". While he still concedes that this is "a rash adventure", no longer is this because it is a "perilous honour" to speak about fairy-stories in Scotland to Scots. Rather, it is because Faërie itself is a "perilous land", with pitfalls and dungeons for unwary visitors. The single most important term in Tolkien's imaginative lexicon, Faërie, is now given pride of place in the second sentence of the essay instead of in the delayed and philological introduction five pages further on as in the *Essays Presented to Charles Williams* version. The danger has been shifted from the audience to the subject matter where Tolkien clearly felt it belonged, and it is there to stay.

Other changes are for the most part less substantial, but all have been noted in the interest of thoroughness and consistency and to make clear that Tolkien's attention to detail was as meticulous in 1963 as it had been in 1947.

EPCW, p. 38 "It is in this case no good hastening to *The Oxford English Dictionary*, because it will not tell you."

T&L, pp. 10–11 "In this case you will turn to *The Oxford English Dictionary* in vain."

EPCW, P. 39 "~~volume F was not edited by a Scotsman~~"

EPCW, p. 39 "Not too narrow for ~~a lecture (it is large enough for fifty)~~"

T&L, p. 10 "Not too narrow for an essay; it is wide enough for many books"

EPCW, p. 43. "That must in that story be taken seriously, neither laughed at nor explained away."

T&L, p. 15 **added** "Of this seriousness the medieval <u>Sir Gawain and the Green Knight</u> is an admirable example."

EPCW, p. 57 "~~And with that I think we come to the~~ children, and ~~with them~~ to the last and most important of the three questions"

T&L, p. 33 "I will now turn to children and so come to the last and most important of the three questions"

EPCW, p. 57 "It is ~~often now~~ assumed that children"
T&L, p. 33 "It is usually assumed that children"

EPCW, p. 59 "~~All children's books are on a strict judgment poor books. Books written entirely for children are poor even as children's books.~~"

EPCW, p. 66 "as they may hope to get suitable introduction to poetry, history and the sciences."
T&L, p. 43 **adds** "Though it may be better for them to read some things, especially fairy-stories, that are beyond their measure rather than short of it. Their books like their clothes should allow for growth, and their books at any rate should encourage it."

EPCW, p. 69 "This is, of course, partly due to the fact that the producers of drama have to, or try to, work with mechanism to represent Fantasy or Magic"
T&L, p. 47 "work with mechanism to represent either Fantasy or Magic"

EPCW, p. 72 "~~As for the disabilities of age, that possibly is true~~"
T&L, p. 52 "As for old age, whether personal or belonging to the times in which we live, it may be true, as is often supposed, that this imposes disabilities (cf. p. 60)."

EPCW, p. 73 "~~(Andrew Lang is, I fear, an example of this.)~~"

EPCW, P. 73 PASSAGE COVERED OVER BY NEW TEXT ON SEPARATE SHEET

We do not, or need not, despair of painting because all lines must be either straight or curved. The combinations may not be infinite (for we are not), but they are innumerable.

It remains true, nevertheless, that we must not in our day be too curious, too anxious to be original. For we *are* older: certainly older than our known ancestors. The days are gone, as Chesterton said[1], when red, blue, and yellow could be invented blindingly in a black and white world. Gone also are the days when from blue and yellow green was made, unique as a new colour. We are far advanced into Chesterton's third stage with its special danger: the danger of becoming knowing, esoteric, privileged, or pretentious; the stage in which red and green are mixed. In this way a rich russet may (perhaps) be produced. Some will call it a drab brown (and they may be right); but in deft blendings it may be a subtle thing, combining the richness of red and the coolness of green. But in any case we cannot go much further, in the vain desire to be more 'original'. If we

pp. 73–74 cancelled

~~add another colour the result is likely to be much like mud, or a mere dead slime. Or if we turn from colour allegory to fantastic beasts: Fantasy can produce many mythical monsters: of man and horse, the centaur; of lion and eagle, the griffin. But as Chesterton says: 'The offspring of the Missing Link and a mule mated with the child of a manx cat and a penguin would not outrun the centaur and the griffin, it would merely lack all the interesting features of man and bird: it would not be wilder but much tamer, not fantastic but merely shapeless.~~

~~This stage was indeed reached long ago: even in fairy-tales it is sometimes found (not in good ones). But before we reach it, there is need of renewal and return. We must hark back, to purple and brown, to dragons and centaurs, and so maybe recover cameleopards and green; even (who knows) we may~~

[1] The reference in this passage is to G.K. Chesterton's article in *The New Witness* of September 6, 1917 on "New Things and the Vagabond". A long quote from his article was included in Maisie Ward's "Introduction" to *The Coloured Lands*, Chesterton's collection of stories and poems published in 1938. For more on this, See the note on Chesterton's Third Stage in the Commentary to MS. A, pages 204–5.

see again yellow, blue, and red, and look upon horses, sheep, and dogs! This recovery fairy-stories help us to make. In that sense only, a taste for them may make (or keep) us childish.

T&L REPLACEMENT PASTED
OVER TEXT PP. 52–3

We do not, or need not, despair of drawing because all lines must be either straight or curved, nor of painting because there are only three 'primary' colours. We may indeed be older now, insofar as we are heirs in enjoyment or in practice of many generations of ancestors in the arts. In this inheritance of wealth there may be danger of boredom or of anxiety to be original, and that may lead to a distaste for fine drawing, delicate pattern, and 'pretty' colours, or else to mere manipulation and over-elaboration of old material, clever and heartless. But the true road of escape from such weariness is not to be found in the willfully awkward, clumsy, or misshapen, not in making all things dark or unremittingly violent; nor in the mixing of colours on through subtlety to drabness, and the fantastical complication of shapes to the point of silliness and on towards delirium. Before we reach such states we need recovery. We should look at green again, and be startled anew (but not blinded) by blue and yellow and red. We should meet the centaur and the dragon, and then perhaps suddenly behold, like the ancient shepherds, sheep, and dogs, and horses – and wolves. This recovery fairy-stories help us to make. In that sense only a taste for them may make us, or keep us, childish.

EPCW, p. 78 note "'Why is the stockbroker less beautiful than an Homeric warrior or an Egyptian priest? Because he is less incorporated with life: he is not inevitable but accidental . . .'"

EPCW, p. 79 "aimlessness of the internal-combustion engine."
T&L, p. 60 "extravagance of the internal-combustion engine."

EPCW, **p. 83** "It is a serious and dangerous matter. ~~I am a Christian and so at least should not be suspected of willful irreverence. Knowing my own ignorance and dullness, it is perhaps~~ presumptuous"

T&L, **p. 64.** "It is a serious and dangerous matter. It is perhaps presumptuous"

EPCW, **p. 83** "They contain many marvels – peculiarly artistic, beautiful, and moving: 'mythical' in their perfect, self–contained significance; ~~and at the same time powerfully symbolic and allegorical~~ and among the marvels is the greatest and most complete conceivable eucatastrophe.

T&L, **p. 65 adds** "But this story has entered History and the primary world; the desire and aspiration of sub-creation has been raised to the fulfillment of creation."

EPCW, **p. 83 note** ~~The Gospels are not artistic in themselves;~~ the Art is here in the story itself, ~~not~~ in the telling. For the Author of the story was not the evangelists. ~~'Even the world itself could not contain the books that should be written', if that story had been fully written down.~~

T&L, **p. 65** The Art is here in the story itself rather than in the telling, for the Author of the story was not the evangelists.

EPCW, **pp. 88-9 note** ~~It is a curious result of the application of evolutionary hypothesis concerning Man's animal body to his whole being; that it tends to produce both arrogance and servility. Man has merely succeeded (it seems) in dominating other animals by force and chicane, not by hereditary right. He is a tyrant not a king. A cat may look at a king; but let no cat look at a tyrant! As for men taking animal form, or animals doing human things, this is dangerous indecent nonsense, insulting to the *Herrenvolk*. But strong or proud men talk of breeding other men like their cattle, and for similar purposes. For a self-chosen *Herrenvolk* always ends by becoming the slaves of a gang, a *Herrenbande*.~~

By 1988 the sales of *The Lord of the Rings* (and on its success the sales of many of Tolkien's less-known creative works), had taken a leap into the stratosphere of publishing statistics, and showed (and continues to show) no signs of flagging. In that year an expanded edition of *Tree and Leaf* was published with an Introduction by Christopher Tolkien and including the complete text of Tolkien's poem "Mythopoeia", part of which is quoted in the essay.

THE TOLKIEN READER

In September 1966 a mass-market paperback published by Ballantine Books under the title *The Tolkien Reader* gathered under one cover *Tree and Leaf*, Tolkien's verse play "The Homecoming of Beorhtnoth", plus the complete texts of *Farmer Giles of Ham* and *The Adventures of Tom Bombadil*. In this volume, "On Fairy-stories" has been continuously in print in the United States ever since. However, the text is a poor one, with numerous typographical errors – for example *adventures* instead of *aventures* – that are not only incorrect but also misleading. There is no evidence that Tolkien undertook any revisions for this edition.

THE MONSTERS AND THE CRITICS AND OTHER ESSAYS

In 1983 the essay was given in definitive form in *The Monsters and the Critics and Other Essays*, a collection of his father's work edited by Christopher Tolkien. As well as "On Fairy-stories", this volume included Tolkien's all-important Sir Israel Gollancz Memorial Lecture on "*Beowulf*: The Monsters and the Critics" delivered to the British Academy on 25 November 1936; his 1940 essay "On Translating *Beowulf*" printed as Prefatory Remarks to C.L. Wrenn's new edition of John R. Clark Hall's 1911 prose translation of *Beowulf and the*

Finnsburg Fragment; his W.P. Ker Memorial Lecture on *Sir Gawain and the Green Knight* given at the University of Glasgow on 15 April 1953; his O'Donnell Lecture on "English and Welsh", given at Oxford on 2 October 1955; "A Secret Vice" delivered in the early 1930s; and his "Valedictory Address" given on his retirement as Merton Professor of English Language and Literature on 5 June 1959. All but one of the essays, the one "On Translating *Beowulf*", had their beginnings as lectures.

POSTSCRIPT

While it is our hope that the present volume will be an authoritative (and useful) edition of the essay and its history, it should not be taken as presenting Tolkien's last word on the subject. In 1964, the same year that saw the publication of his final authorial revision of "On Fairy-stories" for *Tree and Leaf*, Tolkien began to write *Smith of Wootton Major*, the last of his short stories to be published in his lifetime and the one that comes nearest to capturing imaginatively all that he wanted to express about fairies and Faërie and the human interaction with both. He companioned *Smith* with another essay on Faërie and fairies[1], this one considerably shorter than "On Fairy-stories", and unlike it, keyed directly to a particular piece of fiction. Here, he tried once more to set in order his ideas about the relationship of the human and Faërie worlds.

Like overlapping stereopticon photographs, the two essays are most productively viewed with and in the context of one another for the fullest, three-dimensional understanding of what the concept, the world, and the consistent inner reality of Faërie meant to Tolkien. Definitive as it seems to be, "On Fairy-

---

[1] Recommended reading for anyone interested in Tolkien's ideas, the essay, like the story for which it was written, is called "Smith of Wootton Major". Together with the story itself, the accompanying Time Line and Character Scheme, and some of the more readable of Tolkien's notes and drafts, it has been published in 2005 by HarperCollins in a new edition of *Smith of Wootton Major*.

stories" was not Tolkien's concluding word on fairies nor on Faërie nor on enchantment. There probably is no single, ultimate summing-up. It seems safe to say that Tolkien never really stopped thinking about fairy-stories or writing on fairy-stories or trying to set down on paper all that he felt and thought about the relationship between the real and the imaginative, the sensory and the super-sensory levels of experience.

PART TWO

CONTEMPORARY
REPORTS ON THE
1939 LECTURE

THE 1939 NEWSPAPER REPORTS

Three Scottish newspapers, *The Scotsman*, *The St. Andrews Citizen*, and *The St. Andrews Times* reported on Tolkien's lecture within a few days of its delivery. Since two of the reports, those of *The Scotsman* and *The St. Andrews Times* are almost identical, and both are obviously derived from the much longer account in *The Citizen*, we reproduce only those accounts from *The Citizen* and *The Scotsman* as representative of the lecture's reception. Since this coverage provides the only accounts of the lecture as given, it functions as a bridge leading back in time from the essay proper to the much earlier manuscripts on which it was built, the extensive work and research immediately preceding and subsequently following the lecture which was the essay's basis and starting-point.

The reports are significant as well for what is *not* included in them. While they were obviously written in some haste and from memory and on-the-spot notes, they are indices of the lecture's emphasis and of the major areas covered. Thus they are as close as we are likely to come to what Tolkien actually said at St. Andrews on 8 March 1939. The lecture title, for example, was simply "Fairy Stories", without the preposition. The entire matter of the "Epilogue" was apparently not part of the lecture as given, nor, for obvious and practical reasons, was Tolkien's appended and extensive "Note" section which immediately follows the published essay.

The Scotsman, 9 March 1939, p. 9 column 2.

FAIRY STORIES

LANG LECTURE AT ST ANDREWS

THE "ESCAPIST" FUNCTION

Professor J. R. R. Tolkien, M.A., Rawlinson and Bosworth Professor of Anglo-Saxon in the University of Oxford, delivered at St Andrews University last night the eleventh lecture under the Andrew Lang Lectureship Foundation, and took for his subject "Fairy Stories."

The lecturer, in the course of his address, said he could never understand why "escape" should be used as a term of abuse in literature. He did not see why, if a man was in prison, he should not try to get out and go home; nor why, if he could not do that, he should not think of something else than jailers and prison walls. The world outside was not less real because he could not see it, or could glimpse it only through a narrow window. Escape should not be compared with "The Flight of the Deserter."

The Oxford don who welcomed the proximity of mass production factories and the endless roar of traffic because it was "a contrast in real life" caused the escapist to laugh. The realness and ugliness of modern European life was the sign of a biological inferiority, of an insufficient or false addition to environment. Mechanised industrial civilisation would seek to eliminate all waste and movement in work, and so make the operative the perfect complement, or slave, of the machine.

The full Victorian panoply of top-hat and frock coat undoubtedly expressed something essential in the idyllic culture all over the world as no fashion of clothing had ever done before. It was possible that our descendants would recognise in it a kind of grim Assyrian beauty, fit emblem of the ruthless and great age that created it, but however that might be, it missed the direct and irresistible beauty that all clothing should have, because, like its parent culture, it was out of touch with the life of nature – indeed, with real life. Why should we not escape from the grim Assyrian fantasy of top-hats or the horror of machines and the places where they were made.

Fairy stories had always had, to a large extent, this "escapist" function. There were things more grim to fly from than the ugliness of the internal combustion engine. There were hunger, pain, poverty, injustice, and death.

"LIVED HAPPY EVER AFTER"

Referring to the old desire to escape from death, the lecturer said that fairy stories provided many examples of this. Folk stories were made by human beings, not by fairies. The human stories of fairies were mostly full of the escape from death. In any case, our fairy stories could not be expected to rise above our common level, yet, in fact, they often did so rise.

The consolation of fairy story – "and they lived happy ever after" – was not necessarily fugitive. It did not deceive one, not even children. Such phrases were to be compared with margins and frames of pictures, no more to be the real end of the story than the picture-frame was of the visionary scene or the window-casement of the outer world.

The St. Andrews Citizen, 11 March 1939, p. 4, columns 3–5.

ANDREW LANG'S UNRIVALLED FAIRY STORIES.

OXFORD PROFESSOR'S ST ANDREWS ADDRESS.

What was their Origin?

"Fairy Stories" was the title chosen by Professor J. R. R. Tolkien, Rawlinson and Bosworth Professor of Anglo-Saxon in the University of Oxford, for the eleventh in the series of lectures under the Andrew Lang Foundation, which he delivered in the United College Hall, St Andrews University, on Wednesday evening.

Professor Rose, who presided, said the subject chosen certainly fell within the province of the student of literature. He regretted that much of the fairy stories of Scotland would be lost because they had no one to follow on the lines and example of Andrew Lang.

LANDS OF MYSTERY.

Professor Tolkien said he was a reader and lover of fairy stories, but not a student of them as Andrew Lang was. The land of fairy story was wide and deep and high, and was filled with many kings and all manner of men, and beasts, and birds; its seas were shoreless and its stars uncounted; its beauty an enchantment, and its perils ever present; both its joy and sorrow were poignant as a sound. In that land many might perhaps count himself fortunate to have wandered, but its very mystery and wealth made dumb the traveller who would report. And while he was there it was dangerous for him to ask too many questions, lest the gates shut and the keys be lost. The fairy gold often turned to withered leaves when it was brought away.

There were some questions that one who was to speak about fairy stories could not help asking, whatever the folk of Fairyland might think of him or do to him. What were fairy stories? What was their origin? What was the use of them? In defining a fairy story it was no good hastening to the New English Dictionary, because it would not tell one. That might be, perhaps, because of the fact that the author was not a Scotsman. It contained, in any case, no reference whatever to the composition of the fairy story, and was unhelpful on the subject of fairies generally. Its leading sense was said to be (a) a tale about fairies, or generally a fairy legend, with developed senses; (b) an unusual or incredible story; and (c) a falsehood. The last two senses would obviously make his topic hopelessly vast, but the first sense was too narrow to cover actual usage.

SOPHISTICATED PRODUCT OF LITERATURE.

Supernatural was a dangerous and difficult word in any of its uses, looser or stricter, but to fairies it could hardly be applied unless super was taken as a superlative prefix. For it was man who was, in contrast to fairies, supernatural, and often of diminutive structure, whereas they were natural, far more natural than man. Such was their doom. The road to fairyland was not the road to heaven, nor even to hell, though some had held that it might lead thither indirectly.

He did not deny that the notion of diminutive size as applied to fairies was a leading one in modern use, and the quest to find out how that had come to be so, would, he felt sure, be interesting. Of old there were indeed some inhabitants of Faerie who were small, though hardly diminutive, but smallness was no more characteristic of them than it was of human people. It was perhaps not unnatural that in England – the land where the love of the delicate and fine had so often reappeared in art – cultured fancy should in this matter have turned toward the dainty and diminutive: in France it went to politeness, powder, and diamonds. Yet, he suspected that this flower and butterfly minuteness was also in origin a sophisticated product of literary fancy.

The diminutive being was in England largely a product of "rationalisation" which forsook the true realm of fairies to indulge a mere botanical and entomological fancy, and to which minuteness was convenient as an explanation of invisibility. It seemed to begin not after the great voyages had begun to make the world seem too narrow to hold both man and elves. In any case it was largely a literary business in which William Shakespeare had a share.

He was not there to discuss fairies, or elves, but fairy stories. In one sense "stories about fairies" was too narrow, even if one rejected the diminutive size; for fairy stories were not in normal English use stories about fairies (or elves) but "stories about Faerie," stories concerning all that realm which contains many things besides fauns (great or small); besides elves or fairies, dwarfs, witches, giants, or dragons; it holds the sea, and the sun, the moon, the sky, the earth, and they themselves, when they are enchanted.

BEAST FABLES.

None could rival the twelve books collected by Andrew Lang and his wife. The first of these came out fifty years ago and was still in print. But if they looked only at the contents of the first of these books, the Blue Fairy Book, they would see at once the difficulty of any description that would cover all that it contained, without bringing in many other things that were not to be found in that or in any of the later volumes. Of the stories in the Blue Book few referred to fairies, none was directly about them. Most good fairy stories were about men, women, and children in the presence of the marvellous. For if elves or fairies were true, really existed apart from our tales about them (often sadly garbled), then also this was true – they were not primarily concerned with us nor we with them. Their fates were sundered and their paths rarely crossed. Even on the borders of Elfland they met them but at the chance crossing of the ways.

The beast fable had, of course, a connection with fairy stories – among other things because beasts and birds and other creatures could so often talk as men in fairy stories. Where no human being is concerned or where the animals (no enchanted shapes) are the heroes and the heroines, they had rather the beast-fable than the fairy story.

THE "MONKEY'S HEART".

The "Monkey's Heart" was a beast-fable, and the speaker suspected that it owed its inclusion in a fairy book not primarily to its entertaining quality, but just to that heart supposed to be left in a bag. That was significant to Lang, the student of folklore, even though that curious idea was here used only as a joke; for, of course, the monkey's heart was really quite normal and in his breast. But even so there was plainly a reference to a very widespread folklore or fairy tale idea, according to which the life or strength of a man or a creature resided in some place or other; or in some part of the body (especially the heart) that could be detached and hidden in a bag or an egg.

ORIGIN OF FAIRY STORIES.

Discussing the origin of fairy stories, Professor Tolkien said that to ask what was the origin of stories was to ask what was the origin of mind and of language. Actually to ask what was the origin of the fairy element landed us ultimately to the same question; but there were many elements in fairy stories that had to be detached from the main question.

That stage was reached indeed long ago and was ever present in fairy tales. But before they reached it, or after they reached it, there was need of renewal and return. They must track back to red and green – and even to elephants and giraffes if not indeed to horses, sheep, and dogs. And that the old fairy stories helped them to do. In that sense, they might become childish.

THE ESCAPE FUNCTION.

As for escape, he never could understand why wit [sic] could be used as a term of abuse in literature. He did not see why if a man was in prison, he should not try to get out and go home; nor why if he could not do that, he should not think of something else than jailers and prison walls. The world outside was not less real because he could not see it, or could glimpse it only through a narrow window. Escape should not be compared with "The Flight of the Deserter."

The Oxford don who welcomed the proximity of mass production factories and the endless roar of traffic because it was "a contrast in real life," caused the escapist to laugh.

The realness and ugliness of modern European life was the sign of a biological inferiority, of an insufficient or false addition to environment. Mechanised industrial civilisation would seek to eliminate all waste and movement in work and so make the operative the perfect complement, or slave, of the machine.

VICTORIAN PANOPLY.

Referring to fashions, the lecturer said that the full Victorian panoply of top-hat and frock coat undoubtedly expressed something essential in the idyllic culture all over the world as no fashion of clothing had ever done before. It was possible that our descendants would recognise in it a kind of grim Assyrian beauty, fit emblem of the ruthless and great age that created it; but however that might be, it missed the direct and irresistible beauty that all clothing should have, because, like its parent culture, it was out of touch with the life of nature – indeed with real life. Why should we not escape from the grim Assyrian fantasy of top-hats or the horror of machines and the places where they are made?

Fairy stories had always had, to a large extent, this "escapist function." There were things more grim to fly from than the ugliness of the internal combustion engine. There were hunger, pain, poverty, injustice, and death.

Lastly, they had to consider the old desire to escape from death. Fairy stories provided many examples of this. Folk stories were made by human beings, not by fairies. The human stories of fairies were mostly full of the escape from death. In any case our fairy stories could not be expected to rise above our common level, yet in fact they often did so rise.

The consolation of the fairy story, "and they lived happy ever after," did not deceive any one, not even children. Such phrases were to be compared with margins and frames of pictures, no more to be the real end of the story than the picture-frame was of the visionary scene or the window-casement of the outer world.

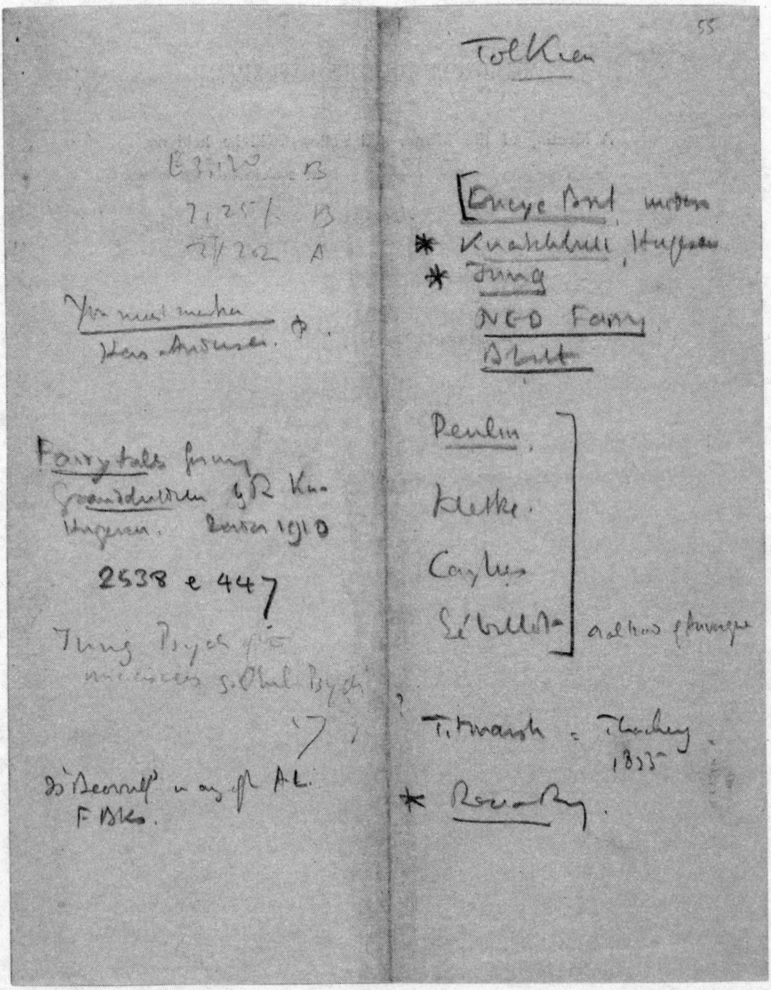

Bodleian Tolkien MS. 14 Folio 55 Recto.

PART THREE
THE MANUSCRIPTS

MANUSCRIPT A

All the evidence suggests that what we have called Manuscript A represents Tolkien's initial draft of the lecture.[†] As the earliest known expression of many of the ideas and concepts which guided his fiction, Manuscript A is valuable both for itself and as a benchmark for comparison with later versions, showing the ways in which those ideas and concepts were subsequently developed and refined.

Unfortunately, both the beginning and end are missing. As we have it, MS. A consists of pages numbered five through twenty-eight, lacking introductory pages one through four and much of its probable conclusion as well.

What appear to have been these original pages were possibly recycled[†] into a subsequent draft (which we have called Manuscript B) whose introductory pages overlap closely the presumed but missing beginning of A, and which picks up and continues from where A breaks off.

For the present publication, we have tried to be faithful to the text while making it as readable as possible, with minimal editorial intrusion. Tolkien was not consistent in using single or double quotation marks, and this text reflects his inconsistency. Words or phrases which defy decipherment are marked as [illeg]. Words written above other words where neither is cancelled are divided by a slash: /. Where Tolkien used abbreviations (e.g., "&", "F. st.", "A. L.", or numerals) we have spelled out the words in full ("and", "fairy-story", "Andrew Lang", "one"). We have regularized some punctuation and (when called for) inserted Tolkien's marginal notes in the appropriate places in the main body of the text. Tolkien occasionally wrote abbreviated thoughts instead of full sentences, and while this has sometimes resulted in a syntactical incoherence, we have preferred to let these stand rather than to intrude editorially. Square brackets are used to denote editorial material. A dagger "†" following a word or phrase signals that there is a note on this material in the subsequent commentary, referenced by page number.

[FAIRY-STORIES]

[MS. A PROPER: BODLEIAN LIBRARY
TOLKIEN MS. 14, FOLS. 59–72]

In these things Spencer [*sic*] is a better guide — to him an Elfe was
a knight of Faierie such as the Red Cross Knight or Sir Guyon,
no mothlike Pigwiggen armed with a hornet's sting.

The first quotation in the Dictionary† for <u>fairy</u> is significant.
It is taken from the poet Gower (<u>Confessio Amantis</u> Book V): <u>as
he were a faierie</u>. But it turns out not to be so, for Gower wrote
<u>as he were of faierie,</u> as were he come from fairyland. And we
~~perceive~~ see by ~~description of the~~ He is describing a gallant
young man who is seeking to bewitch the hearts of the maidens
in church

> His croket kemd and thereon set
> A nouche with a chapelet
> Or elles one of grene leves
> Which late come out of greves
> All for he shoulde seme freish
> And thus he loketh on the fleish
> Riht as an hauk which hath a sihte
> Upon the foul there he schal lihte
> And as he were of faierie
> He scheweth him tofore here yhe.

This is a real young man of flesh and blood, but he gives a much
better picture of the inhabitants of Fairyland than the definition
under which he is by double error placed. For the trouble with
the real inhabitants of Fairy is that they do not always look like
fairies – and at least a part of the magic that they wield for the

175

good or evil of men is power to play on the desires of our hearts and bodies.

upon Fairies (which are not my business)

Now although I have touched ~~upon~~ wholly inadequately upon Fairies (which are not my business) I have already digressed from my theme. I am not here to discuss fairies – or elves, a subject for many lectures (I have written a history of them) – but Fairy Stories. I said 'stories about fairies' was too narrow, for Fairy stories that have any are not generally 'stories about <u>fairies</u>' but about Faery – stories ~~of which~~ covering all of that land or country which holds many things besides 'fairies' (of any size), besides elves or ~~dragons~~ fays or dwarves, witches, or dragons it holds the ~~earth the sun & moon & ourselves~~ sun the moon the sky the earth and us ourselves.

~~But this is a large matter.~~

It is true that the narrow sense is sometimes really used – for instance in McDougall [*sic*] and Calder's Folktales and Fairy Lore.[†] The ~~second part~~ first part is Folktales, the second Fairy tales ~~the first~~. That is tales about the 'fairies' used to translate <u>daoine sìthe</u> <u>sithiche</u>.[†] But that is a special case of the misfit between languages. The English <u>fairy</u> or the fairy kindred is in the tales never to be had: English legacy has owed more and more of recent years to Ireland or Scotland to the <u>sìthe</u> – but it has other ancestors, French fée and the native elf. And a glance at any book that calls itself a collection of fairy stories or fairy tales is enough to show ~~that all~~ that tales about sìthichean or Elves, or any of their remote relatives give small idea of their content. The number of such books is legion – some very bad (the most dismal products of commercialism) some poor, and some very good. For me the standard, the ~~irreplaceable~~ unrivalled, are the twelve books of twelve colours collected by Andrew Lang and his wife. And yet a glance at their contents reveals at once the difficulty of a definition. Few refer to 'fairies', none are directly about them. In fact the stories actually about fairies are few (and the whole poor) but about men women and children in the presence of the marvellous. For we are not con-

cerned with Elves nor they with us: our fates are sundered and
our paths rarely cross.

One of the worst fairy stories ever written, Drayton's
<u>Nymphidia</u> is about 'fairies' and fairies only. There the palace
of Oberon has walls of spider legs "and windows of the eyes
of cats and for the roof, instead of slats is covered with the
wings of bats." Pigwiggen rides on a lively earwig: and sends
Queen Mab a bracelet of emmets' eyes, and makes an assignation in a cowslip flower. But the only tale to tell in all this gossamer silliness is a ~~degraded and off~~ dull story of courtly
cuckoldry silenced by the waters of Lethe. The unhappy tale
of Lancelot and Guinevere – tragic and full of good and evil is
a fairy story rather than this. For fairy-stories proper are ~~grim,
serious and high matter~~ of matters simpler or higher than
these.

Let us take the *Blue Fairy Book*. The main sources are French
and so powerful has been the influence of Charles Perrault (since
he was Englished in the eighteenth century) and of such other
excerpts from the vast storehouse of the Cabinet des Fées as
have, translated, adapted or garbled, become fairly well known
that still I suppose, if anyone was asked ~~what they~~ to name a
typical well-known fairy story he would name one of Perrault,
or perhaps Madame d'Aulnoy[†] or Villeneuve.[†] Besides the traditional French there are ~~three or four~~ six from Grimms. ~~A few~~
four from Scandinavia, a couple [inserted] three from the
Arabian Nights (Aladdin) (Forty Thieves, ~~and a~~ [Paribanou?]
Achmed[†] [illeg] [illeg] [illeg] a couple of English chapbooks[†]
Jack and Dick Whittington. A couple of traditional tales from
Chambers. Then practically a pantomime selection. For
Cinderella, ~~Mother G~~ Little Red R[iding Hood], Puss in Boots,
~~Beauty and the Beast~~ Mother Goose, The Sleeping Beauty are
Perrault. Forty Thieves, Aladdin are Arabian Nights. Jack and
Babes[†] and Dick Whittington are Chapbooks. Robinson Crusoe
is a curious intruder in the Pantomime but not more so than the
Voyage to Lilliput in the *Blue Fairy Book*.

But if we cannot define a fairy-story positively we can do negatively. Lilliput does not belong here—~~unless because~~. It cannot

come in. Lilliputians are small (and that is just an accident in Fairy land as in real life. Pygmies are no more real to us than Wenusians† or Patagonians.† ~~But we cannot admit mere tales travellers Not because~~ It is not ruled out by the satire – for that is present in many genuine fairy stories (probably more often than we suspect). But we cannot admit all travellers tales of the merely marvellous or unusual, or we should become ~~thinking~~ all the other genre tales of time and space, ghost stories and whatnot. ~~H G Wells~~ and all his voyages to the moon and stars upon our hands. The Time Machine Eloi and the Morlocks. And why not indeed? The Morlocks are like ~~dwarves~~ goblins and ~~cannibals~~ with right. Because they are not thought of as existing in their own right. They are derived from man or exist in precisely the same plane. But elves or fairies do not

~~Mon~~ Others too I would exclude such as the Monkey's Heart ~~relating to~~ (a Swahili Tale), which is given in one of the Fairy books (Lilac 1910) about the wicked shark who carried off the monkey halfway to his own land, where the sick sultan needed a monkey's heart to cure him. But the monkey tricked him into ~~leaving~~ taking him back by [stating?] he had left his heart hanging in a bag in the tree. The beast fable has of course its connexion with fairy tale because beasts and birds ~~usually~~ can so often either talk as human beings or by some magic be understood. But we cannot include the genre beast fable – Brer Fox and Reynard or whatnot. At least they do not come in my department.

But this heart introduces another point. I suspect the story owes its inclusion not only to its humour but to that heart left in a bag. Here it is a joke (because of course the monkey's heart was in his breast), but it reminds us of or refers to the wide spread folklore motive according to which the life or strength of a man or creature resides in some other thing or place, a bag or an egg, or in some part that can be removed. Often it is a heart. Cf. the giants heart ~~Campbell~~ Asbjornsen and Moe† revised by George Macdonald, or the heart of Bata.

But this is a folklorists and scientists approach. It is the folklorist, the ~~scientist~~ anthropologist, the scholar concerned with comparisons or with the stories as evidence concerning other things about which they are interested rather than themselves who finds these similarities important. Or saying like Dasent: that the Bechuana Story of Two Brothers[†] has the groundwork of the Machandelboom and the Milk White Doo[†] and commonly traits with the Egyptian Story of Anpu and Bata[†] reminds us of Katie Woodencloak.[†] He is inclined to say that two stories that contain the same folktale motive or the same or similar combination of them is the same often <u>are</u> the same.

Thus Andrew Lang says Black Bull of Norroway <u>Goosegirl</u>

Andrew Lang says[†] Tertullian knew the story of Rapünzel. Turris lamiae, Pecten Solis * Master Maid = Medea and Jason.

Now this is true in that sense, but not in a fairy tale sense. It is precisely the colouring, atmosphere and details that really count. I have said elsewhere that the comparison of skeleton plots, or of abbreviated incidents and motives is simply not a critical literary process at all. [In left margin Red Riding Hood]It is any rate only one part (and not usually the most important) part of it – if we are interested in fairy tales as tales, as literature. So then, personally, I know enough to perceive both the fascination and the intricately ramified difficulty of the discussion of Fairy tale origins – of fairy tales as a branch of historical lore, descending in long line often (plainly) from a very distant past. That tickles me on the philological side but I am not learned enough in this highly developed – specialized branch. In any case I am much more interested in our fairy-stories as they are, and what they have become for us by various strange alchemic processes (in worlds and time). I conceive that as child grows to man (and does not necessarily become contemptible), so the fairy tale as it is now has a value and a meaning of its own kind.

Therefore – not only because I am incompetent to deal with it, nor even because there is not time – but because it is (though interesting) not of the first importance. In this question of which Lang was deeply interested and wrote brilliantly and originally. And others have of course followed. The literature of the subject is large. I am dimly aware of the anthropological and archaeological wars that rage or raged between.

I am hardly going to touch on origins. As Dasent said, we must be satisfied with the soup that is set before us[†] and not desire to see the bones of the ox out of which it has been boiled. Though oddly enough by the soup he meant a mishmash of bogus prehistory founded on early Comparative Philology, and by the bones a demand for proofs. By the soup I mean the story as it is now served to us and by the bones the analysis of its sources.

It is plain that fairytales – or at least tales that could be included in any collection of fairy stories like Andrew Lang's – begin with the earliest records (like the Orsigny Papyrus); and are found universally among all peoples. We are therefore faced with the same problem concerning them as meets us in archaeology and comparative philology. The old (and still present) debate between independent evolution of the similar, inheritance from a remote common ancestry preceding even the major racial and linguistic divisions now apparent, and diffusion (at various times) from one (or more centres). Most debates depend on an attempt at over-simplification. The history of fairy-stories is probably no less complex than that of the human race and its languages. And all three things – independent invention, inheritance, diffusion – have played their part in producing an intricate web that is now beyond any but the Fairies to unravel, except in chance or particular cases or details.

Of these, <u>invention</u> is the most interesting, and ultimately the most important. To <u>an</u> inventor, to <u>a</u> story-maker or story re-maker all lead back. <u>Diffusion</u> (borrowing) whether of culture or stories or stories only push the history and problem back a stage. At the centre of diffusion through place there was an inventor. The same is true of inheritance – (borrowing down time). And independent striking out of similar ideas, theories, etc. ~~reposes~~ only enlarges the constant operation of the inventive force.

Diffusion easier because if ~~travel~~ stories then artifacts – easy to carry. Mere knowledge of languages is needed to peddle tales to [crowds?] but still that is easier managed than we now think. Wider diffusion a slender thread. Myths in Armorica. Story of Raimondin and Melusine.[†]

It is indeed easier to unravel a single thread in the web – that is a detail, or motive or incident – than to trace the history of the picture defined by many threads. And that is the weakness of the analytical method: we learn much more about things in stories and very little about the stories themselves.

Here put <u>diffusion</u>?

~~Dasen   Philologyhas been move~~   or

^<u>Philology see 13b</u>^

[insert from p. 13b] Philology has been dethroned from this place since Dasen wrote (in admiration of the theories of the day) "The philology and mythology of the East and West have met and kissed each other; . . . they now go hand in hand."[†] They have since had a tiff. Max Müller's mythology as a disease of language has been abandoned. But language cannot be forgotten. Mythology is language and language is mythology. The mind, and the tongue, and the tale are coeval. ~~And able [to?]~~ The human mind was endowed with powers of "abstraction", of not only seeing green grass and discriminating it from other things, or of finding it good to look upon, but of seeing that it was green – as well as grass and hence of inventing a word <u>green</u>. But how powerful ~~and potent~~ even stimulating to the very faculty that gave birth to that invention is the <u>adjective</u>: no spell or talisman in a fairy story is more so/potent. In fact many of these ~~charms~~ enchantments that are [narration?] from a fairy tale are closely related in the mind to the very linguistic power that could invent all of those and set them free. When we can take green from grass and paint the sky or a man's face with it, or blue from heaven and red from blood we have already an enchanter's power: the world of ~~golden~~ silver leaves and that ~~golden~~ fleece of gold and the blue moon appear. Such fantasy is a new form, in which man is become a creator or sub-creator[†]. But to that I will return ~~when~~.

More interesting if origins are discussed is the question of relation of ~~the hi~~ what Andrew Lang called the higher and lower mythologies (and of both to religion strictly so called). The biographer of Andrew Lang in the Dictionary of National Biography[†] held that he had proved that "folk-lore was not the debris of a higher or literary mythology but the foundation on which that mythology rests." The nature myth being tied up with early Comparative Philology (wholly by Max Müller) was that the Olympians were personifications of the Sun Dawn Night and so on, and the stories originally told about them [were?] myths (better said allegories) of the greater elemental ~~manifes~~ phenomena, changes and processes of nature; but saga or heroic epic localized these as real places and attributed them to ancestors, and that these sagas, legends broken down again became Märchen and finally nursery tales.

Max Muller Chips <s>13b</s>

That would seem to be very nearly an inversion of the truth. The nearer the nature-myth (or grand nature allegory) remains to nature the less interesting is it (either as a story ~~or~~ in itself or as [true?] light on Day or Night, Sun or Moon.) But no object "in Nature could wear a personal significance or glory if it were not cast upon it from the human spark itself, the one that is the form of all marvels." The gods draw their colour and splendour/glory from the high splendours of nature but their personality from man and their divinity from the primitive universal belief concerning the invisible [real?] world behind the [word?] which is present wherever [illeg illeg illeg] so called uncivilized men can be sympathetically studied from within.

Rather than deriving the conception of the soul from ghosts, and so extending to any strange or uncontrollable phenomenon. So that, in Tylor's words the conception of the soul served as the model for men's ideas in general "from the tiniest elf which sports in the long grass to the heavenly Creator and Ruler of the land – the Great Spirit".[†] But this does not [illeg] be in the least. The whole mind of primitive man is religious and the belief in spirits is only one aspect of his thought. His conception of reality is never limited to what he sees or touches. See Kingsley quoted by Christopher Dawson p. 86.[†]

'Ocean of supernatural energy'.[†]

There is no rigid distinction between the higher and lower mythologies – they live (if they live at all) by the same life, as do kings or peasants. The higher mythology as Andrew Lang said and religion in this strict sense of the word are two distinct things which have become inextricably entangled but are distinct in origin (Christopher Dawson p. 91).[†] But only distinct in origin. And is it not truer to say ~~that~~ neither has become inextricably <u>entangled</u> but they have slowly approached to a form.

Fairy Stories have two faces.   Land of Shadows   Satire
1 Mystical toward God Man 2 the Magical towards the world ~~Thus it is a question without meaning:~~

The Mystical (towards God divine) the Magical (towards the word) and the Critical (towards man in laughter and tears). And though the essential centre of fairy-story is the Magical, both of the other things may be present separately or together.

Thus to take a clear case of nature-myth: Þór, whose name means thunder and whose hammer is not difficult to interpret. Yet he has a character which[†] while relatable to thunder and lightning – since a red beard is red and so is fire –but a hot [illeg] temper is hot and so is fire but is not in flames. It is a question almost without meaning to enquire which came first, nature myth stories that personalized thunder in the hills or stories about strong, irascible, not very clever redbeard farmer of great strength not unlike the Northern <u>bóndar</u> by whom Thór was chiefly beloved. To such Thor ~~became~~ may be said to have "dwindled". But from such he may also be said to have grown. Of much about Thor (who I suppose belongs to the higher mythology, though in Thrymskvitha nature school approach) was confounded from the beginning.

But through all this runs the vein of invention. Sugar plum.[†] Youth who could not fear? [†]

The pot has always been boiling, and it continues to boil. For this reason the fact that a story similar to that known as The Goose Girl in Grimms' collection was told in the thirteenth century of Bertha Broadfoot mother of Charlemagne really proves nothing either way: neither that the story was descending from Asgard or Olympus by way of an already legendary King to become a Hausmärchen; nor the reverse. It ~~makes it merely~~

~~suspect~~. All we could deduce (even if we knew nothing of the real history of Charlemagne) would be that it was not true/ just unhistorical of his mother. For while it seems moderately plain that King Arthur was originally an historical character, around whom in legend both other matters or stray bones of history (such as King Alfred's successful resistance against Danes), and of the higher and lower mythologies gathered; it can hardly be denied that <u>Gawain</u> is higher altogether: a mirror of humanity or human courtesy and true virtue. He is descended (if that is the word) from a figure more mythical, waxing and waning to his strength at noon like a sun hero.[†] Grendel and the fairy-story yet Hrothgar and all his court were historical.[†]

We have far back a certain fairy story which becomes literary in Arabian Nights, is diffused in European tradition e.g Galland's[†] adaptation > ~~abridged~~ early modern translation > and abridged or retold dwindles back to a fairy tale of Paribanou[†] in the *Blue Fairy Book*.

But when we have done all that research or comparison can do – and have explained many of the elements embedded in fairy-stories (stepmothers, younger sons, taboos, cannibalism and the like) as relics of ancient customs once usual and not strange, or of beliefs once held as beliefs not as fancies – there is still a point often forgotten. That is the <u>effect</u> now produced by these old things in the stories as they are preserved. That they have become <u>old</u>, and appeal with the appeal of all antiquity, is a fact – that may be brushed/~~neglected~~ aside by the student of origins, or worse regretted; but cannot be neglected/disregarded by the lovers of literature or of tales. The beauty and the horror of the <u>Machandelboom</u> with its exquisite beginning and the horrible/abominable stew, and the gruesome bones, the sly vengeful bird-soul rising in a mist from the ground has dwelt with me since childhood (when I read a less tamed and mollified Grimm than that which I find on my children's shelves): but I do not think I was the poorer for the horror – into whatever dark reality or imagination of cannibalism; or of beliefs about graves it may reach back. Such stories have now (at any rate) a mythical significance, but as a total significance unanalysed and by marking a picture of other time (good or evil) enable us to view our own and thus to stand a little outside our time. Yet if we ask <u>how</u> such elements have been presented (taboos against speaking names[*] by the father and son) we must realize that this must long have been true.

These elements have indeed often been preserved precisely because they had this appeal – they are not thrown away ~~The modern with his panto collection is not the first to~~ as we see beginning in clearly modern minds, (and fairy stories are by no means reluctant to throw away or lose ancient elements) because they appealed instinctively or even consciously to their oral narrators in the same way as to us.[insert from bottom margin] It is now well known that myths and themes and motives in tales are often far more wide spread than the explanations attached, or the custom that a supposed taboo refined. ~~What of tabu has [illeg] Prohibition~~ Even where the prohibition is attributable to some old dead <u>tabu</u>, it has been preserved because of the intense mythical value of <u>Prohibition</u> with a capital P. A sense that was [insert from side margin] doubtless behind the <u>taboo</u> itself and certainly behind the prohibitions in fairy-stories. Thou shalt not – or else the ~~universe will quake~~ the world will quake; all will be ruined. They shall have or else you shall go forth beggared into endless regret like Peter Rabbit left without hope in a garden and lost his blue coat and yellow shoes. <u>The locked Door</u> stands as eternal temptation. [Return to text] And on the other side neither we nor they are so forgetful: there is in our hearts a memory of both the evil and the sorrow and the joy of our fathers and mothers long forgotten. Something stirs within us in its sleep at these echoes from the past.

And with that I turn to the children – Because it is usually assumed that they are the proper, or specially proper audience for Fairy Stories. In describing as fairy-story which they think a grown-up may read for their own amusement reviewers ~~are~~ usually indulge in such waggeries as "this book is for children from the ages of six to sixty." But is there any essential associa-

[*] as among Zulus still[†]

tion between children and fairy stories, or anything that calls for an apology or even comment in an adult that reads them for himself. Reads them, I say, not studies them as evidence.

It cannot be denied that children are <u>connected</u> with fairy-stories <u>Kindermärchen</u>. Nursery rhymes we say – and sometimes nursery tales. But the contents of nurseries are (or were when such things were commoner) of various sort: not all designed originally for a place there. Folk-lore may not be/in all cases be the <u>detritus</u> of a higher mythology but the foundation on which it rests. The tendency may perhaps be rather upward towards the heroes on Mt. Olympus than downwards. But though we might say that the toy-cupboard is not the debris of the drawing-room china cabinet, but rather its humble model, it cannot be denied that the chairs, the tables, pictures (and even sometimes the books) are (or were) frequently things which had ~~had as they so seem~~ (as they say) "seen better days". And children play/played in attics where all kinds of forgotten and damaged goods used to be found. To the nursery or at least the care of children the old women also were (and still sometimes are ~~found~~) appointed, and have been so long before the stories told by ma mère l'Oye and to this they provided the foundation for the tales of Charles Perrault. I often wonder if the ~~choice of~~ audience could [be] said to be <u>chosen</u> deliberately by Mother Goose, or the subject to be <u>chosen</u> by the child/Master Perrault. Both took what they could get. Fairy-stories are primarily associated with children, because men ~~or would be [illeg] those~~ fathers and mothers ordained it so. (It was at any rate better than mechanical toys, which after having filled nurseries and playrooms with so much ennui have run wild off the nursery floor and now rush about dealing death to ~~the aged or to children~~ both Mother Goose and children. It would not be wholly regrettable if Father and Mother would play less constantly with modern toys and take again to fairy stories.)

~~I have given~~ My children have had many fairy-story books (good and bad) – usually given them by others in accord with tradition. But they are by no means their natural taste. They like other things better at any rate at first. The liking ~~of~~ fairy-tales comes with a beginning of liking for <u>literature</u>. So that I think Lang was to some extent wrong in saying that it seems almost cruel to apply the methods of literary criticism to Nursery Tales. "He who would enter into the Kingdom of Fairy should have the heart of a little child, if he is to be happy and at home in that enchanted field."[†] Is that true? If it is literally there is little more to be said; we must just read on (uncritically). But children don't – especially not those who have a real liking for fairy-stories (as distinct from the general appetite for any food of the young and hungry). They may have children's hearts (and the ignorance or humility which constrains them to accept what is given to them) but they have also heads. In my experience it is notable how frequently their choice and liking for this or that tale [illeg] coincides [with] literary criticism – stories are liked because they are well told. It is good art that commands it.

Andrew Lang's famous collections were of course a by-product of ~~research~~ adult research into mythology and folk-lore, specially drawn off and adapted for "children". The introduction to the first of the series, *The Blue Fairy Book* speaks of "<u>children ~~for~~ to whom and for whom they are told</u> They represent the young age of man true to his early loves, and have his unblunted edge of <u>belief</u>, a fresh appetite for marvels". There may be some truth in that: ~~though I doubt the belief~~ certainly the fresh appetite for marvels, though I doubt very much the <u>belief</u>. The great question "Is it true?" is more often a desire of the children to be sure which kind of literature they are faced with. Their knowledge of the world may be so small that they cannot judge offhand and without the help of ~~a parent~~ an adult (trusted until he betrays) between (1) fairy tale and phantasy (2) strange and rare but true fact (3) everyday facts pertaining to their parents' world with which they will probably soon become familiar. But they know the three classes, and like each according to its kind.

~~It is true that children trust grownups~~

It is very easy to mix things. Of all that is pernicious in children's books, I suppose the most pernicious is the serving up in "true books" under the aegis of the then busy Science of statements which are often nothing more than the first ugly by-products of the science of questions

Once I was one of the <u>children</u> whom Andrew Lang was addressing. I was born about the same time as the *Green Fairy Book*, and the colour volumes were natural gifts for a child, ~~then as [now?]~~. Andrew Lang speaking of me and my contemporaries seems to place fairy-stories as the child's equivalent for <u>novels</u>, saying 'Children's taste remains like the taste of their naked ancestors thousands of years ago, and they seem to like fairy tales better than history, poetry, geography, or arithmetic" (Preface to Violet Fairy Book).

[The next three lines, struck through, are indecipherable.]

But it seems likely that if we have fairy stories because they had them, then we have history, poetry, geography and arithmetic because they had them too (or as far as they could get them). and as far as they had yet succeeded in differentiating the branches from a general interest in everything. Yet really we do not know much about those naked ancestors. Our fairy-stories (however old may be certain things in them) are certainly not the same as theirs.

So I will not say children have changed. I will say they had changed. I never believed in fairy-stories – not at least in the sense in which I believed in books purporting to be <u>true</u>. That was part of their appeal. Almost one <u>wished</u> they were true, impossible if you had <u>believed</u>. Which is quite different from saying that I did not believe in <u>fairies</u> or <u>dragons</u>: as representing possibilities in [england (*sic*) now]. For myself an almost intolerable desire (drawn from adaptations of the Faierie Queen or Malory) that knights in their armour should be <u>true</u> vexed me sore. But in general I disliked most of the more fairyish fairy stories (to which I ~~[illeg]~~ vastly preferred novels: stories of my own day). [illeg] the children and was I was most attracted by the older tales that had not come through the frippery and folly/finery of <u>Cabinet.</u> The adaptation of the Story of Sigurd (done by Andrew Lang himself from Morris's transl of <u>The Volsunga Saga</u>) was my favourite without rival. Even as it stands in the Red Book it is no Conte des Fées. It is strong meat for nurseries. A real taste for fairy stories came long after the nursery or pre-school childhood. ~~Often Heroes had for me as for Lang~~ /nursery sense In that distant day I preferred such astronomy, geology, history or philology as I could get, especially the last two. We do I think an injustice to fairy-stories (and to children) if we conceive of fairy-stories as ~~nursery bread~~ a kind of mental cake or sweetmeat to be set against the bread of knowledge and to be slyly introduced by indulgent uncles. But this idea that fairy tales were childish was firmly fixed in the nineteenth century and still persists [illegible phrase overwritten]. In the year I was born G.K. Chesterton, then about eighteen, wrote a fairy story, "The Wild Goose Chase at the Kingdom of the Birds". He dedicated it to a school friend. "This nonsense is affectionately dedicated by <u>another Baby</u>";[†] reveal[ing?] the current opinion [as?] high irony[:] therefore current opinion: he recognized that the critic was "still enough of a critic to be fond of Fairy Tales". Interesting Andrew Lang had felt it necessary (*Blue Fairy Book* introduction) to admit that some might think a liking for fairy-stories "not a taste to be proud of".

~~The Def[inition?] is thus meant [illeg] of pretext~~
The fairy-story is not then essentially connected with children – though there exist (or existed) a host of them especially made or adapted (according to notions more or less erroneous or foolish) to what was conceived as the needs or measure of children. Dasent critics. Dasent on folly in forbidding children to look at the end.[†] And there exist old and battered fragments thought good enough for them. If they are not thought fit for adults it is because they are not good enough fairy-stories in themselves.

I do not deny there is a truth in Andrew Lang's words: "he who would enter into the Kingdom of Faery should have the heart of a little child." For that possession is necessary to all high adventure (into kingdoms both less and infinitely greater than Faery. ~~But that possession is~~ But that possession does not lead to a mere uncritical wonder nor to blindness. Chesterton remarks of the ~~dissatisfaction~~ of ~~some~~ children ~~at~~ he took to see

Maeterlinck's <u>Blue Bird</u> were dissatisfied because it did not end with a Day of Judgment; and it was not revealed to the hero and heroine that the Dog had been faithful and the Cat faithless. "For children" he says "are innocent and love justice; while most of us are wicked and naturally prefer mercy".[†]

~~Yet while using child in a good sense (it has also legitimately a bad sense) we must note~~

Andrew Lang was at pains to defend the slaying of the Yellow Dwarf by Prince Ricardo in one of his own fairy-stories.[†] "<u>I hate cruelty</u>", he said, "but that was in fair fight, sword in hand, and the dwarf, peace to his ashes, <u>died in harness</u>".[†] Yet it is not quite clear that being ~~stabbed~~ pierced by a sword is less <u>cruel</u>, as it was certainly no more <u>just</u> than the execution of wicked kings and stepmothers which he abjures – sending them to retirement on ample pensions.

~~Let no that drive us to the sentimentality of only using 'grown up' in a bad sense (it also has legitimately a good one). To children~~

But that plea is not made to children – if it had been necessary to make it to children I suppose the slaying of the Yellow Dwarf would not have appeared. The plea was made to <u>parents and guardians</u> to whom Lang was recommending ~~playfully~~ his own Prigio and Ricardo as good, suitable for their charges (in the preface to the *Lilac Fairy Book* 1910).

Nevertheless if we use <u>child</u> in a good sense (it has also legitimately a bad one) we must not let that drive us to the sentimentality of only using adult or 'grown-up' in a bad sense (it has also legitimately a good one). The process of growing up is not necessarily allied to growing wickeder: though that is too often ~~true~~ what happens. Children are meant to grow up and to die, and not become Peter Pans (a dreadful fate). Not to lose innocence and wonder, but to proceed on the appointed journey: that journey upon which it is certainly <u>not</u> better to travel hopefully than to arrive, though we must travel hopefully if we are to arrive. ~~But the very big word~~ But it is the lesson (if one can call it such) of many fairy stories that on callow lumpish and selfish youth sorrow, peril and that shadow of death bestow dignity and even sometimes justice, wisdom – and mercy. Let us not divide the human race into Eloi and Morlocks.

pretty feckless fearful fren affection Children ~~beings old~~ after ~~dark [illeg illeg]~~

[lemure?] [illeg] darkly [telurian?] ~~from~~ earth   dark and deeply
[illeg illeg]

We thus come to the last and to me the most important (or at least the most interesting) question, or questions.

What is the function of Fairy Stories still or now as read and shall we, grown-ups, go on with them – write them for ourselves (and therefore also for our children), read them to ourselves (and therefore also to our children). Quite a different matter to <u>studying</u> them. ~~That~~ Studying is simply one of many legitimate enquiries: it tangles us in a problem of relationships and kinships such as is met everywhere if in comparing genetically trees, dogs or brambles backwards. And we have not studied ~~long~~ before we begin to notice. It warns us, too, that we only collect a few leaves (some already broken and decayed) of the countless leaves foliage of the ~~Forest of Man Mansoul~~ tall Tree of Tales with which the Forest of Days is carpeted that lies about the city of Mansoul†. And each leaf that is lost or blown away had a value. That may make it seem vain to add more to the litter. We can design no new leaf under the sun in fact. The patterns for/from bud to unfolding and their colours from spring to winter were fixed by men of old. But reading (or even writing) will show us that this is not so. The ~~tree~~ seed of the tree can be re-planted in almost any soil, even one so smoke-ridden (as Lang would say) as that of England. New combinations of these patterns and colours will arise. Old elements recombined are surely new.

That spring is not less fair for being like other springs, ~~tre~~ life is never quite the ~~same~~ same.   beech leaves

In a study of fairy stories from this point of view – their vitality not their origin – it is of less interest that the garbled or retold versions of Red Riding Hood in which Red Riding Hood is saved by the woodcutter is a version of Perrault. The important thing is that it is not the same story: it has a happy ending. And how that alters the whole thing from beginning to end

We need not despair of painting or drawing pictures because there is only <u>red</u> <u>blue</u> and <u>yellow</u>, and all lines must be either <u>curved</u> or <u>straight</u>. ~~Red blue Cheerful~~ fantasy is then one of the functions of the Fairy tale. ~~Not gloo~~ both of that same kind which Chesterton called <u>Mooreeffocish</u>; a queer fantastic word yet to be seen often in England. Coffee-room read backwards or through a glass door when read by David Copperfield one night in London; ~~and the cheerful fantasy by which man subcrea~~ blue and what is normal and has become trite seen suddenly from a new angle: and cheerful fantasy[†] by which or where man becomes sub-creator[†].

> Though now long estranged,
> Man is not wholly lost nor wholly changed.
> Dis-graced he may be, yet is not de-throned
> and keeps the rags of lordship once he owned:
> man sub-creator, the refracted light
> through whom is splintered from a single White
> to many hues, and endlessly combined
> in living shapes that move from mind to mind.
> Though all the crannies of the world we filled
> with elves and goblins, though we dared to build
> gods and their houses out of dark and light,
> and sowed the seeds of dragons – 'twas our right
> (used or misused). That right has not decayed.
> We make still by the law in which we're made.

[in side margin:] That fantasy which any have ignored is an extension of belief or jest. Chestertonian Fairy tale very true thrown [away?]

Of the two I am really more suspicious of <u>Mooreeffoc</u>. For if Chesterton in his Napoleon of Notting Hill period as he says "felt impelled to write about lamp-posts as one eyed giants or ~~horse cabs~~ . . . painted omnibuses as coloured ships or castles["][†] – that feeling that the suburbs ought to be glorified by romance and religion to a charm – or destroyed by fire from heaven. A poetry of misfits. [†] Colour world on the train as meaning.

[circled at bottom of page:] Fantasy that made of mean

Anyone can see why the priest's vestment† on common days. Ch[esterton] 110.

[Illegible]

There need be no limit to the mythical monsters produced by the creators finding them made of man and horse like centaurs or the lion and eagle as griffin. But as Chesterton says†, the off-spring of the Missing Link and a mule mated with the child of a Manx cat and a penguin would not outrun the Centaur and griffin: it would be lacking in all the interesting features of man and beast or bird: it would not be wilder but much tamer. It would not be fantastic but shapeless. This stage has been reached long ago – long present in fairy tales (which matter). But before it is reached there is need of <u>renewal</u>.

Yet we must not be too curious to be original. For after all we are older; as certainly older than our ancestors as we are older than our children. Gone are the days when red blue and yellow could be invented blindingly in a black and white world. Gone also are the secondary days when from blue and yellow green was made, unique as a new colour. We are still in Chesterton's third stage† – with all its dangers, danger of being too curious to be common, of becoming knowing and esoteric [illeg] a mixture of privilege or more likely pretension: the stage at which red and green are mixed and a russet hue produced. Some will call it drab or brown but to some deft ~~mixes~~ blendings [will?] be a subtle thing combining the richness of red and the coolness of green, in a unity as unique and new as green. (But at this stage there is need of <u>renewal</u>.) We cannot go much further in the new ~~but~~ vain desire to be called inaugurators, inventors, originals. We stand not at the beginning of a long process but at the end. If we add ~~much more~~ another colour the result will be much like mud: a mere dead slime. Before this befalls we must hark back to <u>red and green</u>, to horses and dogs, elephants and giraffes. And this old (and some new) Fairy stories help us to do. In that sense we may become childish, as Andrew Lang says in the dedicatory verses to the Blue Fairy Book. (addressing Elsp†

And you once more may voyage through
The forests that of old we knew
The fairy forests deep in dew,

Where you, <u>resuming childish things,</u>
Shall listen when the Blue Bird sings,
And sit at feast with Fairy Kings.

This is the function of Renewal or Return.

And another function is <u>Escape</u>: that much abused and misunderstood word. For it is a little hard that it should be used of those who read or write Fairy stories (with their strict hard rules and prohibitions) by those who are so often trying to escape from all rules and prohibitions, from the family and its bonds altogether or even with the deserters still. ~~For them~~ Escape into nothing. The <u>escape</u> (if escape it is and not an extension of reality) of fairy stories is an escape from peril and duress: and that is a perilous thing. And Escape may mean ~~going home, and a true es~~ not only getting out of prison and/or deserting, it may mean standing outside and looking at things in a bright/new light situation, going home. Therefore to judge whether <u>escape</u> is good or bad, weak or strong we must know from what we are escaping, and where we propose to go and how. ~~If we prefer Or~~ There is not time here and now to argue that what we seek to escape from in modern life is bad. (For curiously the critic escapist who talks about real life can offer escape more realistically escapist than real life has [won?].)

[The consecutive numbered pages of MS. A end here. However MS. B appears to continue the "escapist" discussion in pages written in ink over pencil which may have been part of A recycled for inclusion in B.]

†MANUSCRIPT A COMMENTARY

[page 173] initial draft of the lecture. MS. A was written with the St. Andrews audience clearly in mind, as its many references to Scotland, Scottish authors, and things Scottish (more than in any other version) bear witness. The deliberate use of little-known Scots Gaelic terms for fairies, such as <u>daoine sìthe</u>, <u>sithiche</u>, <u>sithin</u> and <u>sithichean</u> (to which the B draft added the Scandinavian and Welsh <u>huldufolk</u> and <u>tylwyth teg</u>) are obviously keyed to Scotland and aimed at a Scots audience. Moreover, the many references pointing to immediate oral presentation – "I am not here to discuss Fairies", "a subject for my lecture", "There is not time", and "There is not time here and now" – make it clear that Tolkien was writing for a specific occasion.

Aside from its immediate chronological proximity to the St. Andrews lecture, manuscript A has a special importance as the earliest layer in the archaeology of "On Fairy-stories", the recorded foundation for the build-up of Tolkien's thinking on the subject.

[173] These original pages were possibly recycled. Dual sets of numbers appear on particular pages of B, allowing the conjecture that these were originally pages from A inserted into B and re-numbered accordingly. As we have it, A begins on page 5 and ends on page 28. The fact that A5 matches closely with B5 is strong implication that A's now missing 1–4 might also have matched B's 1–4. In addition, the text of A stops abruptly on page 28, followed immediately by a blank page 31, implying the existence of intervening pages 29 and 30. Pages numbered 42 and 43 in B also carry the out-of-sequence numbers 29 and 30, suggesting that these were originally in A and were taken and re-numbered for B without cancellation of their original numbers.

Such double numberings continue on various subsequent pages, suggesting that they were re-positioned and re-paginated from A so as to fit B.

[175] the Dictionary. The Oxford English Dictionary, on which Tolkien worked as an assistant lexicographer from November 1918 to the spring of 1920, was dedicated to supplying the first recorded use of words in English. It was originally called the New English Dictionary on Historical Principles to distinguish it from other dictionaries based on word meanings or etymology.

[176] McDougall and Calder's Celtic Folktales and Fairy Lore. More properly titled *Folk Tales and Fairy Lore in Gaelic and English Collected from Oral Tradition*, this was a volume of folk and fairy tales gathered by the Reverend James MacDougall and edited by the Reverend George Calder. It was published in 1910 as a dual-language edition in Scots Gaelic and facing-page English by the Edinburgh firm of John Grant.

[176] <u>daoine sìthe</u>, <u>sithiche</u>. These, as well as their variants, *sithin*, *sithichean* are all Scots Gaelic terms for fairies, and are evidently more or less interchangeable. *Sìthe*, *sithin*, *sithiche*, *sithichean* can all mean "fairy", *daoine sìthe* "fairy people" or "fairy folk". The "Fairy Lore" section of MacDougall's book translates the overall title *Sgeoil Mu Shithichean, Daoine-Sithe, Sith-Bhruthaich, No Daoine Beaga, No Daoine Matha* as "Tales about Fairies, Fairy-men, Fairy-Knollers, Little Men, or Good People".

[177] Madame d'Aulnoy. Marie-Catherine Le Jumel de Barneville, Baronne d'Aulnoy (1650/51–1705) was a French noblewoman known for her fairy tales or *contes des fées*. An author rather than a collector, she composed "salon" or fairy tales that were stylistically "literary" but based on folkloric material. She was the first to use the term which has since become synonymous with the genre, *contes des fées* or "fairy tales". Written at the court of Louis XIV, her tales had a strong undercurrent of political criticism.

[177] Villeneuve. Gabrielle-Suzanne Barbot de Villeneuve (1695–1755), French writer best known for "Beauty and the Beast".

[177] Paribanou & Achmed. "The Story of the Prince Ahmed [*sic*] and the Fairy Paribanou" – the third of the three stories in *The Blue Fairy Book* that came from *The Arabian Nights*.

[177] English chapbooks. The English chapbook was a flimsy, pocket-size booklet that flourished from the sixteenth to the late nineteenth century. Typically printed on one or two broadsheets of poor quality paper, the chapbook was aimed at a poor but literate reading audience. The word itself comes from its typical vendor, a chapman or pedlar. The heyday of the English chapbook was the eighteenth century. Chapbooks could contain ballads, poems, political treatises or folktales. Tolkien's reference is to tales of popular or "folk" heroes such as the cited Dick Whittington, or Guy of Warwick or Robin Hood. In a 1951 letter to Milton Waldman of Collins Publishers describing his own "Silmarillion" mythology, Tolkien is at pains to differentiate this from "impoverished chapbook stuff" (*Letters*, 144).

[177] Babes... "The Babes in the Wood" is not in *The Blue Fairy Book*, though it appears in other collections and has been a pantomime production.

[178] Wenusians. A term meaning inhabitants of Venus (more usually Venusians or Venerians), comparable to the Martians invented by writers of science fiction.

[178] Patagonians. Tolkien may mean by this term his contemporary inhabitants of Patagonia, the far southern regions of Chile and Argentina, popularly supposed to be unusually tall. In context, the reference may possibly be to the human sub-species invented by science fiction writer Olaf Stapledon in his science fiction novel *Last and First Men*, published in 1931. Like Swift's Lilliputians though more positively, Stapledon's Patagonians were intended as a comment on human civilization, a stage in evolution marked by peaceful development and high intellectual capacity but early senescence.

[178] Asbjornsen and Moe. Peter Christen Asbjørnsen (1812–85) and Jørgen Moe (1813–82) were major Norwegian nineteenth-century folktale collectors. Their *Norske folkeeventyr*, translated into English by the English folklorist George Webbe Dasent as *Popular Tales from the Norse* (1859), was of considerable influence in the nineteenth century study of folklore, a study in which Andrew Lang was one of the foremost figures.

[179] Bechuana Story of Two Brothers. This jotted phrase refers to Dasent's Introduction to *Popular Tales from the Norse*, pp. liv–lv, where he enquires rhetorically: "How is it that the wandering Bechuanas got their story of 'The Two Brothers', the ground-work of which is the same as 'The Machandelboom' and the 'Milk-white Doo', and where the incidents and even the words are almost the same? How is it that in some of its traits that Bechuana story embodies those of that earliest of all popular tales, recently published from an Egyptian Papyrus, coeval with the abode of the Israelites in Egypt? And how is it that that same Egyptian tale has other traits which remind us of the Dun Bull in 'Katie Woodencloak', as well as incidents which are the germ of stories long since reduced to writing in Norse Sagas of the twelfth and thirteenth centuries?"

[179] the Milk-white Doo. A brief, Scottish version of the story told in Grimm's "The Juniper Tree" published in Robert Chambers's *Popular Rhymes of Scotland*. Where the bones of the cooked and eaten brother are buried by his sister, a "milk-white doo (dove)" arises, comparable to the bird spirit of "The Juniper Tree".

[179] Anpu and Bata. Brothers in the Egyptian Tale of Two Brothers. In the version in Budge's *An Egyptian Reading Book for Beginners*, they are called Anpu and Bata. In Dasent's Introduction to *Popular Tales from the Norse*, these same names are spelt Anesou and Satou (footnote, p. lv).

[179] Katie Woodencloak. A tale from *Norske folkeeventyr* included in Dasent's translation *Popular Tales from the Norse*. Another translation, as "Kari Woodengown", appears in Andrew Lang's *The Red Fairy Book*.

[179] Andrew Lang says. In his essay on "Mythology and Fairy Tales" Andrew Lang wrote: "Tertullian knew the story of Rapünzel, 'Turres Lamiæ, Pecten Solis;' an Egyptian papyrus has been unrolled, and found to contain the myth which the Scotch call 'the Milk-white Doo'" (p. 618). And: "It is incredible that the Scotch should have borrowed the tale of 'Nicht, Nocht, Nothing;' the Russians that of 'Tsar Morskoi;' the Norsemen, 'The Master Maid;' the Finns, part of the feats of Lemminkainen, from the account of the aid which Medea gave to Jason" (p. 624). Lang also discusses (separately) Grimm's story of the "Goose Girl" (p. 621) and, more briefly, the Scottish "Black Bull o' Norroway" (p. 622).

[180] the soup that is set before us. Again, a quote from Dasent's Introduction to his *Popular Tales from the Norse* (see Asbjørnsen and Moe above).

[180] Raimondin and Melusine. A medieval French fairy tale existing originally in two versions from the late fourteenth and early fifteenth centuries. Raimondin marries Melusine, who promises him protection on the condition that he not look at her on Saturdays. He disobeys the tabu, spying on his wife in her bath only to discover that she is a complete serpent from the waist down. Turning into a serpent when he accuses her, she leaves, but makes appearances from time to time to foretell the death and succession of her descendents.

[181] "The philology and mythology of the East and West have met and kissed each other; . . . they now go hand in hand". Quoted from Dasent's Introduction to *Popular Tales from the Norse* (p. xviii).

[181] a creator or sub-creator. This is apparently Tolkien's first use of a term which was to become integral to his concept of fantasy. See below, the second note to page 194, when Tolkien returns to this concept.

[181] The biographer of Andrew Lang in the Dictionary of National Biography. Quoted from the entry signed "G.S.G.", written by George Gordon, for the volume for 1912–21. The quote actually begins: "folk-lore is" not "was" (p. 321).

[182] "in Tylor's words…" This entire passage is quoted from page 81 of Dawson's *Progress and Religion*, chapter IV, "The Comparative Study of Religions and the Spiritual Element in Culture" (page 85 of the Unicorn edition). It presents a complex problem in citation protocol. Beginning with "in Tylor's words", the primary author, Tolkien, quotes a second author, Christopher Dawson, quoting a third author, E.B. Tylor from Tylor's book *Primitive Culture* (87), volume II, pp. 109 ff.

[182] Kingsley quoted by Dawson p. 86. Page 86 in the 1938 Unicorn edition, but page 81 in other editions. Mary Henrietta Kingsley (1862-1900) was a nineteenth-century anthropologist. The quote Tolkien cites is from *West African Studies* (1899), second edition (1901), p. 330, and refers to the African belief in spirit and matter as undivided.

[182] 'Ocean of supernatural energy'. Pages 83–4 of Dawson's *Progress and Religion* quotes a long passage from J.R. Swanton's *Social Conditions, Beliefs and Linguistic Relations of the Tlingit Indians* in which Swanton uses the phrase to describe the primitive belief in the power of the universe: "Thus the sky spirit is the ocean of supernatural energy as it manifests itself in the sky" (Dawson, p. 84). This is on page 90 in the Unicorn edition.

[183] (Christopher Dawson p. 91). Page 91 in the Unicorn edition; page 86 in other editions.

[183] Yet he has a character which. The syntactic incoherence of this sentence is largely due to its patchwork nature, since it is pieced together from a jumble of telegraphically brief marginal notes and interpolations.

[183] Sugar plum. Tolkien is referring to Lang's discussion, in his Introduction to the large paper edition of *The Blue Fairy Book*, that the folktales have become altered or embellished in later times: "the house of sugar-plums in 'Hansel and Grettel' is clearly modern, perhaps the fancy of some educated nurse" (p. xv).

[183] Youth who could not fear? A reference to the story "The Tale of a Youth Who Set Out to Learn What Fear Was" in *The Blue Fairy Book*.

[184] waxing and waning his strength at noon like a sun hero. Early scholars of solar mythology saw King Arthur's nephew Gawain as a "sun hero" whose legendary strength, which increases from morning to reach its peak at noon and declines thereafter, is one of the mythical Celtic aspects of his character. Transferred to the literary realm, as in Malory's *Le Morte D'Arthur*, this aspect is hardly touched on except in Gawain's fight with Lancelot, where Lancelot simply waits him out until his strength wanes and then defeats him.

[184] Grendel, Hrothgar. Respectively the man-eating monster and the ageing Scylding king who are central to the first part of the Old English poem *Beowulf*. There is no evidence for the existence of Grendel, but Hrothgar was an historical figure.

[184] Galland's adaptation. Antoine Galland (1646–1715) was the first European translator of *The Arabian Nights*, more properly titled *The Thousand and One Nights*.

[184] Paribanou. In "Prince Ahmed and the Fairy Paribanou" from *The Thousand and One Nights*. Paribanou, daughter of a genie and the fairy helper of Prince Ahmed, facilitates all Ahmed's deeds and finally marries him.

[185] As among Zulus still. In Lang's Introduction to the large paper edition of *The Blue Fairy Book*, he writes of the woman separated from her lover in "East of the Sun and West of the Moon": "In other forms of the tale she calls him by name, a thing still forbidden to Zulu women" (p. xvi).

[187] that enchanted field. Quoted from Lang's Introduction to the large paper edition of *The Blue Fairy Book*, p. xiii.

[189] "<u>another Baby</u>". Quoted from "The Wild Goose Chase at the Kingdom of the Birds" in *The Coloured Lands*, p. 91.

[189] forbidding children to look at the end. Dasent added thirteen more tales to the second edition of his translation *Popular Tales from the Norse*, and in his introductory "Notice to the Second Edition" he remarked: "And now, before the Translator takes leave of his readers for the second time, he will follow the lead of the good godmother in one of these Tales, and forbid all good children to read the two which stand last in the book" (p. vi).

[190] For children are innocent and love justice. Quoted from "On Household Gods and Goblins" in *The Coloured Lands*, p. 195.

[190] The Yellow Dwarf. The villain in Andrew Lang's book-length fairy tale *Prince Ricardo of Pantouflia*, 1893.

[190] "<u>died in harness</u>". The quotation is from Lang's preface to *The Lilac Fairy Book* (1910), p. vi.

[191] Mansoul. From *The Holy War*, an allegorical work by John Bunyan, (1628–88). Mansoul is the city for whose possession Shaddai (God) and Diabolus (Satan) fight.

[192] cheerful fantasy. Cf. Introduction to *The Coloured Lands*, pp. 14–15. Chesterton calls Dickensian fantasy "Mooreeffocish", meaning haunting, gloomy, "truth read backwards". He contrasts this with "cheerful fantasy . . . the creation of a new form wherein man, become creator, co-operates with God." The concept of man as creator co-operating with God seems strikingly similar to Tolkien's own idea of "sub-creation".

[192] man becomes sub-creator. Here Tolkien follows up on the idea of a sub-creator, mentioned above. Tolkien's use of the term seems directly related to the passage cited above concerning "new form", in which man "cooperates with God" (*The Coloured Lands*, p. 15).

[192] "felt impelled to write about lamp-posts...." Tolkien first quotes from and then paraphrases from "The Artistic Side" in *The Coloured Lands*: "In the days when I wrote a fortunately forgotten work called 'The Napoleon of Notting Hill,' I quite honestly felt that I was adorning a neglected thing, when I felt impelled to write about lamp-posts as one-eyed giants or hansom cabs as yawning dragons with two flaming optics, or painted omnibuses as coloured ships or castles" (p. 107). And: "I still hold, every bit as firmly as when I wrote 'The Napoleon of Notting Hill,' that the suburbs ought to be either glorified by romance and religion or else destroyed by fire from heaven" (p. 108).

[192] poetry of misfits. The phrase comes from Chesterton's essay "The Artistic Side" in *The Coloured Lands*. Here he concludes that the "poetry of modern life" is "in some strange way a poetry of misfits; a tangle of misunderstood messages, an alphabet all higgledy-piggledy in a heap" (pp. 109–10).

[193] see why the priest's vestment. Another phrase from Chesterton's "The Artistic Side". In the context of a discussion on meaning, Chesterton remarks, "Anybody can see why the priest's vestment on common days is green like common fields, and on martyrs' days red as blood," the idea being that there is a meaningful correlation between the colour of the vestment and the ritual meaning of the day on which they are worn. Cf. "the poetry of misfits" above, where the poetry of modern life shows no such correlation.

[193] **But as Chesterton says.** Tolkien is here paraphrasing from an essay by Chesterton, "New Things and the Vagabond", originally published in *The New Witness*, 6 September 1917, but quoted extensively by Maisie Ward in her introduction to *The Coloured Lands*:

"The offspring of the Missing Link and a mule, if happily married to the promising child of a Manx cat and a penguin, would not outrun centaur and griffin, it would be something lacking in all the interesting features of man and beast and bird. It would not be a wilder but a much tamer animal than its ancestors; it would not be another and more fantastic shape; but simply shapelessness" (pp. 13–14).

[193] **Chesterton's third stage.** In this paragraph Tolkien paraphrases more from Chesterton's essay "New Things and the Vagabond" as quoted by Maisie Ward in the introduction to *The Coloured Lands*. Ward wrote: "In this article he analyses where revolution in the arts is right, and where it, almost automatically, goes suddenly wrong. In a black and white world a sudden splendid production of primary colours would be a magnificent achievement. The artist who came next and mixed blue and yellow creating green would 'brighten and refresh the world with what is practically a new colour'." (p. 12).

Ward then quotes an extensive passage from Chesterton's essay (from which we quote only the relevant section):

"Then we come to the third stage, which is much more subtle and very much more disputable; but in which the artistic innovators still have a quite commendable case. It is the stage at which they claim to have new experiences too curious to be common; revelations that can hardly be denounced as a palpable democratic danger, but rather as a very impalpable aristocratic privilege. This may well be represented by the next step in the mixture of tints; the step from what used to be called secondary to what used to be called tertiary colours. The artist claims that by mixing red and green he can produce a sort of russet shade, which to many may seem a mere drab or dull brown, but which is, to a finer eye, a thing combining the richness of red and the coolness of green, in a unity as unique and new as green itself. This sort of artist generally gives himself airs; but there is something to be said for him, though he seldom says it. It is true that a combination in colour may be at once unobtrusive and exquisite; but it is precisely here, I fancy, that the innovator falls into a final error. He imagines himself an inaugurator as well as an innovator; he thinks he stands at the beginning of a long process of change; whereas, as a matter of fact, he has come to the end of it. Let him take the *next* step; let him mix one exquisite mixture with another exquisite mixture, and the result will not be another and yet more exquisite mixture; it will be something like mud. It will not be all colours but no colour; a clay as hueless as some antediluvian slime out of which no life can come." (pp. 12–13)

[193] **addressing Elsp.** This refers to the introductory dedication in verse "To Elspeth Angela Campbell" published only in the large paper limited edition of *The Blue Fairy Book*. The phrase "resuming childish things" is not underscored in the original.

MANUSCRIPT B

Manuscript B differs from A in several respects, the foremost being in terms of composition. Manuscript A can be viewed as the first expression of Tolkien's thoughts on his topic. Manuscript B is both an expansion and a refinement of Manuscript A, and in it we find numerous passages (ranging in length from a few sentences to several paragraphs) that were written out as complete thoughts, but at some later point in the process of revision were struck through and cancelled. Whether these passages were rejected for reason of length or because Tolkien felt they were peripheral to his topic is unknown. Nevertheless many of these rejected passages are of enormous interest, and in presenting a readable text of Manuscript B we have endeavoured to represent as much of these rejected passages as possible (while also distinguishing precisely which passages were cancelled or struck through). Manuscript B is also a less consecutive text than A, comprising a main body with a large number of ancillary pages. For our text of Manuscript B, we present first what is basically the main running text of B, and we follow that with numerous miscellaneous pages, so designated.

[BODLEIAN TOLKIEN MS. 4, FOLIOS 73–120]

To be invited to lecture in St. Andrews is a huge compliment to any man; to be allowed to speak about Fairy Stories is (for an Englishman in Scotland) an honour difficult to sustain. I feel like a mortal conjuror who finds himself, by some mistake, called on to give a display of magic to the court of an Elf-king. After producing his rabbit, he may consider himself lucky if he is allowed to go home in his proper shape, or to go home at all. There are

dangers in Fairyland for the overbold. And overbold I am –
because I am a reader and lover of fairy stories, but not a student
of them, as was Andrew Lang. I have neither the learning, nor
the still more necessary wisdom, which the subject demands.

For me at any rate fairy-stories are especially associated with
Scotland: not through any special knowledge – such knowledge
of the rich lore of Scotland was late acquired; but simply by
reason of the names of Andrew Lang and George MacDonald.
To them in different ways I owe the books which most affected
the background of my imagination since childhood.

A man who brings fairy-stories to Scotland is likely to be less
welcome than one who takes coals to Newcastle. But I have not
come bringing fairy-stories. I wish I had. I have a gnawing suspicion that to relate here and now a good fairy-tale, or to
produce a new one would be more profitable, and more entertaining than to talk about such stories. Yet that is what I have
rashly engaged myself to do. Very rashly: because I am a reader
and a lover of fairy-stories, but not a student of them, as was
Andrew Lang. I have not the learning and still less the still more
necessary wisdom to justify the boldness.

The Land of Fairy Story is wide and deep and high, and is
filled with many kings and all manner of men, and beasts, and
birds; its seas are shoreless and its stars uncounted, its beauty an
enchantment and its peril ever-present; both its joy and sorrow
are poignant as a sword. In that land a man may (perhaps) count
himself fortunate to have wandered, but its very mystery and
wealth make dumb the traveller who would report. And while
he is there it is dangerous for him to ask too many questions, lest
the gates shut and the keys be lost. The fairy gold (too often)
turns to withered leaves when it is brought away. All that I can
ask is that you, knowing all these things, will receive my withered leaves, as a token at least that my hand once held a little of
the gold.

But there are some questions that one who is to speak about
fairy-stories cannot help asking, whatever the folk of Faery may

think of him or do to him. What are fairy-stories? What is their origin? What is the use of them? Now, today. The answers (often only broken hints of answers) to some of these questions that I have gleaned primarily from the stories themselves rather than from books about them, I will try and give.

What is a fairy story? It is in this case no good hastening to the New English Dictionary; because it will not tell you. That may be, perhaps, because the volume F editor was <u>not</u> a Scotsman. It contains, in any case, no reference whatever to the combination "<u>fairy story</u>", and is unhelpful on the subject of <u>fairies</u> generally. In the Supplement it records fairy-tale since 1750; and its leading sense is said to be (a) a tale about fairies or generally a fairy legend; with developed senses (b) an unreal or incredible story, and (c) a falsehood.

The last two senses would obviously make my topic hopelessly vast(~~, involving me not only with a large part of fiction, journalism and popular history and popular science, indeed with a substantial portion of all that has ever been said or written~~). But the first sense is too narrow – not too narrow for a lecture (it is large enough for fifty); but too narrow to cover actual usage. Especially so, if we accept the lexicographer's definition of <u>fairies</u> as "supernatural beings of diminutive size in popular belief supposed to possess magical powers and to have great influence for good or evil over the affairs of man".

<u>Supernatural</u> is a dangerous and difficult word in any of its uses, looser or stricter. But to <u>fairies</u> it can hardly be applied unless <u>super</u> is (as it is or was in modern school colloquial) taken as a superlative prefix. For it is man who is, in contrast to fairies supernatural (and often of diminutive stature); whereas they are natural, far more natural than he. Such is their doom. The road to fairyland is not the road to heaven, nor even to hell I believe (though some have heard that it may lead thither indirectly) by the Devil's tithe.

> "O see ye not yon narrow road
> So thick beset wi' thorns and briers?
> This is the path of Righteousness
> Though after it but few inquires.

And see ye not yon braid, braid road
    That lies across the lily leven?
That is the path of Wickedness,
    Though some call it the Road to Heaven.

And see ye not yon bonny road
    That winds about the fernie brae?
That is the Road to fair Elfland,
    Where thou and I this night maun gae."

As for the <u>diminutive size</u>: I do not deny that that notion is a leading one in modern use. I have often thought that it would be worthwhile trying to find out how that has come to be so. The quest I feel sure would be interesting: but my knowledge is not sufficient for a certain answer. Of old there were indeed some inhabitants of Faerie that were small though hardly diminutive – but smallness was no more characteristic of them than it is of human people .

~~Elves they may have been (though elves are not usually diminutive). But fairies were not heard of before the Middle Age was nearly over. There is a strong occurrence of fayryes in a glossary of about 1450 A.D. – which says nothing of their size; but in general it was not until the Tudor period and after that the word comes into use and begins to compete with elf (from which it has never been clearly distinguished).~~

The diminutive being (elf or fairy) is, I guess, in England largely a sophisticated product of literary fancy. It is perhaps not unnatural that in England – the land where the love of the delicate and fine has often reappeared in art – cultured fancy should in this matter turn toward the dainty and diminutive, as in France it went to court and put on powder and diamonds. Yet I suspect that this flower and butterfly minuteness was also in origin a product of 'rationalization' which forsook the true realm of Faerie to indulge a mere botanical and entomological fancy, and to which minuteness was convenient – or an explanation of invisibility. As far as my knowledge [of] it goes, it seems to become fashionable just after the great voyages had begun to make the world seem too narrow to hold both Men and Elves. When the magic land Celtic Hy Breasail in the West had become the mere Brazils the land of red-dye-wood. In any case it was largely a literary business in which William Shakespeare and Michael Drayton had a share. Drayton's <u>Nymphidia</u> is an ancestor of that long line of flower-fairies and fluttering-sprites with antennae that I so disliked as a child and which (~~I am glad to say~~) my children (unprompted) have since detested even more. Some years ago there was introduced into my house a plate, upon which were depicted infantile figures with butterfly-wings, and an inscription: Look at this wee tiny elf! My daughter refused to eat off it. Andrew Lang had similar feelings. In the preface to the last of the Fairy Books he refers to the tales of tiresome contemporary authors. "They always begin with a little boy or girl who goes out and meets the Fairies of polyanthuses and gardenias and apple-blossom . . . These fairies try to be funny and fail, or they try to preach and succeed." (~~It is therefore singularly unfair that it should be possible even by error to connect him with this industry. Yet only the other day I came across an explosive outburst of disgust. "Andrew Lang has a lot to answer for: Pink Fairy Book indeed! Who wants Pink Fairies! Bah." But of course the Pink Fairy Book is pink only on the cover. Inside it there is not a single wee tiny elf.~~)

But the business as I said began long before Andrew Lang's day in the nineteenth century, and long ago achieved tiresomeness, certainly the tiresomeness of trying to be funny and failing (though not of preaching and succeeding). Drayton's <u>Nymphidia</u> is <u>considered as a fairy-story</u> one of the worst ever written. (~~To reverse the judgement of a critic it triumphantly achieves the trivial and the burlesque together.~~) The palace of Oberon has walls of spiders' legs

> And windows of the eyes of cats,
> and for the roof instead of slats
> is covered with the wings of bats.

The Knight Pigwiggen rides on a frisky earwig, and sends his love, Queen Mab, a bracelet of emmets' eyes, making an assignation in a cowslip flower. But the tale that is told amid this silly prettiness is a dull story of intrigue, in which gallant Knight and angry husband fall into the mire, and their wrath is stilled by a draught of the waters of Lethe. It would have been better if it had been beer at an inn. Oberon, Mab and Pigwiggen may be "fairies", as Arthur, Guinevere and Lancelot are not; but the good and evil story of Arthur's court is a fairy-story rather than that of Oberon's.

Fairy (as a noun more or less equivalent with elf) is a fairly modern word and the first quotation (the only one from before 1400) in the Dictionary under <u>fairy</u> is significant. It was taken from the poet Gower (<u>Confessio Amantis</u> v): <u>as he were a faierie</u>. But this, it seems, Gower did not say. He wrote <u>as he were of faierie</u>, 'as if he were come from faerie, out of fairy-land'. And he is describing a gallant who seeks to bewitch the hearts of the maidens in church.

> His croket kembd and thereon set
> A nouche with a chapelet,
> Or elles one of grene leves
> Which late come out of the greves,
> Al for he sholde seme freish;
> And thus he loketh on the fleish,
> Right as an hauk which hath a sihte
> Upon the foul there he schal lihte,
> And as he were of Faierie
> He scheweth him tofore here yhe.

This is a young man of mortal blood and bone; but he gives a much better picture of the inhabitants of Elfland than the definition of a 'fairy' under which he is (by a double error) placed. For the trouble with the real inhabitants of Faerie is that they do not always look like what they are; nor other than we should like to look ourselves. And at least part of the magic that they wield, for the good or evil of man, is power to play on the desires of our bodies and of our hearts.

~~There was indeed no need for the Dictionary to make a special sense 4 for Spenser's use of elf as a Knight of Faerie, the Red Cross Knight, Sir Guyon. For this use – apart from the allegory – remains true to older use.~~

The Queen of Elfland that carried off Thomas the Rhymer upon her milkwhite steed swifter than the wind, came riding by the Eildon Tree as a lady, if one of enchanting beauty. So that Spenser was in the true tradition when he called the Knight of his <u>Faerie</u> by the name of <u>Elfe</u>. It belonged to such folk as Sir Guyon rather than to the mothlike Pigwiggen armed with a hornet's sting.

Now, though I have only touched (wholly inadequately) on <u>Elves</u> and <u>Fairies</u>, I must turn back; for I have already digressed far from my theme. I am not here to discuss fairies, or elves, but <u>fairy-stories</u>. I said the sense 'stories about fairies' was too narrow, even if one rejected the diminutive size. For <u>fairy-stories</u> are not in normal English use stories <u>about</u> fairies [*] (or elves), but "stories about Faerie", stories concerning all that realm which contains many things besides fairies (great or small); besides elves, or fays, dwarfs, trolls, giants, or dragons: it holds the seas, and the sun, the moon, the sky, the earth and us ourselves, when we are enchanted.

It is true that occasionally one meets the narrower sense, and finds "fairy-tales" used (in distinction from folk-tale or other term) as a 'story about fairies'. For instance that is the use in MacDougall [sic] and Calder's <u>Folk Tales and Fairy Lore</u>. The second section is headed <u>Fairy Tales</u> and contains only stories concerning "fairies", or more strictly concerning the <u>daoine sìthe</u>. But that is a special case of translation, and of a partial misfit between languages. The English <u>fairy</u> (that is the word fairie in tales now available in the English language) has borrowed more

---

[*] [marked in pencil: "Omit"] Except in very special cases, such as collections of Welsh or Gaelic tales of the <u>tylwyth teg</u> or the <u>daoine sìthe</u>. In these tales about the 'Fair Family' or the Shee-people are sometimes distinguished as fairy-tales from folktales concerning other heroes.

and more in recent years from Ireland and Scotland, (and from Scandinavia) from the <u>daoine sithe</u> (and the <u>huldu-fólk</u>). But it has other ancestors; the French fée (with which it is of course also related etymologically, but I am not concerned with that), and the native, northern elf.

A glance at any book that claims to be a collection of 'fairy-stories' is enough to show that tales about the <u>Tylwyth Teg</u> or the <u>Daoine sìthe</u>, or about <u>Elves</u>, or about the <u>huldufólk</u> of Scandinavia, or even about dwarfs and goblins, are a small part of their content: so small that they sometimes do not appear at all. The numbers of such collections is great. ~~Some are very bad (dismal products of commercialized literature, in which the beastliness of the industrial processes which have killed or nearly killed the art of telling tales is particularly revealed); some are indifferent; and some are very good.~~ For me, partly by accident of old familiarity, but partly, I think by merit, none can rival the twelve books of twelve colours collected by Andrew Lang and his wife. The first of these came out fifty years ago, and is still in print. But if we look only at the contents of the first of these books, the Blue Fairy Book, we shall see at once the difficulty of any description that will cover all that it contains, without bringing in many other things that are not to be found in this or any of the later volumes. Of the stories in the Blue Book few refer to 'fairies', none are directly 'about' them. It is indeed (I believe) a fact that stories that are actually 'about fairies' are relatively rare (and mostly poor). The poem about Pigwiggen is 'all about fairies'. Most good fairy-stories are about men, women, and children in the presence of the marvellous. For if Elves or Fairies are true, really exist apart from our (often sadly garbled) tales about them, then also this is true: they are not primarily concerned with us nor we with them. Our fates are sundered, and our paths touch rarely. Even on the borders of Elfland we meet them but at the chance crossing of the ways.

One of the worst 'fairy-stories' ever written, Drayton's poem Nymphidia (to which I have already referred) is about Fairie, and Fairies only. Therein the palace of Oberon has walls of spiders' legs and

> and windows of the eyes of cats,
> and for the roof instead of slats
> is covered with the wings of bats.

The Knight Pigwiggen rides on a frisky earwig, and sends his love Queen Mab a bracelet of emmets' eyes, and makes an assignation in a cowslip flower. But the only tale that is told amid all this silly gossamer prettiness and is a dull story of cuckoldry, ~~solved by the waters of Lethe and the bumpkin laughter with an angry husband falling into it with~~ in which gallant Knight and angry husband fall into the mire, and their wrath is stilled by a draught of the waters of Lethe. It would have been better if it had been beer at an inn. Oberon, Mab [and] Pigwiggen may be 'fairies'; as Arthur, Guinevere and Lancelot are not. But the story of Arthur's court is a fairy-story rather than that of Oberon's. ~~(For the fairy story is either simpler or too deeper or nobler, or all three, than these fripperies of fancy).~~

In the Blue Book the stories are mainly from French sources. A just choice in some ways then, as perhaps it would be still. Though not to my taste. I have never had much affection for even Perrault. For so powerful has been the influence of Charles Perrault since his Contes de ma Mère L'Oye was first Englished (in the eighteenth century), and of such other excerpts from the vast storehouse of the Cabinet des Fées as have become well-known, that still, I suppose, if anyone were asked to name at random a typical 'fairy-story', he would name one of these French things: such as Puss-in-Boots, Cinderella, Red Riding Hood. With some Grimm's Fairy-Tales might have a chance. And there are six in the Blue Book from Grimm. There are four from Scandinavia; an ingredient not often obtained by English people (or at least children) except in the Andrew Lang books, but one which I liked then and like better now. Three are from the Arabian Nights; there are a couple of English chapbook tales (Jack the Giant-killer and Dick Whittington); and a couple of traditional Scottish tales from Chambers (The Black Bull o' Norroway and The Red Etin).

It is interesting to note that in backbone this might be called a 'pantomime' selection. For among what are still the commonest pantomime titles: Cinderella, Red Riding Hood, Puss-in-Boots, The Sleeping Beauty, are from Perrault; Aladdin and The Forty Thieves are from The Arabian Nights while Jack and the Beanstalk, Dick Whittington and The Babes in the Wood are English. And ~~practically~~ nearly all these are in the Blue Book. Among the pantomime titles Robinson Crusoe is a curious intruder; but not (I think) really much more so than the Voyage to Lilliput is in the Blue Book.

[written in margin, to replace above cancel:] There is one surprising inclusion: The Voyage to Lilliput.

If one cannot hardly describe or define a fairy-story positively one can do a little towards it negatively. Lilliput does not, to my mind, belong there. It cannot be included just because Lilliputians are small (the only way in which they are in anyway remarkable); for smallness is in Fairyland as in our world just an accident. Pygmies are no more like fairies than are Patagonians. It is not ruled out by the satire; for there is satire (sustained or intermittent) in many indubitable fairy-stories, and it may often have been present in some of the traditional tales where we do not now realize it. But we cannot start admitting travellers' tales of the merely marvellous or unusual, or we shall have a host of other things on our hands from Baron Munchausen to the First Men in the Moon. We shall have to admit The Time Machine with the Eloi and the Morlocks. ~~(And why not indeed? The Morlocks are near enough to goblins, are they not? But they are not thought of as existing in their own right, as separate creatures. They are~~

~~descended from ourselves.~~) For the Eloi and the Morlocks there would indeed be a better case than for Lilliputians. Lilliputians are merely men peered down at (sardonically) from a height of a housetop. Eloi and Morlocks live forward in an abyss of time so deep as to a glamour that almost became an enchantment; and if they are descended from ourselves, it must be remembered that giants and ogres and elves were also by the poet of Beowulf derived from Adam through Cain.

Still I should exclude them: on the ground that the Eloi that will be able to make up 'fairy-stories' about Morlocks – their far-sundered kinsfolk – as we can about dwarfs and elves. But I would exclude both Swift's and Wells' creations on the ground that there is no magic in them. They do not really live in or come from Faerie, but in a distant land on the globe, and in a far distant epoch in history. And though distance in time and space may lend enchantment, it is only a very subsidiary effect. A real fairy needs no such adventitious aids 'Once upon a time' may now convey to our minds. 'Once long ago', or 'In days of yore' – but that is part a rationalising process in some ways like the diminishing size: odd things may have happened once that don't happen now. But its primary sense is just 'Once, at a given and wholly undefined time.'

There are other types of story I would exclude – from the title "fairy-story", but ~~not necessarily from collections and~~ certainly not because I do not like them: namely pure beast-fables. I will choose on purpose an example from the Fairy Books: The Monkey's Heart, a Swahili tale which is given in the Lilac Fairy Book. It tells of a wicked shark who tricked a monkey into riding on his back, and had carried him half-way to his own land before he revealed the fact that the Sultan of that country was sick and needed a monkey's heart to cure him. But the monkey outwitted the shark, and induced him to return to the monkey's land by convincing him that he had left his heart hanging in a bag on a tree.

The beast-fable has, of course, a connexion with fairy-stories – among other things because beasts and birds and other creatures can so often talk as men in undoubted fairy-stories. (The magical understanding by men of the proper language of birds ~~contrasts~~ is quite another matter and a more genuine 'fairy' element: to that I return later.) But where no human being is concerned; or where the animals (as animals not enchanted shapes) are the heroes and heroines and men and women only adjuncts; wherever the animal form is merely a mask on a human face, then I think we have rather beast-fable than fairy-story: whether it be <u>Reynard the Fox</u> or <u>Brer Rabbit</u> or merely <u>The Three Little Pigs</u>. <u>The Wind in the Willows</u> is of course a mixed form but the washerwoman and the engine driver are really only adjuncts: the story is about a Toad, a Rat and a Mole. The masterly stories of Beatrix Potter hover on both sides of the border: <u>The Tailor of Gloucester</u> is practically 'fairy-story'; <u>Mrs. Tiggy-winkle</u> is a fairy-story; <u>Peter Rabbit</u> though it contains a Prohibition (a very fairy element), and also Mr. McGregor, is really not; <u>Jemima Puddleduck</u> and <u>The Tale of Mr. Tod</u> are just beast-fable.

<u>The Monkey's Heart</u> is beast-fable and I suspect that it owes its inclusion in a Fairy Book not primarily to its entertaining quality; but just to that heart supposed to be left in a bag. That was significant to Lang, the student of folklore, even though this curious idea is here used only as a joke; for, of course the monkey's heart was really quite normal and in his breast. But even so there is plainly a reference to a very widespread folklore or fairy-tale idea: according to which the life or strength of a man or creature resides in some other place or thing; or in some part of the body (especially the heart) that can be detached and hidden in a bag, or an egg. At one end of history this idea is used by George MacDonald in his fairy-story <u>The Giant's Heart</u>, which derives this central theme (as well as many other details) from well-known traditional stories.

Such as the Norse: <u>The Giant that had no Heart</u> in Dasent; or the <u>Sea Maiden</u> in Campbell's <u>Popular Tales of the West Highlands</u> (where it is no. iv; cf. also no. i); or more remotely in <u>Die Kristallkugel</u> in Grimm.

At the other end, it occurs, indeed, in what is probably one of the oldest fairy-stories in writing: The Tale of the Two Brothers in the Egyptian D'orsigny papyrus. There the younger brother says to the elder: "I shall enchant my heart, and I shall place it upon the top of the flower of the cedar. Now the cedar will be cut down and my heart will fall to the ground, and thou shalt come to seek for it, even though thou pass seven years in seeking it; but when thou hast found it, put it in a vase of cold water, and in very truth I shall live." Wallis Budge, Egyptian Reading Book (1896), p. xxi.

But that point of interest, and such comparisons as these bring us to the brink of the second question: what is the origin of 'fairy-stories'. That, of course, must mean: the origin of the fairyish element. To ask what is the origin of stories, is to ask what is the origin of the mind, and of language. Actually to ask what is the origin of the fairy element lands us ultimately in the same question; but there are many elements in fairy-stories (such as this detachable heart, swan-robes, magic rings, prohibitions and the like) that can be studied without reference to this main question.

But such a study is scientific (or strives to be); and is a pursuit of folklorists or anthropologists or of scholars concerned with the sources of legend: that is, of people studying the stories not for themselves, but as a quarry from which to dig evidence or information on other matters in which they are interested. To them such recurring similarities seem specially important. So much so that they are apt to get off their own proper track, or to express themselves in a misleading shorthand: misleading in particular if it gets out of their books into books about literature as it so often does. They are inclined to say that any two stories built around the same folk-lore motive, or made up of a generally similar combination of such motives, are "the same stories". We read that Tertullian's turris lamiæ, pecten solis is Rapunzel; that The Black Bull o' Norroway is Beauty and the Beast and Apuleius' Eros and Psyche. That the Norse Mastermaid (or the Gaelic Battle of the Birds – see Campbell vol i – and its many congeners and variants) is the same story as the Greek story of

Medea and Jason. In which case, of course, The Battle of the Birds is much further from Medea and Jason.

Now that may be true to some extent on that plane (a low one); but it is not true in a fairy-tale sense, it is not true in art or literature. It is precisely the colouring, the atmosphere, the details, and the general purport that inform the bones of the plot that really count – Shakespeare's <u>King Lear</u> is not the same as Layamon's story. Or to take the extreme case of <u>Red Riding [Hood]</u>: it is of purely secondary interest that the re-told versions of this story in which Little Red Riding Hood is saved by wood-cutters is directly derived from Perrault's story in which she was eaten by the wolf. The really important thing is that this version is a story with a happy ending, and that Perrault's was not. There is a world of difference. ~~A moment's reflection will convince anyone that the unhappy is really better~~ They are different stories. The comparison of skeleton plots, or of abstracted incidents and ideas, is not a critical literary process at all ~~or only acquires a literary interest in those rare circumstances (hardly ever present in old and traditional and far-travelled tales) when the historical connexion between the versions is beyond doubt, and we can see exactly where a story-teller was at work reshaping a tale.~~

Of course, I do not deny, for I feel strongly, the fascination of the attempt to unravel the intricately knotted and ramified history of fairy-tales ~~or one branch of traditional lore, descending as they plainly do often from a very remote antiquity.~~ It is closely connected with the philologist's concern with the tangled skein of language, of which I know a little. But with regard to language it seems to me that the essential quality and aptitudes of a given language in a living moment is both more important to seize (and far more difficult to make explicit) than its history; so with regard to fairy-tales I feel that it is more interesting (and also in its way more difficult) to consider what they are, what they have become for us, and what values the long alchemic processes of time have produced in them. In Dasent's words: "we must be satisfied with the soup that is set before us, and not desire to see the bones of the ox out of which it has been boiled."

Though oddly enough Dasent by the "soup" meant the mish-mash of bogus pre-history founded on early comparative philology; and by the "bones" asking to see the workings and the proofs that led to these theories. By the "soup" I mean the story as it is served up, and by the "bones" ~~the analysis of~~ its sources – even where by luck ~~or analysis or comparisons~~ those can be with any certainty discovered.

I am going therefore to pass lightly over the question of origins. ~~It is a subject in which Andrew Lang was deeply interested and wrote brilliantly and originally. The mass of such writings before and since is now, of course, enormous. I have ideas myself on the subject, though my learning neither in popular tales, nor in the writings about them is quite sufficient to justify this~~ – because I am not really competent to deal with it. ~~I have some ideas, but insufficient learning in folk-tales themselves, not to mention the special literature about them to which Andrew Lang contributed so brilliantly and in his day originally~~, and also because there is no time for all the questions, and if anything must be dropped, this (the least important question) must be the one to go.

It is plain enough that fairy-stories in the wider sense are very ancient indeed; they appear not only in very early records (such as the d'Orsigny papyrus), but they are also found universally wherever there is language. We are therefore obviously faced in dealing with them with the same problem as that which meets the archaeologist or the comparative philologist: with the old (and still continued) debate between (a) the <u>independent evolution</u> (or rather <u>invention</u>) of the similar in similar circumstances, (b) <u>inheritance</u> from a remote common ancestry ~~preceding even the major racial, cultural, and linguistic divisions now known in historical times~~, and <u>diffusion</u> at various times from one (or more) centres. Most debates depend on an attempt at over-simplification; and I do not suppose this debate is any exception. The history of fairy-stories is probably more complex than that of the human race, and at least as complex as the history of human language. All three things: independent <u>invention</u> (primary and secondary), <u>inheritance</u> and <u>diffusion</u>: have probably played their part in producing the intricate Web of Story that is now beyond any but the Fairies to unravel.* Of these <u>invention</u> is the most important and the most mysterious. To an inventor (that is to a storymaker or re-shaper) all three lead back. <u>Diffusion</u> – borrowing in space – whether of culture or story only puts the history and problem back in time. At the centre of diffusion there is a place where an inventor lived. Similarly with <u>inheritance</u> – borrowing in time: we come back at last to an ancestral inventor. While if we believe that sometimes there occurred the independent striking out of similar ideas, means, or devices, we multiply the ancestral inventor but do not necessarily the more clearly understand his gift.

Philology has been dethroned from the high place she once had in all this enquiry – and it was Andrew Lang who played a part in the revolution. Max Müller's view of mythology as a "disease of language" ~~and of heroic legend and folk tale as successive transformations of mythology (less baneful than the original virulent disease)~~ can be abandoned without regret: ~~it was of course as near as possible for any hypothesis to the exact inversion of the truth.~~ It would be far truer to say that language (especially modern language) ~~is much more like~~ is a disease of mythology ~~(and the folk-tale is often nearer to the roots than legend or myth)~~. But language cannot be wholly forgotten. The incarnate mind, the tongue, and the tale are coeval in this world. The human mind, endowed with the power of generalization and abstraction, sees not only green-grass and discriminates it from other things (finding it fair to look upon), but sees that it is green as well as being grass: ~~and there is born a word for green~~. But how powerful, and stimulating to the very faculty that produced it, is the invention of the Adjective: no spell or talisman in

---

* Except in particularly fortunate cases, or in a few details. It is indeed easier to unravel a single *thread*—that is a detail, and incident, or notion—than to trace the history of any *picture* defined by many threads. For with the picture a new element has come in: the picture is greater than the sum of the component threads of the tapestry. That is the inevitable weakness of the analytical method: it teaches us much about things in stories, but very little about stories themselves.

a fairy-story is more potent. Not surprising: because such spells and talismans might indeed be said to be but another view of Adjectives: a part of speech in a mythical grammar. The mind that thought of light, heavy, grey, yellow, still, swift, also thought of magic that would make light things heavy, or grey lead into yellow gold, and the still rock into swift water. If it could do one it could do both, it would inevitably do both.

[Non-sequential notes on reverse of a page:]

This element in 'mythology' – sub-creation – rather than either representation or symbolic interpretation is, I think, too little regarded/considered. Does it belong to the higher or the lower mythology as Andrew Lang called them: meaning I suppose what would probably now be called myth and folktale? There has been much debate concerning their relations, and the question must be glanced at in any consideration of origins however brief. At one time the dominant view (which Andrew Lang especially opposed) was that which derived all such matter from 'nature-myths'. The Olympians.

Not at any rate the fantasies of fallen men. And he has stained the inhabitants of Faerie with his own stain. And he paints the inhabitants of Faerie with his own dark colours. Maybe he traduces them as he traduces all things in his evil mood. At any rate I venture to suggest that if there is any essentially Elvish quality that can be named, any one prime characteristic it is this: the central power of the Elf (or fairy) is the production almos perfect, unalloyed, unbroken by the gap between vision and making with (almost) the immediacy of an act of will of those [creations?] in ([nearly?]) unalloyed perfection which are the ever unachieved aim of the human arts of hand and lyric. The lyre of Orpheus is a prime concept in the world of Faerie.

[slanted, at right:] Faerie is the power to make immediately affective by the will (effortlessly without machinery) these creations of the 'fantastic' creative mind – especially (not alas solely) the beautiful creations: one of its first is the effortless production in excelsis unalloyed, of those beauties for which we strive (laboriously) through the arts of hand and tongue and achieve only impurely.

[text continues from above, "it would inevitably do both":]

When we can take green from grass, blue from heaven, and red from blood we have already an enchanter's power. It does not follow that we shall use the power well. We may put green upon a man's face, and produce a horror; we may make the rare blue moon to shine; that we may cause woods to spring with silver leaves and rams to wear a golden fleece, and put hot fire into the belly of the cold worm: but in such 'fantasy' as it is called new form is made, and man is become a sub-creator.

Among the many interesting questions which an enquiry into origins raises is one we have already just glimpsed: the relation of what Andrew Lang called the higher and the lower mythologies: what would now probably be called myth (or mythology) and folktale. The once dominant view (which he especially opposed) was that which derived all from nature-myths: the Olympians were personifications of the sun, of dawn, of night and so on, and the stories told about them were originally 'myths' (allegory would have been a better word) of the greater elemental change and processes of nature. Epic, heroic legend, saga <u>localized</u> these stories in real places and humanized them by attributing them to ancestral heroes (mightier than men, and yet already men); and then these legends, breaking down again or dwindling, became folk-stories, Märchen, and – finally "nursery- tales".

That would seem to be the truth nearly upside down, almost an exact inversion of the truth: ~~the operative key words person-ification, localization and humanization are at any rate unex-plained: so many questions begged~~.

The nearer the so-called 'nature-myth' – or rather allegory of the large processes of nature – is to its supposed archetype, ~~and indeed to nature,~~ the less interesting it is, and indeed the less is it of a 'myth', capable of throwing any illumination whatever on the world.

It is difficult to conceive how any object of Nature could ever be arranged into a personal significance or glory, if that were not a gift from a person, from the spirit of Men (or of a man). The gods may derive their colour and glory from the high splendours of nature but it was man that obtained these for them; their personality they get direct from him; the shadow or flicker of divinity that is upon them they receive through him ~~from that universal primitive belief concerning~~ the invisible world behind the world, the Supernatural, which is found whenever so-called uncivilized men are studied sympathetically from within.

There is no clear distinction between 'the higher and lower mythologies'. They live – if they live at all – by the same life; just as do kings and peasants. The gods and the lesser figures: all derive their character ~~from man~~ & personality from man. ~~Thus if we~~ Let us take what looks like a clear case of Olympian nature-myth: the Norse <u>Þórr.</u> His name is Thunder (of which it is the Norse form); and it is not difficult to interpret his hammer, <u>Miöllnir</u>, as lightning. Yet ~~he~~ Þórr has (as far as our records go) a very marked character or personality. ~~It is in some details relatable (so to speak) to thunder, fire and lightning;~~ which is not to be found in thunder or lightning even though some details are relatable (so to speak) to these phenomena, e.g. his loud voice, ~~like thunder (though thunder does not speak);~~ his red beard, or violent temper, his blundering and smashing strength. ~~But the character of Thórr cannot be found in lightning or thunder.~~

Nonetheless it is probably a question without much meaning to enquire: which came first – nature-allegories about personalized Thunder on the mountains, splitting rocks and trees; or stories about an irascible, not over clever, red-beard farmer, of strength beyond common measure, a person (in all but stature) very like the Northern <u>bóndar</u> (farmer) by whom Thórr was chiefly beloved? To a picture of such Thórr may be held to have 'dwindled', or from such he may be held to have been enlarged. I doubt whether either is wholly true. I fancy the farmer popped in at the moment Thunder got a voice and a face. And I also fancy that there was a distant growl of thunder every time a story-teller heard a farmer in a rage.

Of course the personification is much older than Scandinavian Þórr; but it is legitimate to speak like this for simplicity. Historically no doubt we have a progressive alteration to suit different cultures, times and tastes of the 'human picture' or 'person' embedded in the personification.

Þórr I suppose must be reckoned as a member of the higher aristocracy (that is of mythology). Yet <u>Þrymskviða</u> is as certainly just a fairy-tale. But there is no real reason for supposing it unprimitive (at least as far as Scandinavia is concerned). If we could go backwards in time the fairy-tale might change in details, or give way to other tales: but there would always be a fairy-tale as long as there was any Thórr. When the fairy-tale ceased there would be just Thunder which no human ears had yet heard.

The distinction one can draw (and that not always) between the higher mythology (the aristocracy of gods) and the lower (the fairy-tale populace of little powers) is one rather of degree than of kind – the aristocracy are captains, and the whole world is their province; the lower orders have more limited sphere and scope.

[pencil at top] I cannot now (as is the duty at this point of one who would properly deal with his topic) take the further step and discuss the relation of mythology to religion.

But something else is of course, occasionally glimpsed: Divinity, the <u>right</u> to power (as distinct from its possession), and the due of worship; in fact 'religion'. Andrew Lang said (and is still commended for saying) that mythology and religion in the strict sense of the word are two distinct things that have become inextricably tangled; though mythology is itself almost devoid of religious significance. This is borne out by the increasing mass of more careful and sympathetic study of primitive peoples. The

hasty survey finds only their wilder tales; a closer their cosmological myths; patience and inner knowledge their philosophy
and religion – the mysterious and intangible of which the gods
are not necessarily an embodiment or only to a variable measure
and degree often decided by the individual.

Yet these things <u>have</u> become entangled – or it is perhaps that
they have marched steadily to a fusion/synthesis. Even fairy-
stories as a whole have three faces: the Mystical (towards the
Supernatural); the Magical (towards the nature); the Mirror (of
scorn and pity towards man). The essential Face of Fairy-tales is
the middle one, the Magical. But the degree in which the others
in variable measure appear may be decided by the individual
story-teller. The mystical may be embodied in the magical and
fairy-tale. This at least is what George MacDonald attempted –
(failing badly when he failed, but producing achieving stories of
power and beauty when he succeeded as (I think) he did in <u>The
Golden Key</u> which he called a fairy-tale), and even when he only
partly succeeded as in <u>Lilith</u> (which he called a Romance).

If we apply another metaphor to the history of fairy-stories, we
may say the pot of soup has always been boiling; and to it have
continually been added new bits (dainty or undainty). For these
reasons the fact that a story similar to that known as <u>The
Goosegirl</u> in Grimm is told in the 13th century of Bertha
Broadfoot mother of Charles the Great, really proves nothing
either way: neither that this story was descending from
Olympus or Asgard by way of an already legendary king of
yore, on the way to become a <u>Hausmärchen</u>; nor that it was on
its way up. All we could deduce from this fact (even if we knew
nothing of the real history of Charles and his family) would be
that this story probably had nothing <u>historically</u> to do with her.
Charlemagne's mother has been put in the pot, in fact has got
into the soup. It seems fairly plain that Arthur once historical
was put into the pot, also and after considerable boiling together
with many other ingredients derived from the higher and lower
mythology and from history (such as King Alfred's successful

~~resistance of the heathen Danes) emerged as a prince of Faerie.~~ It seems fairly plain that Arthur once historical was put into the pot also, and after considerable boiling together with many other older mythological and fairy elements, and perhaps a few other stray bones of history (such as King Alfred's resistance of the Danes), emerged as a fairy king.[*] But of Gawain we cannot be so sure. He emerges in English (as distinct from Welsh and French) as a pattern of courtesy and (true) gracious virtue, yet he wanes and waxes to his strength at noon like a sun-hero. Is that something that has been attached in the pot, or something that has not got boiled off? The latter is commonly assumed: but I do not perceive any proof. The situation in the great northern 'Arthurian' court that of <u>Heorot</u> in Denmark is somewhat similar. Hroðgar and his family have manifest marks of history – far more than Arthur; yet they are mixed up with many fairy-story elements, such as <u>Grendel</u> in the Anglo-Saxon account. The Knight <u>Beowulf</u> has manifest marks of fairy-tale (in act and character) yet he is thoroughly mixed up with real kings. But it cannot <u>a priori</u> (without special reference to evidence in the particular case) be decided that he must be a fairy-tale figure and partly humanized, rather than a minor historical figure that has got into the soup, and been half hurled into fairy-tale.

(And even if we merely consider style, tone, elaboration we can see that processes have not all been in a straight line. A simple illustration will suffice. Far back a folk-tale or fairy-story can be guessed; in <u>The Arabian Nights</u> it appears tricked out with literary raiment; it is diffused in Europe by means of translations and adaptations; it is abridged and re-told, dwindling back into 'mere' fairy-story: the tale of <u>The Fairy Paribanou</u> in the Blue Fairy Book.)

But when we have done all that research (collection and comparison) can do; and have explained many elements embedded in fairy-stories (such as stepmothers, enchanted bears and bulls,

---

[*] That he was made to look again superficially a deal more like an historical king is an accident, and a special process.

cannibal witches, taboos on names, and the like), as relics of ancient customs once practised in actual life, or of beliefs once held as beliefs and not fancies – there is still a point too often forgotten: that is the effect <u>now</u> produced by these old things in the stories as they are. For one thing they are now <u>old</u>, and antiquity has an appeal in itself. ~~The beauty and horror of Der Machandelboom, with the exquisite beginning (in which the nine months of child-bearing are reflected in the life of the tree) and the abominable stew made of the murdered brother, the gruesome bones, and the gay and vengeful bird-soul rising in a mist from the ground has remained with me since childhood.~~ The beauty and horror of <u>The Juniper Tree</u> (<u>Der Machandelboom</u>), with its exquisite and tragic beginning ~~in which the nine months bearing of the~~, the abominable cannibal stew, the gruesome bones, the gay and vengeful bird-spirit coming out of a mist that rose from the tree, has remained with me since childhood – ~~when I read a less tamed and mollified German Grimm than that which~~ and yet always the chief impression was not beauty or horror, but distance: a great backward and abysm of time.[†] Without the stew and the bones (which children are now too often spared in mollified versions of Grimm) that vision would largely have been lost. I do not think I was harmed by the horror <u>in the fairytale setting</u>, out of whatever dark practices and beliefs of the past it may have come. Such stories have now a mythical or total unanalysable effect, an effect quite independent of the findings of Comparative Folklore, and one which it cannot spoil, nor explain: they open a door on Other Time, and if we pass through, though only for a moment, we stand outside our own time, and a little outside Time itself.

If we pause not merely to note that such old elements have been preserved, but to think how they have been preserved, we must suppose that it has happened largely precisely because of this effect: the literary effect I might call it in contrast to the anthropological origin. It cannot have been we, or even the brothers Grimm, that first felt it. Fairy-stories are by no means rocky matrixes out of which the fossils cannot be prised except by [an] expert geologist: the ancient elements can be dropped out or forgotten or replaced easily enough, as any comparison of a story with closely related variations will show. The things that are kept must often have been kept (or inserted) because the oral narrators, instinctively or consciously, felt their curious literary 'significance'. Even where a prohibition in a fairy-story is guessed to be derived from anciently practiced <u>tabu</u>, it has probably been preserved in the later stages of the stories' history because of the intense mythical value of <u>Prohibition</u> with a capital P. A sense of that may even have lain behind some of the practiced <u>tabus</u> themselves. Thou shalt not – or else thou shall go forth beggared into endless regret. The gentlest 'nursery-tale' cannot avoid it. Even Peter Rabbit was forbidden a garden, lost his blue coat, and took sick. The Locked Door stands as an eternal Temptation.

And with that I think we come to the children. It is often (now) assumed that children are the natural or the specially appropriate audience for fairy-stories. In describing a fairy-story which they think adults might possibly read even for their own entertainment, reviewers frequently indulge in such waggeries as: 'this book is for children from the ages of six to sixty'. (But no one begins the puff of a new motor model with: 'this toy will amuse infants from seventeen to seventy' – although that would be much more appropriate. Is there any <u>essential</u> connexion between children and fairy-stories; or anything that calls for comment in an adult that reads them for himself? <u>Reads</u> them as literature, not <u>studies</u> them as collector's items. Adults are allowed to study anything: even old theatre-programmes, and paper-bags.

[arrow pointing left, referring to passages written on the reverse of previous page:]

The writing of fairy-tales – even for (though not down to) children is perhaps one of the most adult activities: it is best left to [illeg, illeg,] politicians, ~~instructors~~, logicians, ~~philosop~~ and theologians. If there is any Neigung[†] – it is to a beast-fable.

I could say a great deal on this topic – but for brevity's sake I will just be dogmatic. Fairy-stories have often been <u>relegated</u> to children like battered furniture to the play-room. But there is no more an essential connexion between children and fairy-stories than between children and linoleum. Children do not specially like them – that is not more than unspoiled grown ups like them, and not more than they like other things. Fairy-stories may be specially written for children and so become distasteful to grown ups (and probably to the children): but so may novels, verses, botany and history.

It is a [certainly?] dangerous process. In the case of literature and the arts and sciences it is indeed saved from disaster only by the fact that here they are not relegated to the nursery. The nursery is really given such hosts of the things as seem fit for it. If fairy stories were relegated to the nursery they would be ruined, indeed in so far as they have been so relegated they have been ruined.

Now if there was an essential connexion between fairy-tales and the nursery then talented children who early show a bent for writing should (a) most often try first to write or tell fairy-tales and should (b) in any case succeed more often in that form than any other. But I think this is the reverse of the truth. Talented children seldom try to write fairy-tales (properly so called) and if they do they fail with a special completeness.

It cannot be denied that children and fairy-stories are especially associated – in that world that buys or borrows books.[*] Fairy-stories are thought of (even when that name is not used) as 'nursery-tales'. But the contents of nurseries are (or were, when such things were commoner) of various sorts, not all designed originally for a place there. Andrew Lang maintained that folk-lore was (as a rule) not the débris of a higher mythology, but the foundation on which that rests. So we might say that the nursery toy-cupboard is not the débris of the drawing china-cabinet, but

[*] In the world that is unlettered, or still preserves habits of an unlettered period (a world which still lingers in many parts of Europe, even in these islands, and even in England was lingering until not so very long ago) that association with children is not so plain. Stories that are indubitable fairy-stories are (or were) told by adults for the entertainment of adults, and with an appreciation on both sides of skill in narrative art. And the traditional tales were, of course, preserved in memory by adults.

rather its humble model. Yet it cannot be denied that the toy-cupboard <u>may</u> have seen better days (as they say), and that the chairs, the table, the pictures, and even sometimes the books, found in the children's room are often enough things that were once held good enough for dining-rooms and guest-chambers. Children play too in attics, where all kinds of half-forgotten and damaged goods are found. And the 'nurse', the woman young or old specially deputed to mind children, was an institution already very very ancient when <u>ma Mère l'Oye</u> told the stories to his son that provided the foundation for the tales of Charles Perrault. Yet I often wonder if the audience could be said to be <u>chosen</u> by Mother Goose <del>(or Uncle Remus)</del>, or the subjects to be chosen by Master Perrault; any more than nurse or children usually choose the play-room furniture. Both, I fancy, took what they were given, and did the best they could.

Fairy-stories are then associated with children primarily because parents or guardians have ordained it so. Sometimes their reasons have been no better than the reasons for giving children other things that had seen better days: because they did not want them themselves. Sometimes the reason has been because they once enjoyed them themselves. That is an excellent reason. But do children <u>specially</u> enjoy fairy-stories, that is more than unspoiled adults do, or more than other things (if they can get them)? I can only speak of myself and my own children. My children have had many fairy-story books (good and bad) – given them by many people (wise and unwise). I gave them some myself that I liked such as <u>The Princess and the Goblin</u>. They liked such things because it is a natural human taste to like them; but they did not specially like them (more than I do, or more than other things). They did not even like them much at all, until they reached a certain but variable age: the age of the awakening of taste for <u>Literature</u>.

So that I think that Lang was wrong in saying that "it seems almost cruel to apply the methods of literary criticism[*] to

---

[*] By which I suspect he meant not literary criticism, but analysis and an enquiry into sources, which was then especially (but is still) often so miscalled.

Nursery Tales. He who would enter into the Kingdom of Faery should have the heart of a little child, if he is to be happy or at home in that enchanted field." [†] Is that true? ~~Not if you mean 'lit-erary criticism', rather than (what I suspect he meant) research, and analysis, and comparison, devoted to the analysis and an enquiry into origins.~~ If it is literally true, then there is little more to be said: we must just read on uncritically. But it is a very dull child that so treats a collection of fairy-stories: even enchanted fields have brighter patches. Especially critical are those who have real liking for fairy-stories (as distinct from the general appetite for literary food of the mind by all young and hungry). They may have childish hearts (and the humility or ignorance which makes them accept what is given to them); but they have also heads. And as far as my experience goes it is notable how fre-quently their choice of liking for this or that tale coincides with an adult judgement of literary merit. (Their dislike is more often due to bad narrative, inappropriate style, or the damage done by forgetful tradition or inept 'adaptation' than to the horrible or the sad) or it is the tale well-told in its own style that pleases; rather than the specially marvellous or the very sweet.

Andrew Lang's famous collections were, of course (though partly a by-product of adult research into mythology and folk-lore) specially intended for <u>children</u>. The introduction to the first of the series speaks of "children to whom and for whom they are told. They represent the young age of man true to his early loves, and have his unblunted edge of <u>belief</u>, a fresh appetite for marvels."

I doubt the <u>belief</u> – if by that is meant <u>belief</u> in the marvels for which there is appetite.

"Is it true?" is (he says) the great question children ask. But that often comes merely from a child's desire to be certain of which kind of literature he is faced with. Children's knowledge of the world may be so small that they cannot judge off hand and without the help of an adult between the fantastic, the marvel-lous, and merely grown-up. That is between (1) fairy-tale and make-believe, and (2) the rare or remote Fact, and (3) the ordinary things of their parent's world which they don't yet know but are busy learning. But they know the three classes, and like each in its own kind. The first two classes have, of course, a shadow-border – but that is not peculiar to children. We are all sure of the difference in <u>kind</u>, but we are not sure where to place all the things we hear. The child may well believe a report that there are ogres in the next county; many grown-ups find it only too easy to believe of another county; and as for another planet: there are very few grown-ups who can imagine it as peopled (if at all) by anything but monsters of iniquity.

Now I was one of the <u>children</u> whom Andrew Lang was addressing – I was born about the same time as the <u>Green Fairy Book</u> – the children for whom he seemed to think that fairy-stories were the equivalent of the adult <u>novel</u>; and of whom he said: their "taste remains like the taste of their naked ancestors thousands of years ago; and they seem to like fairy-tales, better than history, poetry, geography or arithmetic."[*] Yet really we do not know much about those naked ancestors (except that probably [they] were not naked). Our fairy-stories (however old may be certain things in them) are certainly not like theirs. But if it is assumed that they had fairy-stories, because we have them – then probably we have history, poetry, geography, and arithmetic, because they liked these things too, as far as this could get them, and in so far as they had yet separated the many branches of their general interest in everything.

There is in children naturally (since they have human minds) a perception (if an unpractised one) of the different planes of truth – I never imagined that a dragon was of the same order as a horse or stud. I am clear that this was not solely because I had seen many horses but never seen a dragon. The dragon had 'faerie' written plain upon him (whether you knew the word or not). In whatever world he had his being, it was an Other World. I can vividly remember, re-feel, the vexation (such emotions bite

---

[*] Preface to the <u>Violet Fairy Book</u>

deep and live long) caused me in early childhood by the assertions of instructive relations (in their gift-books) that e.g. snowflakes were (or were more beautiful than) fairy jewels, or that the marvels of the ocean depths were more wonderful than the strangest creatures of Fairyland. I thought snowflakes and fishes very beautiful and very wonderful – but neither wonderful nor beautiful [*sic*] exciting – but not wonderful. The beauty and wonder seemed of two quite different kinds, and I thought it quibbling and cheating to try and compare them. I was ready enough to study nature scientifically – very ready, quite as ready as to read fairy-stories. But I was not going to be quibbled into science nor cheated out of Faerie.

I thought early about these things (and was not exceptional in that) before I was eight (when my childhood reading or hearing of fairy-stories ceased) the question of <u>belief</u> had a matter not only of personal [pondering?] but of debate with fellow children. One spared the grown-ups. They were embarrassed. I could not guess why, then. It now appears plain that it conflicted with their views of fresh young folk. But were they really like that when children. Was there a hidden-breach between the generations. I don't think so. My children have been just the same as I was.

So I will not say children have changed since Andrew Lang's time. I will say that I wonder if they were ever like that. I never <u>believed</u> in fairy-stories any more than I believed in stories about rabbits, children, policemen or railway-engines – unless I was solemnly assured that they were <u>true</u> by somebody who played fair. Of course the question naturally arose: do all the things in the story commonly happen in my world; are they possible in my world; are they possible at all. But wondering whether there <u>are</u> such things as <u>fairies</u>, <u>dragons</u>, <u>giants</u>, <u>policemen</u>, or <u>cities paved with gold</u> is quite different from believing any particular account of them. I preserve to this day a fairly open mind on the existence of these things (concerning which there are so many garbled or wilfully fantastic stories). There seems also a fair evidence for the existence of policemen; but the romances that have gathered round these mysterious beings I now find are for the most part frankly incredible (as I always thought).

I must say I hoped or wished that some of the creatures of fairy-story were <u>true</u> – the hope or wish showing the absence of <u>belief</u>. In particular I had a deep longing to see and speak to a Knight of Arthur's Court, whom I should have regarded much as Peredur did. But that is a special case; for owing to the accident of the development of Arthurian legend it was and became thus so presented largely as History. It was not quite fair. In general I disliked the more fairyish kind of fairy-stories – to which I vastly preferred <u>novels</u>: that is stories about people of my own day: I liked my magic in small purposeful doses (the proper way to take it); and I preferred the older tales that had not acquired the frippery and finery of the <u>Cabinet des Fées</u>. The <u>Story of Sigurd</u> (adapted by Andrew Lang himself from Morris' translation of <u>The Volsunga Saga</u>) was my favourite without rival. Even as it stands in the Red Book that is no light matter: it is strong meat for nurseries. But a real taste for fairy-stories came long after nursery days or the brief golden years, when learning to read and going to school. In that happy time I liked a good many other things as well (or better): such [as] astronomy, or natural history (especially botany) as I could get. If I preferred fairy-stories to arithmetic, it was merely because (alas!) I did not like arithmetic at all.

We do (I think) an injustice to fairy-stories and to children, if we conceive of fairy-stories as a sort of [mental?] cake or sweet to be provided by indulgent uncles: ~~and of a taste for them as babyish or "not a thing to be proud of".~~

The fairy-story is not <u>essentially</u> connected with children – though it has (among the nominally educated) been largely relegated to them; and also it has been adapted to what has been conceived as the needs or measure of children (according to notions more or less erroneous or foolish).[*]

---

[*] Dasent replied with vigour and justice to the prudish critics of his translations from Norse popular tales; yet he committed the astonishing folly of specially forbidding children to read the last two. That a man could study fairy-stories and not learn better than that seems almost incredible.

I do not deny that there is a truth Andrew Lang's words: "he who would enter into the Kingdom of Faerie should have the heart of a little child". For that possession is necessary to high adventure.

I do not deny that there is a truth in Andrew Lang's sentimental sounding words: "he who would enter into the Kingdom of Faerie should have the heart of a little child". For that possession is necessary to all high adventure – into Kingdoms both less and far greater than Faerie. But that possession does not imply a mere uncritical wonder. Chesterton once remarked that the children in whose company he saw Maeterlinck's <u>Blue Bird</u> were dissatisfied "because it did not end with a Day of Judgement, and it was not revealed to the hero and heroine that the Dog had been faithful and the Cat faithless." "For children" he says, "are innocent and love justice; while most of us are wicked and naturally prefer mercy."

Andrew Lang was at pains to defend the slaying of the Yellow Dwarf by Prince Ricardo in one of his own fairy-stories. 'I hate cruelty', he said, . . . 'but that was in fair fight, sword in hand, and the dwarf peace to his ashes! died in harness.' Yet it is not clear that piercing a dwarf with a sword is either less cruel or more just than the execution of wicked kings and evil stepmothers which Lang abjures – he sends them (as he boasts) to retirement on ample pensions. Which is mercy untempered with justice. However that plea was not addressed to children but to the <u>parents and guardians</u> to whom Lang was recommending his own <u>Prince Prigio</u> and <u>Prince Ricardo</u> as suitable for their charges (Preface Lilac Book 1910).

[written in margin:] It is parents and guardians that have classified fairy-stories <u>Juvenilia</u>.

All the same if we use <u>child</u> in a good sense (it has also legitimately a bad one), we must not let that push us into the sentimentality of only using <u>adult</u> or <u>grown-up</u> in a bad sense (it has also legitimately a good one). The process of growing-up is not necessarily allied to growing wickeder (though the two do often happen together). Children are meant to grow up and to die, and not to become Peter Pans. Not to lose innocence and wonder (which no man need lose save by his own fault, and which he can regain by [illeg]), but to proceed on the appointed journey: that journey upon which it is certainly <u>not</u> better to travel hopefully than to arrive, though we must travel hopefully if we are to arrive. But it is the lesson (if we can use the word of things that do not deliberately teach) of many fairy-stories that on callow, lumpish, and selfish youth peril, sorrow, and the shadow of Death can bestow dignity, and even sometimes wisdom. Let us not divide the human race into Eloi and Morlocks: pretty children (elves as the [7th?] often idiotically called them) with their fairy-tales, and dark Morlocks with their machines. If the fairy-story is worth reading at all a grown-up will (of course) get more out of it than the child. All that is the matter with some fairy-tales it that they are not fit for anybody to read.

We thus come to the most important of questions. What are the values or functions of good fairy-stories now – for grown-ups to read (or even to write) – not necessarily to study. Fairy-stories I should say (in addition to the general value of Literature) offer especially these things[:] Return Fantasy Escape Consolation. (Some of these are often supposed to be bad.) Return being particularly liable to confusion with Fantasy and Escape. It can in any case hardly be dealt with separately.

[in left margin:] Things of which children have much less need than adults.

I will look at the problem from the point of view of someone writing or retelling a fairy-story for this makes it clearer I think.

Fantasy is of two kinds: <u>Mooreffoc</u> or Chestertonian Fantasy, and Creative. <u>Mooreffoc</u> is a queer fantastic word, yet it is can be seen in this island. It is Coffee-room as seen from the inside through a glass door, as it was seen by Dickens in a dark London day; and it was used by Chesterton to denote the queerness of what has become trite when seen suddenly from a new angle.

That kind of fantasy can be wholesome enough, and can never lack for material. ~~Creative Fantasy which I have already alluded to and the allegory of adjectives may seem to be hampered by age.~~

The study of fairy-tales (as distinct from enjoying them) has the disadvantage – it is apt to be depressing. We do soon feel that we are only collecting a few leaves (many now broken and decayed) from the countless foliage of the tall Tree of Tales, with which the Forest of Days is carpeted – but each leaf that has been blown away had a value. It seems vain to add to the litter. We can design no new leaf. The patterns from bud to unfolding, and the colours from spring to winter were all fixed by men of old. But that is not really true. The seed of the Tree can be re-planted in almost any soil, even one so smoke-ridden (as Lang said) as that of England. Spring is not really less fair for being like other springs, and is never quite the same. We need not despair of painting and drawing because there is only red, blue, and yellow, and all lines must be straight or curved. There are many combinations.

The Oxford don who welcomes the proximity of mass-production factories and the roar of a largely mindless traffic because it is a "contact with real life" causes the escapist to laugh. The theory that motor-cars are more living than centaurs or dragons is uncanny; that they are more real (in any sense whatever) than horses is pathetically absurd.

The roof of Paddington Station is not more real than the sky; and as an artifact it is less interesting than the legendary dome of heaven, or the rainbow Bridge of Bifrost guarded by Heimdall with the Gjallarhorn. Much that is called serious literature is no more than play under a glass roof by the side of a municipal swimming-bath. Fairy-stories may invent monsters that fly the air or dwell in the deep, but at least they do not try to escape from Heaven or the Sea.

I do not think the fairy-story reader (or maker) need ever be ashamed of the wild escapism of "archaism" – of preferring not only horses but castles, sailing ships, bows and arrows; not only fairies, but Knights and Kings and priests.

For it is possible – it is at least a show of reason – to defend the condemnation (implicit in the so-called 'escapist' silence in fairy-stories concerning progressive things like bombs, heavy machine guns, tents, factories). The process of urbanization can even by people unconcerned with the fairy-tale be held to be one of degeneration or disease of modern European culture.

"The rawness and ugliness of modern European life is the sign of a biological inferiority, of an insufficient or false reaction to environment. . . . mechanical, industrial civilization will seek to eliminate all waste [and] movements in work and so make the operative the perfect complement (say slave) of the machine: a vital civilization will cause any functions and any acts to partake of (vital) grace or beauty. To a great extent this is entirely instinctive as in the grace of the old agricultural operations, ploughing, sowing & reaping . . . Why is a stock broker less beautiful than a Homeric warrior or an Egyptian priest?" (Christopher Dawson p. 72) Because he is less incorporated with life, he is not inevitable, but accidental almost parasitic (One feels inclined to say less Real.) . . . "So too with dress, the full Victorian panoply of top-hat and frock-coat undoubtedly expressed something essential in the nineteenth century culture, and hence it has spread with that culture all over the world as no fashion of clothing has ever done before. It is possible that our descendants will recognise in it a kind of grim Assyrian beauty, fit emblem of the ruthless and great age that created it; but however that may be, it misses the direct and inevitable beauty that all clothing should have, because, like its parent culture it, was out of touch with the life of nature and of human nature as well." – (indeed with Real Life).

Why should we not escape from (or condemn by silence) the "grim Assyrian" fantasy of Top-hats or the Morlockian horror of machines and the places where they are made. The wildest castle that ever came out of a giant's bag in a Gaelic story is not only a deal more beautiful than a machine-factory: it is also (to use a very modern phrase) "in a very real sense and deal more real". Our silence is not so much Escapism as a refusal to bow unto any person's whim of fashion.

The anti-escapist should beware. The fairy-story may prove not to be Escape but propaganda of another revolutionary kind.

> Sæt secg monig sorgum gebunden
> wean on wenan wyscte geneahhe
> þæt þæs cynerices ofercumen wære.[†]

> Many a man sat chained in sorrow,
> with no hope by woe, and wished often
> that an end had come of that domain

So said a Poet of the tyrant Eormanric.

Of course fairy-stories have to a large extent always had this "escapist" function – and have not only now become "escapist" in the distaste men feel for their own handiwork. There are things more grim and ineluctable to fly from than the stench and ugliness and terribleness of the internal combustion engine. There are hunger, pain, poverty, injustice, Death. But even when we are not facing hard things like these, we see that there are old ambitions and desires to which fairy-stories have offered a kind of satisfaction or consolation. There are pardonable weaknesses or curiosities: such as the wish to visit (free as a fish) the deep sea; or the longing for the flight of a bird – which the aeroplane so cheats (except in rare moments seen high and by distance noiseless turning in the sun, that is precisely when imagined and not used). There are profounder wishes: such as the desire to converse with (or at least eavesdrop on) other living things. On this desire is largely founded the talking of beasts and creatures in fairy-tales or the magic understanding of their speech – rather than our own. This is quite distinct from the beast-fable – which is (of its nature) largely satirical.

So I think, at least – rather than on "confusion" ancient or modern; rather than on "an absence of senses of separation of themselves from beasts" (Andrew Lang Fortnightly Review).[†] A vivid sense of that separation is very ancient; but also a sense that it was a severance. A strange fate and a guilt lies on us. But all living things are at least our step-brethren. Even Frogs. In speaking of that rather odd but widespread fairy-story of the Frogking (der Froschkönig)[*] Max Müller asked in his rather prim way (he was very prim about mythology: a disease less virulent, he said, in modern languages, but the bane of the ancient world): "How came such a story ever to be invented? Human beings were, we may hope, at all times sufficiently <u>enlightened</u> to know that a marriage between a frog and the daughter of a queen was <u>absurd</u>."[†] Indeed we may hope so. For if not, there would be no point in this story at all! We need not let folk-lore origins and beliefs about frogs and wells lie behind this story, the frog-shape is and was preserved in the fairy-story precisely because it was so queer and the marriage so preposterous.

And, of course, in the versions which concern us, Gaelic, German, English, there is in fact <u>no</u> wedding between a princess and a frog: the frog was an enchanted prince. And the point of the story lies not in thinking frogs possible mates, but in the necessity of keeping promises that (together with Prohibitions) runs through all Fairyland since the days of Orpheus.

I knew a boy who used to visit a certain violet that came on a bank in a dell and call it long names lying his face on the grass. I do not think he was confusing that violet with his sisters or his mother; but rather grieved by the fact of that he was suffering from ancestral [memories?]. I think he wished to understand the violet.

And lastly there is the old desire, the <u>Great Escape</u> = the escape from Death. Fairy-stories provide many examples of this. It may be called the genuine escapist, or (I would say) <u>fugitive</u> spirit. But so do other stories, and studies. Fairy-stories are made by human beings not by fairies. (The human-stories of the fairies are probably full of the Escape from Deathlessness.) In any case

---

[*] Campbell xxiii: The Queen who sought drink from a certain Well and the Lorgann; English: The Maid and the Frog; German: Der Froschkönig.

our fairy-stories cannot be expected always to rise above our common level: in fact they often do so rise. Few lessons are taught more clearly in them than the burden of that kind of immortality (or rather endlessly serial Life) to which the Fugitive would fly. For the fairy-story is specially apt to teach such things, of old and still today. Death is the theme that most inspired George MacDonald ~~, whether in fairy-stories such as the Princess and Curdie, or the Golden Key; or in what he called the 'romance' of Lilith.~~

[the following passages are on paper different from the rest, and datable to 1943:]

And another function might be called <u>Escape</u>. I do not use this as a term of scorn (for which its uses outside criticism give no cause). Those who do use it as a term of contempt would seem too often to confuse Escape of the Prisoner (a hard and perilous feat) with the Flight of the Deserter. And also to confuse the Acquiescence of the Quisling with the Diehard patriot of a doomed kingdom. This confused label – to make the confusion worse – they stick not only on to Flight, and on to real Escape but on to Disgust, Condemnation, and Revolt. Not to mention (indeed not to parade) say Electric Street-lamps in your tale is 'Escape' (in the bad sense), though it may in fact derive from a considered disgust for so typical a product of the mechanical and robot age: combining elaboration and ingenuity of means with ugliness, waste, and inferiority of result, it is possible to exclude such things from your Secondary World simply because they are inferior things.

But Electric Lamps have come to stay, they say. Not if the Escapist can persuade you to the contrary. They forget, too, that Chesterton long ago truly said: "As soon as we hear that anything 'has come to stay' we know that it will swiftly be replaced." The Electric Lamp may be ignored, not only for its intrinsic demerits; but because it is so insignificant and transient. (One of the best accidental virtues of good fairy-stories is their love for the fundamental and permanent things.) The

Escapist is not so subservient to the whims of fashion as this is apparent. He does not make real [illeg] his master by worshipping them as 'inevitable'. And that opponent has no guarantee that the Escapist will stop there: he may quite well rouse men to pull down the Electric Lamps.

Once upon a time at the beginning

This is justly typical. See Terrible Head in Blue Fairy Book. It begins Once upon a time. It is Andrew Lang's adaptation of Perseus and Andromeda. It does turn mythology into fairy-story. So in a sense fairy-story is vaguer than mythology. On that side it is debased: just forgetful. But that is not the whole matter. The timelessness (though not the namelessness) is significant. It produces at once a sense of a great uncharted abyss of time, of other worlds and other modes.

Why are fairy-stories fond of these endings?
Partly because they have really a greater [grasper?] on the infinitude of the world of story than modern 'realistic' stories. They need a sharp outline because they set your mind winging through the endless worlds, and your eye straying, and need something to keep their attention on the corner of this antique unended tapestry.

Life of the less changeful kind – humanised. It lies out just beyond the cruel modern world. I was born in a time when it was still recognizable.

[end passages on smaller paper datable to 1943]

But the 'consolation' of fairy-stories, the joy of the happy ending (which is one of the things that fairy-stories can do supremely well) is not necessarily fugitive. For it is not a 'happy ending' in its fairy-tale setting, it is a sudden and miraculous grace – never to be counted on to recur: a fleeting glimpse of joy, Joy beyond the walls of the world, Joy as poignant as sorrow. Even of the phrase (held to be as typical of the end of fairy-stories as <u>once upon a time</u> is of the beginning) – <u>and they lived happily ever after</u>, that is true. It does not deceive anyone, not even children. Such phrases are rather to be compared to the margins and frames of pictures, no more held to the real 'end' of the total Web of Story than the picture-frame is of the visionary scene, on the window-casement of the Outer World. "Who ever does not believe this tale must pay a dollar".[†] "And if they have not gone away, they are there still." "My story is done – see there runs a little mouse; anyone who catches it may make himself a fine fur cap of it." "And when the wedding was over they sent me home with paper shoes on a causeway of pieces of glass." Fairy-stories are fond of such endings, plain or elaborate, as artificial and as necessary as plain frames or gilded.

It is the mark of a good fairy-story of the happy-ending kind that, however wild its events, however fantastic its adventures, it can give to child or man who reads it, when the turn comes, a catch of breath and a beat and lifting of the heart as keen as that given by any form of art, or keener. When that sudden turn comes we get a piercing glimpse of joy or heart's desire: of heart's mending, of joy that can only come after pain – that seems for a moment to pass outside the frame, to rend indeed the very web of story and let a gleam come through:

> "Seven long years I served for thee,
> The glassy hill I clamb for thee,
> The bluidy shirt I wrang for thee,
> And wilt thou not wauken and turn to me?

He heard and turned to her"

"They will not waken and turn to us, our lost loves, our lost chances, for all our service, all our singing, nor for all our waiting, séven or twice seven long years" said Andrew Lang. So spake the man. But the child feels it, too. It is not that such joys have no foundation. They do happen within time, more often than do wicked stepmothers (who are nonetheless founded on fact). But the fairy-story puts them in their real setting.

Even modern fairy-stories can do this sometimes. It is not an easy thing to do and depends really on the whole story which is the setting of the 'turn'. It happens even in Andrew Lang's own (not altogether successful) fairy-story – <u>Prince Prigio</u>. When "each knight came alive and lifted his sword and shouted 'long live Prince Prigio'", the joy has a little of that curious mythical quality, greater than the event described.

Joy can tell us much about sorrow and light about dark but not the other way about. A little joy can often tell more about grief and tragedy than a whole book of unrelieved gloom. The trappings of fairy-stories are not easily come by – each a unique rescue on the edge of a precipice over which mythological ends have fallen

[On smaller paper, probably dating from 1943:]

[on page in light pencil:]
I have already given a hint in calling the 'eucatastrophe' of fairy-story 'evangelium?'

This I say with due reverence and humility – even if what I say has any kind of validity, it is only one of a myriad facets of truth. But I do not think that the Gospels are a fairy-story can be deemed – those who believe can not [illeg illeg] for fairy-stories are not a [title?] of abuse.

Gospels contain 'marvels'—- [illeg] θαυμάσια [thaumasios]: among them the greatest and most complete conceivable 'eucatastrophe' [illeg] the Blessed Ending.

Art—— or rather [illeg] the Christian Story. For the Gospels are not Art: it is the events <u>themselves</u> that show the [illeg] are artistry. ([World?] of books esp. S. John).

The marvels. Marvels, yes. But the marvels are 'primarily' true. Therefore the marvels are true: occurred in history.

Therefore they are 'miracles'. Therefore the teller of the tale (author) and actor (hero) are <u>the same</u> – and knows God.

[on another page in ink:]

Inner consistency and reality and Joy

'Joy' is felt at the 'turn' of a fairy-story. Prob. every Subcreator making a secondary world wishes to be a real maker, or hopes he is drawing on Reality: that the peculiar quality (if not the details) of this Secondary World are derived from Reality, or are flowing into it (?) [*sic*]. How else can one explain that quality denoted in the dictionary definition 'inner consistency of reality', if it does not in some way partake of Reality. Hence the peculiar quality of the Joy: it is a glimpse, or breaking through to the source-reality. N.B. – it is usually caused by a Triumph of Right, of eternal Justice, of Good (or its representatives) over evil (and its representatives).

How else – if one dare put it that way – could God have redeemed the (corrupt) 'making creatures' Men, except in a way suitable to their own kind. The Gospels are fairy-stories – of course they are: they contain marvels, peculiarly artistic, beautiful and moving ones: 'mythical' in their perfect self-contained significance, and yet symbolical and allegorical as well. They have, preeminently, the 'inner consistency of reality'. There is no tale ever told that men would rather find was 'true' in the Primary World. It is not difficult to imagine the peculiar kind of excitement and delight – joy – which you would feel, if any specially beautiful fairy-story were found to be Primarily true: its narrative to be history (without of course thereby losing any allegoric or mythical significance it possessed, indeed intensifying these). One does not need to imagine it. It would have precisely the same quality (if intenser) of joy that the turn in a fairy-story gives – such joy already has the taste of Truth transcending its Secondary World and coming, as it were, up into the Primary. But Christian Joy – Gloria – is of the same kind, only preeminently high, and pure, and great: because the 'story' is supremely great. The greatest artistry has 'come true'. God is the master of angels and of Elves and of Men. Legend and History have fused.

But the presence of the Greatest does not (in God's Kingdom) depress the small. Redeemed Man is still Man. Stories and Fantasies still go on, should go on. The Gospels have not abrogated Legends: they have hallowed them. As they have not abrogated motherhood or fatherhood, or supper. Horses have been ennobled by Pegasus: and still may be. For all we know, indeed we may fairly guess, in Fantasy we may actually be assisting in the evolution of Creation.

[in light pencil:]
Fairy-stories have kept alight the truth; for there the mind is supreme, The March of Science conceivably is inexorable but if they wish to stop it it is not to Science that men will pray.

[End of smaller paper]

To conclude, then, with the last Question. Shall we go on writing them, and how, and for whom? I do not see why we should not go on. The resources of theme and technique are now so rich and varied that the chief danger is that over-refinement which I have spoken of, the turning of russet into mud.

Stories are now written that are quite unclassifiable like <u>The Wind in the Willows</u>: a little of the beast-fable, a little comedy, an ingredient of <u>contes des fées</u> (or even of pantomime), a little satire, and a happy ending. I personally think that in Pan we have that addition of an extra colour that spoils the palate: but it only comes in one corner of the delightful picture.

And the art or industry has never ceased: old stories have been constantly repatched to mend the holes made by forgetfulness; or 'improved' (in good or bad taste); or newly invented, more or less upon old models. That literary and sophisticated touch that treats horror as a grim jest, amusing for itself, can be detected long before Lord Dunsany. According to Andrew Lang it is present in the 'ugsome' incidents of <u>The Youth who set out to</u>

learn what Fear was out of the way of popular tradition. The sugar windows of the witch's house in Hansel and Grettel were added, says Lang, 'by a high-class nurse', quite independently of the influence of the Cabinet des Fées.

But do not let us consider 'children' too closely. We may certainly read or hand our tales to them; but do not let us write only for them, certainly not 'down' to them. They do not like it now, and I do not suppose they ever have liked it; and certainly if they are old enough to enjoy any fairy-story, they are already old enough to detect it. Children prefer adult conversation – when it is not infantile in all but idiom. But being talked down to (even in verbal idiom) is a flavour that they perceive quicker than any 'grown-up', whether it be at home, at school, 'on the air', or on the printed page. The flavour so quickly spreads from the idiom to the thought. We have to beware in talking about fire in a language which we conceive to be fit for children, lest we begin to think about it like a man who is 'going to talk to children'. If we cannot see Fire like a child (or uncorrupted man), that is freshly and mythologically, for ourselves, we should leave fire alone, or at any rate fire in a fairy-story.

I once received a salutary lesson. I was walking in a garden with a small child. I was only nineteen or twenty myself. By some aberration of shyness, groping for a topic like a man in heavy boots in a strange drawing room, as we passed a tall poppy half-opened, I said like a fool: 'Who lives in that flower?' Sheer insincerity on my part. 'No one' replied the child. 'There are Stamens and a Pistil in there.' He would have liked to tell me more about it, but my obvious and quite unnecessary surprise had shown too plainly that I was stupid so he did not bother and walked away.

Five was young for such good sense; but I think (I hope) I should have said much the same at much the same age (at seven at the latest). For I was interested also in the structure and particularly in the classification of plants; and never at any age that I can recall had any interest in 'fairies' that a frivolous adult fancifulness may put to dwell in them. The child certainly later became a botanist, while I have only become (or almost become) a philologist. But neither study bars the gate to Fairyland the Vera Faerien; though they may slam the door on Pigwiggenry, a most spurious imitation.

It remains a sad fact that adults writing fairy stories for adults are not popular with publishers or booksellers. They have got to find a niche. To call their works fairy-tales places them at once as juvenilia; but if a glance at their contents show that will not do, then where are you? There is what is called a 'marketing problem'. Uncles and aunts can be persuaded to buy Fairy Tales (when classed as Juvenilia) for their nephews and nieces, or under the pretence of it. But, alas, there is no class Senilia from which nephews and nieces could choose books for Uncles and Aunts with uncorrupted tastes.

If there were more time, I should like to speak more of modern fairy-stories: revealing, as they do, all the excellencies and defects possible. By modern I mean fairy-stories that were written or re-written in my life-time, or were still new enough to be books natural to give as presents when I was a child. My reading has been very chancy: I have never pursued or collected (heaven forbid!) fairy-stories, I am not a student but an occasional reader of literature. And yet how large is the field! How many hands have been busy on it: Robert Southey, John Ruskin, Charles Kingsley, Knatchbull Huges[s]en, Thackeray, George Macdonald, Andrew Lang – to name only a few at random of the older moderns. The work still goes on.

I should like to linger on E. Nesbit, and consider how Andrew Lang narrowly missed in Prince Ricardo (a bad failure as a story) the triumphant formula of The Amulet. I should like, also, to turn aside in an attempt at the classification (impossible) of Alice in Wonderland and Through the Looking-Glass; or of The Wind in the Willows. This is an almost perfect blend, at the russet stage, of many pigments: beast-fable, satire, comedy, contes des fées (or even pantomime), wild-wood and rivers of Oxfordshire – with just in one corner that colour, too much, the beautiful colour in itself that muddies the exquisite hue. Pan has no business here: at least not explicit and revealed. I should like to record my own love and my children's love of E.A. Wyke-Smith's Marvellous Land of

Snergs, at any rate of the Snerg-element in that tale, and of Gorbo
the gem of dunderheads, jewel of a companion in an escapade. [*]

But in the short time at my disposal I must say something
about George Macdonald. George Macdonald, in that mixture of
German and Scottish flavours (which makes him so inevitably
attractive to myself), has depicted what will always be to me the
classic goblin. By that standard I judge all goblins, old or new.

And beside The Princess and the Goblin, and The Princess
and Curdie, and other things, he wrote shorter fairy-stories,
some with a tone (not at all for their good) of addressing children; some whatever their tone, not at all for children (as
Photogen and Nycteris); and one (I think) nearly perfect tale (in
his kind and style), which is not for children but children do read
it for pleasure: The Golden Key.

Quote [as?] ending from Golden Key p. 146–148

LAND OF SHADOWS LAND OF [SOULS?]

Andrew Lang of the French historical satirical school of the
'domestic history of the palace' kind. Prince Prigio – in spite of
that lack of apt or beautiful name-invention or even devising,
which is (with all the stores of antiquity and of Celtic, Germanic
and [Frankish?] middle age to imbibe or choose from) so usual a
mark of the nursery tale – succeeds. It has of course a Rose and
Ring element. Andrew Lang was very fond of Rose and Ring
and often recommended it. Indeed he made Giglio the ancestor
of Prigio. Its satirical elements are kept at bounds. It has the right
heartbeats at the happy turn. And it has a very neat semi-satiri-
cal semi-magical ending which is much appreciated by myself
and my children. But it has the germ of the many faults which
destroyed Ricardo and still more Tales from the Fairy Court:
Preaching! Worse – too much magic, wishing caps, seven-
leagued boots, invisibility cloaks, magic spy glasses, and much
else. There is also the magic of an altogether wrong kind –
stupidity (stupidity found in how boots on [illeg illeg illeg]

[*] I do not think the name Snerg happily invented, and I do not like the
bogus 'King Arthur' Land across the river.

fetched from the moon) is not the right kind of weight for the bringing down of an earth-[shaking?] monster. Too much real history, Terra Factalis and Terra Mirabilis cannot be arranged in geographical sequence, or their histories chronologically aligned with some place in time. But the interest of Ricardo and his Tales to me is that Andrew Lang was groping for – and only narrowly missed – the triumphant formula which E. Nesbit found in the Amulet and the Phoenix and the Carpet. But he started out not from a real Family but from a Court on the model of the Contes de Fees.

MANUSCRIPT B
MISCELLANEOUS PAGES

[BODLEIAN TOLKIEN MS. 6 FOLIOS 6–8:]

It is difficult to define the borders of that Realm, as they lie today. In the past they have advanced and receded bewilderingly. Essentially <u>Faierie</u> is the land of Wonder; but slowly we have learned to distinguish between the many things that men have called "wonderful": between <u>Miracle</u>, <u>Magic</u>, <u>Marvel</u>, and <u>Mechanism</u>. <u>Faierie</u> is indeed something different from all of these in quality, though at a glance it may resemble each of them in turn. <u>Mechanism</u> has always been rejected when recognized: it has only intruded itself through the charlatanry of the weaker or spurious magicians. The "magic lantern" was never magical, though it may have deceived the ignorant, while it was a novelty.

The <u>Marvel</u> is simply the unfamiliar which we cannot at once classify. In which class a man will tend at [a] guess to place it, depends on his mood, his education, and the prevailing thought of his day. To-day in Western Europe he will usually assume that a "marvel" is due to <u>mechanism</u>, as uncritically and with as wide a margin of possible error, as in other times he would have assumed that it was due to <u>miracle</u> or <u>magic</u>. But a marvel, even a lying and fantastic marvel taken from a traveller's tale, does not as such belong to <u>Faierie</u>: not as long as it is presented or accepted as something actual or possible without magic in this mortal world, in some corner of time or space.

<u>Miracle</u> and <u>magic</u> are not so easy to distinguish from one another. They have in fact only become distinguished by Christian theology. The profundity of the cleavage that separates them both from the merely marvellous, novel, or ingeniously devised seems to establish a close relation between them, that

obscures their radical difference. The <u>miracle</u> produces real effects, and alters either the past or the future or both. It is effected, as a creative or recreative act, only by God, or by the power specifically and for the nonce delegated by God transcendent, outside the World but master of it. It can therefore only be (humanly speaking) good, in purpose and in ultimate effect. It is essentially moral. It is not possible to perform <u>miracles</u>, it is not possible to be the agent for miracles for an immoral purpose, or a frivolous purpose, or for no purpose at all.[*] God performs <u>miracles</u> in answer to prayer, or through the mediation of a person (human or angelic) who is in that particular operation the agent of a specific divine purpose. The power comes from outside the world, and is 'supernatural'.

<u>Magic</u> does not come from outside the world. Magic is the special use (real, imagined, or pretended) of powers that, though they must derive ultimately from God, are inherent in the created world, exterior to God. It may well be as immoral in purpose and as evil in effect as <u>mechanism</u>: it is perhaps protected from being casual and frivolous, as the purposes of <u>mechanism</u> may be, by the nature of the power wielded, and the character and training required for the wielding. It differs thus primarily from 'scientific' operations in the kind of power inherent in the world that is used. A scientific operation consists simply in the arrangement of objects so that the effect of those conjunctions (in themselves inevitable) will be convenient to the contriver. Water will inevitably boil in a kettle over a fire: the scientific operator merely places the kettle there at an appropriate time when he wishes for boiling water. Much of 'magic' has or had a similar appearance. Partly because magicians were also

---

[*] As begins like the one in Wells's miscalled short story.[†] The 'miracles' of legends (for example of Saints) though their object may seem slight, are always clearly distinguished from 'magic' (good or bad) by the ultimately moral object: testimony to God. When not (as most often) performed by God himself in answer to particular prayer, they are as it were an efflorescence of sanctity (the close union of the Saint with God), or performed unsolicited by God in witness of that sanctity.

trying to discover scientific modes of operation, or any modes that would 'get what they wanted'. But in an essentially 'magical' operation the arrangement of objects is not the efficient cause of the result. The spell, the use of numbers, signs and words is often enough mere ritual happening, at most it is supposed in some way to induce or compel the powers that lie behind the appearances of things to exert itself.

Faierie This has no exact modern equivalent. Magic is often used but that is tainted. It stands for Ars Magica, the magician's art, which at best is but a means of exploiting (for good or more often purely personal and therefore evil ends) the power of faierie by a mortal. But in and by faierie fairies live. They do not exploit it. They have their being in it, and all their acts are 'fay'. What then is faierie. Who can say save the philosophers. It is a state wherein will[,] imagination and desire are directly effective – within the limitations of the world. Above all where beauty – of all the three the most magical – is natural and relatively effortless.

Leaving aside the Question of the Real (objective) existence of Fairies, I will tell you what I think about that. If Fairies really exist – independently of Men – then very few of our 'Fairy-stories' have any relation to them: as little, or less than our ghost-stories have to the real events that may befall human personality (or form) after death. If Fairies exist they are bound by the Moral Law as is all the created Universe; but their duties and functions are not ours. They are not spirits of the dead, nor a branch of the human race, nor devils in fair shapes whose chief object is our deception and ruin. These are either human ideas out of which the Elf-idea has been separated, or if Elves really exist mere human hypotheses (or confusions). They are a quite separate creation living in another mode. They appear to us in human form (with hands, faces, voices and language similar to our own): this may be their real form and their difference reside in something other than form, or it may be (probably is) only the way in which their presence affects us. Rabbits and eagles may be aware of them quite otherwise. For lack of a better word they may be called spirits, daemons: inherent powers of the created world, deriving more directly and 'earlier' (in terrestrial history) from the creating will of God, but nonetheless created, subject to Moral Law, capable of good and evil, and possibly (in this fallen world) actually sometimes evil. They are in fact non-incarnate minds (or souls) of a stature and even nature more near to that of Man (in some cases possibly less, in many maybe greater) than any other rational creatures, known or guessed by us. They can take form at will, or they could do so: they have or had a choice.

Thus a tree-fairy (or a dryad) is, or was, a minor spirit in the process of creation who aided as 'agent' in the making effective of the divine Tree-idea or some part of it, or of even of some one particular example: some tree. He is therefore now bound by use and love to Trees (or a tree), immortal while the world (and trees) last – never to escape, until the End. It is a dreadful Doom (to human minds if they are wise) in exchange for a splendid power. What fate awaits him beyond the Confines of the World, we cannot know. It is likely that the Fairy does not know himself. It is possible that nothing awaits him – outside the World and the Cycle of Story and of Time.

But leaving the question apart – faierie as it has been conceived by men, or as it has now become conceived (after much that did not belong to it has been winnowed away) is a state in which will and imagination and desire are directly effective. Since our 'fairy-stories' rarely even pretend to deal with fairies as they are in and for themselves, we can say little or nothing of what use they make or ought to make of faierie; we know chiefly how it affects mortals. Today for various reasons it affects nature mainly on the side of beauty.

faierie a state of being in which the will can more or less directly cause things imagined or desired actually to be, or can at least present them to the senses; and the very immediacy of the operation enhances the quality of the product: beautiful things produced by faierie retain the beauty of the vision that precedes the making; the desirable thing presented by faierie is commensurable with desire or so really satisfying without satiety.

faierie is a state of being in which Will can directly cause things aesthetically imagined or desired to be, present and sensible; and the very immediacy of the operation enhances the quality of the product: beautiful things produced by faierie retain unalloyed the beauty of the vision that precedes the making, the desirable things presented by faierie is commensurable with the desire, and therefore wholly satisfying without satiety. (Indeed we may say that this is so because faierie is a power drawn from the same reservoir as that from which the vision and the desire proceed.)

This is pure faierie unalloyed with evil purpose, and unclouded by doubt or theological suspicion. In fact owing to theological suspicion I am of course not discussing whether such faierie does exist or can exist philosophically or theologically. I am merely attempting to define it as an assumption – the basic assumption of fairy-stories. But fairy-stories come from various periods. Most have come down through Christian apostolic writers. It is philosophical and theological suspicion that has presented faierie as a deception – its products were not 'real' (as in case of miracle) it deceived the senses; and when the illusion was over the senses were undeceived. This 'doubt' at first makes "fairies" all take on a devilish aspect: álfamaer ekki var hún Kristi kaer;[†] lost later as our longing for beauty became stronger than our fear of devils – it has produced that curious wistful evanescent quality of Faierie which is the mark of much modern fairy-story writing. A thing beautiful or desirable happens – vividly 'reality', and yet farther away, without being definitely characterized as 'dream' as illustrated by Mrs. Tiggywinkle.[†]

Our rejection of the diabolical. Less fear. Our great sickness of ugliness, and aimless meaningless 'beauty'. We cannot really conceive of beautiful evil. Hence faierie as an escape from (1) mechanism (2) ugliness. We are not much disturbed by its moral dangers.

It is difficult to define the borders of that realm, as they lie today. They have advanced and receded bewilderingly in the past. Only slowly have we learned to distinguish between the many things that men have called 'wonderful'. Essentially Faerie is the land of Wonder. There all things are either strange, or else seen in a strange light which reveals them (even when their shape is unchanged) as things ominous and significant. In that land a tree is a Tree, and its roots may run throughout the earth, and its fall affect the stars. It is enchanted. And what does that mean? It means, I think, that when we cross the borders of Faerie we believe (or, if our interest is only literary, we put ourselves in the mental posture of believing) that the scientific, measurable, facts and 'laws' of the relationship of things and events are only one aspect of the world. There is a world where things are not so: where will[,] imagination and desire are directly effective.

It is not the Moral Law is in abeyance – it is in fact very much in evidence more plainly revealed./ For what they are effective depends still on the will and the/moral law; but for those things which are indifferent.

Where therefore good and evil are at once arrayed in strange symbolic forms, and nakedly revealed with startling suddenness and clarity; and where beauty (in all its aspects majestic and delicate) is natural, ready to hand of those that wish for it, like the free water of an unfailing spring. In <u>Faierie</u> one can conceive of a demon or ogre that possesses a castle of hideous nightmare shape (for that is his will or nature); but one cannot conceive of a house built with a 'good' purpose – a hospital, an inn or refuge for travellers – being ugly or squalid.

[BODLEIAN TOLKIEN MS. 6 FOLIO 9:]

To me elves are immortal: that is they are the hum[an?]

Elves are in the <u>main</u> (i.e. as they appear in our stories and without prejudice to the question whether <u>fairies</u> really exist – in which case their nature and the plane on which they exist is a subject for investigation independent of nearly all our fairy stories) an effort of human creative impulse: they are made by man in his own image and likeness; but freed from those limitations which he feels most to press upon him. They are immortal, and their will is directly effective for the achievement of their imagination and desire.

> *Gloria in excelsis deo et in terra*
> *pax hominibus bon voluntatis laudamus*
> *te benedicimus te glorificamus te adoramus*
> *te gratias agimus tibi propter magnam*
> *gloriam tuam Domine deus rex cælestis*
> *deus pater omni potens Domine Fili unigente*
> *Iesu Christe Domine deus Agnus dei Filius*
> *patris qui tollis peccata mundi miserere –*
> *nobis que tollis peccata mundi suscipe dep-*
> *recationem nostram qui sedes ad dexteram*
> *patris*[†]

It is not easy to define Faerie or <u>faierie</u>, for many ancient ideas and beliefs have contributed to it, and the sense of the word has shifted and changed. Today it is charged with at least very different kinds of <u>emotion</u> from those that formerly attached to it. This can [illeg] be illustrated by the word <u>enchant</u> which is too often almost emptied of emotion and significance, but has alongside lost its sinister [sound?].

Faerie is essentially the realm of Wonder but we now have slowly learned to distinguish between the many things that [men?] have called wonderful.

[BODLEIAN TOLKIEN MS. 6 FOLIO 10:]

I am not discussing 'magic' in general, nor its origins. I should say to it there is no answer to the question that does not become theological. The peculiar function of magic is a product of a supernatural religion. In essence 'magic' has become power to make <u>imagination</u> effective.

To define <u>magic</u> (in a fairy-tale not an anthropological sense) is not easy. I have said that fairies are not 'supernatural' but rather supra-natural, that is children of the world in which man is but a traveller or sojourner. To this world their 'immortality' binds them. In it and from it they have their being. What then is their 'magical' power. ~~A man (or wizard, for instance) may acquire control over 'magic', but he can not become a 'fairy'. For fairies live and are by virtue of 'magic'.~~ For though one may attempt to establish an opposition between the supernatural (the spiritual) and the elvish (the magical) and the natural: i.e. the normal, the 'humanly possible', the scientifically explicable or credible. How can elves be both natural and magical? For 'magic' is that by which fairies live and have their being: they are creatures of faierie. A man may acquire control of 'magic' and become a wizard but that will not make him a 'fairy'. He may command the services of fairies, but he will remain mortal. I do not know the answer to this. I am, of course, only attempting to deal with the present situation: that is the nature and function of elves and their magic as I perceive them now in European tradition as it has become, and as I think others perceive.

It is difficult to define the bounds of this realm; and I at least know no pass-word or sign post that will tell of itself where the border is crossed. Magic [illeg] for this was indeed one of principal senses of faierie in the Middle Ages. But this magic

It is easier to tell when you are out on the [lakeside?]. On the border there would be Magic (the chief senses of faierie in the Middle Ages), though it will not [illeg] be open as now. But this magic is not merely marvellous: no mechanism or [something?] more [illeg] tricks can [illeg illeg illeg] nor is it the strangeness of a traveller tale (true or lying). For such marvels are conceived as [presented?] or possible in the mortal world in some time or place. The marvels of Faerie are there only, if still, on different plane[s]. They could not be or intrude into tales about human creatures. But from a power or state of existence outside and [illeg] of our mortal world of fact. The uniped however odd cannot be admitted into Fairyland just by his oddity.

This [might?] say that what was once merely 'odd' becomes magical when it is not yet believed in sufficiently (as possible in some time or place). Then it is [illeg illeg illeg] of 'fairy', if it has. It then perishes, or if it has some beauty or significance that is [illeg illeg] to real[m?] of Faerie.

[BODLEIAN TOLKIEN MS. 6 FOLIO 11:]

As such it draws [virtue?] from the well of creative energy that a man feels to lie behind the visible world.

'Fairies' may exist independently of Men. But that is a wholly separate question. Ghosts may really walk but ghost stories are mainly man-made, and reflect a certain philosophy or philosophies concerning human personalities. We can discuss those philosophies largely without reference to the objective truth of individual ghost-stories. So fairy-stories are mainly man-made and reflect a philosophy or philosophies concerning the nature of the world. We can discuss these largely independent of the objective truth of any account of human [illeg] with fairies. The disappearance in 1691 of the Rev. Kirk author of the "Mysterious Commonwealth of Elves and Fairies"[†] hardly concerns the criticism of the contents of Campbell's Popular Tales of the Highlands. There is at any rate no objective evidence for historical [illeg] mortal [illeg] who could produce castles out of their bags. The magic of fairy-stories is a projection of will and desire upon the natural world. The world itself – like [illeg] [minds?] to lessen a horror, to [turn?] [illeg] minds to beaut[y?] and delight. He will [illeg] the magic to no effect. But his [peril?] [illeg] with a word. The makers of fairy-stories believed that [illeg] to what shape by will, and we [illeg illeg]

Magic the power to make the will directly (or more directly) effective. Now "fairies" or faierie has a good or bad aspect because desires may be good or ill. If 'fairies' exist – objectively and quite apart from fairy-stories (which are obviously largely man-made, based on his ideas, and seldom even in convention purporting to be a report of objectively 'true' events) – then we know very little about them. Would that in a separate class all anecdotes or stories that purport to be about <u>real</u> occurrences, i.e., accounts of 'fairies' the object of which to record events. That is things that are not like the Ghost Stories of an Antiquary[†] but are the records of the Psychical Research Society. Nonetheless it is plain that just as literary ghost-stories repose on a definite philosophy or philosophies – and that these have been partly constructed to meet the evidence or supposed evidence for the real occurrence of ghostly phenomenon; so fairy-stories repose on a philosophy or philosophies that are a report or response to the evidence or supposed evidence for fairy phenomenon. If there <u>are</u> ghosts, and if there <u>are</u> fairies, the philosophies of ghost stories and of fairy-stories must to a certain extent cover <u>ghosts</u> and <u>fairies</u>. We still see that man has [illeg] come to realize that the desires to overcome the limitations on his will and imagination may be both good and ill. Art is the most legitimate form of 'escape'. Only in a fairy-story can lead be turned into gold without serious damage. There are certain profound desires – desires to know and share the [long?] [experience?] of other living things (like trees, birds, beasts) – that are good. Magic is evil when it is sought as a means of personal power (especially over our fellows). Hence the sinister light on wizards and witches. The good wizard is a servant not a master.

[BODLEIAN TOLKIEN MS. 6 FOLIO 12:]

It is difficult to define the boundaries of this realm, even as they exist today: they have advanced and receded bewilderingly in the past. I find myself obliged to say that when you are over the border you will find <u>faierie</u>, though it may not be open or narrow. What is the <u>faierie</u> in which and by which <u>fairies</u> have their being? Magic is the nearest modern equivalent, but that word is dangerous to use, because it has chiefly been used for the operations of mortal men (magicians), and has thus become burdened with all the evil of their purposes, and all the deceit and trickery of their practices. The magic lantern is not <u>magical</u> whatever fear and wonder it may have excited in the ignorant when it was a novelty. It would be magical only if there were no lantern. <u>Faierie</u> can hardly be [clearer?] defined than the hidden controlling powers of nature which the magician tried or pretended to use, but in which and by which fairies have their actual being. (In our garbled tales, often by stupid people, <u>fairies</u> may behave like magicians [illeg] spells and waving wands but clearly this is untrue: they can vanish or appear at will; leaves and gold are [commonplace?] terms to them.)

It is difficult to define the boundaries of this realm. What is <u>faierie</u> or 'magic' to use the nearest modern equivalent. (It need not be a good thing – the virtue of fairy in fairy-stories does not depend on.) I have said that fairies are not super-natural but rather supra-natural, that is children of the world in which man is only a traveller or a sojourner. To this world their "immortality" binds them: in it and from it they have their being. How then are they 'magical', <u>of faierie</u>? For though one may now clearly (as always intuitively) perceive the distinction between <u>supernatural</u> (the spiritual) and the <u>fairy</u> (the magical), there is at first sight also a wide difference between the <u>magical</u> and the <u>natural</u> – i.e. the normal, the humanly possible, the scientifically explicable or credible. How can <u>faierie</u> be both <u>natural</u> and <u>magical</u>. (In the Middle Ages <u>natural magic</u> excluded the invocation or use of 'spirits', but included operations whose efficacy depended on occult power – occult sometimes only because the scientific relation of cause and effect was not yet understood; but also <u>occult</u> because it depended on the use or tapping of the underlying powers of nature.)

[BODLEIAN TOLKIEN MS. 6 FOLIO 13:]

It is difficult to define the borders of this realm. They have shifted many times in the past. First of all we must here leave out of consideration the question whether <u>fairies</u> really exist – objectively, independent of man, or of tales (which in any case are largely inventions) about them. Just as we could define a ghost-story with reference to the genre (and the ideas therein contained) without discussing the nature of human personality, death, and immortality.

The characteristic of Fairyland is <u>faierie</u>. What is this? Now if we were discussing the real objective existence of <u>fairies</u> we should find the answer to this question difficult perhaps (like the answers to what is <u>life,</u> <u>death</u>, <u>mind</u>, <u>matter</u>) but relatively simple. Since we are discussing what is <u>faierie</u>, the common atmosphere, and one might say the very life, and medium of living and acting, of Fairy-stories we are faced with the fact that these stories contain an immense mass of <u>Wonders,</u> which depend on very ancient philosophies. (Many of them were never devised to fit with any philosophy of the actual or possible, but are sheer flights of human creative Fancy.) I can only discuss (therefore) what this atmosphere of <u>faierie</u> is now (in Western Europe and to me in particular!) <u>Faierie</u>, of course, is often used in the Middle Ages in senses closely similar to our <u>Magic</u>. But the two things cannot here be regarded as synonymous.

> Power
> Beauty
> Zauberfluidum[†]

Sanctus sanctus dominus deus sabaoth[†]

[BODLEIAN TOLKIEN MS. 6, FOLIO 13, SMALL PAPER, VERSO:]

Zauberfluidum Brahman R.t.a. Wakan Orenda[†]

It is not easy to define the borders of this realm. But once you cross over you will find <u>faierie</u>: I adopt this medieval word (<u>the ancestor of our fairy</u>) for lack of a better one. We need some word to describe the essential principle of Fairyland as it now is felt by us, not as was understood or conceived in the various periods and according in the various stages of belief out of which Fairy-stories or elements in them have descended to us.

'Magic' by which the modern and [even?] [illeg] often has [illeg illeg] us: from several reasons (its use in anthropology some) the chief is that it is shut from <u>ars magica</u> Magic art and this primarily refers to the attempt of mortals (of magicians) to control [and] use the power for their own ends, and is tainted with the evil of their purposes and their charlatanry and deceit.

In essence <u>faierie</u> is the occult power in nature behind the usable and tangible appearances of things which may tend or pretend to tap, but in which and by which fairies have their being. In origin the belief in this power is an early stage in religious and philosophical thought, but in a [rend.?] especially that in [northern?] Europe of the proper in religious and moral thought and is come to be [in] opposition with religion – fairies have thus acquired a diabolical aspect.

te deum laudamus te dominum confitemur te aeternum patrem omnis terra veneratur tibi omnes angeli tibi caeli et universi potestates tibi cherubim et seraphim incessabili voce proclamant[†]

[BODLEIAN TOLKIEN MS. 6 FOLIO 14:]

And so, I suppose, even Travellers' Tales that use only the lesser magic of Other Place, not the greater of Other Time, may draw near the borders.

But Swift did not try to work this enchantment. The Lilliputians are small mainly to be comic, futile, or despicable. If I chose one of Gulliver's travels for a 'fairy-story', I should choose (or adapt) Brobdingnag. Not so much because Giants are in the tradition, as because of Gulliver's adventures as a <u>small</u> creature in the great grass and corn, in the great marshes, flies and frogs. This approaches to a fairy-story satisfaction: of the desire to know what the world feels like to, say, a field mouse.

So a visit to another planet, a journey to the Stars. Or even if the Other Place is not so remote, it may report something desirable in the faiërian mode – largely aesthetic. Even extreme delicacy and fineness may have an enchanting quality. But Swift did not try to

The Recovered Thing is not quite the same as the Thing-never-lost. It is often more precious. As Grace, recovered by repentance, is not the same as primitive Innocence, but is not necessarily a poorer or worse state.

[BODLEIAN TOLKIEN MS. 6 FOLIO 15:]

It is difficult to define the boundaries of this realm, for they advance and recede <u>bewilderingly</u>. I at least know of no password or signpost that will announce infallibly when the border is crossed. It is easier to tell when you are certainly on the hither side. Over the border there will be <u>magic</u>, though it will not always be open or named. But this <u>magic</u> is not the merely marvellous: no mechanism or conjuring-trick can achieve it; nor is it the same as the strangeness of a traveller's tale (false or true). For such marvels are conceived or presented as possible in this mortal world, in some time or place. The marvels of Faerie are true, if at all, only on a different plane. They exist, and intrude into the lives of human creatures, in virtue of a power and state existing outside and independent of our private and peculiar mortal limitations. The uniped, however odd, cannot be admitted into Fairyland merely because of his oddity. A crocodile is strange indeed, and still more a Jurassic monster (as depicted); but he remains in Zoology and cannot enter where the dragon goes, unless a spell is laid upon him, so that becomes more than crocodile and has personality and significance.

One of the chief senses of <u>faierie</u> in the Middle Ages.

One might say that what was merely <u>strange</u> becomes <u>magical</u> when it is no longer believed in scientifically (as possible or true in some time or place). It then either perishes, or if it has some beauty or <u>significance</u>, it is gathered into the realm of Faerie. But to say that the marvellous, the strange, the odd or unfamiliar <u>becomes magical</u> (after belief is withdrawn) if it is <u>significant</u> begs several questions. I can almost hope to suggest some answers to these questions: how does it become so? Why is it not merely forgotten? What is the <u>significance</u> that gains entrance to Faerie?

[BODLEIAN TOLKIEN MS. 6 FOLIO 16:]

But his magic is not merely the "nameless: [a smudged and illegible line]"
    When 'fairies', or other inhabitants of Faerie appear in fairy-stories wholly about 'fairies' (or their remoter relatives) a small part of their content: so much that often do not appear at all. Such stories are indeed rare and seldom good. Most good fairy-stories are about men, women, and children and

<u>about Fairies</u> or <u>about</u>

It is difficult to define the bounds of this realm and I at least can offer no exact formula or sure signpost. Magic (even if not explicitly named) is one of the tokens by which you shall know it: Most of our fairy-stories are about the men who in the presence of the marvellous: but the marvels must not be primarily those of strangeness they must be also about a [test?] of enchantment; of beauty that intrudes whether mortal eyes [would?] [illeg illeg]

[BODLEIAN TOLKIEN MS. 6 FOLIO 17:]

It is difficult to define the boundaries of that realm, as they lie today. They have advanced and receded bewilderingly in the past. Only slowly have we learned to distinguish between <u>miracle</u>, <u>magic</u>, <u>marvel</u> and <u>mechanism</u>; and to feel that <u>faierie</u> is something different from them all, in quality, though superficially it may resemble each in turn. <u>Mechanism</u> was always dismissed when recognized: it only intrudes because of the charlatanry of magicians. The 'magic lantern' was never magical though it may have deceived the ignorant when it was a novelty. The <u>marvel</u> is simply the unfamiliar which we cannot at once place. In which class a man will tend to place it at guess, pending the discovery of further evidence, depends on his temperament, his mental training, and the prevailing culture in which he lives. Today in Western Europe he will assume that this is due <u>mechanism</u>, or uncritically and with as large a possibility of error as in other times he would have assumed that it was due to <u>miracle</u> or <u>magic</u>. <u>Miracle</u> and <u>magic</u> are the most easily confused: the profundity of the cleavage that separates them from the merely marvellous, novel or ingenious (but explicable), establishes a relation between them, which obscures their own profound difference. This difference is theological and philosophical. The miracle produces real effects and alters both past and future: it is affected only by God or by a power directly proceeding from God transcendent, outside the world and yet ruler of all. It can therefore only be Good (viewed from a human standpoint) in purpose and in effect; it is essentially moral. It cannot be reduced or perverted to any lesser purpose. Were it possible (as it is not) to perform a miracle for an immoral or even a frivolous object (that is by a person who was not precisely in that particular operation the agent of a specific Divine Purpose wholly absorbed in the will of God) it would become a mere act of magic.

Magic in evil hands may counterfeit or seek to counterfeit Marvels.

Magic does not come from outside the world: it uses (or pretends to use) powers that must of course theologically considered derive ultimately from God, but which are inherent in the world as created, external to God. It differs thus only from scientific power – which may be used well or ill for selfish or diabolical ends or for unselfish and moral ones – in the kind of power inherent in the world that is used. Whether we believe in the objective [criteria?] of the occult powers which magic uses or seeks to use, we must if we are to discuss even the literary effect of 'magic' in a story, seek to understand what they are supposed to be. It may be as immoral in purpose and effect as mechanism or scientific operation. Frequently its effect was thought of as unreal – that is as not actually altering past or future, but as producing illusion (though often as a particular kind of illusion that would submit to all normal tests of objective facts). Thus phantom and faierie could be equalled. Yet the head of [a] fairy 'phantom' was solid, had weight, and could drip blood that could be felt, and all present would experience the same impressions. It would not fade like a dream, but had to be set on its own plane (or in its superior supernatural one).

Faierie is the underlying power that the magician only taps or pretends to tap. On this theory it exists in itself – independent of the magician and of what may be found to be by the wickedness or chicane. Fairies exist in faierie and whether they are diabolical or angelic hardly affects the question. The question is (for some) whether faierie exists independent of man, or whether it is creation. Today we feel less strongly the diabolical; and that is because we are less frightened. Not wholly for good reasons. Good is the result of a supernatural religion, and are understanding of the awe and terrible sanctity of miracles. Since Europe became Christian the thought expressed in Beowulf concerning the ogre Grendel has lifted a shadow of fear: þaet waes yldum cuþ þaet hìe ne moste þa Metod nolde se scyn-scaþa under sceadu bregdan[†] "Men knew that the dangerous ogre could not draw them under shadow, if God willed it not." But we are also less frightened of exterior evil, because of the vast evil that we have brought out of ourselves, because religion has protected us so long that we are only just being [open?] to feel its shadow: science (so noble in origin and original purpose) has produced in alliance with sin nightmare horrors and perils of the night before which the giants and demons grow pale. And sick as we are of these horrors, we are still more sick because of the ugliness of our own work, because this meets us not only in moments of crisis and panic, but at every turn of the daily path, slowly grinding all that is fair into a squalor more ruthlessly and ineluctably than a dragon.

[BODLEIAN TOLKIEN MS. 6 FOLIO 18:]

It does not spare the trees nor the hills nor the houses from which first we learned the meanings of these words: it defiles the very sea.

We feel more strongly therefore a kinship between evil and ugliness, and the alliance between beauty and evil (which at times so terrified men of other times) seems to us hardly possible, or a danger wholly remote compared with the rising tide of ugliness. Thus <u>faierie</u> to us is essentially the power to achieve beauty (a magic related to the mystery of art) or to achieve desires more gentle and wholesome than those proved by mechanized science: as talking to animals, or flying like birds. At its very lowest this 'magic' of fairyland achieves the things purposed by mechanism without its disgusting consequences. Our magic carpet or flying trunk may have no object rather than that of the aeroplane – to get quickly from place to place, or to drop death on an enemy, for instance – but it will perform these objects more efficiently (without the unreliable fragility, the ghastly noise, the uncouth and comparative slowness of the aeroplane) but above all without the horror of the aeroplane factory. That seems to us so great a superiority that we do not always sufficiently reflect that the evil that machines have wrought is proceeds from the same moral errors as those that perverted magic. Machines and magic may both be merely "improved means to deteriorated ends":

both have an inherent tendency when use[d] by mortals to deteriorate the ends. But in <u>faierie</u> we are not concerned with 'ends': there magic exists in its own right as the principle of being and action: I do not mean that there is no moral law. The same moral law runs throughout the universe. Fairies are wicked if their purposes are wicked: but it is not wicked or even foolish for them to use magic as it may be for a man. <u>Fairy-stories</u> which are mainly about men women and children are full of morals.

What is this <u>faierie</u>? It reposes (for us now) in a view that the normal world, tangible visible audible, is only an appearance. Behind it is a reservoir of power which is manifested in these forms. If we can drive a well down to this reservoir we shall tap a power that can not only change the visible forms of things already existent, but spout up with a boundless wealth forms of things never before known – potential but unrealized.

[BODLEIAN TOLKIEN MS. 6 FOLIO 19:]

mechanical success) into this quasi-magical secondary world, a further fantasy or magic is to demand, as it were, an inner terti-ary world. It is a world too much.

For this very reason – that the characters and even the places are in Drama not imagined but actually seen – Drama is, even though it uses a similar material (words, verse, plot), of all the arts the one actually most rem[aining?] an art fundamentally dif-ferent from narrative art. Thus, if you prefer Drama, as so many 'literary' critics seem to do, or are dominated by the excellencies of Shakespeare, you are apt to misunderstand pure story-making, and to measure its aims and achievement by the limita-tions of plays.

I have often thought that something can be learned from chil-dren in this respect. Children are, as I have said, probably not more susceptible to secondary belief than adults; but they may be, by lack of experience or by mis-instruction,[*] more liable to confuse secondary worlds (especially when suddenly presented in a blaze of light and living, speaking, much more frequent than their fright at books or stories, may thus be due to these among other causes:

<u>The visible and audible material</u> of Drama is too strong for their natural, and unsurfeited artistic sense. They do not take what they see as Art, but as the Primary World; or (if properly instructed) they start by taking what they see as a Secondary World, and are overcome: they suddenly fear that they are mistaken (or have been deceived). And that is in itself frightening, whether the actual events seen be alarming or not. Adults would feel the same, on evidence sufficient to convince their wider experience. They would be upset and alarmed (and not only by their personal peril), if a gangster on the stage suddenly turned and fired on the audience. It must be a peculiarly horrible experience to be present, as can happen, when the audience suddenly realizes that the droll or idiot in the play is a man who has truly become insane.

<u>They dislike confusion of worlds.</u>[**] Small children are often frightened, if a character – even one that they love on the stage – comes off the stage to speak to them. This offence against artistic decency is becoming increasingly common; so much so that many children are now inured to it. It is a lamentable habit, ruinous of what good fun there may be in plays for children or for anybody.

---

[*] The language used by adults to young children is often calculated to make them think that they are <u>really</u> going <u>to see</u> primary fairies, or ogres, or what not at a pantomime.

[**] Seen very commonly in the dislike children (especially boys) have for the intrusion of the home upon the school-world, and vice-versa.

[BODLEIAN TOLKIEN MS. 6 FOLIO 20:]

omitted between 33 & 34 [Cf. page 237]

But of course, wondering whether they are (or have been) such things, or wishing that there could be such things, or even believing that there are such things as elves, dragons, giants, magicians or policemen, was quite different from believing in any particular account of them. I preserve to this day an open mind about the existence in history of these things, concerning which there are so many garbled and ill-invented tales.

I perceive now that there is fair evidence for the existence of magicians (if not for their claims), and even better evidence for policemen, though I never saw one or the other in early childhood. But the romances that have gathered round these potent beings I now find are largely incredible: many are the inventions of people with little or no direct knowledge of the creatures, drawing on older books and their own fancy. The same is true of fairies.

Comment on p. 42 [Cf. note F, page 82]

Drama can, of course, be made out of the impact upon particularly human characters of some event of fantasy or faerie. But this is not fantasy in dramatic result, but character-study, no different in essential quality from drama made out of the sudden invasion of human lives by strange or rare events of a 'possible' kind: lightning, a comet, an eruption, or the sudden acquisition of great wealth. Or it should be so. By the dramatic form the human characters hold the stage, and it is upon their fate, joy or suffering, that the spectator's attention is concentrated.

Stories telling how men and women have disappeared and spend years with the fairies in which they grew no older and did not know of the passing of time in the mortal world, are well-known, and are (inevitably) tragic or horrible: in so far as they affect the victim. But in the stories the 'fantasy' also exists for its own sake, with all its general and abstract implications. In <u>Mary Rose</u> Barrie made a play on this theme: Successful in the sense that no machinery was required, and the fantastic events were by his art made 'credible'. But nothing whatever is done with the horrible suffering inflicted upon the rest of the family. It is as if Barrie, expending his art upon making a Celtic fantasy credible in the centre of the stage, had ignored the human torment going on in the wings. The play is diabolic, or at least it can only stand as a diabolic drama: that is, if an interpreter or producer says: "Yes, the sufferings of the characters are the thing, watch them squirm and die; the fairies do not matter, except as being malicious, and inhuman: no explanations given, there aren't any." So it was presented when I last saw it. Mary Rose walked out finally to a summons of the same elvish tone as those which had called her away before. But not so Barrie. With characteristic shirking of his own dark issues, in the printed play there is at the end a sentimental falling star, and the calling voices are angelic. Why? Why at all? Why at any rate only for Mary Rose? On any interpretation realistic, symbolic or allegorical, charming and elvish child as she may have been, she is not the natural dramatic centre of the play, and she the least deserving of such (in this story) inappropriate mercy. This is the woodcutters rescuing Red Riding Hood from Perrault's ferocity, and as they it comes too late.

[BODLEIAN TOLKIEN MS. 6 FOLIO 21:]

note to p. 42 [Cf. note F, page 82]

Drama can, of course, be made out of the impact upon human characters of some event of Fantasy or Faerie, that requires no machinery, or that can be assumed or reported to have happened. But that is not Fantasy in dramatic result; it is character-study, not differing in essential quality from drama made out of the sudden invasion of human lives by strange events of a 'possible' kind: lightning, volcanic eruption, the loss or gain of great wealth, the blinding of the eyes. By the dramatic form the human characters hold the stage, and it is upon their joy or suffering, victory or defeat, that attention is concentrated. If the

Fantasy is taken seriously – it may be degraded to mere comedy – it must become allegory, or devilry. Since Barrie was successful in making the Fantasy credible, the result leaned inevitably to the diabolic, but characteristically he shirked or sought to shirk his own dark issues, both in <u>Dear Brutus</u> and in <u>Mary Rose</u>.

Stories telling how men and women have disappeared and spent years among the fairies, without noticing the passage of time or themselves appearing to grow older, are well known and usually tragic or horrible, in so far as the human victims are concerned. But in the stories not only the human characters are presented, and the Fantasy also exists for its own sake: the Fairies are in themselves interesting; and indeed their effect upon mortals is often only a way of indicating the strange powers of Faerie, and its mode of being. In <u>Mary Rose</u> Barrie made a play on this theme, but no fairies were seen. Horrible suffering was inflicted on all those who loved Mary Rose, but with this accumulating dramatic stuff nothing was done. It was as if Barrie, expending his art in making a notion of Celtic fantasy 'credible' in the centre of the stage, had ignored and enchanted with his elvish heroine, had simply ignored the torment in the wings. Taken as a diabolic drama it is moving: that is, if the producer says: 'the sufferings are just cruel, valueless, purposeless; the Fairies do not matter, except as being inhuman and malicious; no explanations are given, there are none'. That at least is a theory. But not so Barrie. When I last saw the play, Mary Rose walked out finally to a summons of the same elvish tones as those which had called her away before. But not so Barrie. In the printed play there is at the end a sentimental falling star, and the calling voices are angelic. Why? Why at any rate for Mary Rose? On any interpretation, realistic, fantastic, or allegorical, charming and elvish child as she may have been, her ghost is the least deserving of such (in this play) inappropriate mercy.

But Barrie's mercy may have been: they suffered and died – that is human fate, and God's redress beyond the grave is not now my concern. But even for those entangled in 'Faerie', pinned in a kind of ghostly deathlessness to the earth God will grant release in the end.

[BODLEIAN TOLKIEN MS. 14 FOLIOS 22–3:]

Conjuring (in the modern sense) is an interesting special case. It differs, of course, from Art in that its effects are used for their own sake, not for an artistic purpose. Even if the conjuring show employs a 'story', this is a mere frame-work. Conjuring may be a kind of bogus wizardry: ~~as its~~ that is the conjurer's object may be to obtain 'primary belief'; he may be a charlatan trying by trickery to get money out of the credulous; he may be trying, by machinery or legerdemain, to create the belief that he has <u>magical</u> powers. It is possible that nearly all 'wizards' (in the Primary World, not in stories) were and are conjurers in this sense. In modern times, perhaps at all times in proportion as the conjurer was an 'artist', or more an artist than a cheat, he may have a different object, one allied to the making of puzzles or of detection-stories: to make play between <u>basic disbelief</u> and <u>apparent reality</u>, so as to pose the question: how was it done? The real applause from an intelligent audience would come, if they were in the end told how it was done; and that applause would increase in proportion as the effects were 'convincing' and the means of deception simple. Conjuring will never wholly escape from charlatanry and become a pure if minor amusement-art, like detection-stories, until revelation in a final scene is a normal part of the entertainment.

The N.E.D. under FANTASY notes in as Sense 4, which is the same as that of Imagination, is in early use not clearly distinguished from Sense 3: delusive imagination, hallucination – 'an exercise of poetic imagination being conventionally regarded as accompanied by belief in the reality of what is imagined'. I do not know whether this convention ever really existed. There was a convention that a narrative-poem recounted either a 'history' or a 'dream'.

Note on Internal Combustion Engine. p 56. [Cf. paragraph 96, page 73]

This curious device, in its motor-car form, affords some pleasures, either minor and inferior, or druglike and obsessive. It may have some practical uses, though one suspects that these consist rather in alleviating problems whose radical cure lies elsewhere; and certainly from the supposed profits a multitude of new problems and disadvantages have to be deducted. But the motor-car is, essentially a mechanical toy that has run off the nursery-floor into the street, where it is used as irresponsibly as before and much more dangerously. It is a dubious piece of 'escape mechanism'. For of course it would not be made in 'mass' (which means that it would hardly be made at all), nor would millions be made out of its purchasers, but for its invention at a time when we have made our towns horrible to live in – a process which it has itself accelerated. The motor-car attracts, because it enables people to live far away from their noisome and inhuman 'works', or to fly from their depressing dormitories to the 'country'. But it cheats: for the motor-factories, and their subsidiaries (garages, repair-shops, and pumps), and the cars themselves, and their black and blasted roads, devour the 'country' like dragons. This is the splendid gift of a magician: he offers to a caged bird that has defiled its cage and perch – what? a little length of chain so that it can flap to a near-by twig and foul that. Magnificent! This is freedom! And to make the chain hundreds of the magician's prisoners sweat like morlocks. This is the Real Life that is so beneficial to the University of Oxford. It might seem simpler to clean the bird-cages.

As for the aeroplane, that has been even more unfortunate. It was fledged just in time to be baptized in blood, to become a chief exemplar in our time of the dreadful potency of Original Sin. Clumsy and, in spite of its growing complexity, inefficient machine, in comparison with its high object, it has taken the menacing shape not of birds but of fish-like or saurian monsters, and it defies and overrides all privacies, and scatters over all quietudes the deadly roar of its parent den; at unawares it may fall in ruin on the frail houses of men, burning and crushing them at play, or by their hearths, or working in their gardens. This 'in peace'. War it has raised to a mass-production of slaughter. Yet a man – yes, in the middle of this war – trotted out this argument to me: 'You can talk', said he, 'but if your child was dangerously ill, and the only specialist was in America, you would be only too glad to use a plane'. That dates it: a little earlier the specialist lived in Vienna. So to save the life of that hypothetical child by the supposed skill of an imaginary specialist (who might not succeed), hundreds of thousands of men, women, and children, are to be blown to rags and burned, and half the remaining beautiful things of saner centuries with them. It would seem rather more economical to have a few more doctors more handily placed. I would be too brutally 'realistic' to suggest that the poor child must die, if it can only be saved by a machine with so terrible a potential of murder. It is all right if it is done by a machine. It might be regarded as odd if I sacrificed even one other man on an altar to gain the favour of the gods.

The question to be asked, of course, is not "Would you try to save your child's life by using an aeroplane now – in a situation that you did not make or will?"; but "Would you will such a situation to save your child's life?" The answer to the first question is: yes, let Moloch bring doctors for once, if he can. The answer to the second is just: no.

[BODLEIAN TOLKIEN MS. 14 FOLIO 24:]

them as tales, not <u>studies</u> them as a collector's item. Adults are allowed to study anything: even old theatre-programmes, and paper-bags. ~~I could say, I should like to say, a great deal on this topic, but I must at this time be content with brevity, though that to achieve it I must be dogmatic.~~

Fairy-stories have often been relegated to children like old-fashioned furniture to the play-room. But there is no more essential connexion between children and fairy-stories than between children and linoleum. Children do not specially like them, that is they do not (as children) like them or understand them more than adults do, or more than they like other things. Fairy-stories may be specially written for children; but so may music, verse, novels, botany and history. And that is a dangerous process. It is indeed saved from disaster only by the fact that the arts and sciences are not as a whole 'relegated to the nursery'; the 'nursery' is merely given such tastes of the adult thing as seem fit for it in adult opinion (often grossly mistaken). Any one of these things, or any one of their branches, would, if left altogether in the nursery, become irreparably damaged. So would a beautiful table, cast off in some foolish change of taste or fashion, probably be defaced or broken, if long left unregarded in a schoolroom. Fairy-stories banished in this way would in the end be ruined; indeed in so far as they have been so banished, they have been ruined.

If there was an essential connexion between fairy story and the nursery, then talented children who early show a bent for writing should most often try first to tell or write a fairy story, and should in any case more often succeed in that form than in others.

But this is not what happens. Talented children seldom try to write fairy-stories, even when they have been provided with many models; and if they do, they fail, more obviously in this form than in any other. The making of fairy stories – even of those written for (not down to) ~~children — is in fact a peculiarly adult activity: it is best left to poets, bankers, logicians, philologists, and the clergy.~~

If children as a whole have any special leaning, it is to Beast-fable (which many adults confuse with fairy story). The better stories of children that I have seen have been either realistic (in intent), or have as their characters animals and birds who ~~show~~ are in the main the zoomorphic human beings usual in Beast-fable. But I imagine that is so often selected primarily because it allows a large measure of realism: the representation of domestic events and conversation that children really know. The form itself is suggested or imposed from without: it has at any rate a curious preponderance in the 'literature' (good and bad) that is nowadays presented to the nursery, and it is reinforced by the bears and rabbits that have in recent times almost ousted the human dolls even from the play-rooms of little girls. Children make up long sagas about their dolls. If these are shaped like bears, bears will be the characters of the saga – in shape; but they will speak and behave like 'People'.

The connexion between children and fairy stories is thus, I believe, accidental, of the same kind as their connexion with many other things, battered, out of fashion, or forgotten in attics and lumber-rooms. That is why collections of fairy stories are now like the lumber-rooms: their contents are disordered and often defective; a jumble of different times, purposes, and tastes; and among them may occasionally be found a thing of permanent virtue (undamaged or at least recognizable), which only stupidity would ever have cast aside. Then the child is fortunate, but the credit is seldom due to the grown-ups.

Andrew Lang's famous collections are not perhaps lumber-rooms. They are more like stalls in a rummage-sale. Someone with a duster and a pretty good eye for things that retain value, has been round the lumber-rooms. His collections were, of course, partly a by-product of his adult researches in mythology and folklore. But he intended them for children; and as he was both intelligent and interested in children he did not do this without reason. Some of the reasons he gives are worth considering.

[BODLEIAN TOLKIEN MS. 14 FOLIO 25:]

traditional Scottish tales from Chambers' <u>Popular Traditions of Scotland</u>, (<u>The Black Bull of Norroway</u> and <u>The Red Etin</u>). There is one surprising inclusion: <u>A Voyage to Lilliput</u>.[*] I may

---

[*] It may be noted that in its main matter this might be called a 'pantomime selection'. For among what are still the most usual pantomime titles: <u>Cinderella</u>, <u>Red Riding Hood</u>, <u>Puss-in-Boots</u>, <u>The Sleeping Beauty</u> are from Perrault; <u>Aladdin</u> and <u>The Forty Thieves</u> are from <u>The Arabian Nights</u>; while <u>Jack and the Beanstalk</u>, <u>Dick Whittington</u>, and <u>The Babes in the Wood</u> are English. Nearly all these are actually in the blue book. Among the pantomime titles <u>Robinson Crusoe</u> is an intruder, but no more so than <u>A Voyage to Lilliput</u> in Lang's collection.

have shirked defining a 'fairy story', but I will nonetheless assert that this at any rate is <u>not</u> one, neither as its author made it, nor as it appears 'condensed' by Miss Mary Kendall. It cannot be included just because Lilliputians are small, even diminutive – the only way in which they are at all remarkable; for smallness is in Fairyland as in our world just an accident. Pygmies are no nearer to fairies than are Patagonians. I do not rule out this story because of its satirical intent: there is satire, sustained or intermittent in many indubitable fairy stories, and it may have often been intended in traditional tales where we do not now perceive it. I rule it out because, apart from the satire, it belongs to the class of travellers' tales, concerning the marvellous and unusual things which may be seen in this mortal world. It has no more right of entry than the yarns of Baron Munchausen; or than, say, <u>The First Men in the Moon</u> or <u>The Time Machine</u>. Indeed, for the Eloi and the Morlocks there would be a better case than for the Lilliputians. Lilliputians are merely men peered down at (sardonically) from the height of a house-top. Eloi and Morlocks live far away in an abyss of time so deep as almost to work an enchantment; and if they are descended from ourselves, it may be remembered that an ancient English thinker once derived the <u>ylfe</u>, the very Elves, from Adam through Cain.[*] So much for the mere marvels of distant space and time. There are other types of tale that I would exclude from the title 'fairy story', certainly not because I do not like them: namely pure 'beast-fables'. I will choose on purpose an example from Lang's Fairy Books: <u>The Monkey's Heart</u>, a Swahili tale which is given in the <u>Lilac Fairy Book</u>. It tells of a wicked shark who tricked a monkey into riding on his back, and carried him half way to his own land, before he revealed the fact that the Sultan of that country was sick and needed a monkey's heart to cure him. But the monkey outwitted the shark: he induced the shark to return to the monkey's land by convincing him that he had left his heart hanging there in a bag on a tree.

[*]   <u>Beowulf</u> l. 112

The beast-fable has, of course, a connexion with fairy stories because, among other reasons, beasts and birds and other creatures can often talk as men in undoubted fairy stories. The magical understanding by men of the <u>proper</u> language of birds or beasts is quite another matter, a far more genuine element of Faerie to that I return later. But where no human being is concerned; or where the animals (as animals, not as enchanted shapes) are the heroes and heroines, and men and women are only adjuncts wherever the animal form is, in fact, only a mask on a human face, then we have beast-fable not fairy story: whether it be <u>Reynard the Fox</u>, or <u>Brer Rabbit</u>, or merely <u>The Three Little Pigs</u>.[*]

The stories of Beatrix Potter lie near the borders of fairy story, inside and outside, mostly outside: <u>Peter Rabbit</u>, though it contains a Prohibition, and there are Prohibitions in faerie (as, probably, in every corner and on every plane of the Universe), is not a fairy story: it and The Tale of Mr. Tod are outside, I think. Their nearness (or semblance of it) is due to their strong moral element inherent not allegorical. But <u>Peter Rabbit</u>, though it contains

[BODLEIAN TOLKIEN MS. 14 FOLIO 30:]

The 'fantastic' element in other verse and prose – even when only decorative or occasional – help in this process. But not so thoroughly as fairy-story a thing built on or about 'fantasy'; of which fantasy is the core. Fantasy is made out of the Primary World.[**] So Green is made out of Yellow and Blue; but redirects attention to them, throws indeed a new light on them. By

---

[*] I would include <u>The Wind in the Willows</u>. <u>The Tailor of Gloucester</u> perhaps comes nearest to the borders of fairy tale.

[**] So we may say for simplicity's sake. But Man's position is infinitely and recessively derivative. He needs not only Grace to do well, but grace to cooperate with the Grace. The material of fantasy is derived from the Primary World as perceived by the senses, but the Image conceived and the Art to express them are also derived from the Source which original.

making swords we come to some appreciation of steel, by a dragon carved in wood to a feeling not only of bestial life and form, but even for the texture of wood, and the flesh & being of trees. By the making of Pegasus horses are ennobled. (In Bakelite and plastics it seems we may be doomed to have all our household goods made of that mud and stone which Chesterton warns was the product of this excessive synthesis.)

Fairy-stories also of course deal much with simple fundamental things, not fantastic: and these simplicities are all the more attractive for their setting. I first acquired a feeling for the force of the words and the marvel of the things <u>bread</u>, <u>stone</u>, <u>water</u> and so on, in fairy-stories or myths.

No gap in time is so great as that which separates the world we live in from all the ages past (since the nineteenth century as that time of the creeping cloud the eighteenth). I lived and the majority of people of my generation (much fewer of later ones) – for I lived in childhood in a cottage at the edge of a really rural country – on the borders of a land and time more like (in spite of the ever changing details) even the lands and hills of the most primitive and wildest stories, incalculably more like them, than the present life of Western Towns (in fact and wish). This 'virtue' of fairy-story may appeal only to a kind of <u>nostalgia</u>, to mere regret. Yet <u>nostalgia</u> means an '(aching) desire to go <u>home</u>'. If you do not think that <u>home</u> for men will ever be found in the ghastly visions of Scientifiction (that wild escapist literature in which men are seen as struggling to escape from the open air into [illeg] [prisons?]) then at least temporarily and as a by product fairy-stories are one of the 'genres' [illeg] those values of precious memory of home and some inklings of whether to or not to seek it. It is at any [rate] a fact that over-synthetic things won't 'go' in a fairy-story. Not even as in wicked wizard's spell. And that may be very significant.

[BODLEIAN TOLKIEN MS. 14 FOLIO 31:]

Note to 46 [Cf. note G, page 83]

Indeed fundamental. The absence of that sense is a mere (unlikely) hypothesis concerning men of the lost past, whatever wild confusions men of today, degraded or deluded, may suffer. It is as legitimate an hypothesis, indeed one far more in accord with what little is recorded concerning the <u>thoughts</u> of men of old – that this sense was once stronger not weaker. It was probably always strong in our western world, until quite recent times. In our days it has become attacked: by the hypothesis (in dogmatic guesses) of 'scientific' writers that classed Man not only as an animal ([illeg] done), but as <u>only</u> an animal. There has been a consequent distortion of sentiment. The natural love of uncorrupted men for animals, and this natural desire to 'get inside the skin' of living things, ran riot. You now get men who love animals more than men; who pity sheep so much that they curse men as wolves; who weep over a slain war-horse, and vilify a dead warrior. It is now, not in the days when fairy-stories were begotten, that we get 'an absence of a sense of separation'. It was a curious result of the application of evolutionary hypotheses concerning Man's animal body, to his whole being, that it produced at first a sort of arrogance. Man had it seemed merely succeeded in dominating other animals, like a tyrant. So let no cat look at the King. And as for men taking animal forms, an animal desires humane things.

These were nonsense, dangerous indecent nonsense. But in the end it destroyed human dignity; and strong or proud men talking of breeding men like their cattle, for ends not dissimilar.

[running upwards in lefthand margin:] It is on these very senses that their fantasies and strange gods are founded.

[BODLEIAN TOLKIEN MS. 14 FOLIOS 32-34:]

them as tales, that is, not studies them as curios. Adults are allowed to collect and study anything, even old theatre-programmes, or paper-bags.

Among those who still have enough wisdom not to think fairy-stories pernicious, the common opinion seems to be that there is a natural connexion between the minds of children and fairy-stories, of the same order as the connexion between children's bodies and milk. I think it is a delusion; at its best an error of false sentiment, one that is therefore most often made by those who (for whatever private reason, such as childlessness) tend to think of children as a special kind of creature, almost a different race, rather than as ordinary members of a particular family, and of the human family at large. In reality, the association of children and fairy-stories is an accident of domestic history. Fairy-stories have, in the modern lettered world, been relegated to the nursery, as shabby or old-fashioned furniture is relegated to the play-room, primarily because the adults do not want it and do not mind if it is misused. ~~And children have a habit, true, of playing in attics and lumber-rooms. But adults are not necessarily good judges even of furniture. In the lumber-rooms of one generation are found the treasures of another, the works of art of the next. With the revival of better taste it is in the play-rooms and attics of literature that fairy stories. But children as a class (which in most mental characteristics they are not) neither like~~ It is not the choice of the children which decides this. Children as a class (except in a common lack of mere experience they are not one) neither like fairy-stories more not understand them better than adults do, and no more than they like many other things. They are young and growing and they normally have keen appetites, so the fairy-stories as rule go down all right. But actually only some children (and some adults) have any special taste for them; and when they have it, it is not exclusive, nor even dominant. It is a taste, too, that would not, I think, appear very early in childhood without artificial stimulus; it is certainly one that increases with age, if it is innate.

~~In my case it was innate, but artificially stimulated very early.~~
~~It became dormant from about my eighth birthday to the thresh-~~
~~old of manhood – then I discovered it via Philology.~~

It is true that in recent times fairy-stories are usually written or
'adapted' <u>for</u> children. But so may music be, or verse, or novels,
or history, or scientific manuals. And it is a dangerous process,
even when it is necessary. It is indeed saved from disaster only by
the fact that the arts and sciences are not as a whole 'relegated to
the nursery'; the nursery and school-room are merely given such
tastes and glimpses of the adult thing as seem fit for them in adult
opinion (often grossly mistaken). Any one of these things, or any
one of their branches, would, if left altogether in the nursery,
become seriously damaged. So likely enough would a beautiful
table, a good picture, or a useful machine (such as a microscope)
be defaced or broken, if it were left long-unregarded in a schoolroom. Fairy-stories banished in this way, cut off from a full adult
art, would in the end be ruined; indeed in so far as they have been
so banished, they have been ruined.

However, the making of fairy-stories, even the modern
writing of them *for* children, is actually an adult activity: judging
by the results, it is best left to bankers, logicians, philologists,
philosophers and theologians. At any rate, they perform, if not
always well, at least better than do children, or than those professionally concerned with their instruction. In fact, those who
have a talent for story-making in general, and no special concern
with children (or similarity to them), but have some training in
the Arts (notably those entailing some discipline of thought) are
likely to write the best fairy-tales. I fancy fairy-stories are really
an adult business, after all, requiring some experience of life, and
some acquaintance with (indeed some genuine training in) the
arts and sciences: especially those which discipline thought.

Well there it is: you will at least have gathered that in my
opinion fairy-stories should not be <u>specially</u> associated with
children. They are associated with them: (a) because children are
human, and fairy-stories are a natural human taste, though false
fashion and false philosophy may obscure this; (b) because fairy-
stories are a large part of the literary lumber that in latter-day

Europe has been stuffed away in attics, and play-rooms; and (c) because of erroneous sentiment about children – a sentiment that has increased with the decline in children.

Fairy-stories were, of course, made by and orally preserved by adults, and even in the age of 'Golden Age' sentiment they are written by adults. But we do fairy-stories and children an injustice, if we conceive of fairy-stories as a sort of mental cake or sweet to be provided by indulgent parents, uncles or aunts. It is true that the age of childhood sentiment has produced some delightful books of or near the fairy kind; but it has produced also a dreadful undergrowth, vast in extent, of stories written or adapted to what was or is conceived as the measure of children's minds and needs. The old stories are mollified or bowdlerized;[*] the imitations are often merely silly (Pigwiggenry without even the intrigue) or patronizing, or (deadliest of all) covertly sniggering with an eye on the other grown-ups listening.[**]

But of course, wondering whether there are such things, or wishing that there could be such things, or even believing that there may be such things as <u>elves</u>, <u>dragons</u>, <u>giants</u>, <u>magicians</u>, or <u>policemen</u>, is quite different from believing in any particular account of them.[***] I preserve to this day an open mind about

---

[*] Dasent replied with vigour and justice to the prudish critics of his translations from Norse popular tales. Yet he committed the astonishing folly of particularly forbidding children to read the last two. That a man could study fairy-stories and not learn better than that seems almost incredible.

[**] A plate was once given to my daughter. On it was inscribed: Look at this wee tiny elf, Fido caught it all himself. I am happy to say she refused to eat off it. But this is the inevitable fate of Elves—not all [their?] beauty, power and terror can save them—if fairy-story and nursery-tale are equated.

[***] I do not remember any particular desire to find that the creatures of fairy-story were (primarily) true. But I do remember a very deep desire to see and speak to a Knight of Arthur's court. If I had, I should have regarded him much as Peredur did. ~~But that was a case of the desire to visit past time. For Arthurian legend, owing to the accidents of its development, took on an historical guise; it was represented to me or appeared to me as History.~~ But that is a special case: the desire was in large part a desire to visit or see Past Time. Owing to the accidents of its mediaeval development Arthurian legends had taken on an historical guise. They did not occur 'once upon a time'.

the primary existence of these things (concerning which there are so many garbled or wilfully invented stories). I perceive now that there is fair evidence for the existence of magicians, and even better evidence for policemen, though I never saw one or the other in early childhood; but the romances that have gathered round these mysterious beings I now find are for the most part frankly incredible (as I always thought): many are inventions written by people with little or no direct knowledge of the creatures, drawing on older books and their own fancy. The same is true of fairies.

In any case, speaking for myself as a child, I can only say that a taste for fairy-stories was not a primary characteristic of early days. A real taste for them awoke long after nursery days, and after the years, few but long, between learning to read and going to school. In that (I nearly said, so habitual in modern linguistic idiom as the false sentiment, 'happy' or 'golden'; it was really sad and troublous) time I liked many other things as well, or better: such as history, astronomy, natural history (especially botany), and more than all philology. I agreed thus with Lang's generalized 'children' not at all in principle, and only in some points by accident: I was quite insensitive to poetry (I skipped it, if it came in tales); and stupid at arithmetic. Poetry I discovered much later through being made to try and write Latin and Greek verses, and especially to translate English verse into classical. A real taste for fairy-stories was wakened by philology on the threshold of manhood, and quickened to full life by war.

It seems fairly clear that Lang was using <u>belief</u> in its ordinary sense: belief that a thing exists or can happen in the real (Primary) World. This, I fear, when stripped of sentiment, makes Lang imply that the tellers of tales to children must, or may, or at any rate does trade on their <u>credulity</u>: that is, on the lack of experience which makes it less easy for children to distinguish fact from fiction in particular cases, though the distinction in itself is fundamental to the human mind, and to fairy-stories. Children are capable, of course, as adults are, of <u>literary belief</u>, when the story-maker's art is good enough to produce it. That state of mind has been called 'willing suspension of disbelief'.

But this is not, I think, a good description of what happens. What really happens is that the story-maker proves a successful 'sub-creator'. He makes a Secondary World which your mind can enter. Inside it what he relates is <u>true</u>: it accords with the laws of the world. You therefore believe it, while inside. The moment Disbelief arises, the spell is broken: the magic or rather art has failed. You are then out in the Primary World again, looking at the little abortive Secondary World from outside. If you are obliged, by kindliness or circumstance, to stay, then Disbelief must be suspended (or stifled), otherwise listening and looking would become intolerable. But suspension of Disbelief is a substitute for the genuine thing, a subterfuge we use when condescending to games or make-believe, or when trying (more or less willingly) to find what virtue we can in the work of an art that has (for us) failed.

A real enthusiast for cricket is in the enchanted state: Secondary Belief. I, when I watch a match, am on the lower level: I can achieve (more or less) willing Suspension of Disbelief, when I am held there and supported by some other motive that will keep away boredom: for instance, a wild, heraldic preference for dark blue rather than light. This Suspension of Disbelief may thus be a somewhat tired, shabby, or sentimental state of mind and so lean to the 'adult'. I fancy it is often the state of adults in the presence of a fairy-story. They are held there and supported by sentiment (memories of childhood, or notions of what childhood ought to be like): they think they ought to like the tale. But if they really liked it for itself, they would not have to suspend belief; they would believe – in that sense.

Now if Lang meant anything like this, there may be some truth in what he said. It may be argued that it is easier to work the spell on children. It may be so, though I am not sure of it. The appearance that it is so, is, I think, often an adult illusion produced by children's humility, their lack of critical experience and vocabulary, and the voracity (proper to their growth). They like or try to like what is given to them; if they do not like it, they cannot express or give reason for their dislike (and so may conceal it); and in any case they like a great mass of different things indiscriminately, without troubling to analyse the plans of their belief. In any case I doubt if this potion – the enchantment of fantasy – is really one of the kind that becomes less effective in time, after many draughts.

commonly assumed, but I do not perceive any proof. The situation in the great Northern 'Arthurian' court of the <u>Scyldingas</u> is somewhat similar. King Hrothgar and his family have manifest marks of true history, far more than Arthur; yet in the ancient English accounts of them they are associated with many creatures and events of fairy-story: they have been put in the Pot. But I do not here refer to the remnants of the oldest English fairy-stories – too little known in England – to discuss the knight Beowulf and the ogre Grendel. I refer to them now because they contain, I think, a singularly illustrative example of the relation of the 'fairy-tale element' to both Gods and Kings and nameless men: bending to show that this element does not rise or fall but is there waiting for the great figures of Myth and History, for the moment when they fall into the Pot and become the characters of Story. The great enemy of King Hrothgar was Froda King of the Heathobards. Yet of Hrothgar's daughter Freawaru we hear echoes of a strange tale: the son of the enemy of her house Ingeld son of Froda fell in love with her and wedded her. What of it? Just this: in the background of this ancient feud looms the figure of that god whom the Norse called Frey (the Lord) and the English Ing: a god of the ancient Northern mythology (and religion) of corn and fertility. The feud of the royal houses has a religious basis: Hrothgar is called lord of the friends of Ing, he calls his daughter the Freawaru Protector of Frey the lord. Both Froda and Ingeld are by name and other traditions connected with the same cult. Yet of all the Norse stories told about Frey the best known is that in which Frey falls in love [illeg] of a [illeg] the day when of the enemies of the gods with Gerda the Great [illeg] and weds her. Does this prove F. I. [illeg illeg] wholly 'mythical'. I think not. [illeg line]

If no young man had ever fallen in love with a maiden at first sight and found old friends to be between him and his love, the

God Frey would never have seen/Gerda the giantess. And yet at the same time such a love is most likely to be told of characters of history – indeed is more likely actually to happen in an historical [illeg] – whose [illeg] are those of golden Frey and [illeg] rather than of Odin the [illeg] the necromancer the [illeg] of [illeg].

[BODLEIAN TOLKIEN MS. 14 FOLIO 35:]

"<u>Is it true? is</u>," Lang said, "<u>the great question children ask</u>". They do ask that question, I know; and it should not be rashly or idly answered. But that question is hardly evidence of 'unblunted belief', or even of desire for it. Most often it proceeds from the child's desire to know which kind of literature he is faced with. Children's knowledge

of the world is often so small that they cannot judge off-hand and without help between the fantastic, the marvellous, and the merely 'grown-up': that is between fairy-story; rare or remote facts; the ordinary things of their parent's world, much of which remains still unexplored; or nonsense and unreason. But they recognize the different classes, and they like each in its own kind. The borders between them are often vague, of course, but that is not peculiar to children. We are all sure of the differences in kind, but we are not always sure where to place everything that we hear. A child may well believe a report that there are ogres in the next county; many grown-up persons find it easy to believe of another country; and as for another planet: there are very few adults who can imagine it as peopled (if at all) by anything but monsters of iniquity.

Now I was one of the <u>children</u> whom Andrew Lang was addressing – I was born about the same time as the Green Fairy Book – the children for whom he seemed to think that fairy-stories were the equivalent of the adult novel; and of whom he said: 'their taste remains like the taste of their naked ancestors thousands of years ago; and they seem to like fairy-tales better than history, poetry, geography, or arithmetic.'[*] But do we really know much about those 'naked ancestors', except that they were certainly not naked? Our fairy-stories, however old certain elements in them may be, are certainly not like theirs. Yet if it is assumed that we have fairy-stories because they had them, then probably we have history, poetry, geography, and arithmetic, because they had and liked these things too, as far as they could get them, and in so far as they had yet separated the many branches of their general interest in everything.

I can only say children have changed since Andrew Lang wrote, or were changing while he was writing. I will say that I do not think they were ever like that.[**] I at any rate never believed (in the primary sense) in fairy-stories, any more than I believed in stories about rabbits, children, railway-engines or policemen, except on some kind of evidence, my own senses and experience or the assurances of older people. Of course, the questions naturally arose: do all these things in this story commonly happen in This World; are they possible in it; are they possible at all? But wondering whether there are

As far as my experience goes children (who have an early bent for writing) have no special inclination to attempt the writing of fairy-stories (unless that is almost the sole form of literature presented to them); and they fail most markedly when they try. It is a difficult form.

If children have any special leaning, it is to Beast-fable (which adults often confuse with fairy-story). The best stories by children that I have seen have been either 'realistic' (in intent), or have had as their characters animals and birds, who were in the main the zoomorphic human beings usual in Beast-fable. But I imagine that the Beast-fable form is so often selected principally

---

[*] Preface to the <u>Violet Fairy Book</u>.
[**] My basic evidence is memory of myself, as it is of everyone; reinforced by loving but not sentimental observation of children, my own and others. I cannot escape the arrogance of preferring my own memories and observations.

because it allows a large measure of realism: the representation of domestic events and talk that children really know. The form itself is suggested, or imposed, by adults; it has at any rate a curious preponderance in the literature (good and bad) that is nowadays presented to young children, and it is reinforced by the bears and rabbits that seem in recent times almost to have ousted human dolls from the playrooms even of little girls. If these are shaped like bears, bears will be the characters of the sagas – in shape; but they will talk like People.

The value of fairy-stories is thus not, in my opinion, to be found by considering children in particular. Collections of 'fairy-stories' are, in fact, by nature attics and lumber-rooms only by temporary and local custom playrooms (or school-rooms). Their contents are disordered and often battered, a jumble of different dates, purposes, and tastes; but among them may occasionally be found a thing of permanent virtue: an old treasure not too much damaged, which only stupidity would ever have stuffed away.

Andrew Lang's Fairy Books are not, perhaps, lumber-rooms; they are not like stalls in a rummage-sale. Someone with a duster and a fair eye for things that retain some value has been round the attic and boxrooms. His collections were, of course, partly a by-product of his adult researches in mythology and folklore. But he intended them 'for children'; and as he was both intelligent and interested in children, he did not do this without reason. Some of the reasons that he gives are worth considering.

The introduction to the first of the series speaks of <u>children to whom and for whom they are told</u>. '<u>They represent</u>', he says, '<u>the young age of man true to his early loves, and have his unblunted edge of belief, a fresh appetite for marvels.</u>'

"<u>Is it true? is</u>, he says, <u>the great question children ask</u>. I suspect that <u>belief</u> and <u>appetite for marvels</u> are here regarded as identical or closely connected. They are not. They are radically different, though the appetite for marvels is not all at once by a growing human mind differentiated from its general appetite.

[BODLEIAN TOLKIEN MS. 14 FOLIO 36:]

report that there are ogres in the next county; many grown-up persons find it easy to believe of another country; and as for another planet: there are very few adults who can imagine it as peopled (if at all) by anything but monsters of iniquity.*

Now I was one of the <u>children</u> whom Andrew Lang was addressing – I was born about the same time as <u>The Green Fairy Book</u> – the children for whom he seemed to think that fairy-stories were the equivalent of the adult novel, and of whom he said: 'their taste remains like the taste of their naked ancestors thousands of years ago; and they seem to like fairy-tales better than history, poetry, geography, or arithmetic.' But do we really know much about those 'naked ancestors', except that they were certainly not naked? Our fairy-stories, however old some details in them may be, are certainly not the same as theirs. Yet if it is assumed that we have fairy-stories because they did, then probably we have history, poetry, geography, and arithmetic, because they had and liked these things too, as far as they could get them, and in so far as they had yet separated the many branches of their general interest in everything.

And as for children of the present day, Lang's description does not fit my own memories, or my experience of children. Lang may have been mistaken about the children that he knew; if he was not, then at any rate children differ considerably, even within the narrow borders of Britain, and such generalizations (treating them as a class, apart from the influences of the country-side they live in, and their upbringing) are delusory. I at any rate never <u>believed</u> (in the primary sense) in fairy-stories; for to me their essential quality was <u>desire</u>. It is difficult to be more explicit. To say that I wished them to be objectively true, and

---

* This is, naturally, often enough what children mean when they ask: 'Is it true?' They mean: 'Is it contemporary. I like all this, but am I safe in my bed?' The answer: 'There is certainly no ogre or dragon in England today' is in that case all that they want to hear.

that this wish, combined with recognition that they were not true in my mortal world, produced the peculiar quality of longing which these possessed, and which they satisfied while whetting it unbearably would be too explicit. Of course, I in my timid body did not wish to have ogres and dragons in the neighbourhood, intruding into my relatively safe world, in which, for instance, it was possible to read stories in peace of mind, free from fear. But to ride with Sigurd of the Volsungs, or to sit at the Round Table in the land of Arthur and Merlin, that could be a passionate desire. Only fairy-tales or stories closely allied had that quality. It was no doubt made of various elements, not all of which are felt by all people. Hardihood and desire for adventure may with Actual desire for 'adventure' may [*sic*] for some, of inborn hardihood, be present; but if that is dominant they will turn as gladly to other adventure stories. There is also the enchantment of Antiquity, and above all the creative and recreative wonder of fantasy. And for people (including children) of my time aesthetic Escape – aesthetic escape: nostalgia for a time (real or imagined) when the work of his hands seemed good to man, and things both rare and common were seemly. So much that fairy-tales contained, because they came out of or treated of the past, seemed desirable and untrue: but as though they were not true: they could be true, or could have been true; something had gone wrong with the world, which it seemed was still right in tales.

The real desire is not to enter these lands as a natural denizen (as a knight, say, armed with a sword and courage adequate to this world) but to see them in action and being as we see our objective world – with the mind free from the limited body: a Faerian Drama.

[BODLEIAN TOLKIEN MS. 14 FOLIO 37:]

The use of this word gives a hint of my epilogue. It is a serious and dangerous point – ~~and hope that it may not appear foolish and presumptuous.~~ I am a Christian and so at least should not be suspected of wilful presumption or irreverence. Knowledge of my own ignorance and dullness should perhaps restrain me from touching on such a theme; but if by grace what I say has in any respect any validity, it is of course only one facet of a truth incalculably rich: finite only because the capacity of man for whom this was done is finite.

I have already given a hint of what I am now coming to in calling the 'eucatastrophe' of 'fairy-story' an 'evangelium'.

I would venture to say that approaching the Christian Story from this direction it has long been my feeling (a joyous feeling) that God redeemed the corrupt making-creatures men in a way fitting to this aspect as to others of their strange nature. The Gospels are a fairy-story, or a story of kind which if larger embraces all the essence of fairy-stories. They contain many marvels – peculiarly artistic,[*] beautiful, and moving: 'mythical' in their perfect, self-contained significance; and yet powerfully symbolic and allegorical as well, and among the marvels is the greatest and most complete conceivable 'eucatastrophe'. The Birth of Christ is the eucatastrophe of man's history. The Resurrection is the eucatastrophe of the story of the Incarnation. This story begins and ends in joy. It has pre-eminently the 'inner consistency of reality'. There is no tale ever told that men would rather find was 'true' in the Primary World, and none which so many sceptical men have accepted as true on its own merits. For the Art of it has the supremely convincing tone of Primary Art, that is, of Creation.

Marvels: yes, but the story is true, therefore the marvels are true, occurring in history. Therefore these 'marvels' require a special name: we call them miracles. For the teller of the tale (the creator) and the actor (or hero) are One – and the one God.

It is not perhaps difficult to imagine the peculiar kind of excite-

[*] Or rather the Christian Story has Art. The "gospels" are not "artistic" in themselves: the Art is in the events themselves. For the Authors of the story were not the evangelists. 'Even the world itself could not contain the books that should be written": if that story had been fully written down.

ment and joy that one would feel if any specially beautiful fairy-story were found to be 'primarily true': its narrative to be history, without, of course, thereby losing the allegorical or mythical significance it possessed: indeed having these more intensely. But no effort of imagination is actually required. This joy would have exactly the same quality (if not degree) of the joy which the 'turn' in a fairy-story gives: such joy has the very taste of primary truth. It looks forward or backward (an unimportant distinction in this regard) to the Great Eucatastrophe.

The Christian Joy, the gloria, is of this same kind; but it is pre-eminently (infinitely if our capacity were not finite) high. Because the story is supreme; and it is true. Art has been Verified. God is the Lord of Angels and Men – and Elves. Legend and History have met and fused.

But in God's Kingdom the presence of the Greatest does not depress the small. Redeemed Man is Man. Story, Fantasy, still go on, and should. The Evangelium has not abrogated Legends; it has hallowed them. The Christian has to work, suffer, die and hope; but he may now perceive that all his faculties have a purpose, which can be redeemed. So great is that bounty with which he had been treated, that he may now perhaps fairly dare to guess that in Fantasy he may actually assist in the effoliation and enrichment of Creation. All Tales may come true; and yet at the last, redeemed they may be as like and unlike the Forms we give them; as Man finally redeemed the Fallen that we know.

It is a great error to suppose that true (historical) stories and untrue stories ('fantasies') can be distinguished in any such a way. Real (primarily real) events may possess (must always possess if we can discern it) mystical significance and allegory. Unreal ends may possess as much plain logical likelihood and [some?] factual sequence of cause and effect as history.

†MANUSCRIPT B COMMENTARY

[page 228] a great backward and abysm of time. Shakespeare, *The Tempest* Act I scene ii. Prospero to Miranda.

[229] Neigung. A German verbal noun meaning variously "inclining", "tendency", "leaning".

[232] that enchanted field. Entire passage quoted from Lang's Introduction to the large paper edition of *The Blue Fairy Book*, p. xiii.

[240] Sæt secg monig. Quoted from the Anglo-Saxon poem "Deor's Lament", lines 24–6.

[240] "an absence of senses of separation of themselves from beasts". Misquoted from Lang in the *Fortnightly Review*, p. 627: "But to construct this myth, the notion of enchantment or magic, and the absence of our later sense of separation from the beasts, is required as necessary form . . ."

[241] "How came such a story. . ." Müller quoted by Lang in the *Fortnightly Review*, pp. 625–6.

[244] "Whoever does not believe . . . dollar." From "The Story of a Clever Tailor" in *The Green Fairy Book*.

[253] Wells's miscalled short story. H.G. Wells's "The Man Who Could Work Miracles", published in the *Illustrated London News*, July 1898 and collected in *Tales of Space and Time* (1899) and in *The Short Stories of H. G. Wells* (1927).

[256] álfamaer ekki var hún Kristi kaer. "elf-maiden who was not dear to Christ". We are indebted to Vésteinn Ólason, Director of The Árni Magnússon Institute of Icelandic Studies for this translation and for the source of the quote. It comes from an Icelandic ballad, "Ólafur Liljurós", the story of a young man first beguiled and then killed by an elf-maiden. The entire line of the ballad reads: þar kom út ein álfamær, ekki var hún Kristi kær, "Out came an elf-maiden, who was not dear to Christ" (i.e., she was not a Christian). Variants of the ballad occur in Icelandic, Danish, Swedish, Norwegian and English. The earliest version is derived from a Danish manuscript of 1550, and the theme bears a strong resemblance to "Clerk Covill" one of the influences on Tolkien's Breton-like lay of "Aotrou and Itroun".

[256] illustrated by Mrs. Tiggywinkle. *The Tale of Mrs. Tiggy-Winkle* (1905) by Beatrix Potter. Note appearance in *Songs for the Philologists*!

[258] Gloria in excelsis deo. The part of the Catholic Mass known as the Gloria. It immediately follows the Kyrie ("Lord have mercy, Christ have mercy, Lord have mercy"), and shortly precedes the first Bible reading. Tolkien's text does not complete the Gloria. A translation is given below.

> Glory be to God on high, and on earth
> peace to men of good will. We praise Thee.
> We bless Thee. We adore Thee. We glorify Thee.
> We give Thee thanks for Thy great glory.
>
> O Lord God, heavenly King,
> God the Father almighty.
> O Lord Jesus Christ, the only-begotten Son.
> O Lord God, Lamb of God, Son of the Father.
> Who takest away the sins of the world, receive our prayer.
> Who sittest at the right hand of the Father, have mercy on us.

[260] **"Mysterious Commonwealth of Elves and Fairies".** The original 1691 version of Robert Kirk's book is titled *The Secret Commonwealth; or, a Treatise Displaying the Chiefe [sic] Curiosities as They Are in Use among Diverse of the People of Scotland to This Day.* Andrew Lang introduced an edition of it in 1893, retitled *The Secret Commonwealth of Elves, Fauns and Fairies.*

[261] **Ghost Stories of an Antiquary.** *Ghost Stories of an Antiquary* (1904) is a collection of eight stories by M.R. James.

[263] **Zauberfluidum.** A German word meaning "magical potency", used by Christopher Dawson in describing the progress of Brahmanism. See *Progress and Religion*, page 128.

[263] **Sanctus sanctus dominus deus sabaoth.** "Holy holy holy lord God of hosts." In the Catholic Mass, the last portion of the Preface of the Eucharistic Prayer, the prayer of consecration of the bread and wine.

[263] **Wakan Orenda.** See *Progress in Religion* by Christopher Dawson. *Wakan*, the Dakota word for the spirit of Divine Power in every object of the world, is discussed on page 82 of that work. *Orenda* is an Iroquois term for the supernatural power diffused throughout nature; see page 83.

[264] **te deum laudamus.** The Te Deum is a traditional Latin hymn of joy and thanksgiving, sung on occasions of public rejoicing. The opening lines translate as: "O God, we praise Thee. We acknowledge Thee to be the Lord. Everlasting Father, all the earth doth worship Thee. To Thee all the Angels, the Heavens and all the Powers, all the Cherubim and Seraphim, unceasingly proclaim [Holy, Holy, Holy, Lord God of Hosts!]."

[268] **þæt wæs yldum cùþ** *Beowulf*, lines 705–8.

BIBLIOGRAPHIES

For the reader's convenience, and because it is a significant record of the immense amount of work and research that Tolkien put into both the lecture and the essay that grew out of it, we have separated the biblography into two sections. First is the bibliography of works we have consulted and cited in preparing this edition. Second (and much longer and more important) is the list of works that Tolkien read and/or cited as part of his own extensive reading and preparation.

CRITICAL BIBLIOGRAPHY

——. *Angles and Britons: O'Donnell Lectures*. Cardiff: University of Wales Press, 1963.

Barfield, Owen. *The Rediscovery of Meaning and Other Essays*. Middleton, Connecticut: Wesleyan University Press, 1977.

Budge, E. A. Wallis. *An Egyptian Reading Book for Beginners*. New York: AMS Press, 1976. [Reprint of the 1896 edition published by Kegan Paul, Trench, Trübner & Co., London.]

Carpenter, Humphrey. *J.R.R. Tolkien: A Biography*. London: George Allen & Unwin, 1977.

Campbell, J[ohn]. F[rancis]. *Popular Tales of the West Highlands*. Edinburgh: Birlinn, 1994. [Reprint of the three-volume edition originally published in 1860–1 by Edmonston and Douglas, Edinburgh.]

Chambers, Robert. *Popular Rhymes of Scotland, with illustrations, collected from tradition*. Edinburgh: William Hunter and Charles Smith & Co., and London: James Duncan,1826.

Chesterton, G. K. *The Coloured Lands*. London: Sheed and Ward, 1938.
——. *The Everlasting Man*. London: Hodder and Stoughton, 1925.
——. *Heretics*. London: John Lane, 1905.
——. *The Man Who Was Thursday*. London: Arrowsmith. 1908.
——. *Orthodoxy*. London: John Lane, 1908.
——. *The Outline of Sanity*. London: Methuen, 1926.

Dasent, George Webbe. *Popular Tales from the Norse*. Edinburgh: Edmonston and Douglas, 1859. Second Edition, enlarged.

Dawson, Christopher. *Progress & Religion: An Historical Enquiry*. London: Sheed and Ward, 1929. Reprinted under the "Unicorn Books" imprint of Sheed and Ward, 1938.

Dorson, Richard M. *The British Folklorists: A History*. Chicago: University of Chicago Press, 1968.
——, ed. *Peasant Customs and Savage Myths: Selections from the British Folklorists*. Chicago: University of Chicago Press, 1968. [Two volumes]

Drayton, Michael. *The Works of Michael Drayton*. Edited by J. William Hebel. Oxford: Basil Blackwell, 1932.

G[ordon], G[eorge]. S. "Lang, Andrew (1844–1912)." In *The Dictionary of National Biography 1912–1921*, ed. by H.W.C. Davis and J.R.H. Weaver. London: Humphrey Milford, Oxford University Press, 1927: pp. 319–23.

Gower, John. *The Complete Works of John Gower: The English Works*, ed. by C.C. Macaulay. Oxford: Clarendon Press, 1901.

Green, Roger Lancelyn. *Andrew Lang*. New York: Henry Z. Walck, 1963.
—. *Andrew Lang: A Critical Biography*. Leicester: Edmund Ward, 1946.

Grimm, Jacob and Wilhelm. *Grimm's Household Tales*, translated and edited by Margaret Hunt, with an introduction by Andrew Lang. Detroit: Singing Tree Press, 1968. [Originally published in two volumes in 1884.]

Hart, Rachel. "Tolkien, St. Andrews, and Dragons." In *Tree of Tales: Tolkien, Literature, and Theology*, ed. by Trevor A. Hart and Ivan Khovacs. Waco, TX: Baylor University Press, 2007: 1–11.

Lang, Andrew. *Custom and Myth*. New York: Harper & Brothers, 1885.
—. *Myth, Ritual and Religion*. New York: AMS Press, 1968. [Reprint of the two-volume edition originally published in 1906 in London.]
—. "Mythology and Fairy Tales." *The Fortnightly Review*, 19 (May 1873): 618–31.
—, ed. *The Blue Fairy Book*. London: Longmans, Green and Co., 1889. [Lang's introduction, pp. xi–xxii, was published only in the Large Paper edition, limited to one hundred and thirteen copies.]
—, ed. *The Book of Romance*. London: Longmans, Green and Co., 1902.
—, ed. *The Brown Fairy Book*. London: Longmans, Green and Co., 1904.
—, ed. *The Crimson Fairy Book*. London: Longmans, Green and Co., 1903.
—, ed. *The Green Fairy Book*. London: Longmans, Green and Co., 1892.

——, ed. *The Grey Fairy Book*. London: Longmans, Green and Co., 1900.

——, ed. *The Lilac Fairy Book*. London: Longmans, Green and Co., 1910.

——, ed. *The Olive Fairy Book*. London: Longmans, Green and Co., 1907.

——, ed. *The Orange Fairy Book*. London: Longmans, Green and Co., 1906.

——, ed. *The Pink Fairy Book*. London: Longmans, Green and Co., 1897.

——, ed. *The Red Fairy Book*. London: Longmans, Green and Co., 1890. [Lang's introduction, pp. xi–xvi, was published only in the Large Paper edition, limited to one hundred and thirteen copies.]

——, ed. *The Violet Fairy Book*. London: Longmans, Green and Co., 1901.

——, ed. *The Yellow Fairy Book*. London: Longmans, Green and Co., 1894.

Lewis, C.S. *The Collected Letters of C.S. Lewis*, Vol. II. Ed. Walter Hooper.San Francisco: HarperSanFrancisco, 2004.

——. *Of Other Worlds: Essays and Stories*. New York: Harcourt, Brace and World, 1967.

MacDonald, George. "The Fantastic Imagination," in *A Dish of Orts, Chiefly Papers on the Imagination, and on Shakspere* [sic]. London: Sampson Low Marston & Company, 1895: 313-322.

MacDougall, James. *Folk Tales and Fairy Lore in Gaelic and English: Collected from Oral Tradition*. Edited with an Introduction and Notes by George Calder. New York: Arno Press, 1977. [Reprint of the 1910 edition published by John Grant, Edinburgh.]

Müller, Max. *Chips from a German Workshop, Volume IV: Essays on Mythology and Folk-lore.* London: Longmans, Green, 1898. [Originally published in 1875 and expanded in 1895.]

——. *Lectures on the Science of Language.* London: Longman, Green, Longman, Roberts & Green, 1861.

Nansen, Fridtjof. *In Northern Mists: Arctic Exploration in Early Times.* London: William Heinemann, 1911. Two volumes, translated by Arthur G. Chater.

Schacker, Jennifer. *National Dreams: The Remaking of Fairy Tales in Nineteenth-Century England.* Philadelphia: University of Pennsylvania Press, 2003.

Shippey, Tom. *The Road to Middle-earth.* London: HarperCollins *Publishers*, 2003.

Tolkien, J.R.R. *The Annotated Hobbit. Revised and Expanded Edition.* Ed. Douglas A. Anderson. London: HarperCollins *Publishers* 2003.

——. *The Letters of J.R.R. Tolkien*, Ed. Humphrey Carpenter. London: HarperCollins *Publishers*, 1999.

——. *The Lord of the Rings.* London: HarperCollins *Publishers*, 2001.

——. *The Monsters and the Critics.* London: HarperCollins *Publishers*, 1997.

——. "Mythopoeia," in *Tree and Leaf, including the Poem Mythopoeia.* London: Unwin Hyman, 1988: 97–101.

——. *Return to Bag End*, Part Two of The History of *The Hobbit*, Ed. John D. Rateliff. London: HarperCollins *Publishers*, 2007.

——. *Smith of Wootton Major: Extended Edition.* Ed. Verlyn Flieger. London: HarperCollins *Publishers*, 2005.

Unwin, Rayner. *George Allen & Unwin: A Remembrancer.* Ludlow, UK: Merlin Unwin Books, 1999.

van den Bosch, Lourens P. *Friedrich Max Müller: A Life Devoted to the Humanities*. Leiden: Brill, 2002.

WORKS CONSULTED OR CITED
BY J.R.R. TOLKIEN

[Some of the items listed below are mentioned only in Tolkien's research notes or draft materials, and not in the finished essay.]

Andersen, Hans Christian.
Apuleius. "Eros and Psyche" [from *The Golden Ass*]
Barrie, J. M. *Mary Rose* (1920)
——. *Peter Pan* (1904)
"Battle of the Birds"
"Beauty and the Beast"
Beowulf
Bernhardi, Theodor von. *Volksmährchen und epische Dichtung* (1871)
"Bertha Broadfoot"
"The Black Bull of Norroway" [*see under* Lang, *The Blue Fairy Book*]
Budge, E. A. Wallis. *An Egyptian Reading Book for Beginners* (1896) [Includes "The Tale of the Two Brothers"]
Callaway, Canon [Henry]. *Nursery Tales, Traditions and Histories of the Zulus in Their Own Words* (1868)
Campbell, J.F. *Popular Tales of the West Highlands* (3 vols. 1860–1)
Carroll, Lewis. *Alice in Wonderland* (1865)
——. *Through the Looking-Glass* (1872)
Castrén, M. Alexander. *M. Alexander Castrén's Ethnologische Vorlesungen über die altaischen Völker: nebst samojedischen Märchen und Tatarischen Heldensagen* (1857)
Caylus. [*see under* Lang, *The Green Fairy Book*]
Chambers, Robert. *Popular Rhymes of Scotland* (1847)
Chaucer, Geoffrey. *The Nun's Priest's Tale*

Chesterton, G. K. *The Coloured Lands* (1938)

——. *The Everlasting Man* (1925)

——. *Heretics* (1905)

——. *Orthodoxy* (1908)

——. *The Outline of Sanity* (1926)

Dasent, George Webbe, tr. tr. *Popular Tales from the Norse* (1859) [Includes "The Mastermaid"]

Dawson, Christopher. *Progress & Religion: An Historical Enquiry* (1929)

Deor

Dickens, Charles

The Dictionary of National Biography 1912–1921 (1927), entry for "Andrew Lang"

Drayton, Michael. *Nymphidia* (1627)

Duelin. [*see under* Lang, *The Green Fairy Book*]

Elder Edda, "Thrymskvitha"

Encyclopedia Britannica, entry for "fairy"

"Dat Erdmänneken" [*see under* Grimm]

Eros and Psyche [*see under* Apuleius]

Fauriel, C[laude]. C[harles]. *Chants Populaires de la Grèce Moderne* (2 vols. 1824–5)

"The Frog King" [*see under* Grimm]

Gower, John. *Confessio Amantis* (1386–90)

——. *Mirour de l'Omme*

Grahame, Kenneth. *The Wind in the Willows* (1908)

Grimm, Jacob and Wilhelm. *Grimm's Household Tales* (1884), translated by Margaret Hunt. [Includes "The Frog King" ("Der Froschkönig"); "The Goosegirl" ("Die Gänsemagd"); "The Gnome" ("Dat Erdmänneken"); "The Juniper Tree" ("Von dem Machandelboom")]

Hahn, J.G. Von. *Griechische und Albanesische Märchen* (1918)

Harris, Joel Chandler. "Brer Rabbit"

Hartland, Edwin Sidney. *English Fairy and Other Folk Tales* (1890)

Jason and Medea

Jung, C. G. *Psychology of the Unconscious* (1916)

Kletke. [See under Lang, *The Green Fairy Book*]

Knatchbull-Hugessen, E[dward]. H[ugessen]. *Stories for My Children* (1869)

Knatchbull-Hugessen, R[eginald]. *Fairy Tales for my Grandchildren* (1910)

Lang, Andrew. *The Book of Dreams and Ghosts* (1897)

——. *Chronicles of Pantouflia* (1932)

——. *Custom and Myth* (1884)

——. *Essays in Little* (1891)

——. *The Gold of Fairnilee* (1888)

——. *Myth, Ritual and Religion* (2 vols. 1887)

——. "Mythology and Fairy Tales," *Fortnightly Review*, May 1873.

——. *Prince Prigio* (1889)

——. *Prince Ricardo of Pantouflia* (1893)

——. *The Princess Nobody: a Tale of Fairyland* (1884)

——. *Tales of a Fairy Court* (1907)

——, ed. *The Arabian Nights Entertainments* (1898)

——, ed. *The Blue Fairy Book* (1889) [Includes "The Black Bull of Norroway" and "The Terrible Head".]

——, ed. *The Brown Fairy Book* (1904)

——, ed. *The Crimson Fairy Book* (1903)

——, ed. *The Green Fairy Book* (1892) [In his notes, Tolkien listed four authors from *The Green Fairy Book*: "Duelin. Kletke. Caylus. Sébillot." More fully, these authors and their stories in this volume are: Charles Duelin, "The Enchanted Watch" and "The Little Soldier"; Hermann Kletke, "The Magic Swan" and "The Biter Bit"; the Comte de Caylus, "Rosanella", "Sylvain and Jocosa", "Fairy Gifts", and "Heart of Ice"; and Paul Sébillot, "The Snuff Box", "The Golden Blackbird", and "The Dirty Shepherdess".]

——, ed. *The Grey Fairy Book* (1900)

——, ed. *The Lilac Fairy Book* (1910)

——, ed. *The Magic Ring and Other Stories* (1906) [Compiled with stories taken from *The Yellow Fairy Book* and *The Crimson Fairy Book*.]

——, ed. *The Nursery Rhyme Book* (1897)

——, ed. *The Olive Fairy Book* (1907)

——, ed. *The Orange Fairy Book* (1906)

——, ed. *The Pink Fairy Book* (1897)

——, ed. *The Red Fairy Book* (1890)

——, ed. *The Violet Fairy Book* (1901)

——, ed. *The Yellow Fairy Book* (1894) [About "In the Land of Souls" Tolkien has noted: "Red Indians"]

——, intro. Apuleius. *The Most Pleasant and Delectable Tale of the Marriage of Cupid and Psyche* (1887)

——, intro. Cox, Marian Roalfe. *Cinderella: Three Hundred and Forty-Five Variants* (1893)

——, intro. Grimm, Jacob and Wilhelm. *Grimm's Household Tales* (1884), translated by Margaret Hunt

——, intro. Kirk, Robert. *The Secret Commonwealth of Elves, Fauns and Fairies* (1893)

——, intro. Lamb, Charles. *Beauty and the Beast* (1887)

——, intro. Perrault, Charles. *Popular Tales* (1888)

——, tr. *Johnny Nut and the Golden Goose* (1887), by Charles Deulin

Lang, Mrs., ed. *The Red Book of Heroes* (1900)

——, ed. *The Strange Story Book* (1913)

Layamon. *Brut*

Lemprière, John. *Bibliotheca Classica, or Classical Dictionary* (1788)

MacDonald, George. "The Fantastic Imagination" (1893)

——. "The Giant's Heart" (1863)

——. "The Golden Key" (1867)

——. *Lilith* (1895)

——. *Phantastes* (1858)

MacDougall, James. *Folk Tales and Fairy Lore in Gaelic and English: Collected from Oral Tradition* (1910)

McEldowney, Mary McQueen. "The Fairy Tales and Fantasies of George MacDonald," [B.Litt thesis 1934, supervised by C.S. Lewis, and examined by Tolkien.]

Maeterlinck. *The Blue Bird* (1908)

"The Mastermaid" [*see under* Dasent, *Popular Tales from the Norse*]

Mayer, Charles-Joseph, ed. *Cabinet des Fées* (40 vols. 1785–9)

Milne, A. A. *Toad of Toad Hall* (1929)

Mirour de l'Omme [*see under* Gower]

Müller, Max. *Chips from a German Workshop* (4 vols. 1867–75)

Nansen, Fridtjof. *In Northern Mists: Arctic Exploration in Early Times* (two volumes, 1911)

New English Dictionary, entries for "fairy", "fairies", "fantasy"

——. *Supplement*

Perrault, Charles. *Histoires ou Contes du Temps Passé, avec des Moralités* (1697). [Includes "Little Red Riding Hood" and "Puss-in-Boots".]

Potter, Beatrix. *The Tale of Peter Rabbit* (1902)

——. *The Tailor of Gloucester* (1903)

——. *The Tale of Jemima Puddleduck* (1908)

——. *The Tale of Mrs. Tiggy-winkle* (1905)

——. *The Tale of Mr. Tod* (1912)

Raspe. *Baron Münchausen*.

"Red Riding Hood" [*see under* Perrault]

Review des Traditions Populaires ["Sebillot articles"]

"Reynard the Fox"

Rhys, Ernest. *Fairy Gold: A Book of Old English Fairy Tales* (1922)

Robinson, W. Heath. *Heath Robinson's Book of Goblins* (1934) [Introduction and postscript]

Sebillot. [*see under* Lang, *The Green Fairy Book*]

Shakespeare, William. [*see under* Wieland]

——. *King Lear* [written c.1605]

——. *Macbeth* [written c.1606]

——. *A Midsummer Night's Dream* [written c.1594]

"Sir Gawain and the Green Knight"

Southey, Robert. "The Story of the Three Bears" (1837)

Spenser, Edmund. *The Faerie Queene* (1590–6)

Steere, Edwin. *Swahili Tales* (1870)

Stevenson, Robert Louis. *Treasure Island* (1883)

Swift, Jonathan. *Gulliver's Travels* (1726) [Includes "A Voyage to Lilliput"]

"The Tale of the Two Brothers" [*see under* Budge]

Thackeray, William Makepeace. *The Rose and the Ring* (1858)

"Thomas the Rhymer"

"The Three Little Pigs"

"Thrymskvitha" [see under *Elder Edda*]

Tolkien, J.R.R. "Mythopoeia"

Wells, H.G. *The First Men in the Moon* (1901)

——. *The Time Machine* (1895)

Wieland, Christoph Martin. [German translator of Shakespeare]

Wyke-Smith, E. A. *The Marvellous Land of Snergs* (1927)

INDEX